Arilyn stared into Elaith Craulnober's amber eyes, startled into immobility by his sudden appearance.

"This is most unexpected," the elf said, in a mellifluous voice that fell just short of song. "I had thought to find a rather different messenger."

She shook off his hold and fell into a battle-ready crouch. "If you've a weapon, draw it," she gritted. "Your *'message'* is about to be delivered."

FORGOTTEN REALMS

Coming in 1999 . . .

Baldur's Gate
Philip G. Athans
July 1999

Silverfall: Stories of the Seven Sisters
Ed Greenwood
August 1999

The Spine of the World
R.A. Salvatore
September 1999

Under Fallen Stars
Mel Odom
October 1999

Beyond the High Road
Troy Denning
December 1999

THE DREAM SPHERES

Elaine Cunningham

THE DREAM SPHERES

©1999 TSR, Inc.

All Rights Reserved.

First Printing: May 1999
Printed in the United States of America.
Library of Congress Catalog Card Number: 98-85785

9 8 7 6 5 4 3 2 1

T21342-620

ISBN: 0-7869-1342-8

U.S., CANADA, ASIA
PACIFIC, & LATIN AMERICA
Wizards of the Coast, Inc.
P.O. Box 707
Renton, WA 98057-0707
+1-800-324-6496

EUROPEAN HEADQUARTERS
Wizards of the Coast, Belgium
P.B. 2031
2600 Berchem
Belgium
+32.70.23.32.77

Visit our web site at **www.tsr.com**

To the unknown visionary who planted the old pines, under which white violets grew and where I first dreamed of elves.

Prelude

The half-ogre strode to the open tavern door, carrying the last of that night's customers by the rope that belted his britches. His captive squirmed like a hooked trout and filled the air with the salty tang of dockside curses. These efforts did not seem to inconvenience the tavern guard in the slightest particular. At nearly seven feet of meanness and muscle, Hamish could lift and haul any patron in the Pickled Fisherman as easily as a lesser man might carry a package of paper-wrapped fish by the string that bound it.

"Raise your keel and haul in your sails," Hamish rumbled as he hauled the flailing man back for the toss. "You're about to run aground, one way or t'other."

Fair warning in these parts, but the patron failed to take it. The half-ogre waited a moment for the struggles to subside, then shrugged and tossed the man out into the night. The man's protests rose into a wail, ending in a muffled thud.

Hamish slammed the tavern door with resounding finality. Wood shrieked against wood as the half-ogre slid home the thick oaken bar. Outside, the patron he had just evicted began to pound on the locked door.

Two tavern maids stopped mopping spilled ale long enough to exchange a sidelong glance and a resigned sigh. One of them, a dark, scrawny girl whose dream-filled eyes belied the reality of her underfed body, tossed a single silver coin onto the table and then reached for a large, half-empty mug. She lifted it high, like a swordsman offering challenge, and turned to the pretty, fair-haired woman who shared the late night shift at the Pickled Fisherman.

"What say you, Lilly? Can I finish this off before old Elton passes out or wanders off?"

Lilly cocked her head and listened. The feeble, irregular rhythm of the man's fists was already dying away. She fished in her pocket for a matching coin, despite the fact that this represented the dragon's share of her nightly wages.

"Aye, Peg, that you can," she said stoutly, slapping the coin down with the air of a woman confident of victory.

Lilly looked to the half-ogre, who was watching this familiar exchange with a faintly exasperated smirk. "I'll stand judge," he agreed, rolling his eyes toward the smoke-blackened beams overhead.

The thin barmaid nodded to acknowledge challenge met, then tipped back her head and drank thirstily. Lilly moved around behind, covering Peg's ears with both hands as if to ensure that the wager was played on a level field.

As Lilly had expected, Elton's protests faded off well before Peg's mug was dry. That mattered not and would not change the outcome of the wager.

Lilly waited until her friend had finished drinking, then dropped her hands from the girl's ears and gave her a playful swat on the rump. "You've won again, lass! It's Tymora's pet you are, with such luck. I'm guessing you've tossed a copper or two toward Lady Luck's temple."

Suddenly uncertain, the girl paused in the act of gathering up her winnings. "Aye," she admitted. "There's no harm in helping luck along, is there?"

"None at all, lass." Lilly sent a look of mock severity in the half-ogre's direction, swearing him anew to secrecy. Hamish lifted both hands and walked off, as if he wanted no further part of this ritual he never quite understood.

It seemed to Lilly a harmless way of putting a bit of much-needed money in Peg's hands, as well as giving the girl an excuse for eating and drinking a bit of the leavings. This was a reality of their lives, something many a down-on-her-luck tavern worker did when need arose, but a thing that Peg's pride would not otherwise permit her. Dipping outright into the tavern's supplies could get a girl fired, and often times a bit of leftover ale and bread and salty pickles might be the only nourishment available to such as Peg. Not that Lilly was overburdened with personal wealth, but she had certain advantages: a merry laugh, a quick bawdy wit, thick hair in an unusual shade of palest red-gold, and delightful curves. Tavern wenches thus blessed could count on the occasional extra coin.

But these days, extra coin was in scant supply in Waterdeep's rough-and-tumble Dock Ward. Lilly sent a wistful glance toward the silent door. "If this were last summer, Elton and his mates would be drinking still."

"And we'd be working still," Peg retorted. "Working til we were fair asleep on our feet."

Lilly nodded, for they'd proven the truth of that often enough. The Pickle, like most dockside taverns, stayed open as long as any man or monster could put down good coin for thin stew and watered ale, but the summer of 1368 had been a hard one. Too many ships had gone missing, which meant less cargo coming in through the docks, lower profits for merchants, fewer hands needed on ship or wharf or warehouse, more masterless men

with nothing to do but turn predator. Many of the sailo
and dockhands who routinely came to soak themselv
in the Pickle's brand of brine were coming into ha
times. Lilly had even heard uneasy whispers from t
young lords and ladies who came into the rough tave
from time to time for novelty's sake. A few among t
merchant nobility were getting cautious, and there w
even talk of finding alternate ways to move goods
and out of the port city. Of course, when they realiz
that someone was listening, Waterdeep's lords and me
chants and sages spoke soothingly of endless prosperit
Lilly wasn't buying that at the asking price.

She glanced at Peg. The younger girl was piling wo
on the hearth to keep the fire burning until morn, b
her eyes kept straying to the far wall. There hung a fe
battered instruments on wooden hooks, awaiting t
rare patron who was more inclined to make music tha
mayhem. Peg's too-thin face was poignant with longin

Lilly straightened and placed her fists on her hip
"Off with you, girl!" she scolded. "It's my turn to finis
up."

Peg needed no persuasion. She darted across t
tavern and snatched up an old fiddle and a fraying bo
Her feet fairly danced up the back stairs, as if they
forgotten the long hours of toil in anticipation of t
music to come.

Left alone, Lilly quickly finished setting the tavern
rights. When the task was done she wiped her hands o
her apron, then reached behind her back for the ties.
her annoyance, the strings had been pulled into tig
knots. Not an unusual state of affairs. She could n
count the times some fumble-fingered patron attempte
to pinch her backside, only to tangle himself in th
strings that bound her apron or her waist pocket.

Lilly sighed and gave up. She took a small knife fro
her pocket and severed the apron strings, silently cur
ing all tavern patrons on behalf of the man who ha

condemned her to an hour's toil with needle and thread. Swine, the lot of them!

Yet once, not too long ago, some of the Pickle's guests hadn't looked so bad, and she hadn't always minded their attentions. Lilly tossed aside the apron and walked behind the bar. Hidden there was a bottle of fine elven wine that a visiting lord had given her. She poured a tiny portion of the wine, the better to savor it, and spoke to the nearly empty bottle.

"A dangerous thing it is, to be drinking the likes of you. I've fair lost my taste for the cider and rot-yer-guts we get hereabouts. And what, I ask you, am I to do about that?"

The bottle offered no advice on the matter. Lilly sighed and pushed a stray wisp of red-gold hair off her face. Suddenly she felt very tired and eager for the escape that awaited her in the small room over the tavern. She tossed back the rare wine in a single gulp, then climbed the back stairs to the bedchambers above the tavern.

She paused at her chamber door, leaning against the frame as she surveyed the room with new eyes. Once, it had seemed a near palace—a room all her own, a safe place to put her things, a bed that she need not share unless she chose to do so. Now she looked at it as her lover might.

Her home was a small, dark chamber graced by neither window nor hearth. It boasted a narrow, sagging cot, a cracked washbowl, a cast-off mirror in dire need of resilvering, hooks on the wall to hold her two spare dresses and her clean chemise. In a room down the hall, Peg sawed away at her old fiddle, which retaliated with squawks of protest that brought to mind a stepped-on cat.

Lilly entered the room shaking her head, as if she could deny the dreary reality around her. She shut the door and sank down on the cot. Reaching under the coverlet, she patted the lumpy stuffing until she found the particular lump she sought. From its hiding place she drew a small globe of iridescent crystal.

For a moment it was enough just to gaze at her treasure, to know that she, a simple tavern wench, could possess a dream sphere. This was a new thing in the city, a wondrous magical toy. They could not be found in the bazaars, of course. Naturally the city's wizards frowned on magic that could be purchased and used without coin crossing their palms. There was nothing, though, that could not be purchased in the City of Splendors, provided one knew where to look.

There was little about Waterdeep's hidden byways that Lilly did not know. She had bought dream spheres before and counted every copper well spent. This one, however, was special—a gift from her lover. A nobleman, he was. Surely he had chosen this particular dream with great fondness, knowing how she longed to enter his world!

Lilly closed her eyes and willed the man's handsome, roguish face to mind. As she closed her fingers around the glowing sphere, she slipped into the waking trance that was the corridor into the dream.

She heard the music first, lovely music that was far removed from the occasional tune brayed out by patrons of the Pickled Fisherman. The poor chamber faded away. Lilly raised her hands, turning them this way and that as she marveled at their unblemished whiteness. Wonderingly she smoothed them over the cool blue silk of her gown.

Suddenly, she was standing in a great hall filled with glittering guests. She saw her lover at the far side of the room, sipping wine and scanning the crowd with obvious anticipation. His face lit up when he saw her. Before she could move toward him, another gentleman broke away from the dancers and approached, dipping into the courtly bow that no woman of her lowly station ever received. Lilly nodded graciously and floated into his arms. Together they joined the intricate circle of the dance.

Her lover watched from the sidelines, smiling fondly. When the first dance was through he came to claim her. Together they danced and made merry until the melting wax of the hundreds of scented, glittering candles hung from the silver chandeliers like fragrant lace. Lilly knew every dance step, though she had never learned them. She remembered the taste of sparkling wine, although no such vintage came within a giant's shadow of the rough tavern where she spent most of her waking hours. She laughed and flirted and even sang, feeling more beautiful and witty and desirable than ever she had been in her life. Best of all, she was a lady among the nobility of Waterdeep, those lofty beings who glittered like winter stars and who would never, ever see her as one of their own.

Except, of course, in dreams.

The squawk of an old fiddle insinuated itself into the lilting rhythm of the dance music. Startled by this intrusion, Lilly missed the step and stumbled. Her lover's arms tightened around her waist to steady her. His eyes were warm with approval at what he clearly thought was a flirtatious ploy.

The dream was fading, though. There would be no time to fulfill the promises offered by her lord's bedazzled smile.

A surge of bright panic assailed Lilly. She tore herself from the gentleman's embrace, gathered up the skirts of her silken gown, and ran like a dock rat.

Frantically she raced down the sweeping marble stairs that led to the anonymity of the streets. She had to get away before the dream faded! She would die if she had to watch the chivalrous wonder in her lover's eyes change to the condescending charm he bestowed upon pretty, willing serving wenches.

Lilly's pace slowed. Her weariness returned, magnified by the fading dream until she felt as if she were running through water. She awoke abruptly and found herself still sitting on the edge of her sagging cot, staring at her own too-familiar reflection in the mirror that was no longer good enough for some unknown noblewoman.

Lilly stared bleakly at the image revealed in the scratched and faded glass. Gone were the silk and jewels. She was a serving wench once again, clad in a drab skirt of linsey-woolsey and a low-laced chemise that was too vigorously scrubbed and neatly pressed to be truly tawdry. Her eyes were wide and dark in her face, and the deep circles of exhaustion beneath her eyes and the impossible dreams within made them look as bruised as trod-upon pansies. One white-knuckled, grimy little hand clutched the dream sphere, which was now dull and milky, utterly and irrevocably drained of magic.

With a sigh, Lilly set aside the spent dream sphere and reached for a shawl. She draped the dark material over her bright hair and then hurried down the creaky back stairs toward the alley. Her feet nimbly avoided the loose boards, the spots that would draw groans of complaint from the ancient wood.

With a grim smile, she remembered the sweeping marble staircase that the dream sphere had shown her, the click of her delicate slippers as she fled the hall. In real life she was as silent as a shadow. That was the first skill a thief learned, and those who failed to do so rarely survived childhood.

Lilly didn't like her work, but she did it well. After all, a girl had to live. In a few nights more, she could enjoy another respite from the Dock Ward. In the meanwhile this was her life, and like it or not, she had to get on with it.

Her first mark was easy enough. A fat warehouse guard sprawled in the alley behind the Pickled Fisherman. His head was propped up on a discarded crate and his jowls vibrated with the force of each grating, ale-soaked snore. Lilly slid a practiced eye over him, then drew a knife from her pocket and dropped into a crouch. A single deft flick opened the worn leather of his boot, sending a few unspent coppers spilling into the street. She gathered them up and slipped them into her pocket as she stood.

She melted into the mist and shadows that clung to the alley wall as she considered her next move. A circle of greasy lamplight marked the alley's end. Beyond that, the distant murmur of voices and laughter from the Soaring Pegasus tavern suddenly swelled as the door opened for what was certainly the last time that night. The congenial babble spilled out into the street and then broke apart, as tavern mates took their leave of each other to stride or stumble off into the night. Lilly's experience indicated good odds that at least one of them would come her way.

The barmaid and thief pressed herself into the slim crevice between two stone buildings. Before long, a single set of footsteps began to tap along the cobblestone toward her.

A man, she surmised from the sound, and not a very large one. He wore new boots with the hard leather soles that marked the work of expensive cobblers. The uneven rhythm of his steps proclaimed that he'd imbibed enough to leave him tangle-footed, but he was still sober enough to whistle a popular ballad, more or less on tune.

Lilly nodded with satisfaction. One drunken man a night was her limit; robbing them was poor sport indeed. She drew a small, hooked knife from her pocket and waited for her mark to amble past.

And worth the wait he was! Richly dressed and fairly jingling with coin—a wealthy guildsman, or perhaps one of the merchant nobility. Lilly started to reach for the purse that swung from his belt.

"Maurice? Ah, *there* you are, you hopeless rogue!"

The voice came from the alley's end. It was female, dark with some exotic accent, full of laughter and flirtation and the sort of confidence that came only with wealth and beauty. Lilly gritted her teeth as "Maurice" spun toward the sultry speaker, his face alight and his purse strings now completely out of reach.

"Lady Isabeau! I thought you had gone on with the others."

"Oh, pooh," the woman proclaimed, packing so much drama into that small disclaimer that Lilly could almost see the artful pout, the dismissing little wave of a jeweled hand. "Cowards, all of them! Boasting of the dangers around them, while they ride in closed carriages with guards and drivers. But you!" Here the sultry voice dipped almost to a purr. "You alone are man enough to challenge the night."

There was a world of meaning in the woman's words. A bright, unmistakable flame leaped in the man's eyes. The spark was quickly quenched by the return of his distinctly pinched expression.

Lilly smirked as she discerned the true reason for the man's digression. He would not be the first to seek the comfort of a dark alley after a night's hard drinking. No doubt he intended to take care of business, then hail down his comrades' carriage when it turned the corner at Sail Street. Lady Isabeau's arrival had thwarted his design, and he looked deeply torn between the demands of nature and the teasing promise in the noblewoman's words.

Necessity won out. "Even the main streets are dangerous," Maurice cautioned the lady. "These alleys can be deadly. I must insist that you go back with the others."

But the dainty click of Isabeau's slippers came steadily closer. "I am not afraid. You will protect me, no?"

No, Lilly answered silently and emphatically. Two pigeons were nearly as easy to pluck as one—not for a simple pickpocket like herself, of course, but hadn't the silly wench heard tell that many Dock Ward thieves were willing to cut more than purse strings? The woman came into view, and Lilly forgot her scorn.

Lady Isabeau was very attractive, with a dark, exotic beauty that was a perfect match for her voice. Thick, glossy black hair was coiled artfully around her shapely head, with enough length left over to fashion ringlets that spilled over her shoulders. Her eyes were large and velvety brown, her nose an aristocratic arc, her lips full and curved in invitation. Lavish curves tested the resolve of the laces binding her deep red gown, and an embroidered girdle decorated with precious stones encircled her narrow waist. Lilly sighed in profound envy.

Lady Isabeau quirked an ebony brow. For one heart-stopping moment, Lilly thought the noblewoman had heard her, but the woman's eyes remained constant in their admiration of the heroic Maurice, never so much as flickering toward Lilly's hiding place.

"If you say the danger is too great, then it must be so." Isabeau tucked herself under the man's arm. "You would not leave me here alone, surely?"

"I will see you safely to Sail Street, then I must be on my way," he said grandly. "Certain matters cannot await the light of day." His tone hinted at clandestine meetings, honor challenges, maidens languishing in prison towers.

Lilly lifted a hand to her lips to keep her smirk from bubbling into laughter.

Isabeau nodded, then produced a small silver flask from the folds of her skirts. "As you say. Let us at least share a last drink?"

The nobleman accepted the flask and tipped it up, and together they walked beyond the range of Lilly's vision. The thief waited until all was silent. Then she ventured out, creeping stealthily toward the main street.

She almost stepped on Maurice. He lay sprawled at the end of the alley, face down, just beyond the reach of the lamplight's dim circle. His fine clothing was stained with strong-smelling spirits, but Lilly doubted he had succumbed to drink. She cautiously stooped and touched her fingers to the nobleman's neck. A thin but steady pulse leaped beneath her fingers. Curious, she smoothed her hand back through the man's hair and inquired around for an explanation to his current state. A small knot was forming at the base of his skull. He would awaken with a fierce headache—and, of course, without his purse.

Lilly rose to her feet, angry now. Noble or common, no decent woman turned tail and ran at the first sign of danger, leaving a friend alone! Why, the spoiled trollop hadn't even taken the trouble to raise an alarm!

She silently padded into the lamplight and scanned the streets for a sign of the fleeing Isabeau. A flash of red disappeared into a nearby alley. Lilly set her jaw and followed. Though she rarely plucked female pigeons, this woman was the most deserving mark Lilly had seen in a month of tendays.

Following the noblewoman was easy enough. Not once did Isabeau look back, so intent was she upon the faint rumble of a carriage approaching the end of the alley. Lilly caught up to her near the midpoint and glided silently up behind. She noted the deep pocket attached to the woman's bejeweled girdle: a large, smooth sack of the same deep crimson as Isabeau's gown, and devised in such a way that it blended into the skirt's folds.

A canny design, Lilly thought. Even though the pocket was full and heavy, a lesser thief might not have seen it at all. She sliced the strings, her touch as light as a ghost's, and then fell back into the shadows to count her booty.

Her eyes widened as she opened the sack. Inside it nestled the richly embroidered coin purse recently worn by the unfortunate Maurice.

"You are good," intoned that dark and sultry voice, "but I am better."

Lilly's gaze jerked up from the twice-stolen coins into the cold, level stare of her noble "pigeon." Before Lilly could react, Lady Isabeau's jeweled hands shot forward. The noblewoman seized the bag with one hand and dug the fingers of the other under Lilly's shawl and into her hair. She yanked Lilly's head forward and down, bringing the coin-filled bag up to meet it with painful force.

Lilly went reeling back, bereft of the purse and, judging from the burning in her scalp, at least one lock of her hair. She thumped painfully against the alley wall.

Blinking away stars, Lilly pushed herself off the wall, drew a knife, and charged. Isabeau set her feet wide and swung the heavy silk bag like a flail.

There was no time for evasion. Lilly slashed forward in what was half parry, half attack. She missed the woman altogether but managed to slice the dangerous bag open. Coins scattered with a satisfying clatter, but the bag was still heavy enough when it hit her to send her stumbling back. Her knife flew off and fell among Isabeau's scattered booty.

Hissing like an angry cat, Isabeau pounced, her hands hooked into raking claws. Lilly seized her wrists and held on, dodging this way and that as she sought to keep her eyes beyond reach of those flailing hands.

Together they circled and dipped—a grim, deadly parody of dance that mocked Lilly's still-bright dream. So frantic was their struggle, and so painfully poignant her memories, that Lilly did not realize her shawl had fallen off until she caught her foot in the fringe.

A small stumble, a moment's hesitation, was all that Isabeau needed. The noblewoman wrenched her hands free and fisted them in Lilly's hair. Down they went in a tangle of skirts, rolling wildly as they scratched and tugged and pummeled and bit.

Through it all, Isabeau was eerily silent. Lilly would have expected a pampered noblewoman to scream like a banshee over such treatment, not realizing that in this part of town the sounds of her distress could bring worse trouble upon her. Apparently this woman was more familiar with the ways of the streets than her appearance suggested.

Still, Lilly knew a few tricks that this overdressed pickpocket did not. Years of fighting off persistent tavern patrons had left her as hard to hold as a trout—she would wager that not even the elf lord's gladiators could pin her if she were determined to wriggle free. Though she was smaller than Isabeau and lighter by at least a stone, the battle slowly began to turn her way.

Finally she managed to straddle the woman and pin her arms to her sides. Her captive, looking outraged and furious but still holding her preternatural silence, twisted and bucked beneath her like an unbroken mare.

Lilly sucked air in long, ragged gasps and prepared to hang on until the sun rose or her foe conceded. Not even for Peg's sake would she have placed a wager on which might come first.

Isabeau's struggles dwindled, then stopped abruptly as her eyes focused on something beyond the alley. Suspecting the oldest trick known to street urchins, Lilly merely tightened her grip.

After a moment it occurred to her that the expression in the noblewoman's dark eyes was not cunning but naked avarice. Lilly hazarded a glance toward whatever had captured Isabeau's interest.

A lone man approached the lamp, glancing furtively up and down the street as he went. He was a big man, heavily bearded, well but not richly dressed.

"Not a nobleman," Isabeau assessed in a low voice. "A trusted servant, running an errand. At this hour, and in this place, surely the errand lies outside the law."

Before she could think better of it, Lilly added, "He has not yet completed this errand. He is looking for someone."

Isabeau slanted a look up at her captor. "Well said. That means he will still be carrying payment."

"Most likely."

They were silent for a moment. "We could split it," Isabeau suggested.

"Aye, that we could," Lilly scoffed softly. "An easy thing it will be for the two of us to separate that large and earnest fellow from his master's money! You'll forgive me for saying this, but you're not much of a hand at fighting."

Isabeau shrugged as well as she could under the circumstances. "No matter. I can always find someone to do my fighting for me."

"Oh, and that would be me, I suppose?"

"Am I a fool to waste such talent?" retorted Isabeau. "You have good hands and quiet feet. I'll distract this pigeon, and you pluck him."

Strange words from a woman clad in silk and jewels. Lilly sat back on her heels and let out a soft, incredulous chuckle. "Who are you?" she demanded.

"Isabeau Thione, bastard daughter of the Lady Lucia Thione of Tethyr," the woman said in a haughty, self-mocking tone, naming a branch of a royal family so infamous that even Lilly had heard of them. The noblewoman grinned wickedly and added, "Until recently, known only as Sofia, tavern wench and pickpocket. I'm new in Waterdeep and looking to do well, any way I can."

A tavern wench, and a thief of noble birth! These words, this dual identity, struck a deep, poignant chord in Lilly's heart.

Weren't they much akin, the two of them? Yet Isabeau, with her jewels and silks and the open court paid her by fancy gentlemen, had achieved what she, Lilly, had experienced only in dreams. Perhaps she could learn how the woman had wrought this marvel.

Another, even more enticing possibility danced into her whirling thoughts. Was it possible that the dream spheres that both enchanted and tormented her were not an impossible dream but an augury into a possible future? There was great magic in the dream spheres—Lilly had felt this power in ways she could not understand or explain. Perhaps it was no coincidence that two misbegotten thieves had crossed paths this night.

Lilly slowly eased her grip and backed away. The two women rose to their feet and began to smooth their wrinkled skirts and wild hair. "If we're to do this, we must move fast," Lilly said.

Her fellow thief smiled so that her eyes narrowed like a hunting cat's. "Partners, then. What do I call you?"

She gave the only name to which she was legally entitled. One word, nothing more. No family or rank, history or future. It had always pained her that her name was the sort that might be casually bestowed upon a white mare or a favorite lap cat.

The noblewoman seemed of like opinion. "Lilly?" she repeated, lifting one dark brow in a supercilious arch.

Lilly was of no mind to hear her shortcomings from the lips of this woman. The sneer on Isabeau's lovely face prompted Lilly to give voice, for the first time in her life, to her deepest, most treasured secret.

She lifted her chin in an approximation of a noblewoman's hauteur and added, "That would be Lilly Thann."

One

Summer was rapidly fading into memory. In the skies over Waterdeep, the stars winking into view were the first heralds of the wintertime constellations: Auril Frostqueen, White Dragon, the Elfmaid's Tears. Beautiful were these fey and fanciful star patterns, but few inhabitants of the great city took note of them, dazzled as they were by splendors closer to ground.

But the young nobleman hurrying down the shadowed streets was oblivious not only to the stars, but the city, the crowds, and everything else but the prospect of the meeting before him. The image of a half-elven woman was bright in his mind's eye, almost bright enough to bridge the darkness of the many long months apart.

Almost bright enough to eclipse his soul-deep resentment over the source of their many partings.

Danilo Thann thrust aside these thoughts. What part had they in such a night as this? Arilyn had returned to the city, as she had promised, in time for the Gemstone Ball—the first in the season of harvest festivals. Doggedly he pushed from his mind the last two such events he had attended without her: markers of two more summers gone, reminders of promises as yet unfulfilled.

The room Arilyn kept for her infrequent visits to the city was in the South Ward, a working-class part of town, on the third floor of an old stone building that in better days had been home to some guildsman who'd since fallen out of fortune. Danilo shifted the large package he carried, tucking it under one arm so that he could tug open the oversized door.

He stepped into the front hall and nodded a greeting toward the curtained alcove on his left. The only response was a grunt from the hidden guard who kept watch there—an aging dwarf whose square, spotted hands were still steady on a crossbow.

Danilo took the stairs three at a time. The door to Arilyn's room was locked and warded with magic that he himself had put in place. He dispatched the locks and the guardian magic, silently, but with more haste and less finesse than he usually employed. He eased the door open and found, to his surprise, that Arilyn was still sound asleep.

For a moment it was enough simply to stand and watch. Dan had long taken comfort in watching Arilyn at rest and had spent many quiet hours doing so during the time they had traveled together in the service of the Harpers. Only half-elven, she found repose in human sleep rather than the deep, wakeful reverie of her elven forebears. It was a small thing, perhaps, but to Danilo's thinking Arilyn's need for sleep was a common link between them, one she could neither deny nor alter.

Danilo studied the half-elf, marking all the small changes that the summer had brought. Her black hair had grown longer, and the wild curls tumbled loose over her pillow. Though it hardly seemed possible, she was even thinner than she had been when they last parted on the road north from Baldur's Gate. Asleep, she looked as pale as porcelain and nearly as fragile. Dan's lips curved in an ironic smile as his gaze shifted to the sheathed sword beside her.

Resentment akin to hatred filled Danilo's heart as he contemplated the moonblade, a magical sword that had brought them together—and torn them apart.

At the moment the moonblade was dark, its magic mercifully silent. No telltale green light limned it, signaling yet another call from the forest elves.

Danilo shook off his dark thoughts and slipped inside the room. With one fluid motion, he placed the wrapped package on the table and drew twin daggers from his belt.

The soft hiss of steel roused the sleeping warrior. Arilyn came awake at full alert, lunging toward the sound almost the very instant her eyes snapped open. In her hand was a long, gleaming knife.

Danilo stepped forward, daggers raised into a gleaming X. The half-elf's knife sent sparks into the deepening twilight as it slid along the dual edges. Though Arilyn deftly pulled her attack, for a long moment they stood nearly face to face—a lover's stance, albeit over crossed weapons.

"Still sleeping with steel beneath your pillow, I see. It's comforting to know that some things never change," Danilo quipped as he sheathed his daggers. He regretted the words as soon as they were spoken. Even to his ears, the intended jest sounded stilted—a challenge, almost an accusation.

Arilyn flung her knife onto the bed. "Damn it, Dan! Why do you insist upon creeping up on me like that? It's a marvel you're still alive."

"Yes, so I'm often told."

The silence between them was long and not entirely comfortable. Arilyn suddenly seemed to remember her disheveled appearance. Her eyes widened, and her hands went to her tousled hair. "The Gemstone Ball. I don't even have a costume yet."

He was absurdly pleased that she remembered and that she cared enough about his world to consider such matters. "If you like, we need not attend. After all, you've only just got back."

"Late this afternoon," she agreed, "after a long trip, and the last two nights of it steady travel. You're expected, though, and I promised to be with you."

She seemed to hear her words as he might, for her eyes grew dark with the awareness of other promises she had made, and not kept. She cleared her throat and nodded at the table. "What's in the package?"

Danilo allowed himself to be distracted. "When word reached me that you were delayed on the road, I took the liberty of acquiring an appropriately gem-colored costume."

"Ah. Let me guess: sapphire?"

They exchanged a quick, cautious grin. In their early days together, when Danilo went to great pains to convince her and everyone else that he was a silly, shallow dandy, he composed a number of painfully trite odes comparing her eyes to these precious gems. To drive the knife a bit deeper, Arilyn lifted one brow and began to hum the melody to one of these early offerings.

Her dry teasing shattered the restraint between them. Danilo chuckled and pantomimed a wince. "The best thing about old friends is that they know you well. Of course, that is also the *worst* thing about old friends."

"Old friends," she repeated. The words were delivered in level tones, but they held a question. Was this what they were destined to be—old friends, and nothing more?

Danilo had long sought an answer, and he thought he had finally found one that might avail. Arilyn's teasing comments made as good an opening as he could expect to get. Their lives might have changed, but one constant remained: the intense and often inexplicable love born on the day she had kidnapped him from a tavern. He ripped open the paper that bound the package and lifted from it a length of deep-blue velvet—a gown of exquisite simplicity, elf-crafted and rare.

"Sapphire," he confirmed with a grin, "with gems to match. I'll spare you the song I prepared for the occasion."

Arilyn chuckled and took the gown from his hands, then tossed it aside with the same casual disregard with which she had discarded the knife. Danilo opened his arms, and she came into them. "I have missed you," she murmured against his chest.

It was a rare admission from the taciturn half-elf. In fact, Danilo could count on his hands the times they had spoken of such matters since the night, four years ago, when they had planned to announce their betrothal at the Gemstone Ball. Events had forestalled this, rather dramatically, and had set their feet upon a path of deepening estrangement.

That path, he vowed, was to end this night.

He took her shoulders and held her out at arm's length. "Look further in the package. Look carefully at what you find, for you will never see it again so close at hand."

Arilyn gave him a puzzled smile, then did as she was bid. Her eyes widened as she drew a black, veiled helm from the wrappings.

"A Lord's Helm," she murmured, naming one of the magical artifacts that marked and concealed the Hidden Lords, men and women drawn from every walk of life to rule the city. Understanding flooded her face. "Yours?"

Dan nodded ruefully. "An uneasy fit it has been. Khelben foisted it upon me four years ago. I would have told you long before this, but . . . "

His voice trailed off. Arilyn gave a curt nod of understanding. It was common knowledge that the secret Lords told no one of their identity but the person they wed—and even that degree of confidence was frowned upon. Only Piergeiron the Paladinson, the First Lord of the city, was known by name.

"Why do you tell me now?" She glanced over at the sapphire gown, and her face was clouded with memories of the pledge they had meant to speak at the Gemstone Ball four years ago.

Danilo had been prepared for this reaction, but even so his heart ached to see it. "I am free to tell you now, for it is my intention to give the thing up," he said lightly. "There has been some trouble of late between the Harpers and some of Waterdeep's paladins. Lord Piergeiron, as one might anticipate, came out fervently on the side of righteousness. He was graciously willing—one might even say eager—to relieve me of this duty. Likewise, I have given notice to the redoubtable Khelben Arunsun that I have no intention of assuming his mantle as future protector of Blackstaff Tower."

Arilyn frowned at this mention of Danilo's kinsman and mentor—and her former Harper superior. "I thought he had long ago given up that notion."

She was hedging, noted Dan, buying time as she absorbed the implications of his revelation. "On the surface, yes, but as you well know, the good archmage prefers to work in mist and shadows. Some time back, when I declared my intentions of becoming a bard in truth as well as in jest, he was all gracious agreement. Yet he continued to give me valuable spellbooks, to share crumbs of his power, to confide in me secrets that bound me to the Harpers and to him. Before I knew it, I was attending him almost daily. I even had other Harpers under my command." He shuddered. "Insidious, our dear Khelben."

Arilyn smiled at his droll tone, but there was a touch of anger in her eyes. "A better description of Khelben Arunsun could not be cast by his own shadow! You did well to break free. Do you still wear the pin?"

This was a sore spot, for they both had reason to cherish the pins that marked them as Harpers, members of a semi-secret organization dedicated to keeping

Balance in the world and preserving tales of great deeds. Arilyn had grown increasingly uneasy with the direction of the Harpers in general and the directives of Khelben Arunsun in particular. After their last shared mission, the rescue of Isabeau Thione, Arilyn had broken with Khelben and the Harpers.

Danilo, however, was not quite ready to renounce either. He touched his shoulder where, pinned to his shirt and hidden beneath his tabard, a tiny silver harp nestled into the curve of a crescent moon.

"A good man entrusted this pin to me. I will wear it always in his honor and try to be worthy of his trust."

And his daughter.

The words were left unspoken, but the deepening conflict in Arilyn's eyes marked them as heard. "I, too, wear the Harper pin in honor of my father, but for no other reason. My allegiance is elsewhere."

"Yes, I am all too aware of that," Danilo said with more bitterness than he intended. He lifted a hand to forestall her explanation. "No, don't. We have traveled this road. What you did, you did for love of me. I wish the result had been different, but I cannot fault your intentions."

Again his gaze shifted to the moonblade, a hereditary elven sword to which each wielder could add one magical power. For Arilyn's mother it had formed a magical gate between her human lover's world and the distant elven island of Evermeet. This had led to tragedy for the elven folk, and many years later it led to a long string of events that had brought Arilyn to the attention of the Harpers of Waterdeep. Danilo had been assigned to follow and watch her. In the course of this mission, he and Arilyn had formed their own bonds: trust, friendship, and something deeper and infinitely more complex than love. Arilyn had ceded to him the right to her moonblade and its power. In doing so, she had broken a tradition of many centuries, that none but a moonblade's true inheritor could wield the blade. In doing so, she had unknowingly committed him to eternal service of the magic sword.

It was a price Danilo would gladly have paid for the bond it gave them, but he had never had that choice. When confronted by the results of her decision, Arilyn had taken it upon herself to free her friend from a service he never chose. In doing so, she had broken the mystic, elven bond between them. Once that bond was broken, the sword had granted Arilyn a different power and forged another allegiance.

Now the moonblade warned her when the forest folk were in need of a hero's sword. There were small bands of elves scattered through many forests in Faerun, and many were in danger and decline. Arilyn's sleep had become dream-haunted, and her sword gleamed with verdant light more often than not. Though she understood that hers was but a single sword and that she could not stand beside every beleaguered elf, the calls were too strong for her to ignore. Elf and moonblade shared soul-deep bonds. Since that day she had been on the road almost constantly and could not do otherwise.

"You do what you must," Danilo said softly. "I have had my duties here. However, there is nothing more to hold me in Waterdeep. There is no reason why I cannot travel with you."

There was, and they both knew it. Arilyn was an oddity among the forest elves, who seldom had anything to do with strangers among their own kind, much less moon elves with human blood. In the eyes of the forest elves, though, she had become part of the centuries-old legend of the moonblade she carried. Thus she had finally achieved what she had longed for all her life: true acceptance from the elven folk. No human was likely to manage such a feat.

"No. No reason at all," she said faintly and unconvincingly. She met his eyes and manufactured a rueful smile. "You seem to have broken free of all things but one. This night you must meet family obligations. When does this ball start?"

Danilo squinted at the window. Twilight had passed, and the faint glow of lamps rose from the streets below. "An hour, I should think. If you hurry, we can be fashionably late." He punctuated this remark with a sly smile. "If we take our time, we could be scandalously late."

"A tempting suggestion, Lord Thann," she said with prim tones but laughing eyes. "I am in accord with the spirit of it but not the timing. You go on without me, and I'll follow as soon as I can. Since this is your family's party, your absence would be noticed and remarked."

"The Lady Cassandra sees all," he murmured, naming the formidable woman who had given him life and who managed the Thann family fortunes with an iron will and a capable hand.

Arilyn's blue and gold eyes took on the hard, flat gleam common among warriors who heard their nemesis named. "True enough. Even without delay, I'm sure we'll manage to cause some sort of scandal."

"That's the spirit," he said approvingly.

* * * * *

Not much more than the allotted hour passed before Arilyn stepped from her hired carriage at the gates of the Thann family villa. The vast, sprawling white marble mansion commanded nearly a city block of the North Ward, and every pace and breath of it was ablaze with light and sound. Danilo, it would seem, had used a bit of poetic license in naming the starting hour. By all appearances, the festivities were well under way and had been for quite some time.

Arilyn surveyed the scene through narrowed eyes, as a warrior might size up a potential battlefield. Though the Gemstone Ball was one of the last fetes of the summer season, in this bright place the drab and chill of coming winter seemed far away. Even the darkness of night was held firmly at bay. The moon cresting the peaked roofs of the villa was as bright and full as a summer rose, and in the gardens surrounding the villa floating globes of light winked on and off like giant, multicolored fireflies. From the open windows floated the sounds of laughter and festive music.

She followed a small crowd of latecomers, cursing the slim skirts that broke her stride into small, mincing steps. Inside the Thann family villa, scores of guests gathered in a great hall ablaze with the light of a thousand candles. Dancers dressed in vivid gem-toned costumes dipped and spun in time to the music. Other guests sipped the rare wines that were a cornerstone of the Thann family fortunes or listened to the fine musicians who seemed to be everywhere. Paired guests wandered into artfully designed alcoves and garden nooks to gather the last blossoms of a summertime romance.

It was, Arilyn had to admit, quite a spectacle. This party was considered a highlight of the season, and the merchant nobility rose to the occasion, each guest striving to outdo the others in matters of finery, beauty, or gallantry. It was understood—expected!—that on such a night everything must be perfect. Cassandra Thann, the matriarch of her clan and a maven of noble society, would not have it otherwise.

The only discordant note, if merry laughter could ever be thus described, came from the far corner of the great hall. With a certainty born of experience, Arilyn headed in that direction.

She slipped quietly into the crowd surrounding Danilo as he began to recount his misadventures with a riddle-loving dragon. It was a comic retelling and quite different from the story Arilyn had heard. She doubted that those who'd shared that grim encounter would recognize the tale. Or, perhaps they would. Arilyn had noted that truth had a way of ringing through the words of a bard, even when it, and he, were concealed by gilding and motley.

She studied the man who had been her Harper partner and who still held her heart in his hands. By all appearances, Danilo was an agreeable and entertaining dandy, well favored by nature and fortune and good company. He was a tall man, lean and graceful, fair of form and face, and completely at home with the finery and deportment that such evenings demanded. The sleeves of his fine emerald green jacket had been slashed repeatedly to reveal the bright cloth-of-gold lining beneath. Gold glinted also on his gesticulating hands and in the pale hue of the thick mane that flowed past his shoulders.

Golden, she decided. That was the word for him. Offhand, she could not name an advantage he had not enjoyed, a task he could not accomplish with almost indecent ease. Danilo was to all appearances well content with himself. Nor did he seem to be alone in his high opinion, for his roguish grin and the mischief in his gray eyes brought instinctive, answering smiles to many who beheld him.

It amazed Arilyn still that this effortlessly golden, merry person saw anything to cherish in her, an elf whose life was consumed with duty and danger. But nevertheless when he saw her his eyes lit up with a genuine pleasure that gave lie to the bright façade he wore in her absence.

"Arilyn, you must come watch this!" he called, raising his voice over the applause that followed his tale. He beckoned with the object in his hand—a half-blown rose in a rare, true shade of blue.

A murmur of interest rippled through the group. Such roses were the stuff of legend, known only on distant Evermeet. Danilo had somehow managed to charm a few of these treasures away from the fey folk. He had determined to fill the courtyard behind his townhouse with an elven garden in honor of his lady, one that would rival the best Evermeet had to offer. Arilyn had heard that this romantic tale was repeated often by Waterdhavian ladies, always punctuated by wistful sighs. Many eyes turned in her direction now, some envious, some merely curious. The crowd parted, leaving her standing alone.

More than a few stares lingered pointedly on the sword she wore on her hip. She was the only person in the hall thus armed. To be sure, the moonblade was a priceless thing, worth more than the gems that bedecked a score of guests, but it was still a weapon. Most likely, a few of them had heard of her dark reputation and regarded an assassin's sword as not merely a faux pas but a threat.

Arilyn ignored the stares and went to Danilo. Her fingertips brushed his outstretched hand and the symbolic rose he held, then she fell back to observe the spell he clearly planned to cast in tribute.

He held the rose out before him at arm's length as he sang a few words to it. When he drew back his hand, the blue flower remained suspended in the air. Chanting now, he drew from the bag at his belt a pinch of dark powder with a distinctive, unmistakably barnyard aroma. He sprinkled this on the floor beneath the rose, quickly sweetening the burgeoning spell with another layer of powder that smelled of meadows and summer rain. A flurry of rapid, graceful gestures followed, accompanied by a song in the Elvish language.

Power, in the form of green and glowing light, began to gather around the spellcasting bard. Danilo's audience fell into expectant silence as the verdant aura reached out to envelop them, as well. Elsewhere in the room, laughter and conversation faded as the guests awaited the effects of the spell. Their faces showed varying degrees of curiosity, wonder, or—in the case of those who knew Danilo's reputation in such matters—apprehension.

His spell ended in a high, ringing note. Some of the spectators responded to the music with a smatter of applause, but most merely gaped at the transformation taking place before them.

The blue rose was growing—not as roses grew in the normal course of events but with the same eerie speed that a dismembered troll regenerated its limbs or a hydra sprouted two new heads to replace one lost to a warrior's axe. Unlike these regenerated monsters, however, the elven rose did not stop growing once it reached the size ordained by nature.

The rose's stem lengthened into a stalk, which in turn sent new shoots racing toward the ceiling and roots slithering along the smooth marble of the floor. Leaves murmured as they unfurled. Buds quite literally popped open, sounding like tiny bottles of sparkling wine decanted by unseen pixie folk. In moments dozens, scores, hundreds of rare blue roses covered the magical rosebush.

The monstrous rosebush.

Already the thing was half way to the vaulted ceiling, and the limbs were beginning to droop down of their own weight. Its growth showed no sign of slowing. This, Arilyn surmised, could be a problem. She grimaced and dropped her hand to the hilt of her sword.

Gracefully soaring branches described a slow, lazy outward arc, then began a plunging descent toward the marble floor.

Murmurs of wonder fell abruptly silent, and a heartbeat later returned as cries of alarm. The rosebush's many branches lunged toward the revelers like the grasping, thorny talons of a hundred swooping falcons.

Cries went up for Khelben Arunsun, a relative of the Thann family and the most powerful wizard in all of Waterdeep, but the archmage was not presently in the hall. Frenzied chanting mingled with the growing clamor as a few lesser mages tried their hands at containing the runaway magic. The best that any of them could do was to change the hue of the flowers from their elven blue to a more mundane shade. Still the bush came on.

All of this took less time than the telling would take. In the first moments following his spell, Danilo stood in slack-jawed amazement at the very center of the verdant maelstrom, unscathed by the wild growth of thorn and branch. He saw at once that Arilyn might not be so fortunate. Too many times had she witnessed his "miscast" spells, and he feared she would not understand that this night, the danger was real. She stood at alert but did not flee the approaching thorns.

Danilo thought fast. *"Elegard aquilar!"* he called, praying that Arilyn could read the truth of the matter in the old Elvish battle cry.

As he'd hoped, the half-elf's sapphire eyes went flat and level, a warrior's ready stare. Her moonblade hissed free of its scabbard as the racing limbs closed in. She lifted the sword in time to bat aside the first leafy assault, then fell into a deft, practiced rhythm.

Some of the thorny limbs dove into the crowd of retreating guests, tearing at their bright clothing and tangling with flowing hair. Panic set in, and the nobles turned tail and made a frantic, collective dash for the exits. Graceful dancers tripped on their diaphanous skirts and sprawled. Courtly gentlemen leaped over their ladies' prone bodies in their race toward safety. The musicians abandoned their posts—all but for the waggish uilleann piper who struck up the first plaintive notes of "My Love, She is a Wandering Rose."

Through it all, Arilyn's elven blade danced and sliced. Severed limbs piled around her, hampering her attempts to wade forward and cut down the source of the spell.

The rosebush, that is, not the spellcaster.

So Danilo fondly hoped.

Still, he couldn't be completely certain. As Arilyn advanced on him, slashing her way through the persistent growth, the expression in her blue eyes was grim and furious.

Danilo couldn't fault her. He was renowned for his miscast spells, but never had he turned one of his pranks upon Arilyn. He winced as one of the limbs broke through her guard and snagged her skirt. The sapphire velvet gave way with a resounding rip, tearing her gown from thigh to ankle and leaving a thin, welling trail of blood on her exposed leg.

Instinctively Danilo's hand dropped to the place where his sword usually hung, and he started to move toward her before he remembered he was weaponless.

"Hold," she commanded. She lunged forward, her sword whistling in so high and close that Danilo felt the wind of it on his face.

He fell back a step, then began to turn in a circle, looking for some way to bridge the verdant barrier between himself and Arilyn. Suddenly the bush ceased its advance. The halted branches, poised as if for renewed flight, began to shimmer with green light. Severed limbs faded into mist. The bush disappeared—all but for the single, half-blown blue rose lying on the marble floor.

From the corner of his eye, Danilo noted that the guests were edging back into the hall, their faces bright with mingled wariness and curiosity. However, his attention was fixed upon the grim, disheveled woman before him, and his usually nimble tongue felt weighted down with stone as he sought for some word of explanation.

"What a remarkable performance. Again, I might add," observed a cultured, feminine, all-too-familiar voice at his elbow.

Without turning, without seeing the direction of the speaker's ice-blue stare, Danilo knew that his mother's ironic commentary included both his miscast spell and Arilyn's response.

So, apparently, did Arilyn. The half-elf's gaze flicked to Danilo's face in wry acknowledgment, then to the sword still in her hands. She thrust the weapon back into its sheath and turned to her hostess.

"My apologies for the disturbance. Again, I might add," Arilyn responded dryly. She gestured to her shredded skirt. "If you'll excuse me, Lady Thann, I think I'd better change."

Cassandra Thann eyed the half-elf with genteel distaste. "On that," she said, with a pause that silently shouted, *if in nothing else,* "we are in accord. Suzanne will show you to a guest room with an appropriate wardrobe. Choose whatever suits you."

It was a command thinly cloaked in courtesy. Arilyn acknowledged both with a curt nod, then turned to follow the maidservant who darted forward to do her mistress's bidding.

Danilo caught Arilyn's arm as she shouldered her way past him. "We'll talk about this later," he said, speaking only for her ears.

She met his eyes and lifted one ebony brow. "On that," she replied in kind, "you can bet your—"

At that moment the dance music resumed, drowning out the last words of her response. Danilo, however, was fairly certain he got the gist of it.

He watched her leave, her stride back to its normal length now that the slender column of velvet no longer hampered her. He sighed as he turned to face the family matriarch, the other of the two most formidable women he knew.

Cassandra Thann was, or so most of Waterdeep believed, sister to Khelben Arunsun. She was also mother to nine children who had in turn supplied her with a small flock of grandchildren. She had probably passed her sixtieth winter, but despite the lines of displeasure creasing her brow, she appeared no more than a decade older than her youngest son. Her carefully arranged hair was just as thick and fair as his, her figure youthful and trim. The fine, sharp, sleek lines of her cheeks and jaw had not been blurred by age. Rumor suggested that Cassandra's beauty owned a debt to potions of longevity, but Danilo didn't believe it. More likely, the years simply didn't dare to touch her.

"Remarkable party," he commented lightly. He clasped his hands behind his back as he eyed the renewed dancing. "Resilient crew, wouldn't you say?"

"A good thing they are," Cassandra retorted, her sharp tone at odds with her blandly smiling countenance. "That ridiculous stunt of yours was nearly the end of this affair."

Danilo watched as Myrna Cassalanter, a young woman with bright henna-colored hair and the eyes of a hungry predator, closed in on his old friend Regnet Amcathra. Rumor had it that the Cassalanter clan was anticipating a match between their house and the young scion of the wealthy Amcathra clan—a rumor probably started by Myrna herself. Regnet, Dan knew, had other thoughts on the matter. Panic, thinly veiled by gallantry, suffused poor Regnet's face as he led Myrna onto the dance floor. No one, it seemed, was having an easy night.

"An early end to the ball. What a disaster that would be," Danilo murmured.

"You insisted upon attending this year," Lady Cassandra pointed out. Her eyes tracked the path Arilyn had taken out of the hall, then turned their full force on her son. "I trust that no announcement will be forthcoming this year?"

This set Danilo back on his heels. For a moment, he wondered how Cassandra had learned of the plans he and Arilyn had cherished four years past. Upon consideration, he realized that his mother's comment owed more to tradition than augury. It was not uncommon for betrothals to be announced at the harvest and spring festivals. Even so, her words disturbed him.

"And if it were?" he challenged.

"Ah." Cassandra smiled faintly, her face reflecting an infuriating mixture of relief and satisfaction. "I thought as much. The rumors considering your . . . liaison . . . with this half-elf have been exaggerated."

Danilo was frankly and thoroughly puzzled. "Arilyn has been my companion for more than six years now, and apart from the debacle at the Gemstone Ball four years ago, you've made no real objection. Why now?"

"Why indeed?" the woman retorted. "As a hired sword, she was more than competent, and when one hires persons with such skills, one must endure the occasional inconvenience of unexpected battle. No real harm was done at the Gemstone that year. This year is another matter entirely. Do not think I have not heard the young women sighing over your elven garden. A man does not gift mere hirelings with a fortune in sapphires and blue roses."

"Arilyn was never a mere hireling."

Cassandra sighed through clenched teeth. "Then it *is* true. Danilo, it is time you considered your position. You are not a lad, to waste your time with trifles and trollops."

It took every ounce of discipline he possessed to hold back the anger that rose in him like a flame. "Have a care, Mother," he said softly. "There are some things I will not hear, even from you."

"Better you hear them from me than another. This half-elf is unworthy of your regard, and there ends the matter."

Danilo studied the dancers for a long moment before he could trust himself to speak. "No, it most assuredly does not, but this discussion ends now, before matters between us are beyond repair. With all respect, my lady, if you were a man, I would be obliged to call you out for such statements."

"If *you* were a man, there would be no need for this

discussion!" she snapped. Her anger cooled as quickly as it flared. "My son, I must be frank."

"Imagine my astonishment," he murmured.

Cassandra let the comment pass. She accepted a glass of wine from a passing servant and used it to make a sweeping gesture that encompassed the sparkling throng. "Look about you. Have you never noticed that there are no elves among Waterdeep's nobility?"

He shrugged. "Yes? So?"

"Perhaps you should ponder that."

Danilo snapped his fingers. "What about the Dezlentyr family? Corinn and Corinna are half-elven, and Corinn stands to inherit the title."

"The title will be challenged, of that you may be certain," she said in a distracted tone. "These are the children of Lord Arlos's elven wife. His first wife," Cassandra stressed. "Do you remember the circumstances of her death?"

A story Danilo had heard in his youth, long since forgotten, floated to the surface of his mind. "She was found dead in the garden," he said slowly. "If I recall aright, Lord Arlos insisted that it was the work of assassins. He claimed that his enemies were loath to see races other than human introduced into the Waterdhavian nobility and that his lady's death was the result. Surely, though, this was nothing more than the raving of a grieving man!"

Cassandra met his eyes once more. "Was it?"

A long moment of silence passed between them, for Danilo could think of nothing to say in the face of such absurdity. Before his wits returned, his mother glided away, and was swept up into the circle of dancers.

* * * * *

Arilyn stalked down the gleaming halls, ignoring the thorns that had pierced her too-thin slippers. At the moment, she would have happily traded her best horse for a pair of stout, practical boots. Not only would they have saved her feet from the skyflower thorns, but they would also lend conviction to the kick she longed to deliver to Danilo's backside.

Whatever had come over the man? Granted, he was fond of pranks. True, he worked behind the carefully constructed façade of a shallow, silly fop. She could accept that much. Much of the time, she derived a considerable amount of secret amusement from his contrived foolishness. She had learned to look behind the jest to the intent, and usually found herself in full agreement with Danilo's goals, if not always his methods. This stunt, however, was utterly beyond her ken.

As Arilyn's ire faded, however, she remembered the look of astonishment on Danilo's face. Then there was his use of Elvish to warn her. This was strange, considering the pains he took to hide his knowledge of the language from his peers. No, there was considerably more to this night's work than a silly prank.

"Are we almost there?" she asked the maidservant as they rounded yet another corner in the labyrinth of halls and rooms within rooms.

The girl looked back over her shoulder and smiled sympathetically. "It is a lovely party, even with that bit of excitement. You must be impatient to return."

Arilyn cast her eyes toward the ceiling and forbore comment. Perhaps by human standards, this *was* a lovely party, but she could not help contrasting elven festivals with Waterdhavian fetes. Here the heart of festive gatherings was politics, business, and intrigue. Deep, true celebration eluded the city's humans.

What could this girl know of such things? How could she know the joy, the unity, that marked elven festivals? Judging from the servant's clear and untroubled smile, she also knew nothing of the heartaches and complexities that could result. Arilyn wasn't altogether certain whether the girl was to be pitied or envied.

Finally the maidservant showed her into a room. She insisted upon bringing out one bright costume after another, expounding the merits of each. Anxious to get on with it, Arilyn pointed out a silver gown that looked about the right size—and that was loose enough to allow freedom of motion. She peeled off her silk slippers and handed them to the maid to give her something to do. The girl exclaimed in dismay over the thorns embedded in the delicate fabric, then settled down to the task of pulling them out and scrubbing at the stains.

Left to her own devices, Arilyn quickly stripped off her ruined gown and tugged on the replacement. A brisk brushing removed clinging bits of twigs and leaves from her hair and left the black curls floating in a wild nimbus about her shoulders. She shifted impatiently from one bare foot to the other as she awaited the return of her shoes.

"I'm afraid they're ruined," the girl said at last. She cast a reproachful look up at Arilyn. "You've bled on them."

"Inconsiderate of me," the half-elf responded dryly. She nodded toward the room-sized closet adjoining the bedchamber. "You have any boots in there?"

The girl's eyes rounded, and she sputtered in protest. Arilyn let her have her say, then simply raised one eyebrow. With a sigh, the maidservant yielded. In moments she emerged, holding a pair of low, thin-soled leather boots gingerly between thumb and forefinger.

"This is not the done thing," she began. "The Lady Cassandra bade me to attend you and find you suitable clothing. She will not thank me for this."

Arilyn suppressed a sigh. The boots were obviously elf-crafted, for they were of butter-soft deerskin dyed a rich blue shade that no human artisan could achieve, and they fairly shimmered with magic. Most likely they were worth more than the collar of silver and sapphires Arilyn wore.

"Elves wear these for dancing," she assured the girl.

"Well . . ."

"If you come to grief over this, send Lady Cassandra to me," Arilyn said firmly. "I will settle the matter."

The girl considered her for a moment. A slow, speculative smile spread across her face. "That is something I would dearly love to see," she said softly.

Arilyn chuckled. "Hand over the boots. If a fight breaks out later, I won't draw first blood until I'm certain you have a good seat. Agreed?"

"Done."

The boots changed hands, and in moments Arilyn was on her way, alone. After the first few turns, she realized that nothing looked familiar. She had been too distracted by her troubled thoughts to mark the way in. Now she, an elf who could track a deer by moonlight and follow a squirrel's trail through the trees, was completely turned around in the maze of rooms and halls.

"Wouldn't Bran be proud?" she muttered, naming the famous human ranger who had sired her. Once Danilo got wind of this misadventure, she would never hear the end of it. Determined to keep her embarrassment to herself, she kept going, merely nodding to the occasional servant or guest she passed.

Her mood darkened with each false turn. Finally she gave in to the inevitable, and decided to ask directions from the next person she encountered.

She heard the sounds of conversation coming from a room at the end of the hall and set off toward it at a brisk pace, silent as a shadow in her borrowed elven boots. She slowed as she neared the door, and listened to the conversation with a mind toward finding an acceptable place to interrupt.

"It is my considered opinion that there is already far too much magic in Waterdeep."

This statement, emphatically spoken by a familiar, faintly accented male voice, halted Arilyn in mid-stride. It was not the sort of thing one expected to hear from Khelben Arunsun, the most powerful wizard in the city and Danilo's long-time mentor.

Arilyn grimaced at her misfortune. If she inquired directions from this assembly, Danilo was certain to hear of her plight.

"You present an interesting proposal, Oth Eltorchul, but a dangerous one," stated a thin, querulous male voice.

That would be Maskar Wands, Arilyn supposed. Danilo had often described the elderly wizard as being as nervous as a brooding hen.

"Dangerous? How so? The dream spheres have been thoroughly tested. The subjects were willing, even eager, and though none of them were persons of much consequence, I am pleased to claim that no ill effects were suffered. To the contrary, the dream spheres gave them a few moments' respite from their dreary little lives."

The man's voice held the well-trained, almost musical tones of an accomplished mage, but the genteel sneer in it set Arilyn's teeth on edge. That was undoubtedly Oth Eltorchul, a member of a wizardly family who engaged in magical training and experimentation. She knew Oth by sight only. He was a tall man with the flame-colored hair common to his clan and ale-colored eyes that brought to mind the fixed stare of a hunting owl. Danilo had studied several years ago with Lord Eltorchul, Oth's father, but he had no use at all for Oth. At the moment, Arilyn was inclined to applaud Dan's judgment.

"Where do these dreams come from?" asked an unfamiliar voice.

A brief silence followed, broken by Oth's scornful laugh. Arilyn thought it was a reasonable question. All dreams came from somewhere.

"They are magical illusions, Lord Gundwynd, nothing more. A created incident that the dreamer experiences as if it were real. Entirely harmless."

"Magic is never entirely harmless," Khelben pointed out. "Every wise man, mage or not, knows this to be true."

There was an angry scraping as a chair was pushed back. "Do you call me a fool, Lord Arunsun?"

"And insult those assembled here?" the archmage returned, his tone edged with exasperation. "Why point out that the sky is blue, when they have eyes to see this for themselves?"

"Now see here!"

Arilyn decided that no good opportunity for interruption would present itself any time soon. She took two steps before another familiar voice halted her.

"Sit down, Oth," Lady Cassandra said firmly, "and listen to the advice you sought. I will speak plainly. No one will sell these dream spheres of yours, for the city's wizards will oppose them. Any attempt to peddle magical illusions from a stall in the bazaar is a foolish challenge to their power and their right to ply their trade. I will have nothing to do with it, or anyone who does."

A murmur of agreement followed her words. "The dream spheres could become vastly popular," Oth insisted. "There is much profit to be made."

"There is profit to be made in the sale of slaves, poisons, and certain types of pipeweed. But such things are forbidden by law, Oth, and you know it well."

"There are no prohibitions against dream spheres," protested Oth.

"There will be," announced a voice Arilyn recognized as Boraldan Ilzimmer. She also noted that the man seemed none too pleased by his own observation. "The wizards' guild holds much power in this city, and their desires will soon be bolstered by force of law."

"Well said, Lord Ilzimmer. The Watchful Order of

Magisters will seek to have these baubles declared illegal. If for some reason they do not, I will see to it myself."

Maskar Wands's voice might be creaky with age, but Arilyn did not doubt that he would do precisely what he said. The patriarch of the Wands clan was probably the most traditional wizard in the city and was vehemently opposed to frivolous or irresponsible magic.

"There you have it," agreed a deeper, younger male voice that Arilyn did not recognize. "You'll find no investors here, Oth. Who would pledge good money to an endeavor destined for failure?"

"Failure is not quite the word I would use," amended Lady Cassandra. "As Oth pointed out, there probably is money to be made with these toys. A prohibition would put this product into the hands of less scrupulous dealers." She sniffed. "Not our kind of people."

"You surprise me, Lady Thann," retorted Boraldan Ilzimmer. "In the past, your words and deeds have matched admirably well. Yet you speak of unscrupulous rogues, even while you entertain the elf lord Elaith Craulnober under this very roof. Consorting with elves, even if they were the honorable sort, is hardly the done thing."

"That is my son's doing, not mine," Cassandra said in clipped tones. "Perhaps I indulge him too much."

Arilyn blinked, startled by this news. She had not seen Elaith among the revelers but she could hardly blame Lady Thann for her displeasure.

Danilo and Elaith had been foes for as long as she'd known either of them. Matters had changed earlier that summer, when Danilo had repaid the elf's treachery by saving his life. Elaith might be a rogue and a scoundrel, but he was still an elf and he followed certain codes of honor. He had named Danilo an Elf-friend, the highest honor an elf could pay a human. Danilo probably thought including Elaith among his guests was the only natural thing to do. Arilyn could understand why Cassandra would think otherwise.

"I don't trust the elf, and I don't appreciate his inclusion among the peerage," Boraldan said flatly. "If any problems arise—"

"He will be dealt with," Cassandra said firmly, and with great finality. "Are we agreed that Lord Oth will not sell these toys?"

"If I do not, then someone else will," Oth said stubbornly. "Once a thing is made it cannot long be hidden. Word of these marvels will spread. Someone will find a way to profit from them. Better it be one of us."

A long, pregnant silence followed his words, one that Arilyn could not interpret. "There are strictures on trade," Cassandra Thann said carefully, "that are not always obvious to those who buy and sell in the shops and stalls. Those who try to circumvent these restraints often come to grief."

"I am heir to the Eltorchul lordship," Oth said indignantly. "Do you presume to threaten me?"

"Not at all," the woman said in a wry tone, "but you asked for an audience and for our advice. It has been given."

"I understand," Oth said in a stiff voice.

Arilyn did not, but she was not particularly interested in learning more. Nor did she wish to be discovered eavesdropping. She headed for the stairwell at the end of the hall and hurried down the tightly curving spiral. Sooner or later, she reasoned, she would reach the main floor, and the din emanating from the great hall would make tracking easy.

Several moments passed, and Arilyn judged that she had descended a depth sufficient to bring her well past the main floor, but no doors led out of the stairwell. She continued down. The stairwell tightened, and the flick-

~~~ light of the torches thrust into iron wall brackets

~~~~~ darkness. Her eyes adjusted, slipping past

the need for light into the elven range, where heat registered in complex and subtle patterns.

The stairs ended in a dark and silent hall beneath the Thann estate. To one side, a vast, cool room was honeycombed with small shelves filled with dusty bottles. The Thanns were wine merchants, and Danilo had often remarked on their cellars. Arilyn spared this treasure trove no more than a glance. Her attention fixed upon the footprints that led past the door.

They were heat prints, large and faint. Several sets of them, by the looks of it. She dropped to one knee for a better look, and her eyes widened.

The tracks belonged to tren—huge, reptilian creatures that lived beneath ground, surfacing only to ply their trade. Arilyn had reason to know this. Tren were assassins, and she had crossed swords with them before. In her experience, they did not venture this far above ground without deadly purpose. She knew them well enough to realize that tren bodies warmed or cooled with their surroundings, so their heat prints were faint even when fresh.

These were very fresh, indeed.

Quietly, Arilyn rose to her feet and slid her sword from its sheath. Her own feet, elf-shod and magically protected, left no telltale marks as she began to follow the assassins' trail.

Two

Danilo glanced up at one of the tall, narrow windows that lined the great hall. The moon had risen perhaps twice its own width since his miscast spell. Arilyn was taking far more time in returning than he had anticipated.

A hearty clap on the back shook him from his reverie. A tall man with curly brown hair regarded him with mock dismay. "Look at you! Snared like a hare! Tell me, how long have you been waiting for this woman?"

Danilo turned a wry grin upon his friend Regnet Amcathra, then nodded toward Myrna Cassalanter, who was whispering tales to a woman wearing an emerald colored gown and an expression of scandalized delight. "About as long as you have been evading that one."

Regnet threw back his head and laughed. "An eternity, it would seem! And the night is still young! However, I was not speaking only of tonight. In truth, Dan, it seems years since we've gone out drinking and wenching together. There are many woman in this wide world, you know."

"One who matters." Danilo's gaze slid again to the door through which Arilyn had disappeared.

Regnet shook his head. "One woman!" he mourned. "When I consider the straits to which you have been reduced!"

"I have other vices," Danilo assured him, brandishing an empty goblet.

"Well, that's a comfort." The nobleman scanned the room, and his eyes lit up as they settled upon a pretty barmaid at the far end of the hall. "We are in luck. There's a sight to gladden us both."

They sauntered over to the table, and Regnet immediately busied himself with a flirtation. Danilo applauded his choice. The girl was a merry lass with red-gold hair, laughing gray eyes, and dimples that flashed in genuine good humor. Her voice might be rough with the accents of the shantytowns of Dock Ward, but there was nothing blunt about her wit.

"Don't be taking this amiss," she advised Regnet, "but you'd best be moving on. There's a moor fire burning this way."

Danilo followed the line of her gaze and burst out laughing. Myrna Cassalanter advanced, her gaze intent upon Regnet. With her scarlet hair and even brighter gown, she did rather resemble a wind-driven blaze. Moor fires were considered terrible omens, and in practical terms the burning bog gasses left a foul scent behind. Dan could not imagine a better description of Myrna, a gossipmonger by profession and inclination, than that supplied by the barmaid.

When Myrna had dragged her prey away to the dancing, Danilo lifted his glass to the serving girl in silent salute. She responded with a quick, impish smile and then a shrug.

"I've seen enough of such things to name them true."

"Bog fires?" Dan inquired with a grin.

"Wouldn't that be fine!" the girl replied wistfully. "No,

I've never stepped beyond these city walls."

He helped himself to a bottle from the table and refilled his glass. There was no self-pity in the girl's voice, but he recognized the sound of genuine longing— and the echo of his own restless nature. "Where would you go?"

She shrugged again. "Anywhere that doesn't smell of fish and ale would suit me fine."

Danilo laughed and captured a ripe apricot from the tray of a passing servant. "These help a bit, when I'm feeling restless. Taste it, and see if the flavor doesn't conjure images of warm sunshine and distant lands."

"Oh, I dare not eat on duty," she protested, although she considered the fruit as if it were a rare gem. "Besides, if I pocket it, folks might think ill of me."

He nodded, understanding this. Thievery by servants was severely punished. Even so, it didn't seem right to deny them the festive fare they helped to serve. "Give me your name, then, and I'll have some sent to you."

"Will you, now?" she retorted with good-natured skepticism. "Along with a case of that elven wine, I suppose. . . . "

Her words faded as something seized her attention. Danilo followed the line of her gaze and grimaced. Not far away, an exceedingly curvaceous young woman was dancing with an amorous nobleman. Both partners' hands were far busier than their feet. Normally, Danilo would not consider this odd—after all, the attention Myrna lavished upon Regnet was even less subtle—but he had reason to distrust this particular woman. It would seem that Sofia the pickpocket was having a bit of a problem with her transition to Lady Isabeau.

"Excuse me," he murmured as he set down his glass.

A look of deep consternation flashed across the girl's pretty face. "Have a care with that one, sir. Looks fine as frog's hair, she does, but I've seen things. That one is trouble."

"You've a very good eye," he commented as he began to move away. "Thank you for your advice. I shall bear it in mind."

"Lilly," she said abruptly.

He turned back, lifting one brow in inquiry.

"My name," the girl explained. "Just wanted you to be knowing it. Your name, I'm already knowing." She grinned again. "It's been spoken."

"Yes, I can imagine," he said dryly, enjoying the woman's wry, impish humor—even when it came at his expense. He touched his forehead in parting salute. "Lilly, it has been a rare pleasure."

He deftly intercepted Isabeau from her partner and danced her as unobtrusively as possible into an alcove.

As soon as no eyes were upon them, Isabeau pulled away. She squared her shoulders, not so much in defiance as to better frame the expanse of feminine charm displayed between her ruby necklace and her low-laced gown.

"Calling in your debts, Lord Thann?" she said mockingly. "A tryst, in exchange for my rescue and my new position? I have been expecting you to name that coin, but not in so public a place."

Danilo stuck out his hand, palm up. "I've come to collect—you're right about that much. Hand it over."

She pouted, the picture of insulted innocence. "I don't understand."

"Clearly. May I remind you that you are Isabeau Thione, a noblewoman related to the royal house of Tethyr? I know this is all very new to you, but you must learn to comport yourself according to the mores of Waterdhavian nobility."

"Huzzah!" She gave him a cool, mocking smile and a little patter of applause. "Bring him the prize for stuffiest speech of the night! In truth, Lord Thann, the only difference between me and most of these fine people is that *they* steal larger quantities, usually from those who can ill afford the loss. I have been in this city for only a few tendays, and already I know that much!"

Danilo refused to be distracted. "Don't make me sorry I brought you here," he warned her. "There are those who would be only too happy to take you back to Tethyr."

Isabeau abruptly sobered. Her black eyes darted across the room to the silver-haired elf with a hawk's watchful amber eyes.

"Very well," she said petulantly, and began to empty her pocket. In moments Dan's hands were heaped with items she had taken from her dance partners: coins, pendants, a small crystal sphere, even a ring—an unusual piece set with a large stone of rosy quartz.

He regarded the haul with dismay. "Have you any idea how long it will take me to sort through these things and return them without suspicion to their owners?"

The woman folded her arms over her abundant cleavage and smiled. "There is an easy solution. Give them back to me, and save yourself the trouble."

Danilo sighed and spilled the treasure into the bag attached to his belt. "Perhaps you should leave, Isabeau. We'll discuss this later."

"Much later, I hope," she said airily. Her eyes scanned the crowd, no doubt looking for one of her victims. She glided from the alcove and disappeared into the swirling, silken haze of the dance floor.

For a moment, Dan was tempted to follow. After all, he and Arilyn had brought Isabeau to the safety of Waterdeep. Though they had both come to rue and reject the Harper reasoning that had ordered this mission, a personal responsibility remained: they had to keep Waterdeep safe from Isabeau.

* * * * *

Elaith Craulnober saw Danilo whisk the southern woman into an alcove and had little doubt about the reason for it. The wench was a thief, and she was damned good at her work. She had stolen a dagger from him—*him!*—earlier that very summer, and in doing so had nearly gotten him hanged.

This made Isabeau Thione unique in Waterdeep. She was the only person who had seriously crossed Elaith who still drew breath. The elf would not have made her an exception but for the debt he owed Danilo Thann. How could he refuse something so paltry as a woman's life, measured against the worth of his own?

They had traveled a far path, he and the human bard. Elaith had once hired underlings to kill Danilo— a deed he considered too trivial to take upon himself. By now, though, his regard for young Lord Thann had changed from utter loathing to grudging respect. If not for Danilo, Elaith would have been slain by a passel of vengeful gnomes for a murder he did not commit. Elaith had chosen to repay that debt in elven fashion, and named the man Elf-friend.

Elf-friend. It was a rare gift, a pledge of absolute acceptance and loyalty, an honor rarely conferred upon humankind.

It was also without doubt the most stupid thing he had done in decades.

The primary proof of that was Elaith's presence at this wretched party. With the exception of a few hired musicians and Danilo's half-elven love, Elaith was the only elf in attendance. To say that he drew attention would be a vast understatement. Elaith preferred not to garner much notice. It seemed prudent, given the nature of his activities.

Therein lay Elaith's second source of disgruntlement. He was a rogue elf, wealthy through endeavors that ran the whole gamut from sanctioned to suspect to hideously illegal. His life had long ago turned onto a dark and twisting path. Yet of late, he had acquired pockets of virtue that were, not to put too fine a point on it, damnably inconvenient. Honor, loyalty, tradition—these were garments Elaith had long ago cast off, now much moth-eaten and of uncertain fit.

One of the more inebriated guests began to lurch purposefully in the elf's direction. Elaith regarded the man with keen displeasure. He was not a particularly imposing specimen of humankind. Of middling height, he had narrow, sloping shoulders and a meager chest. Most of his weight had settled in his haunches and hams. His sandy hair was shorn close to his head, and his beard was trimmed to a sharp point—no doubt in an effort to suggest resemblance to a satyr. In reality, the overall effect was nothing loftier than a two-legged billy goat.

The merchant immediately began to regale Elaith with stories. Since the only escape the elf could see involved a quick dagger and a faster exit, he merely let the slurred words flow over him as he observed the crowd.

There was much to learn at such gatherings, and the elf's quick eye had already discerned several interesting meetings, some unusual alliances, and some outright deals. He had long been of the opinion that information was as valuable a currency as gold, and already he had gained enough to repay himself for the tedium of attending the dreary affair.

" . . . sell the elf gem right out from under him, I will," boasted the merchant.

Elaith's attention snapped back to his captor. "The elf gem," he prompted.

"Big thing," the man said, beaming at this sign of interest. "A ruby, full of magic." He leaned in and elbowed the elf's ribs sharply. "Getting fuller by the day, too, eh? Eh?"

Elaith grimly added the presumptuous lout to the list of those whose funerals he would dearly love to attend. A list, he added, that was growing nearly as fast as Danilo's skyflower bush. It was so much tidier to kill people as you went along and have done with it. Isabeau Thione might be beyond Elaith's blade, but this man was shielded only by a bit of unlearned information.

"I am remiss," Elaith said in cordial tones. "Your name has escaped me."

The merchant drew himself up, weaving only slightly. "Mizzen Doar of Silverymoon. Purveyor of fine gems and crystals."

"Of course. And the gentlemen who is the target of your clever plan?"

Elaith's questions had an unforeseen effect. As the merchant gathered himself in an effort to form an answer, his vague smile wavered, and his bleary eyes focused and then went bright with fear. "I know you," he said in a clearer tone than he had used thus far. "Damn me for a fool! You're That Elf."

The man spun and reeled off with indecent haste. This garnered Elaith a number of suspicious glances and set a good many tongues wagging.

The unfortunate result, he noted wryly, of a long and misspent life. For decades he had cloaked his misdeeds with his handsome elven features and abundant charm. Eventually, deeds had a way of growing into reputation.

All things considered, he was not very surprised when a servant discreetly handed him a folded note along with a goblet of wine. Probably a request from his redoubtable hostess that he remove himself. Or, just as likely, a summons from one of the apparently staid and proper members of the merchant nobility, who wished to make a deal beyond the gleam of this gilded circle.

A glance told the whole tale. On the paper was a maze of tiny lines—undoubtedly a map. Interesting. It was unlikely that any of the merchant nobility would risk contact with the rogue elf unless the matter held considerable urgency. Most likely, it was a summons from a member of the Thann family or one of their retainers, judging from the complexity of the map. He could always deal with Mizzen later.

With a faint smile, Elaith slipped the note into his pocket. He finished the wine and then drifted out into the gardens, and toward the meeting to which he had been summoned.

*　*　*　*　*

Alone in the alcove, Danilo slumped against the wall and considered his predicament. Isabeau had robbed more than a dozen guests. Lady Cassandra would be mortified and shamed if it became known that a thief had been working her party. Danilo, for all his disagreements with his mother, had no wish to see her suffer such humiliation.

Neither could he hold her entirely blameless. He had warned Lady Cassandra that such a thing might occur. Isabeau Thione had been trouble from the day he'd met her, and he had told Cassandra so. But no—his mother had been too taken with the Thione name, too determined to have a member of the restored Royal House of Tethyr at her harvest festival.

Well, he had done his part. The choice had been Lady Cassandra's, and she would have to find a way to deal with the consequences.

A probable solution occurred to him, one so obvious and yet so chilling that it slammed into his mind like an icy fist. "If there's any trouble, Elaith will be blamed," he muttered. "Damnation! Why didn't I think of this sooner?"

Danilo dug a handful of Isabeau's booty from his bag and regarded the glittering baubles balefully. The markings on the ring caught his eye. Engraved into the rosy stone was a leaping flame surrounded by seven tiny tears: the symbol of Mystra, goddess of magic.

He groaned aloud. Isabeau, either in ignorance or in supreme arrogance, had robbed a mage!

He lifted the ring for closer examination. Tiny hinges were cunningly concealed in the setting, indicating a hidden compartment. He found and released the clasp, then lifted the cover. On the inside lid was etched the tall, old-fashioned wizard's cap—the Eltorchul family crest. The cavity was filled with powder the color of old ivory.

Dan sniffed cautiously at the powder. Pulverized bone, most likely, no doubt a component for one of the Eltorchul's shapeshifting spells.

"Have a care," advised a stiff, patronizing voice. "You could find yourself turned into a jackass."

He glanced up into Oth Eltorchul's narrow, esthetic face. With great effort, he mustered up a good-natured smile. "Some might argue that such a transformation would be redundant. This ring is yours, I take it?"

The Eltorchul mage strode forward. He was too well-bred to snatch the ring from Danilo's hand, but he came as close as proprieties allowed. "I must have left it on the privacy washbasin. How did it come to your possession?"

"A lady picked it up and gave it to me so that I might find the owner," Danilo said, truthfully enough. "I must say, it is a fortunate coincidence that you happened by just now."

"No coincidence at all. I sought you out to ask of you a question."

It did not escape Danilo that this admission seemed to pain Oth. "Oh?"

"The blue rose. The elven swordswoman."

Danilo wasn't sure where this was going, but he doubted he would like the destination. His curt nod held scant encouragement.

The mage hesitated, clearly loath to find himself in the position of supplicant. "I have heard stories claiming that you can cast the elven magic known as spellsong. Such magic is beyond my grasp. If you have this knowledge, I desire you to teach it to me."

That was not the question Danilo had expected to hear and the last he intended to answer.

He had indeed learned and cast a uniquely elven spell on an enchanted elven harp, but he had never since been able to recapture the elusive spirit of elven spellsong. At the time, he had not realized that the magic of Arilyn's moonblade had bound his destiny to that of the elves in deep and mystical ways. When the connection was severed, his fragile link with elven magic had vanished. He had told this to no man, and did not intend to begin by confiding in this one.

"You know how rumors grow in the telling," he said lightly.

"So you cannot cast spellsong?"

Dan wasn't sure whether Oth looked disappointed or vindicated. "No, I cannot."

"Ah. Well, it is no real surprise. Elves are notoriously close-pursed when it comes to such matters."

The man's mixture of arrogance and ignorance floored Dan, though he knew that it should not. After all, Oth sustained his family fortune by creating and selling new magical spells. He had probably approached an elven sage, prepared to barter like a camel trader for magic that elves held dearer than family heirlooms or crown jewels. That image, and the inevitable reaction, brought a quick, wicked smile to Danilo's face. He quickly squelched it, not wishing to insult the mage.

However, Oth's attention had settled elsewhere. He was regarding Isabeau with speculation.

"Lovely woman," Danilo said, hoping that this was the only inspiration for Oth's interest. It was entirely possible that Oth could have tracked the path taken by his lost ring and that his stated interest in spellsong was a story to cover his true intent. There was no trace of anger on Oth's face, though, as he regarded the beautiful thief.

"Very lovely," the mage agreed. "If you will excuse me, I shall attempt to claim a last dance." He slanted a glance back at Danilo. "You might do well, young man, to do likewise. There are many *ladies* of *good family* at this affair."

His meaning was unmistakable and offensive. Danilo had parried one insult too many on Arilyn's behalf, and he reacted as any man of his rank did when his lady's name and honor was maligned. He stepped forward, one hand instinctively dropping to his sword belt in anticipation of formal challenge.

This amused the mage. "I think not, young Lord Thann. You are unarmed. In more ways than one, I might add. If that fascinating horticultural display was typical of your magical talents, you would do well to leave the Art strictly alone, much less challenge an accomplished mage."

The irony of Oth's statement was nearly as powerful a challenge as the insult to Arilyn had been. Power thrummed through Danilo's mind, sang in his blood, and set his fingertips tingling. He could squash this supercilious toad of a man beneath one foot without leaving a smudge on his boots. The knowledge both tempted and repelled him.

Danilo inclined his head, the gesture of one gentleman conceding to another. "I think we agree, Lord Eltorchul, that an uneven challenge does no honor to either man."

For a long moment the mage stared at him, as if trying to decide whether Danilo's words held self-deprecating agreement or subtle insult. Color rose high on his cheeks, making his narrow face nearly as red as his hair. He answered Danilo's bow with a curt one of his own, then spun on his heel and stalked off into the swirling throng.

* * * * *

Arilyn crept along the tunnels, following the faint and rapidly fading trail. All her senses hummed with awareness as she rounded a corner, even though her moonblade's magical danger-warnings were oddly silent. She might not have perceived the ambush at all but for the flick of an anticipatory tongue, like that of a giant hunting snake.

She froze, understanding that the tren's vision required movement. When the creatures paid her no heed, she slowly melted back into the shadows for a better look.

Despite her sharp elven vision, several heartbeats passed before she could discern the creatures from the shadows in which they hid. Chameleonlike, they blended with the color and texture and even the heat patterns of the stone walls. There were five of them—tall, scaly, thick-bodied creatures that walked about on two legs. A stub of vestigial tail spoke of their lizard-man ancestry, as did the wide, cruelly curving mouths filled with sharp, reptilian teeth. All the creatures held long daggers, though the claws on their massive hands made such weapons seem redundant. One of them, the largest of the group and probably the leader, held a small, sickle-shaped knife.

Bile rose in Arilyn's throat as she understood the nature of the tool. The hooked blade was not designed to kill but to disembowel a living victim. The prey would still be alive when the creatures began to feed. Tren were highly effective assassins, voracious killers and feeders who left little trace of their crime. Dimly she saw a line of drool spilling from the corner of the tren chieftain's fanged maw as it anticipated the kill. All the creatures were poised for a sudden spring, yet they did not attack.

It was clear to Arilyn that the tren did not sense her

presence. Well enough. She would bide her time and aid whoever fell unwitting into this trap.

A light hand rested on her shoulder, another grasped the wrist of her sword arm in the elven signal for peace. Arilyn whipped around, startled and chagrined that anyone could approach her unheard.

She found herself face to face with a tall, silver-haired moon elf—an elf she knew far better than she wished to.

Three

There was no sense in putting the task off—the rest of Isabeau's booty had to be returned. Danilo took a silver bracer from his bag and began to examine it for signs of ownership.

A short, sandy-haired man burst into the alcove, pulling up when he saw he was not alone. With his bulging eyes and scant, pointy beard, the man reminded Dan of a panicked billy goat. Resigned to an eventful evening, the nobleman rose. "Is something amiss, sir? Can I be of some service?"

The man sank down on the chair Dan had vacated and sucked in a wheezing, ragged gasp. "No. No, he's left. Just need to catch my breath."

The sheer terror in the man's eyes set off alarms in Danilo's mind. He knew full well who at the party could best inspire this emotion. "If someone offended you, the Lady Cassandra would certainly wish to know," he prompted.

"No need. Already been dealt with," the man said shortly. He gathered himself and rose to his feet. Squaring his meager shoulders, he gave Danilo a curt nod and then lurched into the crowd.

Danilo followed, his eyes sweeping the crowd for the slim, gleaming figure of Elaith Craulnober. The elf had, appropriately enough, chosen moonstone for his gem color. In a throng of jewel-bright reds and greens and blue, his silvery hair and the pale satin of his costume—milky white swirled and shadowed with blue—made the elf look like a living blade. Danilo wondered, briefly, if Elaith had deliberately fostered this image.

But no. That was unlikely, given his choice of gem color. The moonstone was a semiprecious stone, a powerful conductor of magic. It was often used in elven magic and was the magical cornerstone of the moonblades' power. Elaith possessed such a sword, though it had long ago gone dormant to proclaim him an unworthy heir. For many years the moonblade had been to Elaith a symbol of disgrace and failure. He had gone to great trouble to reawaken the sword, which he held in trust until his only daughter came of age. What could the elf's costume mean but a reclaiming of his honor?

On the other hand, why wasn't Elaith in the hall?

Why had the goatlike little man been so afraid?

Knowing Elaith as he did, Danilo could summon up any number of answers to the second query. With a sigh, he thrust the stolen bracelet back into his bag and headed toward the door. It might be wise to inquire of the grooms whether or not Elaith had left—and if not, to find him and put a stop to whatever mischief he was engaged in. For a moment Danilo understood his mother's exasperation with him. Thanks to his efforts, Lady Cassandra's guest list included a Tethyrian pickpocket, a reputed half-elven assassin, and a deadly elf who was, among other things, possibly the most successful crime lord north of Skullport.

"In order to exceed myself," he murmured as he strode through the garden, "next year I shall have to produce a pair of illithids and a red dragon."

* * * * *

Arilyn stared into Elaith Craulnober's amber eyes, startled into immobility by his sudden appearance.

"This is most unexpected," the elf said in a mellifluent voice that fell just short of song. "I had thought to find a rather different messenger."

She shook off his hold and fell into a battle-ready crouch. "If you've a weapon, draw it," she gritted. "Your *'message'* is about to be delivered."

With a single, deft motion, Elaith drew two knives from sheaths hidden beneath his sleeves. His puzzlement and hesitation were clear even to her heat-reading vision.

The tren came on in a rush, and a mixture of comprehension and relief flooded the elf's visage. This was a foe he could fight without reservation. With the speed of a striking snake, he darted forward, blades raised high to intercept the first slashing blow.

Arilyn heard the clash of steel on steel, but her gaze was fixed upon the two creatures charging her. They held their knives in their massive fisted hands, blades pointed straight down for a quick, stabbing attack.

It was a difficult assault to defend against. Arilyn sidestepped the nearest tren and lifted her sword in a glancing parry, point slanted back over her shoulder. The descending knife slid harmlessly down her blade.

She disengaged quickly, ducked under the slashing blow of the second tren, and spun around as she rose. Careful to keep beyond reach of the wicked spikes that thrust back from the tren's elbows, she whirled past the creature, bringing her sword around level in a hard, slashing, two-handed attack.

With speed and agility remarkable in a creature so large, the tren managed a nimble two-step dodge and leaned sharply away from the attack, its long arms flung up to retain balance.

Arilyn had anticipated this. She changed the direction of her stoke, shifted to her back foot, and then came in straight ahead with a hard thrust. Her sword bit deep into the tren's exposed armpit. She felt the blade grate against bone, and she threw her weight into the attack.

The moonblade sank deep into reptilian flesh, piercing the lung and seeking the creature's main heart. Blood burst from the creature's maw, a sign that she had struck true.

Arilyn planted one foot against the tren's body and kicked herself off. As the sword came free, she spun back toward her first attacker. The moonblade cut through the air with an audible swish, which ended with the rasp of metal against reptilian scales. A line of blood welled up across the breadth of the creature's chest.

She retreated a few steps and assessed the situation. The cut she had dealt the tren was not a mortal wound. Grunting with outrage, the tren reached up with clawed hands to pinch the edges of his hide together. His reptilian eyes glazed as he called upon his next attack.

Immediately a foul miasma filled the tunnel. Arilyn fell back, choking and gagging at the stench. Elaith was at her side in a moment, pressing a square of linen into her hands. Though she doubted this would prove much of a barrier to the debilitating spray, she clapped the cloth over her nose.

A faint, floral scent swirled deep into her, filling her with a sensation like sparkling wine drunk too quickly and deeply. The terrible stench faded into memory as the antidote took effect. Arilyn blinked tears from her streaming eyes and brought her sword up in guard position.

Just in time. The wounded tren, thinking her beyond battle, was coming in confidently for the kill. One of his clawed hands still clutched at the wound, the other

reached for her throat. Behind him came the leader, hi
sickle blade raised in anticipation.

Arilyn danced beyond the reach of the wounde
tren's grasping claws. Before she could take the offen
sive, a small, silver knife spun between her and he
attacker, burying itself deep into the narrow gas
Arilyn's sword had opened.

She glanced over at Elaith, wondering how he coul
consider her situation in the midst of his own battl
That was all but over. He had felled one of the crea
tures, and his twin daggers dealt with the last as
shark might dispatch a wounded whale—slicing off on
bloody bite at a time.

Anger rose in her like a hot, bright tide. Elaith migh
have aided her, not once but twice, yet what of his ow
battle code? There was little honor in his methods, non
at all in the dark pleasure written on his face.

She set her teeth, determined to end this as quickl
as possible. Two of her assailants were finished. Th
knife-struck tren had stopped its advance as sharply a
if it had hit a magic wall. Its claws made small, flutter
movements in the air and then groped for the hilt
Elaith's thrown blade. The creature's body stiffened an
began to topple forward.

The leader let out a roar of outrage and charged th
half-elf. Its sickle blade slashed the air in anticipatio
of deadly harvest.

Arilyn stepped aside, putting the dying creature be
tween herself and her attacker. The tren kept on, to
enraged to pull his attack. His curved blade hooke
deep into the soft folds under the dying tren's throat
Before he could pull the weapon free, his comrade'
falling weight bore him down. Arilyn lunged, her swor
diving for the assassin's eye.

The tip of her sword struck the bony ridge, slid wetl
across the scales and sought the narrow socket.

The tren was too quick for her. With another roar, h

tossed his enormous head and threw her sword wide. Wrenching the sickle free of his comrade's slack throat, the tren backed away from the carcasses of his clan. He melted into the shadows as completely as a drop of water might merge with the sea.

Arilyn's first impulse was pursuit, but years on the battlefield prompted her not to turn her back too soon on any opponent. She spun, sword held in guard position before her, prepared to face the final tren—or its elven opponent.

The last tren was weaving on its feet, bleeding from scores of wounds. There was no fight left in the creature. Its long arms hung slack, claws scraping the stone floor as it rocked on unsteady legs.

Yet Elaith showed no signs of ending the game. Arilyn had seen barn cats show more mercy in torturing a captured squirrel, and less pleasure.

"End it!" she snapped.

The elf shot her a quick, startled glance, as if he'd suddenly recalled where and who he was. For a moment Arilyn could have sworn that his handsome features wore an expression of shame.

Elaith turned aside quickly, as if from some unwanted truth. He dropped one dripping weapon to the floor and produced a slender knife from some hidden fold of his festive garb. A quick flick sent the blade hurtling into the inner corner of the creature's slack mouth. The silver tip burst through the hide on the opposing side of the tren's throat, opening the way for a bright, quick flow of lifeblood. The tren sank quickly, almost gratefully, to the blood-soaked floor.

For a long moment elf and half-elf regarded each other. Disgust and gratitude warred for possession of Arilyn's first words. "I should thank you," she began.

"Much against your personal inclination," Elaith cut in smoothly. He lifted one hand to forestall the words one elf spoke to another after shared battle. "There is no debt, Princess. I have been pledged from birth to serve the royal house. My sword is yours."

That shut Arilyn up, as no doubt Elaith had intended it to do. The rogue elf was one of the few who knew of her heritage and the only elf who openly acknowledged it. Among the Tel'Quessar—the elven term which meant simply and exclusively "The People"—there was little honor in being the half-breed daughter of an exiled princess. Elaith, for his own reasons, seemed to think otherwise.

She turned away and busied herself with cleaning her sword. "We should follow that last tren."

"Undoubtedly," Elaith said, and smiled faintly. "Unless I miss my guess, however, another battle awaits you above. This has been a most eventful evening."

Arilyn did not dispute that. First Danilo's mishap with the skyflower spell, then the odd conversation she'd overheard.

The words Cassandra Thann had spoken came back to her—the promise to promptly deal with any trouble Elaith might cause. In the aftermath of battle with paid assassins, these words held a new and sinister meaning.

She shook her head, denying this absurd thought. Lady Cassandra might be a two-legged dragon, but Arilyn could not picture her hiring assassins to deal with misbehaving guests. On the other hand, there was the risk that Elaith might believe this to be true, and take action accordingly.

The elf kicked at one hulking carcass. "I wonder who hired this crew," he mused, echoing her concerns with discomforting accuracy.

Arilyn cleared her throat. "Any thoughts?"

"The possibilities are nearly endless," he said lightly. "Do you think this is the first time such a thing has occurred? Don't trouble yourself over it. I do not intend to."

Arilyn mistrusted his easy dismissal of the matter. "I will speak to Danilo of this," she said softly. She studied

Elaith as he absorbed the many levels of meaning in her words.

The elf cut sharply to the foundation of her fears. "Do you believe that Lord Thann invited me to his family home so that I might meet with these assassins?"

"No!"

"Neither do I." Elaith seemed ready to say more, but he shook his head and turned away.

Arilyn let him go. As he had observed, she had another battle ahead. Once Elaith was well out of sight, she began to follow his trail through a maze of underground paths. This ended with a hidden door and then a short flight of stone stairs leading to an open bulkhead. Arilyn glanced up into what appeared to be a garden shed. Above her was the black velvet sky, and a moon well past its zenith. Her side trip had taken far longer than she realized.

The Gemstone Ball awaited. Offhand, Arilyn could name a dozen bloody battlefields she had faced with more enthusiasm and less dread. With a sigh of deep frustration, she squared her shoulders, hitched up her borrowed gown, and resolutely climbed the stairs.

* * * * *

The oil lamp on the bedside table flickered and went out. By the dim light of the hearth fire, Oth Eltorchul regarded the woman stretched out languidly at his side.

"A pleasant end to an otherwise regrettable evening," he said.

Pleasant was she? That was the best he could do? Not trusting herself to speak, Isabeau bared her teeth in a brief, answering smile.

Her gaze flicked to the mage's discarded garments, which he had hung neatly on pegs. Isabeau's practiced eye measured the weight of the hidden pockets and estimated the worth therein. It would have to be considerable to make the evening—and the man—worth her while.

Her own ruby-colored gown pooled on the floor like spilled wine. Rings, eardrops, and a necklace of matching red stones were scattered on the bedside table. They were glass, of course, clever copies that were all Isabeau could currently afford—a situation she intended to remedy as soon as possible. So far, the night had been less than profitable. Danilo Thann's intervention had set her back considerably. Eager to get on with things, Isabeau impatiently studied Oth's face for signs of slumberous contentment.

The mage, however, was in an expansive mood, ready to reprise the complaints she had endured all the way to The Silken Sylph. "They will regret refusing me, you know. They treated me like some importunate commoner, with none of the honor due a member of the peerage. A small investment, a moment's endorsement—what is that to such as Thann, Ilzimmer, and Gundwynd? The dream spheres could have made all three families exceedingly wealthy!"

Isabeau twined a strand of Oth's flame-colored hair around her finger. "They are wealthy already, my lord."

Oth sent her a sharp, angry glance, a movement that tugged the red lock from her grasp. He did not seem to notice. "You do not regard the dream spheres with appropriate respect. You would if you tasted but once of their magic!"

This notion seemed to galvanize him. He sat up abruptly, absently smoothing back his tousled red hair. "What is your heart's desire? What wonders do you wish to experience?"

She gave him a slow, warm smile. "My lord, at this moment I am well content."

The mage waved aside this flattery. "You are of the Tethyrian royal house, but I hear that you were raised in fosterage and have never stepped foot in your native land. Would you like to claim what might have been yours, if but for a moment? Would you like to see the palace? Enjoy an audience with the new queen?"

Not waiting for her reply, Oth leaped to his feet and paced over to his cloak. He flipped back the folds and took a small, softly glowing sphere from one pocket. This he placed in Isabeau's hand.

"Hold this. Close your eyes and envision the sun upon towers of pink marble," he instructed.

Isabeau did as he bade, more to humor him than from any desire to experience the illusion. Why would anyone content herself with a fleeting dream? She had always lived by a simple rule: What she wanted, she took. No longer were her horizons defined by the boundaries of the out-of-the-way, gnome-run tavern that was the only home she had ever known. Now her territory was a vast, glittering city, and her fingers fairly itched with the desire to grasp all that her eyes had seen so far.

Nevertheless, a strange fragrance beckoned her, seduced her. Isabeau breathed in deeply, letting the scent of the southern sun flow through her in all its complexity of thick, flower-filled heat, musky-sweet fruits, and rare spices. The aroma suddenly burst into light, like festival fireworks, which in turn slowly focused into a scene so lavish that Isabeau's heart throbbed with longing.

Lords and ladies, viziers and courtiers were finely dressed and seated at tables draped with embroidered linens and set with silver plate. Behind them were the pink marble walls of the palace, enlivened by wondrous tapestries. The table was set with a royal repast. Rare tropical fruits were piled high on silver platters. Fragrant steam rose from plates of tiny, savory pastries. On each table was a roasted peacock. Their bright blue and green tails had been reattached in unfurled splendor, creating the impression that the proud birds were courting the diners to partake.

At the moment, no one ate of the feast. All present lifted their goblets in salute. It occurred to Isabeau that they were all looking at her, Lady Isabeau Thione of the House of Tethyr. She nodded graciously, regally, to accept their acclaim.

"To Queen Zaranda!" exclaimed a fat man with oiled black hair.

"Zaranda!" echoed the others in one voice.

Isabeau swallowed her mortification and hastily reached for her own goblet. She barely had time to lift it to her lips before the toast was drunk. To her relief—and her chagrin—no one seemed to notice her faux pas. All eyes were fixed upon the woman seated at the royal table behind and to the right of Isabeau's seat.

Isabeau cast a careful, sidelong look at the queen. Zaranda was a handsome woman in early middle life. She possessed the sparse body of a warrior, strong features, and thick dark hair emblazoned by a streak of white. She was simply dressed and wore no jewels but a silver crown, and she looked not at all impressed by the acclaim or the splendor. It seemed to Isabeau that the new queen was ridiculously out of place—a commoner and a northerner, a minor mage and mercenary who had inexplicably grasped the throne.

Her throne.

Where the thought came from, Isabeau could not say. She had never seen her newfound heritage as a path to be pursued but as an opportunity to exploit. Now she saw the subtle glances sent her way, the slight inclination of several dark, southern heads in her direction as they lifted their glasses in false tribute to the false queen.

Isabeau awoke abruptly, her eyes still dazzled with the vision. She glanced down at the crystal sphere in her hand and willed the magic to continue, but the little ball was cool, quiet, and as milky as a baby's smile.

Furious, she whirled toward Oth. "Bring it back! It was not enough!"

The mage threw back his head and laughed delightedly. "That is the beauty of it, don't you see? One dream is never enough! New vistas open, new possibilities beckon. Since few men have the wit, talent, or character to turn their dreams into reality, they will happily turn over coin again and again for dreams more easily purchased."

His heedless words restored Isabeau's resolve. She had the wit and the will to make her own way, but this dream sphere had suggested a whole new world of possibilities.

"A wondrous toy, my lord," she said, inclining her head in a gesture of one swordsman conceding a point to another. "The merchant lords were fools to refuse you. That I would never do." She smiled in blatant invitation and patted the rumpled sheets.

Oth was still absorbed with other matters. "What my peers do not realize is that the dream spheres will be sold, whether they wish it or not. There have been attempts to steal them, to ferret out their magical secrets. Mizzen, the wretched cur, is the worst offender!"

"Mizzen," she repeated, remembering the name from some chance-heard gossip. "The crystal merchant?"

"The same." Oth's glare turned sly. "I endured his inept ambitions as long as I had need of him. He has mined and shaped sufficient crystals for now. Most have been enspelled. All that remains is to ship the finished dream spheres to Waterdeep." His brow furrowed in remembered anger. "That, and to find a manner of bringing them to market that circumvents the merchant lords!"

As to that, Isabeau had a few ideas of her own. First she had to coax this man into slumber.

She rose from the bed and walked into the path of Oth's restless pacing. "Tell me, my lord," she breathed as she entwined her arms about his neck, "have you a dream sphere that two can share?"

He looked at her sharply, with new respect. "That is something I had not considered," he marveled. "Imagine the possibilities! A bored nobleman with a watchful lady could stay within propriety's bonds, yet fancy himself entertaining a queen! His lady, on the other hand, could experience her lord in whatever manner pleased her."

"Such toys would sell by the gross," Isabeau agreed. She glanced pointedly at the mage's cloak. "We should perhaps test out the possibilities?"

Much later, when the moon was nearly set and the hearth fire nothing but a few burning embers, Isabeau crawled gingerly out of bed. She had no idea what dark fantasy had gripped Oth and did not wish to know. That the dream spheres would sell, she had no doubt. She herself would never use one again. The sooner she could profitably rid herself of them, and of Oth, the better.

Isabeau crept over to the mage's clothing and quickly emptied his pockets. Oth had some fine jewelry, a well-filled coin purse, and a small silver knife such as gentlemen carried for table use. These she tucked into pockets hidden in her discarded clothing, cunningly sewn into her heavy petticoats and between the stays of her corset.

She hesitated just a moment before looting the mage's cloak. Resolutely she dug her hand into the folds and began to take out the dream spheres, one at a time. There were nearly a score of them—a small fortune! She ignored the silent hum of their compelling magic and hid her booty, along with her own jewelry, in the prepared hiding places.

It was by far the boldest, riskiest theft of Isabeau's life. Her hands were moist and shaking by the time she'd finished. She wiped them dry on the skirts of her petticoats, took a long, steadying breath, and climbed back into bed beside the sleeping mage.

* * * * *

Arilyn hurried through the garden toward the great hall. The affair was almost over, judging from the steady stream of carriages rattling past the villa and the subdued tone and languid pace of the music emanating from the hall.

Danilo met her at the door with a smiling face and concern-shadowed eyes.

"Sorry," she snarled.

He looked startled, then burst out laughing. "You've no idea how much I've missed your unique brand of charm!"

Her lips twitched in a reluctant response. "I was held up."

"So I surmised." He took her arm and led her out into the garden. "A faint aroma clings to that gown. That's not quite the bouquet of an undead creature."

"A tren zombie. Now, there's an appealing thought," she said with a grimace. "As if the live ones weren't bad enough."

Danilo drew back, looking startled and deeply concerned. "Tren? Here in the family compound?"

"You know of them?"

"Nasty creatures. Assassins by trade, aren't they?"

Arilyn nodded, glad that she would be spared explaining that part. Years had passed since she had posed as an assassin, but the weight and darkness of that time still pressed heavily upon her. "There's more."

As they walked, she recounted in detail the conversation she had overheard and the attack upon Elaith Craulnober. Danilo did not interrupt, but his face grew increasingly troubled.

"I don't know what Elaith is up to now," Arilyn concluded, "but it's possible that someone arranged this situation to deal with it."

Anger flashed in Danilo's eyes as he threaded together her bits of information. "You think Lady Cassandra is responsible for this?"

"I'm not making any judgment," Arilyn retorted. "I'm merely telling you what I heard. Regardless of who commissioned this attack, you should consider the possibility of trouble ahead. Elaith Craulnober is not one to let a slight go unavenged."

A troubled expression crossed his face. "You still mistrust Elaith."

"You don't?" she retorted. "Before we tread that path, why don't you tell me what possessed you to fill the great hall with skyflowers?"

Danilo flicked one hand in a small, insouciant wave. "I had intended to present you with a bouquet, not a garden maze."

"So what happened?" she pressed.

"I wish I knew," he said in a more serious tone. "It troubles me. The spell's misfiring seems more ominous in light of your story."

"I'm not sure I follow."

Danilo stopped and pulled her into a vine-covered alcove. His face was as grim as she had ever seen it. "How is it that you stumbled into a tren ambush?" he asked in a low voice. "How did Elaith catch you unaware?"

That cut a bit too close to the bone. She folded her arms and glared. "Get to the point!"

His gaze dropped to the sword on her hip. "Your moonblade's magic should have warned you of danger."

That had bothered her too, but until this moment she hadn't had time to consider the matter.

"I know the skyflower spell exceedingly well," Danilo continued softly. "It is a minor elven spell, such as any human mage with a surplus of gold and time could learn. I can cast it as easily as your sword can slice through a melon. Why do you think they both failed, your elven magic and mine?"

His tone held an acrid tinge of bitterness. Arilyn suspected what was coming next. She took a step back. "You blame the moonblade for this?"

"Why not? When has anything between us *not* been defined by that thrice-bedamned sword?" he demanded. "It brought us together when its magic destroyed a score of Harpers—my friends, many of them! It bound us together when you were too stubbornly elven to see and follow your heart. Its demands tore us apart when you chose to break that bond."

The naked pain in his eyes smote her heart. Gone was the good-natured dandy, the attentive courtier. Never had she seen so clearly, so painfully, the toll that her well-meaning sacrifice had taken on her closest friend.

"Dan," she said softly, holding out a hand to him.

He was not looking at her. He had turned aside to study the setting moon as if all the wisdom of the elven gods were written on its shining surface. "I have been a fool," he said softly. "Nothing I do can change the fact that you are pledged elsewhere. The moonblade's magic will make sure that you are not deterred by other, conflicting pledges."

Her jaw dropped as his meaning hit her. "You can't believe that!"

He sighed and dug one hand into his hair. "I'm not sure what I believe. I've been around magic all my life, though, and I know that some forces show antipathy toward others. Maybe your sword senses me as a threat to your chosen path and is forcing you to choose between us."

"That's absurd!" she said, trying to imbue her words with more conviction than she felt. In truth, Danilo's words seemed utterly, disturbingly plausible.

His smile was both bleak and perceptive.

"I gave up the sword once," she said stoutly.

Finally he turned to face her. "To free my spirit from a servitude I did not choose for myself," he stated. "Do you think so little of me that you believe I would accept the sacrifice of *yours?* For that is what you would give up, if you knowingly turned away from the pledge you made as the sword wielder."

Arilyn had no words to refute that simple truth. She turned and strode out of the alcove, as if she could somehow outpace the shadow Dan's words had revealed.

He fell in beside her. For a time they walked together in silence, a silence broken only by the faint sounds of guests bidding farewell and the crunch of dried leaves that spoke of a summer gone beyond recall.

When they reached the far gate, Danilo reached for her hand and raised it to his lips. The expression in his eyes was bleak but resolute. "You freed me once, though I did not ask it of you. How can I do less?"

They had shared many farewells, but this was different. Soul-deep desolation assailed Arilyn at the thought that this might be their last. Stifling pain and cold, numbing shock racked her, rivaling any battle wound she'd taken. She shook her head, trying to force words of denial through her constricted throat.

It was too late. Danilo was gone, but for a cloud of faint, silvery motes. They shimmered in the air for a moment, then fell like tears into the dying garden.

At her side, the moonblade began to hum with faint, familiar magic—the first she had felt since entering the Thann villa.

Four

In the tavern room of The Silken Sylph, Elaith Craulnober sipped his ale and watched as the staff prepared for the morning meal. Good smells filled the air: smoked fish, oat porridge sweetened with honey and dried fruits, fresh bread, and the rich, smoky tang of the apple-wood fire. The tavern was exceedingly well run and very prosperous. Elaith had seen to that. It was a happy coincidence that his quarry had gone to ground in this particular den, but the elf would have found him regardless.

"Your standard fee," he said, placing a small leather bag on the table. "Good work, Zorn. Give an extra coin to the driver who brought us here so swiftly."

The mercenary's large, bronzed hand seemed to swallow the bag as he hefted it to measure the coin within. Zorn was a big man, sun-browned from many years as a caravan guard. Though the warrior was thick with muscle and short on conscience, Elaith found him rather amusing. The man's head was utterly bald, but his upper lip and chin were thicketed with curly black hair. To the elf's eyes, the effect was that of a wholesale southern migration. In another few years, if matters continued apace, Zorn should be as hairy-footed as a halfling.

"Only forty gold," Zorn stated sullenly. "I've called in favors."

A prickle of irritation marred Elaith's good humor. This was the first time the man had dared imply that his compensation might be lacking. It was not a precedent that Elaith could allow to stand.

"Of course you did," Elaith said, as if he were explaining something to a slow-witted child. "That is how you gather information—which is, if you recall, what you are paid to do."

Zorn scowled behind his beard. "You didn't give me much time," he complained. "Twenty men and more have I roused from their beds. Some demanded double fees, and some swore they'll not deal with me again."

"Soothe their tempers with those coins, and they will be ready enough when I have need of you and you of them."

"Do you know what'll be left for me?"

Elaith's patience was at an end. "Your life, provided you silence your whining tongue at once!"

The mercenary sat back. A dull flush rose from behind his beard and stained his face with suppressed rage. "As you say," he muttered as he hauled his massive frame from the chair.

With a curt bow the man turned and walked from the tavern. Elaith sighed and nodded toward the small, watchful woman who sat in the shadows of the cloakroom. The apparent servant rose and slipped out after Zorn. She would allow him to finish his business, then ensure that this task was his last.

A shame to lose a good informant. Zorn had contacts among the city's mercenaries and carriage guild, and he was adept at coaxing or bullying information from hired guards, but Elaith had many such men in his employ.

His stewards and lieutenants would pay at least a dozen similar purses before highsun. And no man would know of the efforts of the others.

That was the way of things. Elaith saw his business concerns as a deep, underground river fed by the trickle of many converging streams. The loss of Zorn would not greatly affect the whole, and Elaith knew better than to suffer even a fledgling challenge. His hirelings were utterly loyal because they knew they would be well paid and fairly treated—and because they understood the cost of even the smallest treason.

Elaith lifted his mug in salute to the departing mercenary and then drank to his memory.

*   *   *   *   *

The white whirl of magical travel faded away. Danilo found himself standing in a dark, cold room—not the comfort he expected from his lavish townhouse or from Monroe, his capable halfling steward.

Danilo was too heartsick to care overmuch about domestic incompetence. Monroe could burn the damn place down, for all he cared. He closed his eyes and heaved a profound sigh.

"What are you doing here, and at this hour?" demanded a low, furious, and slightly accented male voice.

Khelben Arunsun's voice.

Danilo's eyes popped open, then narrowed as he peered at the large, dark figure at the far side of the room. "Uncle? Is that you?"

"Considering that this is Laerel's bedchamber and that I expect her back directly, I should hope that it is no other! Explain yourself, boy, and be quick about it."

Danilo's hands flashed through the gestures for the globe of light cantrip. In response to the minor casting, a glowing sphere bobbed into life between them. A mixture of light and shadows revealed the strong, stern features of Waterdeep's archmage.

Khelben Arunsun appeared to be a man in vigorous middle life, tall and broad and well-muscled. His hairline was in retreat, but what remained was thick and black and only lightly threaded with silver. His beard was full and neatly trimmed, with a distinctive silver stripe in the middle. Dark brows drew together in a scowl of consternation over nearly black eyes.

Even in his current state of mind, Danilo could see a certain humor in the situation. "I swear before Mystra, Uncle, you are the only man alive who could manage to look formidable when clad only in his nightshirt."

The archmage's scowl deepened. "Only a handful of mortals can pass the magical wards that guard this tower. If you wish to remain among them, speak quickly and speak sense!"

Danilo's wan grin disappeared. Without doubt Khelben deserved some word of explanation, but if Danilo had devoted serious thought to the matter, he could not have contrived a place, a person, or a conversation he would rather avoid.

"A miscast spell, Uncle, nothing more. Accept my apologies, and I'll be on my way."

The archmage would not let the matter lie. "What has come over you? Are you ill? Bewitched? Utterly given over to stupidity? I heard tell of the jest you played at Cassandra's party—as who did not?"

"Uncle—"

"And now this! Have you not incurred enough wrath to enliven one evening? I do not imagine Cassandra was amused by the skyflower trick, or Arilyn either, for that matter. If you must play these frivolous jests, you would be wise to inflict them on those less able to retaliate. Furthermore— "

"*Uncle.*" Dan cut off the wizard's tirade with a sharp tone and an upraised hand. "Believe me, I did not design the skyflower spell as a prank. Nor did I intend to come here."

The cloud of ire slowly lifted from the archmage's face, to be replaced by dawning concern. "This is plain truth?"

"Unadorned."

Khelben nodded slowly, his eyes intent upon the young mage. "This could be serious. There are some magicks—not many, Mystra be praised—that can have such effects. Have you bought another singing sword or some such nonsense?"

"No, nothing. Must we speak of this now?"

The archmage merely lifted one brow. Danilo sighed and began to gather words to explain what he suspected—and what he had done. "As you know, the magic of Arilyn's moonblade has not always been stable," he began.

"That is true enough, and I perceive the feel of elven magic about you."

It was on the tip of Danilo's tongue to confess that the moonblade's magic had also been affected, until he remembered his mother's words, and Oth's, and Regnet's, and the many other small remarks that had warned him away from following his heart. Anger surged through Danilo at the thought that Khelben would add his considerable weight to the argument.

"You need not concern yourself," he said angrily. "I would not ask Arilyn to choose between me and the moonblade. That is the only thing in this world or any other that would make me foreswear her, half-elf though she may be. If that notion offends you, I would thank you to keep it to yourself."

Khelben looked genuinely surprised. "Why would it? Arilyn is a good woman. Probably far better than you deserve."

This was not the response Danilo had anticipated. "You approve?"

A wry smile touched the archmage's lips, and he made a sweeping gesture that encompassed the bed-chamber and came to rest on the portrait of a wondrous, silver-haired lady. "How could I not? You know that Laerel's mother was half-elven."

"No, I didn't," Dan responded. In truth, little was known of Laerel, one of the famed Seven Sisters.

"Laerel's mother was a fine woman, though like many half-elves, she did not have an easy life. Nor did my father, for that matter," Khelben continued.

That bit of intelligence stole the starch from Danilo's legs. He sank down on the edge of Laerel's bed and regarded the archmage with astonishment.

"Your father was half-elven," he said in wondering tones, regarding the mage from whom he had descend-ed. "So there is elven blood in the Arunsun family! The Lady Cassandra carries it and passed it to me."

"Yes, that sounds like the normal order of things," Khelben said testily. "However, there is reason why Cas-sandra would not thank me for telling this tale or you for repeating it."

Danilo smothered a grin. Though Khelben Arunsun was not, as was commonly believed, Cassandra Thann's younger brother, he still seemed to hold the woman in genuine awe.

"Your secret is safe, and I thank you for speaking it," Danilo said from the heart. A small thing, perhaps, but it seemed to him nothing less than a key to most of his life's questions. Since boyhood, he had been drawn to all things elven and knew not why. He better understood why an elf woman had claimed his heart so completely—and why he cared enough about elven ways that he was prepared to give her up if he must.

"What will you do now?"

The archmage's question surprised Danilo, as did the gentle tone in which it was broached. Usually Khelben gave opinions and orders or asked questions designed to extract information. He was particularly strict with Danilo, in whom he took an oppressively paternal interest, but the archmage's normally stern face was softened by genuine concern. All of this prompted Danilo to do something he had not done for many years: ask advice.

"What do you suggest?"

Khelben's gaze shifted to the portrait of Laerel, then back to the young man. "Find Arilyn and set right this matter between you. If things are as you suspect, and the moonblade's magic has gone unstable, then she will have need of your counsel and aid. But be wary in the use of magic. Perhaps you should devote yourself entirely to bardcraft until this matter is settled."

"Strange words indeed," Danilo murmured.

"Not at all. Magic is a great gift, but some things are more important."

"I am glad to hear you say that, my lord," said an amused, silvery voice behind them. Both men turned to regard Laerel, who stood listening without shame and who seemed not at all concerned by the fact that she was clad in little more than her own silvery hair. She nodded to Danilo, then turned a smile of such intimacy upon Khelben that the younger man wondered if she had truly seen him at all.

Danilo rose at once. "I must be going."

Neither of the great wizards of Blackstaff Tower gave any indication that they had heard him. Despite Khelben's warning, Danilo quickly summoned magic's silver path and stepped into the weft and warp of it. This time the spell held true, and he emerged in his own study.

A low fire glowed in the hearth, and a tray of breakfast pastries had been arrayed under a glass dome and placed on the table beside his favorite chair. All was as he had come to expect from the capable Monroe.

Danilo sank into the chair and rubbed both hands briskly over his face. His unintentional interview with Khelben had not given him much hope. The archmage had mentioned that he felt elven magic at work. Arilyn and Elaith had been the only elves in attendance. That left the moonblade as the most likely source.

It was true that Khelben had not advised Dan to stay away from Arilyn, but he had evoked Laerel to support this reasoning. That was hardly reassuring. Not too many years back, Khelben had given up a considerable amount of his own power in a struggle to wrest Laerel from the Crown of Horns, an evil artifact that held her completely in its sway. Danilo agreed that Laerel was worth any cost in magic lost. So was Arilyn. He would gladly strip his hard-won skill down to the most basic cantrip and count the loss as nothing.

But what of *her* magic? Elf and moonblade were inseparable, joined in mystic bonds. How could he possibly justify disrupting that, and what would be the cost to Arilyn if he did?

He pondered these questions until the fire burned down to ash and the night sky faded to silver. When all the argument had been made and countered, not once but a dozen times, Danilo merely stared at the eastern window, praying that the coming of dawn might bring illumination.

* * * * * *

The rising sun burned through the sea mist that shrouded the port city and curtained the upper windows of The Silken Sylph. Through it all, Isabeau feigned sleep—no easy task once Oth Eltorchul awakened and discovered his loss.

She held her false repose while he searched and muttered and cursed and fumed. She lay unmoving until he seized her shoulders and shook her. With a gasp, she sat upright in bed, hoping that her expression was sufficiently dazed and frantic for credulity.

"You are alive," he said grimly, staring into her wide eyes. "Good. I was beginning to fear that the thief had smothered you in your sleep."

"Thief?"

Isabeau's hand flew to her throat, as if seeking her necklace. She lunged for the bedside table where she'd left her jewels, palmed them, and then came up on her knees with both empty hands fisted and flailing.

"How could this happen?" she shrieked as she pummeled the startled mage. "Did you not set wards? Have you no servants to stand guard? My rubies! Gone, all of them!" Her voice rose into a wail, then broke into impassioned weeping.

Oth tossed her aside and began to pace again. "This was no common thief," he fretted. "It would take considerable magic to overcome the wards I placed upon the doors and windows. Perhaps there is a hidden door. I did not think to check."

He hurled an accusing look at Isabeau, as if blaming her for the distraction she offered. Not willing to give up the offensive, she tossed back her head, wiped her eyes, and returned his glare with equal heat. "What do you intend to do about this?" she demanded.

The question set Oth back on his heels. Isabeau had expected that it would. If the nobles and wizards were as opposed to dream spheres as Oth claimed, they would not be pleased to learn that a score or so of the forbidden objects would soon be in circulation. Nor would they believe Oth was innocent. The theft of his precious dream spheres, so soon after his presentation was soundly rejected, would appear far too convenient a solution.

"Well?" she pressed. "Will you call the Watch and report this, or shall I?"

After a moment of intense, silent struggle, the mage snatched up her clothing and tossed it to her. "Forget the matter. It is of no consequence."

Isabeau stopped in the act of pulling her chemise over her head, as if his words had stunned her into immobility. She tugged on the undergarment with a single quick, furious motion and rose from the bed. Stalking over to Oth, she stabbed him in the chest with an angry forefinger.

"My rubies were of considerable consequence! If you wish me to remain silent on this matter, I insist upon reparations."

Oth's narrow face turned pale with fury. "Extortion is hardly a wise course of action for a woman alone."

There was a cold, dangerous note in his voice. Isabeau's frightened expression was not completely feigned. She took two steps back, her hands turned palms up in supplication.

"I meant no such thing, my lord. I was distraught over the loss of my gems. You have my word that I will say nothing of this matter. I would not in any case, for fear of damaging your good name and mine. There were many who saw us leave the Thann estate in one carriage."

She kept her gaze wide and ingenuous while Oth tried to ascertain whether her words held a second, subtler threat. Finally he threw up his hands in surrender. "Shed no more tears over your baubles. The Eltorchul family will see to their replacement. Before you carry tales, though, know that your new rubies will place a geas of silence upon the wearer!"

A little fact that Isabeau did not intend to pass along to the fence who would resell these gems. She sank into a low curtsy. "More than I dared ask, my lord."

Oth hauled her to her feet. He stripped a ring from his finger and pressed it into her hand. "Take this. Show it to the seneschal of any of the Eltorchul estates and bid him handle the matter."

Isabeau took the proffered ring. "Will you see me safely on my way, my lord?" she asked in tentative tones.

The mage scoffed. "The thief has come and gone.

What more can he take that you have not lost? Or eagerly given," he added in nasty insinuation.

She gasped in genuine outrage. "You are no gentleman!"

Oth sneered. "I will not gainsay you. How could I? Though you have not been long in Waterdeep, I dare say you have already sampled enough of my peers to be considered an expert in the matter."

Isabeau lunged for the oil lamp and hurled it at the mage. He stood his ground and made a short, sharp gesture with both hands. The lamp shattered in mid air and fell to the ground in a shower of glass shards and droplets of scented oil. Without another word, Oth turned and stalked from the room, leaving Isabeau shaking with rage.

And fear. And triumph and excitement blended in a sudden, wonderful, waterfall burst of relief.

The moment she was alone, Isabeau flung herself back onto the bed and opened her mouth in a long, silent scream of victory. She had done it! Oth's treasure was hers, and no suspicion would touch her!

She quickly finished dressing, then slipped down the back stairs and dived through a hidden exit in search of a man who could market these treasures for her and set her feet more firmly on the path that she had chosen.

* * * * *

When Oth Eltorchul came storming down into the tavern room of The Silken Sylph, Elaith was waiting for him.

"A carriage," the mage demanded of a serving maid, "and wine while I wait. One small goblet. Mark me, I do not wish to wait long."

Elaith caught the woman's eye and held up two fingers. She moved off to tend to the amended order. The elf rose and came over to the mage's table, sliding silently into the empty chair.

The mage studied him with ill-concealed distaste. "The tavern is nearly empty, elf. Surely you could find another seat."

Before Elaith could reply, a large, well-armed tavern guard stepped forward and nodded politely to Oth. He then leaned down and said confidingly, "Lord Craulnober can sit wherever he pleases. He owns this tavern, you see."

"Ah. I do indeed." Oth smiled thinly across the table at his host, who spread his hands in a parody of self-deprecation. "It would appear that I am your guest."

"A paying guest," Elaith said cordially, just so there would be no misunderstanding on the matter.

"Quite." The mage looked up when the servant brought a bottle of wine, and his face darkened when she placed two goblets on the table. "Won't you join me," he invited through gritted teeth.

"How very kind." Elaith took up the bottle and poured two generous portions of elven wine. Usually he would not waste the precious liquid on a human, but the light, almost floral taste of the wine masked a kick more powerful than that of an angry centaur.

Oth drank more deeply than prudence dictated. When the goblet was empty, he thunked it down on the table and glared at his host. "What manner of establishment do you run here, elf?"

Already his tone was fuzzy, lacking focus. Certainly his judgment was affected, for he would not otherwise dare to speak with such belligerence. Elaith let the insult pass for the moment.

"It is my desire that the service at The Silken Sylph be without peer. If you have reason for complaint, speak, and the matter will be set right."

Oth snorted and held out his goblet for a refill. "So easy, is it? What was taken from me cannot be replaced."

Elaith began to see the shape of things. He poured a second goblet and waited until the mage had drained it.

"Perhaps it could be recovered."

"Hmph," scoffed Oth, but without much conviction. His face went slack with despair, as long and morose as a pack mule's.

"If you were robbed during your stay, then the reputation—and the profitability—of this fine establishment is at risk. Confide in me," Elaith said earnestly, "and I will ensure by any means available to me that your loss is made right, and avenged, if you are so minded."

Oth peered at him with drunken cunning. "No small foe," he cautioned. "The treasure was stolen while I slept, despite wards I myself placed."

The elf carefully hid his surprise and anger. He had anticipated a tale that pointed to a misplaced belonging. Guests were more inclined to ascribe their losses to theft than to their own carelessness, but the inn should have been protected against a theft. If Eltorchul's tale were true, Elaith's servants would answer for it.

"Do not concern yourself over the finding or the foe. Only tell me what is missing, and I will carry on from there."

"Some coins, perhaps a hundred platinum," Oth said in a sly tone. Elaith suspected the amount was probably a third of that. "A few pieces of jewelry: a gold ring, an embossed wrist bracer, also of gold. A ruby necklace set in silver filigree, with ear drops and rings to match."

Elaith pricked up his ears. "A lady was with you? Where is she now?"

"Gone," Oth said shortly. "She was most unhappy about her loss."

"I can imagine," the elf murmured, making a note to find out the identity of this lady. "Was that the extent of your loss?"

The mage hesitated. Indecision waged battle on his face, then gave way before the potent persuasion of greed and elven wine. "There was more. Dream spheres, at least a score of them."

"Dream spheres," Elaith repeated.

"Small crystal orbs," Oth explained. "They hold magic. A single illusion, which is experienced as a vivid dream in which the dreamer places himself."

Elaith had heard rumors of the things for quite some time now. They were becoming quite popular among the city's servants and mercenaries. The tale Arilyn told had raised enormous possibilities in Elaith's mind and convinced him to track these new magical toys to their source.

"An ingenious notion. I imagine many in this city would pay a small fortune for such a thing."

"Would and do," Oth boasted. He leaned toward the elf. "You offered to help. Find them. Return them. I'll make it worth your while."

Elaith tamped down a surge of elation. This was more of a concession than he had expected from the mage. Perhaps he could do better still. He tilted his head to one side as if considering. "I could do that, of course."

Apparently Oth was not entirely overcome by elven wine. His sharp-featured face became wary. "But?"

The elf smiled apologetically. "I am in business. When confronted with the potential for great profit, should I be content with a simple reward? No matter how generous that might be," he added in a conciliatory tone.

Oth considered the matter, and a sly smile stole across his face. "I have heard of your business affairs. You are not overly hampered by respect for law."

"Laws are admirable things and are often quite convenient. Just as often, they are not."

"Quite." Oth suddenly made up his mind. "You find the dream spheres. I will supply you with others. You will find channels through which these might be sold— channels so convoluted that the sales could not be traced back to me. This can be done?"

"You would be surprised how much business is transacted in this city in just such a fashion," Elaith said, speaking for the first time with complete candor.

"Settled, then," the mage said. The decision made, he abandoned his struggle against the compelling lullaby the elven wine was singing in his veins. He rose unsteadily and looked about the tavern, his face wearing the expression of puzzled concentration as he tried to remember what he sought.

Elaith gestured to the serving girl. "Summon a carriage for Lord Eltorchul," he bade, "and pour him into it," he added in a voice too low for the human to hear.

She nodded and slipped an arm around the mage's waist. "This way, my lord," she said, leading him to the front door and the waiting carriage.

The elf rose and slipped out the back door. He circled around to the back of the building and ran his hands over the smooth stone of the wall. A hidden door swung open. As he suspected, the cobwebs that should have festooned it hung in ragged shreds. Some enterprising thief had discovered the door and used it to good effect.

That made his task all the easier. Anyone skilled enough to find this back way into the building would also be adept at moving the stolen goods. Coins, gems, and magical items. There were perhaps four fences in Waterdeep who could handle them all with moderate risk and at a good profit. Elaith would have the dream spheres in hand before the day was out.

He would not return them to Oth Eltorchul. Nor would he see them sold as yet another mindless amusement in this city full of humans who believed that dreams could be purchased rather than earned.

He wondered if any of the fools, Oth Eltorchul included, understood the true price of these fleeting dreams. Unless he missed his guess, Oth Eltorchul had no idea what sort of tiger he held by the tail. Unless Elaith was very, very wrong, the dream spheres could be the most valuable and the most dangerous magical items he had sought in his long and infamous career.

More important was the promise that he might hold in his hands the elven artifact that he suspected was behind their magic. He would test himself against the power of the elf gem and in doing so would answer once and forever the question that had haunted him for more than a century. He would know for a certainty whether the remnants of his elven honor were a wishful illusion or if he was a creature given over wholly to evil. Either way, the elven gem would light the path to greatness.

"Now *there* is a dream," he murmured with dark irony, "that is well worth pursuing."

*　*　*　*　*

Arilyn welcomed the rising sun as a marker that the worst night of her life was finally at an end. She was not by nature an introspective person, but since leaving the Thann villa she had wrestled her way to several important conclusions. Now all that remained was to persuade Danilo to her way of thinking.

His townhouse was a long walk from the lodge where Arilyn stayed, but it was a pleasant walk. The air was thick with the scent of breakfast fires and the clatter of carts hauling goods to the market. Most of the city's folk were abed when the Gemstone Ball had scarce begun, and half their day's work would be finished before the revelers emerged to face the day.

Arilyn could not help but note that this was yet another difference between her and Danilo. He was accustomed to the patterns of city life, while she spent much time on the road and was attuned to the sun and stars. It was no small consideration, but at this moment it and all other matters seemed insignificant.

She cut up the street behind Danilo's townhouse and climbed the stone fence. She dropped lightly into the enclosed garden and instinctively scanned the area for danger. Finding nothing to hamper her, she plucked a blue rose and crept toward the many-paned window of Danilo's favorite room.

As she had anticipated, he was in his private study. She hauled herself up over the window ledge and eased into the room.

"You were wrong," she said.

Danilo started, then sat staring as if she was an apparition. His eyes dropped to the moonblade at her hip. "Wrong?" he repeated.

"Don't sound so surprised. Surely it has happened before," she said in an attempt at lightness. Without waiting for a response, she let the rest of it rush out. "I am not saying that you are wrong about the sword. Its magic is . . . complicated. It has been compromised before, and I won't claim that it couldn't happen again, but I do not accept that you are responsible."

He shook his head. "What if I am right? I won't let you take that risk."

"Let me? You can't keep me from taking it! I'm not finished," she said when Danilo began to interrupt. "Think back. If I'd had my way, we would have parted ways the first day we met. The first hour!"

His lips twitched with rueful amusement. "Yes, I seem to recall a certain lack of enthusiasm."

She began to pace. "Exactly. You, however, persisted, and we learned to work together. We became friends, which must have been like pushing a boulder uphill. Every step of the way I fought you. Always it has been you pushing, pursuing, getting me to go along by being funny or charming or just plain stubborn. Because of that, I suppose you think this all just stops when you say it does." She leveled a glare at him. "Well, it doesn't. Get used to it."

Danilo rose and walked over to her, stopping just a pace away. "You wish to remain together?"

She huffed and folded her arms. "Didn't I say just that?"

She waited for him to speak or to make some sort of move toward her. When he did not, she continued. "I don't know how we are to go about this. You were right in saying that I cannot give up the moonblade. That means I will be on the road more often than not. You offered to leave the city with me, but do you understand what that will mean? Some communities of forest elves might accept your presence. Most will not. Many times you would have to languish in small towns at woods' edge, while I go into the trees alone."

As she spoke, Danilo began to see the path her reasoning was taking. He could see the logic in it, but he did not like it at all. "So you believe that we should proceed as we have these past four years. You pursue your duties, I follow mine, and we are together only for a few short days here and there."

"If there truly is a conflict between your magic and mine, that might be the best course." She hesitated. "There is another way."

"I am most eager to hear it."

Arilyn nodded, but glanced uneasily around the study. "Can we go to my room? I can't help wondering when that steward of yours is going to sail in with a tea cart."

Danilo extended his hand. Arilyn took it, and together they melted into the roar and rush of the silver-white pathway that he had laid between his sanctum and hers. The trip took but a moment, but Arilyn was relieved to feel the firm reassurance of wood planks beneath her boots. Danilo did not comment on her aversion for magical travel, but his eyes dropped to her clenched hand and the blue rose she had crushed.

Inspiration struck her, and she stepped over to her cot and let the fragrant petals fall onto the coverlet.

Danilo quickly averted his eyes from the bed and

cleared his throat. "You have my full attention."

"For many days now, since I set my course for Waterdeep, I have had no dreams, no summons from the Tel'Quessar. That could mean that all is well. It might also mean that the sword's magic was compromised before I reached the city, in which case it's unlikely that you are the cause. There is a third possibility. Perhaps there is a task for me here, in the city. If so, that will give us time to determine what is disrupting the moonblade's magic and yours. No sense running from a foe you have not even named."

That brought a faint, rueful smile to Danilo's face. "When you put it that way, I sound like a coward and a fool."

"I've noticed that humans often err on the side of caution when dealing with the well being of those they love, but I am puzzled. You can accept that I make my way as a warrior, but not the possibility that my sword's magic might falter. I wonder what you trust: my skills or my sword."

He regarded her with bemused respect. "I had never considered the matter in that light. Your logic is remarkable."

She shrugged. "Problems are like enemies: you name them, track them down, and do whatever it takes to kill them."

Danilo threw back his head and laughed. As he did, the heavy burden of indecision lifted. Perhaps he could not yet see a way clear for them to be together, but Arilyn's forthright approach to the matter made him believe that one did indeed exist. "So what do we do now?"

"Assume that my task is in Waterdeep. As long as I tend the needs of the elven folk, I doubt that any but the most dire emergencies will summon me to the forest."

Hope began to dawn in Danilo's heart. He took her hand and led her over to the cot, and he kept her hand in his as they sat together. "And if the forest elves have need of you, they will have to take me into the bargain. It is that simple."

"I wouldn't put it quite that way," she cautioned him. "Where elves are concerned, nothing is ever simple."

Danilo reached over and cupped her cheek in one hand. "What dream worth having is easily gained?"

"True, but—"

He stopped her argument by sliding his hand over her lips. "Has anyone ever told you that you talk too much?"

"That's rich, coming from you," she mumbled through his fingers.

She did not seem inclined to further conversation. Her eyes drifted shut as Danilo began to stroke her along her jawline with gentle fingers, then moved back up to trace the elegant points of her elven ears. Few humans understood the intimacy of this gesture. Years ago, in the first bright flush of young manhood, Danilo had been well schooled in such matters by an indulgent elven harp mistress.

Arilyn sent him a look of mock suspicion. "How do you know such things?"

"The benefit of a well-rounded education." He held up both hands, palms toward her.

Without hesitation, the half-elf placed her fingertips to his. Slowly their hands eased together until they were palm to palm. It was a simple contact but far more intimate than any kiss or embrace they had yet shared, for it was the beginning of the elven handfasting, a personal ritual as old as the seasons. Their eyes locked, their hearts opened to each other, and the circle was begun.

"The summer is nearly past, the harvest moon beckons the night," she said in a soft, wondering voice, beginning the traditional words of the pledge they were about to make.

Danilo wondered if she realized that she was speaking in Elvish. It was an unconscious acceptance, one he was determined to honor as well as any human man might. By elven standards, their time together would be short. He would die when she was still young; did that mean that he was never to live? Perhaps nothing about elves was ever simple, but this one thing was plain: for him, to deny Arilyn was to deny life.

Their fingers linked, and he repeated the next words of the handfasting pledge. There were more words, accompanied by graceful movements that held the power of spellcasting and the subtlety of starlight. Danilo was not certain when their words melted into silence, and he did not care.

The elven patterns were exquisitely slow, torturously sweet. At some point, the ritual melded with a deeply personal, shared pattern of their own creation, one that was no less sacred for its newness.

Arilyn's patience with elven subtleties shattered before his. She pulled away and tore at her confining shirt with fierce abandon and utter disregard for the laces.

The sound of ripping linen startled her. Danilo burst out laughing at her befuddled expression, and after a surprised moment she joined in. Further bound together in the mirth only he seemed able to inspire in her, they sank down together to her cot, bathed in the mystic blue light of the moonblade's magic.

A moment passed before the implication of that fey light pierced their shared oblivion.

Arilyn sat up abruptly. "Damn!" she spat, glaring at the inconvenient sword.

Danilo let out a long, unsteady breath and nodded in heartfelt agreement. At least the moonblade's light was blue, not the faint green glow that warned of a dream to come and a forest journey to follow. That was some consolation. The danger of which it warned was close at hand. Name it, track it down, kill it. That, he could deal with.

He reached for his sword belt and boots, trying to remember precisely how they managed to end up on the floor. Arilyn was quicker and was dressed and battle ready in moments.

Her eyes took on a distant expression as she drew the elven sword. "Tren," she murmured. "Here in the building."

In a moment she was gone, shouting a warning to the dwarven guard as she raced down the stairs. Danilo followed, drawing his sword as he clattered after her.

The curtain concealing the guard's alcove rustled. Four enormous claws punched through the fabric and sliced down, shredding the curtain. Out leaped a hideous reptilian creature, fully the height of a tall man and at least two stone heavier.

Dan stopped, impressed despite himself. He'd heard that tren were like lizardmen, but that was true only as a dwarf could be said to resemble a human. Compact and powerful, the creature was thick with muscle and armored with leathery green hide. Spikes lined its backbone and jutted from behind each elbow joint. Long, powerful arms ended in hands so enormous that each clawed finger was fully the length of a human's hand. A long, livid cut traced the bony ridge above one eye.

"This time," the creature said, addressing Arilyn in a voice that sounded like rocks tumbling downhill, "we finish this."

"Watch the claws," Arilyn snapped back at Danilo.

"Watch the *dwarf*," Dan riposted. He threw his weight against Arilyn and sent them both tumbling down the last few steps.

Just in time. As he suspected, the tren had already dispatched the dwarven guard. Even as Danilo spoke, the creature reached back into the alcove and hauled out two objects: a small shield and a disembodied dwarven leg—still booted. The tren hurled the latter at the attacking humans.

The gory weapon whirled over them as they fell. It crashed into the stairs with enough force to splinter wood.

Arilyn rolled and came up on her feet. She came in hard and high, sword flashing with a quick, three-stroke attack. Her moonblade clattered against the wooden shield as the tren deftly parried each blow. The creature danced back a step, then leaned forward and swiped at her with one long arm. She dodged the blow and riposted with a quick thrust. The moonblade sank deep into the tren's forearm.

With astonishing speed, the creature pivoted on one massive foot, yanking its arm free of the sword—and pulling Arilyn along. Before she could get her feet back under her, the tren hit her with a brutal shield smash.

The slight half-elf went reeling back. Danilo stepped in, his hands empty but for a bit of bright green silk. He hurled the fabric square toward the creature. Snarling contemptuously, the tren swiped at the puny missile.

However, Danilo had already begun the spell. The silk caught in midair, just beyond the slashing claws, and began to spread into a thin globe, rapidly encircling the tren.

The creature backed toward the open door, thrashing about with shield and claws in an attempt to shred its prison. Glistening beads of black oil began to gleam along its fang-lined jowls. A hint of its foul scent-weapon seeped into the room just before the magic globe closed in.

Rank, swirling mist filled the globe, and the tren's struggles redoubled as it sought to escape the full force of its own stench. The creature quickly saw that it could not escape, and its yellow eyes darted from the young wizard to the angry half-elf. Arilyn stalked in, sword level and ready.

Changing tactics, the tren dropped its shield, spun away from its attackers, and fell forward onto its hands. This sudden motion tilted the globe forward. Running on all fours, the tren set the globe spinning toward the open door. The wooden lintel groaned and shuddered as the encased tren pounded through.

Danilo raced out into the street after it, with Arilyn close behind him. She quickly passed him as they wove through the morning crowds. Not that their passage was hampered overmuch—the tren's flight took care of that. Passersby ran screaming from the weird sight. Horses shied and reared, pawing the air and whinnying in terror. A cart overturned, spilling a load of cabbages onto the cobblestone. Danilo kicked one out of the way as he ran.

"The magic won't hold long," he managed, hard-pressed to keep up with the more agile half-elf.

Even as he spoke, the green globe dissipated like a child's soap bubble. The freed tren scuttled down a side street, its former quarry in close pursuit.

Suddenly the creature stopped and hunched over. Its massive arms corded as it strained upward.

"I don't think so," Arilyn muttered, running straight for the tren.

Before Danilo could guess her intent, she leaped at the creature without pausing to draw her sword. She landed so that she was nearly face to fang with the tren and standing on whatever it was trying to lift. Dan glimpsed the gleam of steel in her hands, then saw her knife flashing toward the tren's heart.

The tren's muscles bunched and heaved. Lock and hinges gave way with a shriek of metal, and the sewer cover burst free. The tren straightened abruptly, sending Arilyn tumbling up and over its massive shoulder. Danilo noticed that her knife was no longer in her hands.

The sudden movement had spoiled her aim. The tren turned back and tugged the weapon out of one shoulder.

Contemptuously it flung the knife aside, its long black tongue flicking out as if to taste the half-elf's scent.

"Mine," the creature rumbled in dire promise, then dropped into the sewer tunnels below.

Arilyn was on her feet and starting down the ladder before Danilo recovered from the shock of her bold attack. He let out a colorful oath and strode toward her. "What now?"

She looked at him as if he'd turned as green as the tren. "We follow."

Danilo regarded his fine suede boots and groaned. They were new and as good as ruined, but there was no help for that. Arilyn would go, whether he accompanied her or not.

Danilo had heard much about the sewers of Waterdeep. Part public necessity, part hidden highway, they wove an intricate web under the city. This was his first direct experience with them, and much of what he saw was surprising. Some tunnels were finished with carefully dressed and fitted stone and might well have been corridors in some castle or dwarf's stonghold. Others were simply dug into the rock. Twists and turns were frequent, and in moments he had lost all sense of direction. Nor was this the only level. More than once the stone floor gave way to iron grating. Stones kicked by their passing fell far to land sometimes with a muffled click of stone on stone, sometimes with a splash. Water marks rose high on the wall, indicating that the tunnels were flushed. After what seemed to be hours wading through ankle-deep sludge, Danilo concluded that it was high time for another such cleansing—provided the mysterious powers who handled such things didn't mind waiting until they had vacated.

"At the risk of sounding ignorant," Dan said, his voice muffled by the hand he held clasped over his nose, "precisely how are you tracking this thing? Surely not by scent! What are we looking for?"

Arilyn stopped at a cross tunnel and considered her path. "I'll let you know when I find it."

"Oh, splendid," he said, throwing up his hands in disgust. "In all fairness, my dear, I should inform you that the mood is now thoroughly broken."

The half-elf nodded absently, then strode forward to study some marks on the wall. "This way."

Danilo sighed and fell in behind. "What are we following?"

"Trail sign. The tren who attacked us was a clan leader. He left marks to direct the rest of the clan." She darted a somber look back over her shoulder. "They met here earlier and split up to attend to different tasks."

"Thoughtful fellow to lead you right past those marks," Dan commented. "A trap, perhaps?"

"It's possible," she admitted, but her pace did not slow. Dan shook his head and followed.

They slogged down the tunnel to its end, then climbed a ladder out into the city. This one did not lead them into an alley but into a narrow, dark passage that rose straight up.

Arilyn gritted her teeth in annoyance. "A garbage shaft," she said shortly. She tapped at the fresh claw marks on the stone. "Up we go."

The shaft was a long one. Climbing it was slow going, for the stone was smooth and the blocks tightly fitted. They tested each possible handhold or footrest carefully, for often what appeared to be a small stone ledge was nothing more than an accumulation of caked-on powder. Danilo soon began to suspect their destination from the scents and substances that layered the stone.

"The good news," he gritted out as he hauled himself up to the next secure handhold, "is that this is not a privy shaft."

Arilyn glanced back at him. "That much I already knew. What's the bad news?"

"Unless I very much miss my guess, this is a wizard's

tower," he said grimly. "You'd better let me go in first."

She nodded and let him take the lead. Before much longer, he caught sight of a faint, fading blue glow in the tower ahead. It beckoned them on, grim evidence of a magical battle waged—and most likely lost. Danilo redoubled his efforts, hoping to get to the unknown wizard while there was still something left to save.

Finally he reached the ledge. He cautiously peered over the edge, alert for attack from either a triumphant tren or an angry wizard.

The room was silent and empty. Danilo dragged himself over the ledge and rolled onto the floor. He reached down and pulled Arilyn up into the room, then turned to survey the tower.

It was a well-equipped study, octagonal in shape. Neat rows of vials and boxes and pots filled the shelves that lined four of the walls. Several small tables had been clustered about. These had been overturned in the struggle, their contents tossed onto the polished stone floor. A faint, acrid scent, like that left by a hundred bolts of lightning, lingered in the air—evidence that defensive magic had been cast. However, there was no sign of the tren, or of the wizard who had fought him.

Arilyn's eyes were sharper. She strode forward and kicked away some of the debris. "Look at this," she said in a grim voice, pointing.

He came forward and swallowed hard. A severed human hand lay on the ground, palm up, fingers curved as if in a final gesture of supplication.

"It's a sign," the half-elf explained in a flat, even voice. "Tren eat their victims, unless their employer wishes to leave a warning or message. Then they leave a single hand or foot."

"There is a ring on the hand," Danilo pointed out.

She prodded the grisly thing with her boot, turning it over. The hand was pale as bleached bone and slightly freckled. A few red hairs on the lower finger joints stood out starkly against the pallor. The ring was gold, and on the rose-colored quartz was engraved a small, leaping flame surrounded by a circle of seven stars.

"Mystra's symbol," Arilyn commented. "That accounts for the wizard."

The ring was familiar. Danilo crouched down for a better look. He gingerly found the clasp and opened the hidden compartment. As he'd expected, the outline of a wizard's tall-peaked hat was engraved into the inner lip. The hidden compartment was empty.

He stood up. "I recall what you told me of last night's overheard conversation. It would appear that Maskar Wands was more right than he knew when he named the dream spheres as dangerous toys."

When Arilyn sent him an inquiring look, he pointed to the severed hand. "That is—or strictly speaking, *was*—Oth Eltorchul."

Five

A premonition raced through Arilyn like a winter chill, or the shadow of a passing ghost. "You think Oth Eltorchul was killed for the dream spheres?"

"In all truth, I wouldn't lay odds one way or another," Dan responded. "Remember, I knew the man. He might just as well have incurred the wrath of a former student or a fellow mage, but it is possible, yes."

"Everyone at that meeting I overheard last night was opposed to the sale of dream spheres. Perhaps one of them hired the tren. Find out who was there, and we've got a place to start looking."

Danilo folded his arms and scowled. "Wait a minute. A place to start? You intend to go after the killer?"

"Don't you?"

"I fail to see how this fits any definition of service to the elven people."

"Maybe not." She shrugged. "Nonetheless, one way or another I might not have a choice."

He gave her a keen look. "I'm not going to like this, am I?"

"No." She began to pace, picking her way through the

clutter. "I can't make sense of this. At first I assumed that the tren attack at the Gemstone Ball was directed against Elaith. But I was there first, and then the same tren showed up at my lodging house. It is possible that second attack was the tren's vendetta—I killed a couple of his clan, I wounded him—but it's also possible that I, not Elaith, was his original target." She blew out a long breath. "There's another possibility. As you pointed out, the markings that led us here to this tower room seemed a little too convenient."

Danilo looked puzzled, so Arilyn reluctantly continued. "It's well known that some assassins occasionally work with tren. The tren provide muscle as well as a means of disposing of the body. You know my reputation. Some people might ask why I just happened to be the first one on hand after a tren attack. The Eltorchul clan is going to want to know the answer to that."

His face clouded. "Surely you have left those rumors behind at last! I have not heard anyone speak of you as an assassin for years."

"Nor would you," she retorted. "Yet I don't imagine that even now your peers are eager to accept me into their midst!"

"Only because you're half-elven," he said heatedly. A look of utter mortification crossed his face as he realized what he had said.

Arilyn quickly turned away, before any reaction of hers could add to Dan's regret. She understood the implications of their friendship in the young nobleman's world, probably far better than he did. To forestall any further discussion, she began kicking at the debris with more force and fervor than the task required.

After the first moments, Arilyn became genuinely absorbed by the puzzle before her. She began to circle the octagonal room, studying the chaos in search of some small pattern.

The wizard's tables had been overturned, and shards

of pottery lay scattered on the floor along with a variety of weird spell components that Arilyn could not begin to name. Oddly enough, none of the shelves had been disturbed by the struggle, as if the mage had deliberately avoided damaging any of the contents. That seemed to fly against logic, but Arilyn had heard of people who protected their possessions more fiercely than their own lives.

"What is the worth of all that?" she asked, pointing to the orderly shelves.

Danilo's gaze swept across the rows of glass and silver bottles, carved wooden boxes, and carefully stacked scrolls. "Almost beyond estimation," he admitted. "This is a most impressive study."

"Worth dying for?"

"I wouldn't say so. Oth might have. I see your point, though. This was an unusual struggle. Another thing puzzles me: there is far less blood than one might expect."

"Not unusual for tren attacks," Arilyn corrected. "They're . . . tidy. They also feed with astonishing speed. On the other hand, it is possible that Oth died elsewhere and that his hand was left here for someone to find."

"That someone being you." Danilo frowned. "I am finding more to dislike about this situation by the moment, but we cannot dismiss the possibility that Elaith was the target of the first tren attack. Perhaps we should see what he knows."

Arilyn had no desire to seek out the rogue elf, but she could see the sense in that. She nodded toward the one door that led out of the room and drew her sword. "The tren is long gone, but we might not be able to leave this place without meeting opposition."

"One moment." He took a carved wooden box from the shelf, emptied the dried herbs it contained onto the floor, and then, to her astonishment, pushed the disembodied hand into it. He carefully fastened the clasp and then tucked the box under one arm.

"What do you think you're doing?"

"It is better that I turn this matter over to the Watch than you," he explained. "After all, I once studied with the Eltorchul family, and I could contrive a reason for entering Oth's tower. No one need hear of your presence here."

Arilyn started to protest, but she recognized the implacably stubborn expression in her friend's eyes. She turned and walked toward the door. "Good thing you're giving up that Lord's helm," she muttered. "I wouldn't call this upholding the laws of the city."

"You haven't actually broken any, have you? Recently?"

"I just got here," she said with a bit of grim humor.

"Well, then," he said, his tone suggesting that the matter had been settled.

She led the way down a winding stairs into the main hall. The building that supported the wizard's tower was small, just a center hall with a few rooms to either side for servants and household functions. There was no sign of anyone in the building, and they slipped out into the courtyard without challenge.

Since they had come that far, Arilyn deemed it safe to begin the search for Oth's killer. She nodded toward the carriage shed, from whence drifted a faint murmur of sound. Tucking away her sword, she went to inquire.

A thin man with lank, yellow hair was busy digging a stone from the hoof of a bay horse. Three matching steeds munched hay in tidy stalls, and a fine carriage stood nearby, its undercarriage still grimed with a layer of street dust.

The man looked up when Arilyn's shadow fell upon him. His lip curled disdainfully, and he brandished the small knife as if he were shooing off an importunate stray dog.

"Be off with you," he snarled, "and be quick about it. There is no work for you here. My master would sooner turn the likes of you into a lizard than hire you."

Dan stepped around her. Even in his current bedraggled state, he was unmistakably a man of wealth and position. The coachman leaped to his feet, chagrin on his thin face as he recognized the raven-and-unicorn heraldry on the young man's pendant as the mark of a noble family. "My lord," he stammered. "I did not—"

"You apparently speak for Lord Eltorchul," Danilo said, cutting off the man's apology. "Perhaps then you can tell me where he is. No one answered our knock."

"Nor will they, my lord," the man said quickly, obviously eager to undo whatever ill will he had caused. "Lord Oth gave the servants a day's holiday to enjoy the harvest festivals. I delivered him myself to the Thann estate last night."

"And from thence?"

The coachman hesitated, clearly at conflict whether or not to speak of his master's business. Danilo held up a large silver coin. "I have forgotten already what you are about to tell me. Try to convince me to overlook the insult you offered my lady."

The man's eyes shifted incredulously to Arilyn. She supposed she could understand why he'd come to the conclusion he had. Clad in worn leather breeches and boots, wearing no ornaments but an elven sword, she looked like any one of the hundreds of mercenaries who thronged the city and made their way the best they could.

The coachman caught the coin Dan flipped him and nodded his agreement to the bargain. "I took Lord Oth to a tavern in the Sea Ward. The Silken Sylph. There was a woman with him." A quick grin jerked across his thin features, and his hands traced a voluptuous outline in the air.

"I am acquainted with the general concept," Danilo commented. "Can you offer something a bit more specific?"

"Red dress, black hair, big dark eyes," the man reminisced. "Dark skin, but not as dark as a Calishite. Nose like a scimitar. Slender, but not scrawny, if you know what I mean." As if there could be any doubt, he cupped the air several inches from his chest.

Arilyn hissed through clenched teeth. Isabeau Thione, beyond doubt. Was it possible the troublesome wench had progressed from thievery to murder?

Yes, she concluded, entirely possible. Arilyn did not know what complaint Isabeau had against Oth, but she had an excellent reason to hire an attack on Elaith Craulnober. Earlier that very summer, the elf had vied with Arilyn and Danilo over Isabeau's fate. Had the matter been resolved differently, Elaith would have sold the woman to whatever faction in Tethyr offered the best price. It mattered not at all to the elf whether the bidders wished to use the Thione bastard as a political pawn or to remove her entirely from the picture. Given Elaith's dark reputation, Isabeau had no reason to believe the elf would not yet do what he had once set out to accomplish. If she found a way to strike first, she would probably take it. Nor did Isabeau hold much affection for Arilyn. What better way to deflect attention than to place both attacks at the doorstep of a half-elven assassin?

Arilyn shifted impatiently from one foot to the other as she waited for Danilo to finish the transaction. After a few more questions, he flipped the man a second coin, and they walked together into the street.

"Isabeau hated Elaith. She was with Oth," Arilyn pointed out. "As far as tren attacks go, that's two out of three."

"And you the third. Why?"

She thought back to Isabeau's rescue and the vicious resistance that the tavern pickpocket had waged when Arilyn had caught up to her outside the gnomish stronghold. "Once Isabeau realized what was awaiting her in Waterdeep, she was in favor of rescue, but getting to that point was like reasoning with a mule. Sometimes you have to hit it over the head with a stick to get its attention."

"Ah. Knowing Isabeau, I'm guessing you had to use a fairly big stick."

"You could say that. It's possible that she's holding a grudge. There's more." She hesitated a moment, not wanting to give words to what seemed incomprehensible behavior. "You didn't seek her out on the trip to Waterdeep. I don't think she's accustomed to being ignored. Since she's not one to blame herself for much of anything, I wouldn't be surprised if she has a grudge on that score. Creating trouble for me would balance the scales for your inattention."

Danilo looked coldly furious. "I am beginning to regret the pledge I took from Elaith for Isabeau's safety. Speaking of whom, we'd better see him at once—provided I can remember which of his properties he currently inhabits!"

He hailed a passing carriage. The crest of the Carriage Guild was painted on the door, marking it as available for hire—as did the presence of its halfling crew. The stout little driver tilted his plumed cap and pulled the horses to a halt. A second halfling scrambled down from the coachman's seat and opened the door, smiling expectantly up at Arilyn.

Too tired to argue, she climbed in and settled back against the plush seat. With a jerk, the carriage took off toward the south to seek out whatever rock the elven snake happened to be sunning himself on this particular morning.

*　*　*　*　*

Elaith Craulnober was not in good humor. He was never so when going over his account books. The numbers therein would have sent many a merchant lord dancing giddily into the streets, and in truth Elaith was not un-happy with the results of his recent ventures in Skullport. It was the ciphering itself that he loathed.

A pity he could not trust another to tend such mat-ters for him. There were scribes, of course, and men who wrote up bills of sale and tallied the day's transaction. There were other men who collected this information and passed it along to their superiors, who in turn passed it along. Groups of men, some small, some num-bering in scores, tended Elaith's vast concerns, but each group was like a single room with windows and doors to the outside word—and none at all to the corridors that led to those other rooms. Only Elaith knew the whole of his empire.

The small brass bell suspended above his door chimed musically. Almost glad for the interruption, Elaith tugged at the embroidered bellpull to grant permission for audience.

The door opened soundlessly. Just as quiet was the elderly elven servant who glided up to Elaith's desk and offered a small, silver tray.

Elaith glanced at the engraved card and smiled faintly. Young Lord Thann had come calling, no doubt with a bottle of elven wine and an apology that would be peppered with foolish anecdotes—but no less sincere for all that. Elaith's words to Arilyn the night before had been simple truth: he did not believe that Danilo had issued the invitation in order to lure him into an ambush. He would not, however, hold other members of the Thann family above suspicion. There was no reason for Danilo to know that, of course.

"Send him in."

"Them, my lord. The moonfighter is with him," the servant said, showing Arilyn the respect due any elf honored with a moonblade. If the servant had an opin-ion about whether a half-elf deserved this honor, he wisely kept it to himself.

Elaith rose as the unlike pair entered his study. His words of welcome died as he regarded their disheveled appearance. They both looked as damp and road-sore as horses run too long and too hard. A wide variety of substances besmudged their clothing, which to all appearances had been donned hastily and without the aid of servants. Arilyn's black curls fell to her shoulders in wild disarray, and her white, angular face was streaked with grime. Both looked as if they had thrust their hands into a gnome's sausage grinder, so torn were the skin and nails.

"What in the Nine bloody Hells have you been about?" Elaith demanded.

Danilo threw himself into a chair, then placed what appeared to be a large, wooden snuffbox on the table beside. "Fighting tren, traversing sewers, climbing walls. Nothing out of the ordinary. How was *your* morning?"

Consternation swept through the elf. He looked to Arilyn for a straight answer. "There was another tren attack?"

"Two." In a few terse words, she described the situation.

Elaith nodded thoughtfully. The pieces fit. Indeed they did.

"Oth Eltorchul and Isabeau were at The Silken Sylph last night," Arilyn said in a flat, even tone.

The elf knew what was coming next. "I suppose you stopped there looking for me, and you were informed, though not without some persuasion, that I was seen in conversation with Lord Eltorchul."

Danilo quickly entered the conversation. "We came here to learn what you know of the matter, not to make accusations. Three tren attacks, in the space of a single day, all of them threatening Arilyn's safety or reputation. There are other common threads: all those attacked were at the Gemstone Ball, all had dealings with

Isabeau Thione. Can you see something I might have missed?"

"Nothing more than I said last night," Elaith said. "This was not the first time someone took steps to hasten my departure from this world. Nor, all things considered, will it be the last. I do not know what occasioned this particular attack, nor have I any knowledge of the other two."

"We will be looking into this matter," Arilyn stated.

Obviously she suspected him, whatever Danilo might say to the contrary. That knowledge stung the elf more than it should.

Elaith gave her a faint smile and a courtly bow. "I will consider myself warned. Lord Thann, what is that box?" he asked, more to distract the conversation than from any real interest.

Danilo shifted uneasily. "It's all that remains of Oth."

"Ah. Turning evidence over to the Watch. Very commendable," the elf murmured without much interest.

"Actually, I thought I'd turn this over to the Eltorchul clan for possible resurrection."

Outrage, quick and sharp and utterly elven, surged through Elaith. He noted that Arilyn's expression mirrored his thoughts. In this, at least, they were of like mind.

Resurrection, was it? Typical human arrogance! The elf could think of nothing more self-centered or more repugnant than disturbing the afterlife of friend or kindred.

"Why do you humans persist in doing this thing?" he demanded.

"Because we can, most likely," Danilo responded wearily. "It is hard to accept that a loved one is lost when magic exists that will call him back."

"You could have mentioned this earlier," Arilyn snapped.

Danilo shrugged and glanced from one angry elf to the other. "I always like to break bad news when I'm grossly outnumbered. It keeps me in good trim."

Elaith stepped between them before the argument could escalate. "Although I regret to hear of your troubles, I can offer you nothing that would assist you. Have you considered the possibility that I have no real part in this drama? That the tren in the Thann tunnels were tracking Arilyn, not lying in wait for me?"

"I have," admitted Arilyn. A wary look entered her eyes. "Lying in wait. They had reason to expect you?"

The elf cursed himself for the misstep. If the persistent half-elf learned that he had been lured to the tunnel, she would not rest until she found out who had sent the note. In the process, she would no doubt come across the connection between him and the dream spheres. That, he could not permit.

"I was speaking from your vantage point," he said smoothly. "Of course you could not know that I caught a glimpse of you in the halls and followed you into the tunnels. You appeared to be lost. I merely wished to offer assistance."

Arilyn shot a quick, almost guilty glance in Danilo's direction, then returned a level gaze to Elaith. "If you think of anything that might help, you will contact Dan?"

It did not escape the elf that Arilyn removed herself from the chain of information. Elaith inclined his head in another bow. "Always at your service, Princess."

His visitors left soon after. As soon as the study door closed behind them, Elaith paced over to the hearth and stared at the fire with unseeing eyes.

What was he to do now? The dream spheres he would and must have; that need had not changed with Oth's death. Now, however, he would have to sidestep, if not actively contend with, the efforts of these two people. Under any circumstances, he would rather count them as allies than adversaries. He had made pledges to them both, evoking the deepest bonds known to elves and stirring the very core of his forgotten honor.

To Danilo he owed the pledge of Elf-friend. No elf Elaith knew in fact or in legend had ever set aside that pledge. Arilyn, half-elven though she was, Elaith regarded as both kin and liege lady. The Craulnober clan was a sept—a minor branch—of the royal elven house. Elaith's first sword had been sworn in service to the Moonflower family, and Arilyn was the daughter of the disgraced and exiled Princess Amnestria. She should have been *his* daughter, but for his own private disgrace.

The elf firmly set aside these thoughts. Despair lay at the end of that path. He had not thrived all these many years away from Evermeet by ruing what was past.

It was easier to ponder the death of Oth Eltorchul. There were few who deserved the fate more and many who might have ordered it. Several powerful wizards had cause to hate the mage. Rumor spoke of several women angered by his treatment of them. Elaith knew of at least four noble families who had reason to squelch the proposed trade in dream spheres—for much the same reason that opposition to his own enterprises in Skullport was growing. Legal trade in Waterdeep was strictly regulated. Illegal trade was even more sternly enforced.

All in all, Elaith's fancy settled upon the crystal merchant, Mizzen Doar. Mizzen had already offered a drunken confession of sorts. Elaith had reason to connect the man's boast of the "elf gem" to Oth Eltorchul's magical toys. If the gem was what Elaith suspected it to be and if the crystal merchant was truly in possession of it, Mizzen was the most likely suspect to murder that Elaith could conceive.

It occurred to him, briefly, to reconsider the wisdom of seeking out the gem. Not long ago, Mizzen had possessed a sterling reputation. Recently Elaith had heard rumors of shady dealings that ranged from counterfeiting to outright fraud. Murder was not out of the question for one under the thrall of the elven stone.

"I am sufficient to the challenge," he muttered.

Was he? A few years ago, he would have undergone this venture in confidence. After all, had he not removed himself from all things elven? The gem would have been to him a rare and legendary treasure, no more. Possession would have been enough.

That was before he had remembered the value of honor, before he had looked into the face of his tiny daughter and dreamed for her things he had long forgotten. It was before he had undergone a quest to reawaken the Craulnober moonblade and hold it in trust for his heir, before he saw and honored the royalty in a rough-edged half-elf. Before he had forged the sacred bonds of Elf-friend.

In doing these things, Elaith had torn pieces from his carefully constructed armor. Ironically, in allowing pockets of virtue into his life, he had opened himself up to the very real danger posed by the twisted magic of the elven gem. If there was yet good in him, the gem would seek to win him. If he were truly a creature of evil, the gem would submit to his will, for that would be the best way of creating mischief. Either way, it would change his life immeasurably, but at least, at last, he would know.

"Better to embrace evil without reservation than to be overcome by it," Elaith mused.

Even as he spoke, the spiral of his thoughts turned again. If he were to deny the only honor remaining him, would he not be overcome indeed?

The elf's mind whirled with the confusion of it. This was not the sort of puzzle that normally occupied him. In his world, a thing was, or it was not. He was an honorable elven warrior of Evermeet, or he was utterly disgraced and dissolute. He could not be both.

Yet he was.

Elaith stalked over to his desk and hurled the ledgers into the open chest beside it. The books disappeared and would not return except to his call.

"Thasilier!" he bellowed.

The elven steward came to his call. "Send word to my captains," snapped Elaith. "I would have them meet me at highsun at Greenglade Tower. Those who lodge there have until that hour to make other arrangements."

Astonishment overcame the steward's inscrutable calm. "My lord?"

"Do it," Elaith said in a cold, dangerous voice.

The elf bowed and turned away, obedient even in this, the dissolution of one of the last elven havens in the city. Elaith owned the enclosed garden and tower, and he would use it however he saw fit.

He was no longer a Guardian, captain of the royal elven guard. Let the elves of Waterdeep fend for themselves, as best they could.

As Elaith intended to do.

* * * * *

Isabeau Thione swept down the street toward the elegant stone building housing Diloontier's Fine Perfumes. She had never had occasion to visit this shop or, for that matter, the coins to finance a purchase. Thanks to Oth Eltorchul, she now possessed both.

She tried not to look impressed as she entered the shop, despite the rows of glittering bottles that lined the walls and the rare, costly spices and tinctures that scented the air. The front room was furnished as well as any noblewoman's parlor. A large, arched door led into the back room, where stood tables heaped with rare, fresh flowers. Two young apprentices were busy with mortar and pestle, crushing blossoms and herbs into paste. Another lad carefully placed herbs or bits of citrus peel into vials of strong spirits, in order to draw off tinctures.

The proprietor bustled up to greet her. Diloontier was a small man, not much taller than Isabeau. He was exceedingly thin of limb and face but wore his belt low under a small, tightly rounded belly. His dark hair had been oiled back, and his thin-lipped smile was exceedingly broad. On the whole, he rather resembled a frog. Isabeau gave him a cool nod, then tugged off her gloves and presented her wrist to him.

"This perfume was blended for me in Zazesspur," she said, speaking not fact, but code. "Can you match it?"

The little man sniffed delicately. "Patchouli, citrus, and snowflower," he mused, "and perhaps one thing more."

It was the agreed-upon response. A wave of relief swept through Isabeau. She had gone to great trouble and expense to seek out such a man, and it was gratifying to know her efforts had been well spent. Diloontier's words indicated that he was available to sell things not offered in the fine shop: poisons, potions, and a variety of services.

Isabeau cast a glance back toward the door to ensure that they were not observed, then took the sack of dream spheres from her bag. "This is the one thing more," she said. "I believe you can sell them for me."

The perfumer reached into the bag and drew out one of the gleaming spheres. His eyes widened. "Indeed I can. I have heard tell of these. So have some of the gentry, and I've had enough discreet inquiries to enable me to move these quickly, as well as any more you might happen upon," he said.

"At what price?"

Diloontier looked scandalized. "A lady of quality need not concern herself with such details. I will handle all, and report faithfully to your steward."

Isabeau refused to be flattered or patronized. She

strolled over to a shelf glittering with decorative silver vials and took from it a small, plain bottle. Turning to face the perfumer, she slowly, deliberately dropped the vial into her bag.

"Half," she specified coldly, staring down the suddenly wary man. "I expect to receive half the purchase price of each dream sphere you sell. Do not attempt to cheat me."

"My lady!" he protested.

"Do not," she said in a low tone as she patted her bag, "or I will feed you one of your own poisons. Now that we are properly acquainted, let us discuss some other matters you can help me with. . . ."

*　*　*　*　*

Arilyn and Danilo walked down the long, black marble stairs that led from the front door of Blackstone House, one of Elaith's favorite residences. Unlike most houses in the city, this one had no windows or doors on the first level. Guests were obliged to climb a steep, narrow stairs to the front door. No rails lined the stairs, which were smooth and slick as a ballroom floor.

Arilyn had to admit that it was a clever design and extremely defensible. Anyone who wished to storm the elf's abode would be obliged to do so one at a time. No one could stand and fight on so precarious a perch, and she would not be at all surprised if the stone griffons that flanked the stairs on the ground below were magical constructs, waiting to pounce upon any who might fall.

Arilyn all but leaped down the stairs and hastily climbed into the waiting carriage. "He's lying," she said flatly.

Danilo did not disagree. He climbed into the seat, leaned forward and gave the halfling driver his address, then slid shut the wooden door. "At least he does not hold the Thann family responsible. I would not care to renew that particular enmity."

"They call him the Serpent, and not without reason," she pointed out. "A snake still strikes whether you name him friend or foe. It's his nature."

"I am not so certain," Danilo argued. "There are some things even Elaith holds sacred. He did not lightly name me Elf-friend. I believe he will honor that pledge."

"As long as it's convenient." Arilyn slumped down in the seat and stretched her booted feet out before her. The look she sent in Danilo's direction bordered on pleading. "At least consider the possibility that I'm right."

"This much I will do." Danilo reached up and tapped on the wooden door. "Change of plan," he informed the beaming halfling driver. "Take us to The Curious Past, on the Street of Silks."

The half-elf sat upright, surprised to hear him name the posh shopping district. "What is this?"

"The dream spheres hold part of the answer to this puzzle," Danilo explained. "Of that much, I am fairly certain. Perhaps Elaith has more involvement in this matter than he is willing to admit. I will have someone follow him, and we will see."

Arilyn nodded. That was more of a concession than she had expected to get. "A Harper?"

"One of the agents assigned to my direction," he agreed, "and recently released to tend her own affairs. You have not met Bronwyn. She is a finder of lost things, a scholar of sorts but ready for just about anything that comes her way. She is most knowledgeable concerning treasures both ancient and modern and deals frequently with the gem and crystal merchants. These dream spheres had to be mined and cut and polished. She would be able to find out who did these things—as would Elaith, if indeed he plans to follow this path."

Arilyn nodded agreement to this plan and settled

back to watch as the city rolled past. The carriage swung eastward toward a place of elegant shops and taverns. The tang of the sea deepened as they rode, and it mingled with the savory odors wafting from the taverns and bakeries and pastry shops that offered respite to those who strolled the broad streets.

The day was fine, and the shops were crowded with people eager to enjoy the last warm days. Before the moon waned and waxed twice, many of the revelers would quit the city in search of softer climes. They poured into the streets for one last, hectic bustle of commerce and festivity.

So many people milled about the streets that passage by carriage was impossible. Danilo settled with the halfling driver and led the way through the crowd toward an elegant, dark-timbered building.

A tilted hourglass decorated a carved and painted sign, and markings proclaimed it to be The Curious Past, using not one language but three: the trade language known as Common, beautifully rendered Elvish script, and the squat, emphatic figures of the dwarven runes. Behind the small-paned windows, each of which was etched with the same hourglass design, was a pleasing jumble of trinkets and treasures.

Arilyn liked Bronwyn at first glance. The Harper was of average height for a woman, nearly a head shorter than Arilyn. She wore neither the weapons nor the manner of a trained fighter, but there was no hint of weakness about her. She was compact and trim and was sensibly clad in tunic and breeches of a matching russet hue. Her large, chocolate-brown eyes were lively with intelligence, and her gaze managed to be both warm and direct. The small hand she offered Arilyn in response to Dan's introduction was ornamented only by ink stains and calluses.

"A pleasure," Bronwyn said with genuine warmth. "Dan has spoken of you."

"And of you, a scholar and adventurer," she repeated, seeing the truth of both.

The woman laughed. "Fine words! That's a sure sign that he wants something from me."

"Guilty," Danilo said with a grin. He quickly described the situation.

"I know of Elaith Craulnober," Bronwyn murmured. She turned a dry smile upon her friend. "Either you have a very high opinion of me or a very low one."

"Dealing with Elaith often requires the best of both philosophies," he admitted.

"Well, that's why you're here," Bronwyn said matter-of-factly. "As it turns out, I do have a legitimate errand to attend—or more accurately, an illegitimate one."

She went to a case and removed from it a waterfall of glittering, pale green stones, artfully woven into a necklace. "The stones are peridot, considered only semi-precious in the north but highly prized in Mulhorand and the lands of the Old Empires as gems fit for royalty. Lovely, aren't they?"

Arilyn shrugged. Jewelry was nice enough, but irrelevant.

"Good eye," Bronwyn congratulated her, misunderstanding her lack of enthusiasm. "There are exactly two genuine peridots in this lot. The rest are crystal. The gem merchant who hired me wants more of the same. If Elaith is nosing about among the crystal merchants, I'll have a reason to follow—or at least bump elbows."

"Splendid," Danilo agreed happily as he rose to leave.

"You've just got here," the merchant scolded him. "Perhaps Arilyn would like to see some of the elven pieces first?"

Danilo pantomimed a pained expression and reached pointedly for his coin bag. "Didn't I tell you she was good at her business?" he asked Arilyn.

"These are not for sale," Bronwyn said with brisk good humor as she led the way to a long, glass-covered box. "I recovered these for the elves of the Pantheon Temple. To be honest, I'm hoping you can shed some light on them. I like to know the history of the pieces I collect. These appear to be personal possessions, but there is apparently some sort of sacred significance to them."

Arilyn's heart pounded as she studied the objects in the case. There was a small flute grown from green crystal, an emerald pendant, a leather bracer dyed green and tooled with beautiful, mystic designs. There was a small, stylized sculpture of Hannali Celanil, the elven goddess of beauty, rendered in green-veined marble.

"The color is significant, isn't it?" Bronwyn went on.

"Yes." Arilyn cleared her throat. "These are Midsummer gifts, given at festival time. They are personal, as you say. They are also sacred, but not in any manner that can be explained with talk of gods and temples."

"How fascinating! What can you tell me about this festival?"

"Nothing." Arilyn softened the refusal with a faint smile. "I am sorry, but there is no way to explain it. Some elven rites are not allowed to be revealed to humans, and even if they were, they would not be fully experienced or understood."

Bronwyn took no offense. She glanced over at Danilo, who was happily leafing through some old tomes at the far side of the shop. "Humans use the Weave," she said, naming the mystic force that shaped all magic, "but elves are part of it. They are also one with the land, and the sea, and the patterns of the sun and stars. This much I know, even though I could never experience it as you would. I have heard that the times of solstice and equinox are sacred to the elves. I know that such times were celebrated with fertility rituals by many ancient human cultures. I did not mean to offend you by implying that elven festivals were the same and nothing more."

"You understand more than I thought," Arilyn

responded. To her surprise, it was not only easy to speak of this, but comforting. "No offense was taken. Yes, these are times of revelry among the elves. Many marriages are made, friendships celebrated in intimate ways, but this is part of a larger, mystic connection—connection to all elves, and to the Weave of magic and the very circle of life."

"And only elves are accepted," the woman repeated. She smiled faintly. "To a limited degree, I understand. Perhaps Dan has told you of my life. I spent most of it searching for my family, my past. This meant everything to me. I found my father and lost him all in the space of a few hours, but I came away from that experience feeling like a whole person for the first time in my life. I can't imagine what it would mean to a half-elf to be invited to take part in such a festival."

Arilyn met the woman's warm, sympathetic gaze. She took from the pocket of her breeches a small stone knife, sharp as steel and carved with a feather pattern. This she handed to Bronwyn. "Add this to the Temple's store. It is as precious as anything there."

The woman hesitated, demonstrating for the first time that her understanding was more human than elven. "You are sure you want to part with this?"

"Midsummer gifts are also part of the whole. The wheel turns, and they are often given anew with the coming of another summer."

Bronwyn nodded her thanks. Arilyn handed her the stone knife, a gift from Foxfire, the elf who had offered her the first true acceptance she had ever received from her mother's people—and who had changed her life. Without Foxfire, she would not have come to terms with her own divided nature or learned that though her soul was elven, her heart belonged to a human man.

A heavy thud drew her attention. She glanced over at Danilo. He stooped quickly to pick up the tome he had dropped, but not before Arilyn saw his gaze dart from the knife in her hand to the green treasures in Bronwyn's case. Not before stunned comprehension flooded his face.

Bronwyn glanced from Danilo back to Arilyn, and her brown eyes widened with chagrin. "He didn't know."

"No."

In truth, Arilyn had never seen need to speak of that Midsummer night. The initial joy of her reunion with Dan had swept aside all other considerations. Shortly after, she had been called back to the forests to aid the embattled elves. There had been little in her life since then to bring to mind the sacred revels of Midsummer.

Now she tried to see the matter as Danilo might. Few humans could understand the true nature of elven festivals. They would see her participation as a shallow indulgence. Danilo, though, knew more of the elves than did most men, and he valued highly what he knew.

That could be more of a problem than a blessing. Just last night, he had been ready to give her up rather than separate her from the magic of her elven sword. Arilyn was not sure how he would respond to the knowledge that she had known an elven love.

"It'll be fine," Bronwyn said with quiet urgency. "Dan has reason to know that lovers can become friends, content to leave the past as it was."

Arilyn looked at her with sudden comprehension. She felt no jealousy over this revelation. Even if she were so inclined, that emotion would have been an unworthy response to Bronwyn's obviously well-meaning concern. "Why do you tell me this?"

"For his own good," the woman said as she took Arilyn's hand in a sisterly clasp. "Use it if you have to. Just don't let him do anything noble and foolish."

The half-elf gave her new friend a small, wry smile. "Apparently you know that that's more easily said than done."

"What of it? Men are not put here to make our lives easy," Bronwyn announced. "They're just put here."

Despite the situation, this amused the half-elf. "Any more words of advice?"

"Yes." Bronwyn nodded toward Dan, who was staring fixedly at the far wall and absently stirring through a tray of fragile coral jewelry. "Get him out of here before he breaks something."

Six

The hum and bustle of the streets enveloped Danilo
and Arilyn as they left The Curious Past behind. Bronwyn's shop was not far from the market, a vast, open-air
bazaar that dominated the northern end of Waterdeep's
Castle Ward.

They walked in silence, weaving their way through
the crowds. Usually Danilo took great pleasure in the
sights and sounds of the colorful district, but today he
felt as if he were walking through an illusion. His
senses noted the ringing, musical cries of the street vendors, the salty warm scent of the pretzels draped over
the T-shaped crook carried by a young man with a
much-freckled countenance and a jaunty purple cap. He
heard the loudly whispered boasts of the two small lads
who leaned out from a second story window and
attempted with twine and wooden hooks to snare some
of the pretzels.

He led the way through the maze of shops with the
surety of long experience. Over the years, Danilo had
spent a great deal of time in the market. Almost everything a wealthy man could desire flowed to this place,

Merchants from up and down the Sword Coast brought wares from every corner of Faerun and from the exotic lands beyond. Craftsmen from the Trades Ward rumbled north with their wagons loaded with simple, necessary goods: barrels, tack and saddles for riding horses, iron utensils for tending fires and stirring pots. Blacksmiths, coopers, brewers, cobblers—all plied their wares in the market alongside the silks and gems of distant lands. Fragrant smoke rose with the sun as vendors and tavern keepers stoked fires in anticipation of the midday meal.

The only thing lacking, and the only thing Danilo required at present, was privacy. The answers he wished to know would be hard enough to hear under any circumstances. He could hardly shout delicate questions over the bustle of morning commerce.

He turned up Bazaar Street toward the quieter residential area. Arilyn fell into step without argument. The crowd thinned as they moved west from the market, and before long they strode the broad, cobbled walks along Suldoun Street.

The townhouse he called home was tall, narrow, and elegant. It was tucked neatly alongside other, similar homes, most of them owned by young members of the merchant nobility. The front was finished stone, the peaked and gabled roof tiled with multicolored slate. Tall windows of many small panes, some of them colored glass, flanked the door. Decorative iron gates enclosed the small front courtyard and led into the narrow walkways on either side of the building and the garden courtyard beyond.

The tinkling song of the bellflowers drifted out to the street. Danilo's hand paused on the latch of one gate. He had intended to lead the way into the garden, which he'd spent nearly four years designing and perfecting. The elven garden was remarkable, boasting flowers that chimed with the passing of sea breezes, blue roses entwining elaborate arches. Reproductions of a pair of elven statues—the originals he had donated to the Pantheon Temple—stood in hauntingly beautiful repose beside the still waters of a small reflecting pond. It was an astonishing accomplishment and the pride of his elven gardener.

Suddenly, it seemed to Danilo to be nothing more than one of the pretentious excesses so common among his peers. If it accomplished anything at all, it would be to remind Arilyn of how broad a gap remained between him and the elven people she served.

He opened the stout oak door and tossed his hat to the waiting steward. The halfling sent his master a cautious, sidelong glance, and then walked off without offering their guest the usual refreshments.

To the left was Danilo's study, a lavish room paneled with dark Chultan teak and softened by carpets and tapestries in rich shades of crimson and cream. Magic warded the room from prying eyes and ears, ensuring complete privacy.

Arilyn followed him in and took a chair near the hearth. She settled in and turned a steady gaze upon him. "Let's get this over with."

Typically direct, but hardly the most promising beginning. Danilo paced over to the mantle and picked up a small, elven sculpture, which he studied without interest as he collected his thoughts.

"Four years ago, before we parted in Zazesspur, I spoke my heart," he began. "There was no time for you to say yes or no. We were forced into separate paths: I to the High Forest and a madwoman's challenge to the Northland's bards, you to the Forest of Tethyr. When these tasks were completed, I spoke again, and you were of like mind. However, things had changed. I saw that. I did not understand how profound these changes were."

"That's apparent."

This was not the response he'd anticipated. He put down the statue and turned to face her. "Then please enlighten me."

The half-elf folded her arms and stretched her booted feet out before her. "Let's start here. Have I ever asked how you spent each of your days and nights, these past few years?"

"No, but that is different," he said firmly.

She lifted one ebony brow. "Oh? How so?"

"For one thing, the foolish games played in this city are without meaning."

"That's a good thing?"

He regarded her with faint exasperation. "Ever the sword mistress. You cannot yield the offensive for a moment, can you?"

Arilyn considered this, then gave a nod of concession. "I'll speak plainly, then. I knew what was in your heart when we parted, that's true, but I did not know my own. Until I forged a place for myself, I could not answer you yes or no. Now I have found that place."

"Among the elves."

"It was a needed thing. For most of my life, I lived and worked among humans." She touched the sheathed moonblade. "This was my only elven heritage. I always sensed that this weapon defined who I was, but I knew almost nothing about it. Everything that transpired that first summer we spent apart was part of the journey. To understand the moonblade, I had to become fully elven—if only for a short time. My time among the forest elves, including the midsummer revels, was a part of this. Without it, I would not have had the understanding of myself to know my heart."

Danilo could not refute the logic of this, but neither was it something he could easily accept. For a long moment he gazed out the study window, absently noting that the leaves were starting to take on the hues of autumn. He tried and discarded a dozen responses. The words that eventually emerged, however, were utterly unplanned.

"I suppose it would be ungentlemanly to ask for a name."

"Foxfire," she said without hesitation. "He was the war leader of the western clan. He was, and remains, a true friend."

That was hard to hear, and full of possibilities he hardly dared to explore. "You have returned to the forest more than once," he said tentatively.

"That's right. I have responsibilities."

A painful thought occurred to him. "Is there a child?"

Her eyes turned dark with surprise and outrage. "Do you think I would forget to mention such a thing? Or perhaps you envision me slinking at midnight into a home for unwed mercenaries?"

Had he been in a brighter frame of mind, he would have found that incongruous image amusing. "True enough. Accept my apologies—this revelation has left me somewhat distraught." He considered that, then added with a faint, pained smile, "That might well be the most masterful understatement I have ever contrived."

"Let's discuss that." The half-elf rose and faced him down. "I have lived forty years and more, hard years, for the most part. Did you expect to find me an untried maiden?"

"Well . . . "

"I see. And should I assume from this that you have followed a paladin's code?"

"Hardly." He sighed, struggling to explain what certainly did seem to be a code written on both sides of the parchment. "It would have been easier for me to shrug aside a score of lovers, had they been human."

She threw up her hands. "That's ridiculous!"

"Is it? When you left for the forest, you and I were bound in a form of elven rapport through the magic of your sword. When you returned, you swore your heart was mine. Yet your first allegiance was to the forest elves, and you kept from me this secret. What am I to think?"

Exasperation edged onto her face. "Would it have helped if I had spoken of this at once?"

"Probably not," he admitted. He hesitated for a moment as he sifted through the jumble of his emotions. "Forgive me. I desired change, and over the past two days the fates seem hell-bent on granting this wish. I just learned that there is elven blood in my family, courtesy of our dear archmage. This was no small revelation and means more to me than I can begin to express, but as I consider these new developments, I fear that the wine is too well watered."

Comprehension edged into her eyes, then disbelief. "Do I hear you correctly? You fear comparison with an elf?"

"That is putting it rather baldly," he said, wincing a bit at how foolish that made him sound. "Let me try to do a little better. I know how elves regard the half-elven. I have known you for more than six years and have seen how this pained you. In one part of my heart, I am truly happy that you have found the acceptance and community that you sought among the elven folk, but like most lovers, I have a certain selfish interest in this."

He sighed. "Therein lies the dilemma. Knowing you as I do, I wonder if you can be truly happy with a human man."

Arilyn was long in answering. She rose and began to prowl about the room, as if action was required to spur thought. "Happiness," she said slowly. "I have heard many people speak this word, and never once did I understand what they meant. Nor did they, I suspect. Notions of endless peace and bliss and ease, or some such."

His lips quirked in a faint smile. "You speak as if you were describing one of the lower reaches of the Abyss."

"I'm a warrior," she stated simply. "My mother put a wooden sword in my hand as soon as I could stand, and steel not long after. I never thought in terms of ease and comfort and so forth. But this much I know: I would rather fight with you than any other."

He regarded her for a long moment. "*With* me, or *alongside* me?"

A smile rippled across her lips. "Both, I suppose. Will that content you?"

He took her hand and raised it to his lips, kissing the delicate white fingers as he ran the pad of his thumb over the warrior's calluses on her palm. "That strikes me as a better measure of happiness than any man—or elf, for that matter—has right to expect!"

*   *   *   *   *

Their first fight was not long in coming. They hailed another carriage, and all the way to the Eltorchul manor, Arilyn argued against the course Danilo seemed determined to follow. A sudden squall, common during the changing season, swept in from the sea as they rolled westward. The pounding of rain and the grumbling thunder kept counterpoint to their argument.

"Oth Eltorchul is dead," she stated finally. "His spirit has gone to whatever afterlife his days have earned. Who are you to disturb that?"

"Who am I to make such a decision, one way or another?" he retorted. "That belongs to the Eltorchul family. At any rate, they must be told of their kinsman's fate."

She cast a dark look at the box Danilo had placed on the carriage floor between them. "Is that how you intend to make this announcement? Present them with that thing?"

"Credit me with some small measure of sense! Certainly you must admit that once the tale is told, they have every right to this box. Even if they do not elect to seek resurrection, they will want to inter Oth's remains. The Eltorchul family has a tomb in the City of the Dead—quite an impressive one, I hear: a dimensional door, leading into their private catacombs. I suppose they'd need it," he mused. "They are a large family, with a rather high rate of tragedy. A hazard, I suppose, of being in the business of magical research and mage schooling. Now that I think of it, some of my early tutors had rather close calls. Did I ever tell you about the time Athol's beard caught fire from the lighted ink I created?"

She silenced him with a glare, then turned to regard the passing city. The Eltorchul family, like many of Waterdeep's nobility, had more than one property in the city and probably several outside the city walls. Their hired carriage took them through the Sea Ward, the wealthiest and most sought after district of the city.

Arilyn seldom had reason to come here, and she carefully marked the byways and buildings in her mind. The streets were broad and paved with smooth, dressed stone. Lining them were tall walls, behind which lay lavish estates or temple complexes. Towers rose against the clouds. Many were so fanciful in design that they could only have been contrived and sustained by magic. Turrets, balconies, and gables decked the heights. Gargoyles kept stony-eyed watch over the city. Bright banners whipped about in the driving rain and wind.

"This ward will soon be all but deserted," Danilo commented after a few moments of silence. "There's a promise of winter in that wind."

Arilyn nodded glum assent. Her spirits sank still further as they turned off Morningstar Way and the Eltorchul tower came into view.

The elaborate structure defined the easternmost corner of the narrow street known as The Ghost Walk. Even without the name—and without her own wariness of human magic—Arilyn felt distinctly chilled as she eyed the uncanny place.

Towers of mist-gray stone rose into the sky, most of them connected by walkways and stairs that seemed to go everywhere, and nowhere. Several homunculi—small, bat-winged imps that served as wizards' familiars—winged silently through the architectural tangle, disappearing and reappearing without apparent reason or pattern. Wisps of acrid blue smoke rose from one of the towers, evidence of magical activity within.

As they alighted from the carriage, Arilyn noted that the stone walk near the front gate was as blackened as if it had entertained a hundred campfires—or a few bolts of lightning.

"So much for unwanted guests," Danilo murmured as he reached for the bellpull.

A dark-skinned young woman clad in the robe and apron of an Eltorchul apprentice came to answer their summons. Danilo requested an audience with Thesp Eltorchul, the family patriarch. They were shown into the hall. While the apprentice went off to dry their sodden wraps, they took a seat under a tapestry depicting the coronation of some distant monarch—an ancestor of Azoun of Cormyr, most likely, though Arilyn was uncertain exactly which of several Azouns the weaver intended to commemorate.

After a few moments Lord Eltorchul came to meet them. The old mage was a tall man, not at all stooped by his years, with a dignified manner and hair of the indeterminate gray-beige color to which red often faded. It was not difficult to imagine the mage's hair as it once had been, for the young woman who walked by his side was crowned by ringlets the color of flame.

Arilyn's heart sank. She knew Errya Eltorchul, if

only by reputation, as a spoiled, spiteful viper. Though the family fortunes, by all reports, were dwindling, the young woman wore an exquisite russet gown, a fortune in garnets, and a supremely haughty expression. Her emerald gaze slid down Arilyn boldly, and her expression turned disdainful. Dismissing the half-elf with a sniff, she turned her attention upon Danilo.

"You have taken long enough in returning," she said with an artful pout.

Danilo acknowledged her comment with a slight bow but directed his first response to the patriarch, as custom demanded. "It has been quite some time since I studied with Lord Eltorchul." He bowed again to the old mage. "I have been remiss, sir, in not paying my respects sooner."

The mage sent a fond, long-suffering look at his daughter. "It is a comfort to see that not all of Waterdeep's young have forgotten their manners! Lord Thann, my apprentice said you wished to speak to me concerning my son Oth, about a matter you could not entrust to another?"

"That is so. Perhaps we could speak in private?"

Lord Eltorchul glanced at Arilyn for the first time. His brow furrowed in disapproval. Whether his displeasure had to do with her half-elven heritage or the fact that she carried a sword instead of a spell bag, Arilyn could not say. "In private. Yes, by all means," he murmured.

"By no means!" retorted Errya. She stooped to pick up a passing cat and glared at her father over the animal's head. "That wretched apprentice of yours said that our visitors had word of Oth. I wish to hear it."

Lord Eltorchul seemed resigned to let her have her will. He led the way past a display of three sets of plate armor. Though the helmet visors were raised to reveal empty suits, all three "knights" lifted their mailed fists in a sharp, clanking salute. The elderly mage took no notice of this but ushered his guests past the guards into a small side parlor. Once all were seated and offers of wine or tea or snuff made and refused, he settled down with a heartfelt sigh.

"What has my son done now?"

"Sir, I regret to bring ill news. Just this morning, I went to Oth's tower on some impulsive errand." Danilo glanced at Arilyn, silently bidding her to let him tell the tale as he saw best. "The door was ajar. No one was there to answer my hail, so I took liberty to enter and investigate. I found the study in fearful disarray. There had been a struggle, and I was too late to give aid. My lord, I am deeply sorry."

The old mage stared at him, not yet comprehending. "A struggle? What manner?"

Arilyn leaned forward, ignoring Danilo's silent warning. His intentions were good, but she believed that a quick cut was kindest. "It appears that your son was killed by tren—powerful lizardmen who kill for hire. I am sorry."

Lord Eltorchul let out a small, choked sound of dismay. Arilyn's gaze flicked to Errya. The young woman received the news stoically. Her painted lips had thinned to a tight line, and her face was set as if in marble. Arilyn turned back to the mage.

"I am sorry to ask this, but do you know of any who might have wished Oth's death?"

Lord Eltorchul looked down at his clenched hands. "No. None at all." He lifted dazed eyes. "He is gone? You are certain of this?"

"The tren left a sign." Danilo explained the situation as delicately as possible, and then handed the man the ring he had taken from Oth's hand. "I saw this ring in your son's possession, not more than two days ago."

"Yes. It is his," the mage muttered. "I have seen him wear it. It is true, then. He is gone."

"Yes, but perhaps you know of a high-ranking priest. . . ."

A bit of hope lit the old man's eyes as he caught Danilo's meaning. "Yes. Yes! If there is a possibility—"

"There is not," snapped Errya. Her hands clenched at the gray tabby in her lap, drawing a hiss of protest from the animal. "I know my brother better than you do, Father. He would not wish resurrection. He is a wizard, and he despises clerics and their magic! Do you think Oth would want a gift from such hands, even if it were his own life?"

"I suppose you are right," Lord Eltorchul said in a weary, defeated tone. He slumped forward and buried his face in his hands.

His daughter turned a spiteful gaze upon their visitors. "That suggestion was unworthy of you, Danilo, but what more could I expect? This is just the sort of thing that comes of consorting with elven ruffians!"

"That's it." Arilyn rose to leave.

Dan placed a restraining hand on her sword arm. "You are remiss, Errya. This has nothing to do with Arilyn. Quite the contrary. Elves do not believe in disturbing the afterlife."

"She's here, isn't she?" demanded the young woman, leaning forward over the cat in her lap. "Oth is dead, isn't he?"

The cat wriggled and hissed a warning, which Errya ignored. Danilo rose to stand beside Arilyn, his eyes cold. "I understand that you are distraught, but take care whom you accuse."

Errya's lip curled. "Rest easy. The half-breed had nothing to do with it. Oth was killed because he had dealings with Elaith Craulnober. I know it!"

Her voice held a note of hysteria and reached a pitch that was painful to hear. Arilyn noted that the long-suffering tabby turned his ears back against the onslaught, and she wished she could do the same.

"What will be done about it?" Errya went on. "Nothing! Time was when outsiders were dealt with. Ask Arlos Dezlentyr, if you doubt me, and—*Damn!*"

Her voice rose in a shriek of pain as the tabby nipped sharply at her hand. She hurled the cat across the room. The creature twisted in the air with feline grace and landed on his feet, tail lashing as he leveled a baleful stare at the woman. She tossed her head and turned back to the visitors.

"You've said what you came to say. As you can see, my father is overcome with grief. Leave the box with me and go."

Arilyn was only too glad to comply. As she stalked past the polite, empty suits of armor, she heard Danilo offer his condolences to the Eltorchul patriarch and promise to help find who killed his son. This "interference" sent Errya into a fit of shrieking, which finally pushed the old man beyond the edge of his composure. The mage began to weep in low, terrible sobs. Errya left him there, her slippers clicking an angry staccato as she went off after the cat who'd dared to nip at her, as if this insult far outweighed the loss of a brother and the grief of her aging father.

As the door shut on the noble folk of the Eltorchul clan, Arilyn was not certain whether the old mage's deepest regret was for the family he had lost or that which he still had to endure.

* * * * *

Each morning, a number of caravans mustered in the Court of the White Bull, an open area in the heart of South Ward. This was the working district of Waterdeep. Smoke rose from between the tightly packed buildings that surrounded the courtyard. The clang of metal upon metal resounded from the nearby forges, and the nervous lowing of cattle drifted from the stockyard. The cupping sound of hooves on hard packed earth heralded the passing of a dairymaid leading her cow. The warm, earthy scent of leather emanated from the saddlers' shop.

But such common things faded before the unusual sight that dominated the courtyard. Elaith Craulnober had been a merchant and an adventurer for over a century, and never had he seen a caravan as peculiar as this.

Servants bustled about rolling up the canvas tents that had shielded the caravan from the sudden downpour. The vast courtyard was alive with the rustle of giant wings, and the rumbling coos and roars and whinnies of scores of sky-going steeds. Several quartets of pegasi pawed the ground. Grooms wearing the Gundwynd crest fitted the winged horses with long, strong traces. Behind each team was attached a lightweight carriage fashioned without wheels or runners. On the north side of the courtyard, a line of griffons sat like brooding hens, their lionlike front paws tucked under their breast feathers. Enormous leather hoods masked their hawklike heads and kept them from flying too soon.

This typically human device sent a quick surge of anger through Elaith. Keeping a bird from flight was unconscionable, yet the humans did it all the time. They hooded their hunting falcons to keep them docile when they were not flying after game. They cropped the wings of their geese to keep them trapped on mill ponds. Some of the fools even netted songbirds and clipped their wings to keep them as ornaments to their gardens. Of course, those birds died with the coming of winter, but what was that but another task for the servants to tend come spring?

A peal of lighthearted laughter interrupted the elf's angry thoughts. He turned in time to witness a highly unusual game of catch.

A golden steed hopped into the path of a passing half-orc porter—not a horse, but a titanic eagle with a raptor's cold eyes and hooked, rending beak. Just the sight of it was enough to freeze the blood of a brave man. The eagle's beak opened and the gigantic head suddenly lunged forward in a quick, darting strike.

The porter shrieked, dropped his load, and rolled frantically aside. This inspired another burst of laughter—merry and wild but without malice.

An involuntary smile curved Elaith's lips as he remembered this game. The eagle's partner, a young elf probably not much past his second century, tossed a second piece of meat toward his feathered steed. The bird deftly caught it and tossed back its head to let the treat slide down its gullet. The half-orc sent a glare at the mischievous elf and scurried off.

Three more elves stepped from the crowd and fell into conversation with their brother. They were Moon elves, like Elaith: tall and slender and as finely honed as daggers. All of them had silvery hair and eyes the color of precious stones: amber, jade, topaz. Their speech held the accents of faraway Evermeet, and their tunics bore an almost-forgotten insignia.

Elaith's brow furrowed with consternation. Eagle Riders, here on the mainland? These youth were among the most fierce defenders of the elven island. Why were they here?

The young leader noticed his scrutiny. He frowned in concentration for a moment, then his face lit up like a sunrise.

He came toward Elaith, his left palm held out and level in the manner of one elven lord greeting another. "This is an honor, Lord Craulnober! My father served under your command in the Palace Guard, when I was nearly as young—although, gods grant, not quite as silly—as these humans!" He grinned and dipped into a bow. "Garelith Leafbower, at your command."

These words, and the respect with which they were delivered, touched memories that Elaith had thought long forgotten. He acknowledged the greeting with scant courtesy. "Many years have passed since I left the island," he said dismissively, but his irritation with these youth remained, and he could not help adding, "What of you? Has Evermeet no need for her Eagle Riders?"

The young elf laughed. "None that I have heard! The island is as it ever was. Beautiful, inviolate—and boring beyond endurance! These lads and I were hungry for a bit of excitement."

"Which you expect to find as caravan guards."

"Honorable work," the elf said with a shrug, then he grinned again. "There is, at least, adventure in it! We are going to Silverymoon, are we not? I have heard tales of this wondrous city and of the lady mage who rules it."

Garelith's fellow Riders clustered near, their gem-colored eyes alight with curiosity and high spirits. Elaith's irritation melted as he parried their questions and enjoyed the melodious flow of the Elvish language.

A tall, thick-bodied shadow fell upon them. Garelith's animated face fell at once into the calm, inscrutable mask that elves showed to outsiders. "Captain Rhep," he said in formal tones, inclining his head in the small, gracious gesture an elven warrior used to acknowledge, but not reward, an unwanted interruption.

Rhep shouldered past the Eagle Riders and planted his booted feet nearly toe to toe with Elaith's. He was a big man, a half head taller than the elf, and nearly as broad and thick as a bugbear—nearly as hairy, for that matter. Dark brown hair fell in thick waves from beneath Rhep's leather helm. His upper lip and chin were furred with massive, ill-trimmed whiskers. His features were coarse and his nose so broad and flat that it hinted at orcish ancestry in the not-too-distant past. Rhep wore leather armor on his huge frame and a confident sneer on his face. Elaith imagined that the two of them gave the appearance of a catapult and a stiletto standing side by side. The human, no doubt, was fool enough to think himself the better weapon.

"You mighta bought yourself a place on this caravan, elf, but these guards report to me," Rhep snarled.

"Really. Since when does Ilzimmer hire Eagle Riders?" Elaith inquired with a faint smile.

The big man snarled. "I work for Gundwynd," he said, nodding toward the small, gray-bearded man who bustled about securing cargo.

This was a lie, and Elaith knew it well. Rhep was a soldier for the Ilzimmer clan, but both he and the lords of that noble house took great pains to conceal this fact. This might, after all, lead into too close an inquiry into why a family of gem merchants had need for a mercenary army.

"I work for Lord Gundwynd," Rhep repeated, "and so do you, for as long as you ride with this caravan. A shame it is, that Gundwynd has fallen so low to be accepting the likes of you!"

Garelith stepped forward, his green eyes snapping at this insult. "Watch your tongue, human! This was the captain of the King's guard."

The man sneered. "Well, that makes him long out of a job, don't it? That elf king die on your watch, Craulnober?"

"Hardly," Elaith returned mildly, refusing to be baited by this oaf. "King Zaor's death occurred less than fifty years ago. I was well established in Waterdeep at this time and long before your ancestors started having carnal knowledge of goblinkin."

Dark, dull red suffused the big man's face. He unhooked the mace on his belt and began to raise it for the attack.

Elaith ducked under the weapon and stepped in

close, a knife gleaming in each hand. The tip of one slender blade pressed up under the man's chin, and the other stood poised at the opening of his ear.

Rhep looked to the caravan guards for support. All four elves had long slender knives in hand, but their watchful eyes were on Rhep rather than his attacker.

"Treacherous scum," he spat. "You'll be paid in your own coin soon enough!"

"Perhaps you should explain that comment," Elaith said pleasantly. But just so that there was no mistaking this order for a suggestion—and because he simply felt like doing it—he gave the knife at the man's ear a little flick, cutting a small notch in the lobe.

Rhep bleated like a gelded ram. "Didn't mean nothing," he muttered. "Bad coin has a way of circling back, is all."

The elf was not certain whether this was a platitude or an evasion, but the dispute was beginning to draw attention, and Elaith was not willing to jeopardize his place on this caravan over a worthless, orc-spawned cur. He lowered his blades and stepped back, giving the man a small, ironic bow—an insult entirely lost on the clod. Rhep stomped off, muttering imprecations.

The elf watched him go, then turned to the Eagle Riders. "Watch him," he said in a low voice. "I know that man. Trouble follows close on his heels."

"He seems a buffoon," remarked Garelith, "but I will defer to your judgment. You know the clouds that gather around this particular mountain, and I trust you'll warn us of a coming storm."

This led to the next, more difficult warning Elaith felt obligated to deliver. "That will not be possible. You would do well not to be seen with me."

All four of the Eagle Riders looked puzzled. "Why?" demanded the one with eyes the color of topaz.

Elaith's smile held a self-mocking edge. "You will learn soon enough."

Before the young elves could press him, Elaith turned and walked away. Their exuberant adulation appalled him. At this moment, he would welcome almost any other company, so long as they regarded him with a proper, familiar mixture of fear and respect.

"Stones!" exclaimed a deep, gruff voice, with a vehemence that turned the word into a curse.

"A dwarf," muttered Elaith wearily. How could this day possibly get any worse?

"You mean to tell me we have to *fly* out west?" demanded the dwarf.

"A winged horse," said a persuasive female voice. "You're always saying there's nothing on four legs you can't ride."

Elaith whirled toward the familiar voice, and his scowl deepened. He knew of that woman—Bronwyn was a merchant with a refreshingly devious streak. Though he was interested in making her acquaintance, this was hardly the time. He was even less pleased to learn that she had acquired a dwarven traveling companion.

This dwarf was a particularly squat, square fellow. An abundance of auburn curls rioted about his broad shoulders, and a long red beard spilled over his chest. His upper lip had been shaved, and his blue eyes were stormy. A horseshoe hung on a thong about his neck. The dwarf fingered his horseshoe as if laying claim to Bronwyn's words concerning his riding abilities.

"Nothing on four legs," he repeated. "That's true enough, if'n those four legs got solid ground beneath them!"

Bronwyn cast a glance up at the sky, then turned a crooked grin upon her companion. "Clouds look pretty thick today."

The dwarf snorted derisively.

"Look, Ebenezer," she said in the tones of one who had finished with persuasion, "I have business in Silverymoon. You can come or stay, as you please."

"Who said anything about staying?" the dwarf demanded. He pointed a stubby finger at an untethered pegasus. "That one's a spare, most likely. Got my eye on him."

The dwarf ambled off, a lump of maple sugar in one stubby fist. Bronwyn watched him go, and her sweeping gaze settled upon Elaith. After a moment of hesitation she poured wine from a flask into wooden cups and held out one to him in invitation.

Elaith approached and accepted the cup. "Are you always so generous to strangers?"

Her grin was quick and dagger-sharp. "Oh, I know you, at least, as well as I could be expected to. You're Elaith Craulnober, and you seem to own an inordinately large chunk of Waterdeep." She raised her cup in salute.

Amused, he drank to her toast. "Your name is known to me, as well. I take it you will also be traveling with the caravan?"

"One last trip to Silverymoon before winter sets in." She used her cup to point toward a small man with a pointed beard and a wan, wasted countenance. "That's Mizzen Doar—or what's left of him! Looks a bit worse for wear, doesn't he? He has been making the rounds of the harvest festivals, or so I hear. From the looks of him, a clan of rampaging kobolds is better for your health than a nobleman's party."

That brought a wry smile to the elf's face. He had heard that Bronwyn had a warm yet forthright manner that put people at ease, and he found that he was not immune to her brand of charm. Still he remained cautious. "You know him?"

"As well as I need to. He deals in crystals and other minor gemstones."

"So do others," he prodded, "some closer to home than Silverymoon."

"True enough, but none who can touch the variety that Mizzen carries in his shop." She glanced around to see if any were within hearing distance before continuing. "Appearances are important in this city," she said dryly. "Even during times of declining fortunes, no one wants to part with jewelry, so they keep their baubles, but sell the individual stones as needed—"

"—And replace them with crystal," Elaith concluded.

Bronwyn merely shrugged again, as if she found the matter a bit too distasteful for direct words. The elf could understand that, and he also saw the potential for profit in such endeavors—especially for a woman whose first trade had been creating counterfeit copies of coins and jewelry.

He could not help but wonder whether Bronwyn had another agenda. He hoped it was not too similar to his own. In his own way, he rather liked the woman. Elaith genuinely hoped that he could tend to the business at hand without killing her.

"Stones!" erupted the dwarf. "I've a mind to be biting you back, you long-legged excuse for a pigeon!"

The elf cast a glance toward the uproar. Ebenezer was shaking one hand and glaring at the pegasus he'd been trying to befriend. The winged horse munched sugar, then let out a delicate whinny that sounded suspiciously like laughter.

Elaith adjusted his thinking. He still hoped that Bronwyn could emerge from this journey unscathed; on the other hand, he would welcome a chance to reduce Waterdeep's dwarf population by at least one.

"Your . . . companion seems to have met his match," Elaith observed.

This set Bronwyn off into merry laughter. "You're more right than you know. Those two will be firm friends within the hour. The worse-tempered the horse, the more fond Ebenezer is likely to become of it."

"A risky thing," the elf mused, not without pleasure. "One must be able to trust a mount under any circumstances. Pegasi fly high and are notoriously skittish."

Bronwyn's smile didn't falter, but the warmth drained from her eyes. "No friend of mine falls but I do my best to catch him."

Their gazes locked for a moment, unspoken challenges made, met, and countered. Elaith broke first, instinctively making the small, subtle hand gesture used between elves under such circumstance—a proud but gracious gesture that was part apology, part acknowledgment of a battle averted.

"D'rienne," Bronwyn said softly, speaking the traditional Elvish word of acceptance of potential challenge avoided.

Before the startled elf could respond, she turned and ambled over to her dwarf friend.

Elaith's first thought was chagrin over his unconscious lapse into old patterns. The encounter with the Eagle Riders had apparently affected him more than he knew. Bronwyn's display of knowledge troubled him, though, especially considering the real focus of his journey. Was it possible she knew about the elven gem and was giving him fair warning that they sought the same prize?

If so, some might consider it a gesture worthy of an elven adventurer. Obviously Bronwyn had made a study of the cultures whose artifacts she sought. Elaith observed the woman as she stood at ease, stroking the pegasus and nodding with tongue-in-cheek sympathy over Ebenezer's continued rants.

She did not lack for courage or style. It would be a shame to kill this woman. Elaith raised his wooden cup to her in silent salute—and probable farewell.

* * * * *

The squall had blown itself out by the time Arilyn and Danilo left the Eltorchul manor. The gate swung open of its own accord. The couple hurried out into the street, instinctively skirting the blackened walk with the same cautious respect that prompted cemetery ramblers not to tread upon a grave.

"You actually studied with the Eltorchul mages? How could you stand spending time in that place?" Arilyn demanded.

Her companion shrugged and veered down a side street. "Lord Eltorchul is not so bad. He's very serious about the art of magic and dedicated to teaching it well. Oth was too involved in his research to bother much with the students."

Arilyn nodded absently, scarcely hearing his words. A faint, tingling awareness swept through her. She touched her fingers to the sheathed moonblade and concentrated on the magical warning.

"We're being followed," she said tersely.

Danilo glanced behind them. The sudden downpour had all but emptied the streets, and there was no one on the narrow walkway behind them. Water pooled here and there on the large flagstone paving, enough of it to make dry passage impossible. There were no damp footprints but theirs. The sun was resolutely pushing aside the clouds. It was almost directly overhead, leaving no shadows to hide possible foes. He tilted back his head and scanned the rooftops overhead.

"Nothing that I can see—yet."

Without breaking stride, he reached into his spell bag and quickly cast an enchantment that would reveal magic at work. The blue light of the spell settled upon his spell bag, upon the singing sword he kept as a novelty, and upon Arilyn's moonblade. No other enchantment was at work nearby. No one followed them in a cloak of invisibility.

As the light of his reveal-magic spell faded, the moonblade's warning intensified into glowing blue light.

"We're being followed," Arilyn repeated stubbornly.

She put one hand to the hilt of her sword, ready to fight their as-yet-unseen foe.

The stone near their feet shuddered. Arilyn darted a look behind her as one of the flagstones that paved the street exploded into shards.

A large, reptilian head thrust up from the opening. One huge, clawed hand swiped at Arilyn's boots.

She danced back out of reach and drew her sword. As the moonblade hissed free, the tren gripped the stone ledge and hauled itself out in one quick, nimble leap. The beast drew from its weapon belt a curved knife with a stout blade and an elaborate guard designed to trap and break swords.

Arilyn could imagine no better weapon for a tren. With its long arms, the creature could easily reach over a trapped or broken sword and tear out an opponent's throat with a single swipe of its claws. It was a variation on an assassin's trick: focus attention on one threat, and strike with another.

In short, this was not the sort of battle for which Danilo was prepared. She glanced back. He had already drawn his blade and was moving into position beside her.

"Back off. This is my fight," she said. He looked dubious, so she added by way of explanation, "Narrow street." He hesitated for a moment, then moved away to give her room to maneuver.

The unlike assassins circled each other, weapons level. The tren's knife was no longer than a dagger, but its arms were so long that its reach was nearly the equal of Arilyn's. She tested the tren with a quick, thrusting lunge, which it caught on the curved guard of its knife. Without disengaging, it pivoted hard to the side—wrenching the sword with all its considerable strength.

Elven metal shrieked in protest as the iron guard slid along the moonblade's length, then locked and twisted brutally. A lesser blade would have shattered. Arilyn spun in toward the tren, leaning in to ease the pressure on her sword.

The hooked claws of the tren's free hand slashed up to meet her, aiming for her throat. The half-elf tore her weapon free, but she was in too close to parry the blow. She lashed out with her elbow and caught the tren's massive wrist, flinging it up as she ducked under the attack.

The tren's aim was spoiled, but its claws caught and tangled in the half-elf's hair. Arilyn's head jerked sharply to the side, and burning pain exploded in her scalp. She danced back. Curly strands of her hair flowed from the tren's claws like streamers as he came in with another furious blow.

This time she got her sword up. The moonblade cut a deep line in the scaly hide of its forearm. Without pause, Arilyn changed the direction of her stroke, sweeping the sword down low and aiming for the creature's hamstring.

The tren got its knife down for the parry, catching the sword again in the curved guard. It brought up a massive, clawed foot over the joined weapons, clearly intending to stomp on the captured sword.

Arilyn twisted away, turning the blade so that the edge greeted the tren's foot. The tren could not halt its momentum in time and roared in rage and anguish as the sharp edge sliced deep. She threw the sword up hard and high, cutting through the thick pad of scale, severing bone. A clawed toe fell to the cobblestone.

The creature again began to circle her, limping now and emitting panting little hisses of rage. Arilyn turned with it, her sword in guard position. She suspected what its next tactic might be. Sure enough, as soon as the tren had maneuvered her so that her back was to the gaping hole, it tucked in its head like a charging bull and leaped at her, massive arms outstretched in a deadly embrace.

Arilyn deftly stepped to the side and pivoted on her outer foot. Her sword slid along the ribs of the lunging creature, drawing a long deep line. She pulled the blade up high and back, and then plunged it between the beast's ribs.

Holding the sword with both hands, she braced her feet at the edge of the hole and held on for life. The sharp pull of the falling tren's weight almost tore her arms from her shoulders, and the sudden release when its body fell clear sent her staggering back.

She stumbled into Danilo's arms. It occurred to her that he had a grip on her belt—and that he had probably seized it the moment she'd stabbed the tren.

"You shouldn't interfere during battle," she reminded him. "What if things had gone differently, and I'd pulled you down with me?"

He turned her to face him. "That would have saved me the trouble of jumping in after you."

She acknowledged this with a nod, then glanced toward the hole. "We'd better move on. Listen to that. The other tren will be finished soon."

"Finished?" His face took on a pained expression as the meaning of her words came clear to him. "You don't mean to say that these creatures eat their own?" he demanded, although the faint sounds emanating from the tunnel below made the question unnecessary.

"The price of failure," Arilyn said as she kicked into a trot. "I'd say there's at least five or six down there. Now the others will only be more determined. It's a matter of honor now. As tren reckon honor, that is."

Danilo fell in beside her. "Keen motivation! As well, one should not discount the bracing effect of a good meal."

She sent him an incredulous look, but she saw a certain logic in his grim humor. "There's that, too," she agreed.

They ran until they reached a wide, busy street. Danilo flagged down a carriage and promised the halfling driver double his hire if he could get them to the North Ward swiftly. The halfling set a pace brisk enough to inspire angry shouts from some of the passersby.

Arilyn relaxed against the plush seat, certain that their hired driver could outrun any tren that cared to give pursuit.

Why, then, was she still beset by the conviction that she and Danilo were not alone?

Seven

After leaving Arilyn at her lodging, Danilo headed for the North Ward and the Thann family villa. For once the sedate, quiet streets did not have their usual effect on him—the familiar mixture of exasperation and ennui, and the numbing certainty that nothing particularly dangerous or entertaining could possibly occur.

It was an odd belief, one that Danilo had never identified before. Strange, he mused, how a long-held notion could continue to color his thinking, long after he knew it to be false.

The North Ward's serenity was deceitful to one who knew the city and its long, often violent history. Danilo had been well schooled in such matters, and so the repeated tren attacks struck him as having greater portent than they might otherwise have held.

Not many generations had passed since Waterdeep had been torn by the Guild Wars. The merchant families had hired mercenary armies and fought each other in the streets. Many other nobles fell to assassins, poisons, and magic. Entire clans had been destroyed. Though this era was past, Danilo knew enough of history to understand that the pattern was not a line but a spiral. Old wounds festered, sometimes for generations. The last time tren assassins had been used in any number was during the Guild Wars. It was entirely possible that their return signified some sort of holdover from the days of the Guild Wars, the ambition of one family against another.

That was a most disturbing possibility, but if that were true, it provided a possible connection between all the tren attacks. Only one attack had been fatal—that which had killed Oth—but all the others seemed related to the Eltorchul mage. A tren attacked Elaith, who had dealings with Oth. Arilyn had assisted Elaith, thus drawing the ire of the tren clan, and she and Danilo were investigating Oth's death. Twice they had interfered. That was probably enough to add their names to the tren runes scratched in the hidden places beneath the city.

In all, it was a disturbingly plausible explanation. Danilo intended to test it against a mind other than his. Although he knew many of Waterdeep's sages and scholars, he could not name anyone who knew more of the city's history than Lady Cassandra.

The conversation ahead would no doubt prove . . . interesting. In times not long past, she had been very interested in inflicting this knowledge on her youngest son. Dan supposed he had seemed the most likely to follow his mother's scholarly leanings. Somehow, he doubted that at this late date his mother would regard his sudden interest without skepticism.

He found her, predictably enough, in the library. For a moment he lingered in the doorway and observed the remarkable woman who had given him life.

Cassandra was seated on a low bench, clad in a day gown of blue linen and looking as elegant and poised as some legendary queen. Her thick blonde hair was coiled smoothly about her head, and her face was unlined and serene. The long night of revelry had left no mark upon either the woman or the villa she ruled. While half of Waterdhavian society slept, she calmly dictated instructions to a pair of stewards, a dock master, and a scribe.

She glanced up at Danilo's knock. "You are up and about early," she observed.

He sauntered into the room. "I have not had opportunity to sleep. So far this has been a most eventful day. Shall I tell you about it?"

Cassandra stiffened almost imperceptibly and glanced toward the suddenly interested scribe. Danilo suppressed a smile. Scribes were restricted by law—and often by magic—from revealing to others the secrets they entrusted to parchment, but more than one scribe made extra coins on the side by selling bits of chance-heard gossip to such purveyors as Myrna Cassalanter. That was something Cassandra Thann would not countenance.

She turned back to her servants. "Julian, you may advance our vintners in Amn the requested credit. Add an additional forty barrels of spiced winterfest wine to this year's order. Gunthur, I would like to see all Thann shipping records for the moons of Flamerule and Eleasias by highsun tomorrow, if that is convenient."

The sudden panicked expression on the dock master's face indicated that this was far from convenient. Danilo could almost hear the click of beads sliding across on the man's mental abacus as he tallied the hours such a task would take.

Without waiting for a reply, Lady Cassandra rose gracefully to her feet. "We are finished for the day. Attend me tomorrow morning at the usual hour."

She held her look of implacable serenity until the men had left the study and closed the heavy wooden door behind them. The face she turned upon her son, however, expressed a familiar blend of resignation and exasperation.

"You'd might as well tell the tale. Without the usual embellishments, if you please," she said wryly. "I am in no mind to be amused."

Danilo poured himself a glass of deep red wine from the decanter on his mother's table. He inhaled the rich, complex scent of the spices and took an appreciative sip. "Are you quite sure that an extra forty barrels will be sufficient? This is exceptionally good. After the first tasting, word will spread quickly. You will sell all within a tenday to the better taverns and have none to meet orders from wine shops, much less from those who wish to stock their private cellars. As you undoubtedly know, the bards' college will sponsor a winterfest gala for the first time this year. I can guarantee an order of twenty barrels from that source alone."

A flicker of interest warmed Cassandra's ice-blue eyes. "Very well. See to it." She arranged herself on her settee. "But this is not why you are here. I doubt you neglected your bed to improve the family fortune."

Danilo lifted the goblet in salute. "As wise as you are beautiful, my lady. That is well for me, as I find myself in need of your good counsel."

"Is that so?" murmured his mother, eyeing him warily.

"Yes. I've noticed a disturbing trend of late—or *tren*, to be more precise. It seems that more people are being killed and eaten than is usual custom. You have ever been one to dictate fashion, Mother, so I suppose it is fitting for this pattern to begin here."

Cassandra's face paled but for two spots of bright, angry color. "Tren? The lizard assassins, here? What is this nonsense? If this is another of your games, I assure you it is not amusing!"

"Mark me, I am not amused," Danilo said as he took the seat across from his mother. "Arilyn happened upon an attack last night. By the way, you might have your steward see to mopping the corridors between the wine vault and the old mercenary armory. I dare say it's still a bit of a mess."

The woman stared at him as if he were speaking Orcish. "An attack here, during the Gemstone Ball? Upon whom?"

Her surprise seemed total and genuine. Although Danilo had never truly believed his mother had had any part in this attack, he could not deny the sudden easing of his mind.

"Elaith Craulnober. A guest," he said firmly, cutting off the exasperated comment she was so obviously prepared to make, "here by my invitation and protected by the rules of hospitality."

"Do not lecture me on proprieties and social obligations," the noblewoman returned heatedly. "You had no business inviting that rogue to a respectable affair in the first place! Nor did your . . . companion . . . do well to intervene!"

Danilo's eyes narrowed. "I suppose she should have walked on and left a lone elf to face his death at the hands of five tren assassins?"

"Five tren," Cassandra repeated tonelessly. This news seemed to dissolve some of the starch from her spine, and suddenly her posture was less that of a warrior queen than of a woman who could claim a score of grandchildren. The moment quickly passed. "What transpired?"

"They fought. Four were killed, one escaped."

"By the runes of Oghma." Having delivered that oath, Cassandra rose and began to pace, her face deeply clouded with anger and concern. "Perhaps now you will understand my reservations concerning this liaison you insist upon forming with this woman! If you do not understand it, you soon shall—unless you are as great a fool as you have always pretended to be."

This pronouncement startled Danilo for a number of reasons. He addressed the easiest issue first. "You saw through the pretense. I did not think anyone in the family did."

The woman sniffed. "Do you think I know so little of what happens under my own roof? I understand more than you think. As it turned out, your decision to play the fool in the service of the Harpers dovetailed well with the family interests. Wine merchants must know the trade. That you have learned, probably quite by accident, while meddling with Khelben's projects."

"One tavern at a time," Danilo agreed, making a jest to cover his surprise. "There is no substitute for first-hand knowledge."

"Indeed," she said dryly. "And now you are acclaimed as a bard, after all those years of tormenting your tutors and music masters! In all, I would say the choices you made for your life were not so very different from those I would have chosen for you. Until recently, of course."

Her implication was unmistakable and supremely irritating. Danilo set down his wineglass with exaggerated care to compensate for his urge to heave it against a wall. "Which brings us to several other questions," he said evenly. "Why are you so opposed to Arilyn?"

"I suppose I have nothing against her personally. As a traveling companion, you could hardly have chosen better. However, it is time that you considered finding a consort. A half-elven mercenary is not suitable for a man of your position."

"Then I shall change my position," Danilo returned. "Anything I do for this city or this family can be done by another. Why should I not follow my own inclinations?"

Cassandra threw up her hands. "Why stop now?"

He let that pass. "I am also puzzled as to why you think Arilyn erred in giving aid to one of the Thann guests. Would you have felt differently about this matter had the target of the tren attack been some nobleman's daughter?"

The noblewoman gave the question more consideration than Danilo expected—more, he thought, than it warranted. "That is quite different, of course, but even so, she should not have interfered."

Danilo shook his head in astonishment. "You are surely not in favor of giving assassins free reign of the estate!"

The look Cassandra sent him was somber. "You should have listened," she said softly, "to the lessons I tried to teach you in your boyhood."

"Guild Wars, assassinations, chaos," Danilo said impatiently. "Yes, I remember it well."

His mother shook her head. "We are never quite done with the past. Who should know that better than a bard?"

Danilo studied her for a long moment. "There is an untold tale here."

"Better it be so," she said. An expression of chagrin crossed her face, as if she regretted yielding even that much. Her chin lifted, and her eyes cooled to their usual expression of serene control. "Leave it, my son. There is no tavern song here."

"Perhaps there is," he countered. "A man died today. Oth Eltorchul was the victim of another tren attack. Arilyn and I carried word of this to Lord Eltorchul. We were followed and attacked by tren shortly after we left the Eltorchuls' Sea Ward manor."

The color drained from Cassandra's face. "Have nothing more to do with this."

He briefly considered telling her about the attack at Arilyn's lodging. "Finally you give me advice I desire to heed!" he said with dark humor. "I fear, though, it will prove difficult to follow."

"I have none better to offer."

Her tone rang with finality. A long moment of silence passed between them, and Danilo rose to leave. Cassandra followed him to the door, her expression more somber than any she had shown even in the aftermath of his worst boyhood pranks. She caught his arm as he was about to open the door.

"One thing more. Do not ask any more questions about this matter, not of me or any other. Content yourself that you are better off without this knowledge."

He patted her hand and gently disengaged himself from her grip. "Strange words, coming from a lady who prides herself on her scholarship."

"I prize my skin far more highly," she said bluntly. "Though you often give me cause to wonder why, I would like to see *yours* remain firmly attached."

Danilo gave her a puzzled look.

"Those boots you are wearing. I suppose the leather is some sort of lizard?"

"Yes, that's right. Why?"

"The tren have their own notions of fashion, as appalling to us as ours probably are to them. They do not always dispose entirely of their victims. It is possible that one or more of your ancestors ended up as a tren garment or gear bag."

"Ah. I am touched by your concern, but I have no intention of ending my days as some tren's leather loincloth," Danilo said dryly. "It seems to me that some lady recently remarked on the choices I have made and how closely they arrived at the destinations of her own hopes and goals. That same lady gave the opinion that her youngest son is no fool. Trust me to find my way to the end of this path."

"I do," said Cassandra, and her face was clouded by emotions Danilo could not begin to read. "I fear that nearly as much as I do the tren."

*   *   *   *   *

In the craggy mountains that surrounded Silverymoon, the trees were ancient and sociable—huddled together like aging warriors around a hearth fire, exchanging tales of feats long past. So thick was the forest, and so relentless the passage of wild water over rocks and through gorges, that the cloud-going caravan circled the area several times seeking a place broad and tame enough to settle upon.

Elaith saw the hilltop clearing well before the caravan master began the circling descent. He tightened his grip on the rim of the sky chariot as the driver—a gold elf in the employ of Lord Gundwynd—guided the pegasus team down in ever-tightening spirals.

Given the nature of their journey, Elaith had expected the caravan to make a general, immediate, and grateful dismount. However, everyone stood or sat as he was, gazing down in silence at the famous Moonbridge, which led into Silverymoon.

A shimmering expanse, more like a child's soap bubble than the usual, solid comfort of stone and wood, rose in a soaring arc over the River Rauvin. The last tints of sunset seemed to linger in the insubstantial structure. Beneath the bridge—and *through* it—one could see the churning waters of the Rauvin as they tumbled over rock and shoal in a headlong race to the south.

"I'm not for crossing that thing," announced Ebenezer, with what seemed to Elaith to be typical dwarven cowardice.

This comment broke the spell. Bronwyn slid carefully down from her griffon mount. "There was less than that under you all the way from Waterdeep to Silverymoon," she pointed out, reasonably enough.

The dwarf snorted. Before he could respond with more complaints, Rhep leaped from his sky chariot and strode into the center of the merchant band. "We camp here tonight and ride into the city first thing in the morning."

A chorus of murmured protest met the caravan master's words. All of them, other than the Eagle Riders and the grooms in Lord Gundwynd's employ, were new

to flight. Two days had they traveled, under condition
that were both exhilarating and terrifying, and every
person was primed for a night's revelry. Few places in
the Northlands offered more enticements than Silvery
moon. To add further inducement, it was common
knowledge that the hills beyond the city were riddled
with orcs, wild beasts, and other annoyances. With the
coming of night, any securely walled city was attractive

It seemed odd to Elaith that they would travel so far
in a mere two days, using such an unusual and expen
sive means of transport, only to risk all with their des
tination fully in sight.

Nor was Elaith the only person to entertain such
thoughts. Many of the merchants gave loud protest
which the big mercenary answered only with a glare. A
caravan master's word held the force of law, even to the
merchants who hired him. Rhep stalked off and began
shouting orders to the guards, and after a few moment
the protest subsided.

There was not much to unload, as most of the cargo
seemed to be small, precious items. The guards made
short work of the task, then encircled the treasure with
the sky chariots. The formidable steeds they tethered
just beyond, reasoning that the fierce pegasi, griffons
and giant eagles would be a greater deterrent to thef
than any human guards Lord Gundwynd could muster
In the next circle the guards and merchants set up camp
some sharing the companionship of scattered fires
others, less eager for company, finding relative privacy
on the outer edges of the clearing.

Elaith picked the least hospitable spot for himself
Uphill from the clearing, near the edge of the trees, was
a spot strewn with tumbled rocks and fallen limbs. The
boulders formed a barrier between him and the com
pany, yet the site offered good visibility over the clear
ing and well into the tree line behind him. It was a
highly defensible place, which the elf bolstered with a

few snares and half-moon traps—an abomination to most elves, but effective for all that.

The elf finished up by hiding several throwing knives here and there and then quickly built a fire. He pushed aside some of the burning wood and placed a small travel pot amid the glowing embers. Into this he emptied some water from his drinking flask as well as some dried mushrooms and herbs. While that simmered, he settled down to enjoy the solitude—and to watch his fellow travelers.

Bronwyn busied herself with the caravan's bundles, setting to work along with the guards. She exchanged jests with several of the men and slapped away a few grasping hands—but with easy good humor that left most of her companions standing alone, but smiling. The elf had to admire her aplomb in this matter, not to mention her good taste in refusing to have anything to do with the louts.

He was not pleased, however, when the woman began a purposeful approach to his campsite. She paused at the very edge of the circle of firelight and cast an uneasy glance over her shoulder.

"Mind if I join you?" she said tentatively. When he hesitated, she added, "I am the only woman in this camp."

Elaith's eyebrows flew up. "You hardly need to offer that as an inducement. Many would seek you out in a crowd of courtesans."

This response brought a wry chuckle from Bronwyn. "I suppose that did sound like an offer," she admitted. "It wasn't intended to. In truth, I'd like to get some sleep tonight, and I'm looking for a safe place."

"This is it?"

She shrugged, following his meaning. "I haven't crossed you in business, and I've got nothing worth stealing. By all reports, you've got little interest in human women. As I see it, that adds up to about as safe as I'm likely to get. If you've an objection, I'll find another spot."

"None whatsoever." Now that he considered the matter, Elaith could see a definite advantage in keeping a close watch over his probable rival. "Do have a care near that jagged boulder."

She skirted the large rock, nodding approval when she caught sight of the circle trap. "Got many of those around?"

"A few."

"Good. I'll sleep more soundly for knowing it."

Elaith made room for her at the fireside. "Where is the dwarf?"

"Around," she said vaguely. "He pulled first watch. Oh, will you look at that!" she exclaimed suddenly, pointing.

The elf followed her gesture. At the far side of the clearing, a large fire leaped into the night. Multicolored lights and intricate patterns danced amid the flames. Silhouetted against the fey light were the lithe forms of the Eagle Riders. Garelith was telling the tale, judging from his animated face and hand gestures.

"Fireside tales," Elaith reminisced. "A small magic, often taught to elven young."

"This puts to shame all those hours I've spent staring into the flames," Bronwyn said, her tones rounded with wonder and delight. "How I wish I could hear their stories! But the elves would never tell them before me."

"No doubt you are right." A peal of bawdy laughter punctuated the elven tale, and the flames turned blue and rose into improbably entwined figures. "Not necessarily for the reason you think," Elaith added.

Bronwyn peered at the fire for a moment, then sat back looking impressed. "Huzzah! I'll always regard centaurs in a whole new light."

The elf saw no particular place for that conversation to go, so he dipped up soup in his travel mug and handed it to his guest. She produced a similar cup from her bag and handed it to him. For a few moments they ate in silence.

Finally Elaith's curiosity prevailed. "You strike me as exceedingly forthright, yet you haven't asked me my business in Silverymoon."

This amused her. "I'd probably be better off not knowing! Truthfully, this has been a busy season for me. I have a great deal of business to attend. It's all I can do to watch my own affairs, much less mind anyone else's."

"You'll be staying on in Silverymoon for a while, then."

"As long as it takes. A few days, perhaps."

At the far side of the clearing, the Eagle Riders began a raucous game of dice. Bronwyn responded with a quick, sympathetic smile. Her reaction prodded the elf's suspicions about her knowledge of elves, and her true reasons for the trip.

"Their behavior doesn't seem to surprise you," Elaith commented.

"Should it? They're young, high-spirited, and enjoying good company. They are entitled to their fun."

"Most humans do not consider high spirits to be an elven virtue," he persisted. "I think you're more familiar with our ways."

She shrugged again. "I've done business with all sorts. It helps to know the customs."

"I can see how it would," he agreed, approaching the question from another side. "Your work must often present challenges. Forgive me, but I find it difficult to envision the fey folk entrusting their lost treasures to a human."

Bronwyn accepted this with a nod. "Some do feel that way. Others respect results and pay well for them. Why do you ask?"

"I might wish to engage your services some time," the elf said vaguely. He glanced up at the stars to measure the hour, then inclined his head in apology. "I am being a poor host. I have kept you talking, when you expressed desire to sleep."

She stopped in midyawn and then reached for her bedroll. "I won't argue with you."

Elaith sat by the fire long after the woman's soft, steady breathing indicated that she slept. From time to time he drifted into reverie, that watchful dreaming that renewed and restored the fey folk.

However, there was little respite for Elaith this night. For the first time in many years, he saw in reverie the leaping white towers of the Moonstone Palace as he rode his silver-gray horse through the streets of Evermeet's royal city. His heart swelled with the pride befitting one of his race and rank and talents, and it beat with quick anticipation of the meeting ahead. Amnestria, the youngest daughter of King Zaor and Queen Amlaruil, had been pledged to him in betrothal. She had sent word that she was eager to meet with her betrothed when the moon rose.

The crunch of heavy boots against stony ground roused Elaith from his dream. His keenly honed senses recognized the portent of danger, but for a moment or two he didn't care. The dream was so vivid, so poignant, that it left behind a sense of loss that dwarfed all other considerations.

Evermeet was lost to him. Amnestria was long dead. Her half-elven daughter despised him, and not without reason. What could possibly matter, in light of all that?

Elaith watched without interest as a large figure broke away from the trees and stalked toward his camp. A small movement nearby drew his eyes. Bronwyn's small hand curled around a knife. Other than that, she might have been asleep. She did not move and her breathing was slow and even.

"Expecting trouble?" the elf said softly.

"I warned you of the possibility," she responded. Her eyes opened a crack, and fell upon the large, bearded man who was creeping toward them.

"Rhep," she said resignedly. "Some men understand the word *no* only when it's accompanied by a stab wound or a fireball spell."

Elaith found this notion distasteful. He had never been able to understand why any male would wish to force attention upon an unwilling female. There was no joy in such games, and little sport. On the other hand, the prospect of battle offered a diversion, a familiar respite from his despair.

"I would be delighted to distract him," the elf offered.

"Thanks, but I don't want you to get in trouble on my account. No offense, but who will believe that you fought to protect my honor? I'll set up a fuss, and the others will intervene."

"Don't be so sure," he cautioned her. She looked puzzled, so he added, "Rhep is in the employ of the Ilzimmer family. He is caravan master, which means that, although Lord Gundwynd has supplied the mounts and some of the guards, Ilzimmer is funding the dragon's share of this journey. Most of the mercenaries report to Rhep. You would receive little assistance from that lot. Nor would you find recompense, afterwards. The Ilzimmer clan is known for its distasteful habits and would not be particularly concerned about the behavior of its hirelings. If you were a woman of their class, they might manage to dredge up a sense of outrage. As matters stand, you can expect nothing."

Bronwyn did not flinch. "Harsh words, but good knowledge to have. I'll circle back to camp." She slipped from her bedroll and wriggled like a snake behind the stand of boulders that separated Elaith's camp from the trees beyond.

Rhep scowled as his gaze fell only on the watchful elf and the ashes of a solitary campfire. "Where's the woman, elf?"

Elaith rose, a stout stick in his hand. This he tossed

in the direction of the approaching man. A circle trap snapped shut, splitting the wood and sending two neatly sheared pieces flying into the air. The mercenary shied back, both hands flung up to ward off the leaping wood. His furious expression deepened as he realized how his response might be read.

"The camp is warded," Elaith said calmly. "You would be wise to stay where you are."

"Coward!" Rhep grated, as if eager to place that name upon another. "Leave your toys and traps and come out in the open! Name your place, if you're not afraid to fight a real man."

"The forest," Elaith said shortly, and then he turned and led the man away from Bronwyn's hiding place. After a moment, he heard behind him the heavy but cautious tread of the mercenary's boots. He heard also the stealthy rasp of metal against metal as Rhep drew his sword.

Coward indeed, the elf thought scornfully. He subtly quickened his pace to keep his back beyond the reach of the man's treacherous sword.

When he judged they were far enough away that battle would not rouse the camp, Elaith turned to face his challenger. As he did, he pulled a knife from his sleeve and slashed in a single smooth movement so fast it defied the eye to follow. The sharp edge sliced through the shoulder strap that supported Rhep's weapons belt. Belt and weapons sank toward the ground.

Rhep instinctively stooped to grab the falling belt. The elf seized a handful of hair and jerked the man's head down. At the same moment, he brought his knee up hard. The man's face smashed into the thigh greave that reinforced Elaith's travel leathers. Bone was no fit challenger for elven metal, and it gave way with a satisfying crunch.

Elaith flung the man aside. Rhep tripped and fell

heavily back, clutching at a garishly broken nose. His sword clattered to the rocky ground.

The elf hooked a toe in the guard of Rhep's sword. One kick sent it spinning up. Elaith caught the descending blade easily and held it at arms' length for inspection. His lip curled as he regarded the pitted edge, then he stalked in.

"You drew first," he stated. "I defended myself as best I could." This remark he flavored with heavy irony—and punctuated with a vicious kick to the man's ribs. "You would have defeated me but for the fact that you tripped in the darkness and fell upon your own sword. A tragic tale, is it not? To think that you had the honor of hearing it first."

Rhep rolled blindly away. The elf aimed a final kick at the base of his spine and raised the crude weapon for the killing stroke.

A small, stubby hand seized his ankle and jerked him to a halt. Elaith released the sword and twisted, catlike, in an effort to retain his balance. He shifted his weight—and his furious gaze—back toward the direction of the interference.

The red-bearded dwarf whom Bronwyn had called Ebenezer clicked his tongue in reproach.

"Man's down," he pointed out. "Me, I like to see games played on an even field."

Elaith kicked out viciously, but the dwarf released him and danced back out of reach with surprising agility. The meddling little toad lifted Rhep's sword in mock challenge, then he handed the weapon to its owner.

"Set to, if that's what you've a mind to do," the dwarf continued. "I'm all for a bit of fun."

So, apparently, was Rhep. Using the sword like a cane, the mercenary rose unsteadily to his feet. His broken nose was beginning to swell, and his breath whistled wetly through the shattered protuberance, but there was livid hatred in his eyes, and that served to focus and steady him.

The elf pulled twin daggers from sheaths hidden beneath his leg greaves. He whirled toward the mangy pair, one knife coming in high and intended for Rhep, the other aimed at the dwarf's throat.

He heard the heavy thud of a dwarven body hitting the ground and sensed that Ebenezer was rolling toward him. He leaped over the thick, stubby body and leaned into the attack on Rhep, but the evasion had stolen his rhythm, and his stabbing attack on the mercenary fell short of its target. Rhep easily parried the elf's knife and then punched out hard over the enjoined blades.

Elaith leaned away from the blow, but it glanced off his shoulder and spun him to one side. The mercenary leered in triumph and lunged.

The pitted sword never came close. A dwarven axe spun in, knocking Rhep's sword wide. Man and elf turned to regard Ebenezer with astonishment.

"Play fair," the dwarf admonished as he scampered around the combatants to retrieve his weapon. "Looks like it's your turn, elf. Make it good, now!"

Elaith needed no prompting. Ignoring the dull ache in his shoulder, he stood and fought with a quick and ignominious finish in mind.

His opponent seemed equally determined. Rhep used his vast size to advantage, chopping and hewing at Elaith as if the elf were an oak he was determined to whittle into arrow shafts. For all his speed and skill, Elaith was forced to take the defensive. His twin blades flashed in the gray gleam of dawn, catching the first slanting rays of the morning sun. Neither fighter could seize advantage. The dwarf continued to intervene, first on one side then the other, keeping the balance level.

Suddenly Elaith knew the dwarf's game. Bronwyn was long gone—and her companion was making sure that Elaith was kept too busy to follow.

Rage swept through him as he realized how he had been tricked. He quickly mastered the bright surge and studied his opponent. The mercenary's eyes still burned with determination, but he was blowing like a beached whale. The elf parried a heavy, slashing attack and retreated several steps.

"I have had enough of this dwarf," Elaith said firmly. "Why should we fight to amuse him? Let's kill him quickly, then have done with this."

"Nay." Rhep spat bloody foam at the elf's boots. "I wouldn't join you in a lifeboat!" He drew back his sword for another stroke.

The elf ducked under a slashing backhanded blow. As he came up, his sword sliced a thin line from the man's shoulder to elbow.

"Good hit," Ebenezer congratulated. "Took you long enough."

The dwarf's taunting stung, though Elaith took it as more an insult to his wits than his fighting prowess. Determined to end the matter, Elaith landed a stinging smack to Rhep's cheek with the flat of his dagger.

"Listen," he snapped and then stepped back.

The sounds of a caravan readying for departure drifted to them, barely audible over Rhep's labored breathing.

"I do not intend to walk to Silverymoon," Elaith said. "If I kill you now, that's what I'd have to do. Leave this for another time, and let's get on with the matters at hand."

He sheathed his daggers and began to walk back to camp. Rhep let him pass, then lunged at the elf's back.

The attack was drearily predictable. Elaith's patience snapped. He sidestepped and seized the man's wrist as it thrust past. He turned, twisting the arm behind Rhep's back. The sword clattered to the ground, and the mercenary fell to his knees, his arm held unnaturally high. Elaith jerked up higher still. Rhep's arm parted from its shoulder with an audible pop. The man shouted once in pain and outrage, then sagged to the ground, senseless.

Elaith whirled toward the dwarf, but Ebenezer had disappeared.

For a moment Elaith considered pursuit, but he had little doubt of the plan laid against him. The dwarf would no doubt return to the caravan, bearing word that Bronwyn and Elaith—who had been seen sharing a secluded campfire—had decided to go off on their own. If Elaith showed up without her, he would be called upon to explain what had become of the woman. No one would believe he was innocent of foul play. Certainly not once they managed to round up their captain and saw the state he was in.

With a hiss of frustration, Elaith turned aside and melted off into the trees. Moving lightly among the forest shadows, he skirted the camp and headed toward the city below.

The sun was high above the Moonbridge when Elaith arrived in Silverymoon, alone and in a foul temper. He asked directions of a passing town crier, then wove through the streets to a shop bearing a sign depicting a multifaceted gem.

He strode into the antechamber and toward the locked door. The two guards flanking it eyed the grimly approaching elf warily. Elaith threw a pair of knives without breaking stride. Both men jerked upright, pinned through their throats to the door frame.

The elf batted aside the flailing hand of one of the dying men. He pivoted on his right foot and kicked out hard with his left. The door flew open with a sound like a thunderclap.

Mizzen himself was behind the counter, stroking his billy-goat beard with apparent satisfaction. He froze when the elf exploded into the shop, then let out a little bleat of alarm. With a quick, frantic burst of speed, he lunged for the bellpull behind him.

Elaith kept coming, another knife poised in his hand. He hurled it, pinning the cord to the wall. "For form's sake," he told the shrinking merchant. "The alarm would do you little good."

"The guard—" began Mizzen.

"My apologies," the elf said with a mocking little bow. "They are still standing at their post, if that is any consolation."

The merchant paled, then panicked. He reached under the counter, seized handfuls of crystals and gems, and began to pelt the elf with them.

Elaith batted aside a few of the missiles, then snatched a large hunk of jasper from the air and hurled it back. The rock caught Mizzen on the forehead. Both his eyes turned inward, as if the merchant wished to identify the specific rock that struck him, then he tilted slowly back and crashed into a shelf laden with whatnots. Crystal trinkets rained down upon their creator like multicolored hail.

Muttering, the elf found a half-full pitcher of wine and threw it on the senseless man. Mizzen came to, sputtering with indignation. His protests stopped abruptly as he recalled his circumstances and his attacker.

"Take it," the man pleaded, sweeping both hands in a wide arc to indicate the entire contents of the shop.

Elaith glanced around and was not particularly impressed. "Crystal dragon? Perfume bottles? I think not."

"Then w-what? W-Why?" Mizzen stammered.

"I wished to purchase the ruby you spoke of just three nights past, but I believe now that I will simply take it, since I've paid out in annoyance more than the gem is likely to be worth."

"Oh, that!" Mizzen looked relieved at the limited

scope of the anticipated theft. "A young woman came in earlier. She offered me more than a ruby that size was worth. No one can blame a man of business for taking a profit," he said piously.

"Unless he sells for profit another man's goods. I believe that stone belonged to Oth Eltorchul."

"Lord Eltorchul," Mizzen repeated, his voice getting stronger as ire crept into his tones. "That stone will just about cover what he owed me. Cheat and liar, he was! Hiding behind that title, acting as if no commoner had the right to demand pay."

The story rang true to Elaith. In his experience, the wealthier or more titled a man, the less concerned he was about certain financial obligations. Since the Eltorchul clan was not overburdened with ready coin, merchants such as Mizzen were unlikely to see payment. Elaith could hardly blame the man for trying to cover his losses.

"What of the dream spheres?"

Mizzen looked surprised to hear these words, but only for a moment. "Gone," he said shortly. "Lord Eltorchul made arrangements to have them sent to Waterdeep, same way they got here."

Elaith was not pleased to hear this, but he would deal with the inconvenience later. "What of the gem? You know something of its true worth—you let that much slip when you were deep in your cups. The 'elf gem,' you called it. Why did you let it go?"

"I didn't like it," the man said bluntly.

The elf considered this a reasonable response. To inspire the man to elaborate, he removed a dagger from his belt and began to toy with it, flipping it nimbly between his hands. "The dream spheres. Oth was using the Mhaorkiira Hadryad—the elf gem—to create these devices."

"That's right." Mizzen spoke quickly, his eyes fixed in horrified fascination upon the flashing, spinning dagger. "He said it was an ancient elven artifact that held the memories of an entire lost clan. He placed some of these memories in the crystal spheres, to be released by a paying dreamer."

Not a release, but an exchange, thought Elaith. Each time some stupid sod used one of these toys, one of his own memories or dreams went into the kiira stone. No doubt Oth sorted through them, keeping what was useful and turning the rest back into other magical fantasies.

On the surface, it seemed an ingenious way of gathering information. Elaith almost admired the man who'd found a way to profit from the evil artifact. Oth's command of magic clearly outstripped Elaith's. Unfortunately for Oth, he was limited by his arrogance and his human ignorance. While Elaith might be accused with some justification of the first vice, he, unlike Oth Eltorchul, knew what the gem could do, and he knew how incredibly dangerous it could be. Kiira were among the most powerful of elven magical items. The Mhaorkiira, or "dark gem," was the only one that had been twisted to evil. It had somehow absorbed the twisted ambitions of the long-dead Hadryad clan, and in the process had contributed to the demise of that ancient family.

The thought did not deter Elaith. "How are these dream spheres made?" he demanded.

"I do not know. Lord Eltorchul never entrusted the secret to me."

Mizzen understood his mistake as soon as the words were spoken. In speaking too freely, he had outlived his usefulness. His eyes grew enormous with fear, then glazed over in acceptance of death.

The elf obliged him.

On the way out, Elaith tossed aside a gilded mirror—the only ornament on the carved and polished wood of the walls. The hidden door beneath was almost laughably obvious to his keen elven vision. He ran his fingers lightly over the carvings, found and released the clasp.

Inside the safe was a pile of gems—real gem entrusted to Mizzen to be matched with crystals. Elai emptied the safe's contents into his bag and slipped o the back door into the streets. It would be an easy tas finding a caravan of flying creatures. All that remain was for him to find them, and the Mhaorkiira Hadrya and then settle with Bronwyn and her dwarven ally.

As Elaith suspected, Silverymoon was abuzz wit word of the strange caravan, but to his dismay, his si trip through the forest had cost him. The caravan ha already left the city on fresh mounts.

The determined elf sought out the stables where th caravan had taken a brief rest. A pair of elven groom clad in Gundwynd livery tended the hooves and hid and wings of the weary pegasi.

Elaith's hand went to his sword, and then he thoug better of it. These were gold elves, well armed and good trim. Fighting them would take more time than h had to spare.

"I must have one of those horses," Elaith said flatl "I will pay whatever you ask."

The elves looked him over, astonished at such request from a fellow Tel'Quessar—even if he *was* moon elf. "These are not mere horses," one of the pointed out. "Even if they were, they have traveled fa and have earned a day's rest."

"It is important."

"What is so important that it could justify flying tired pegasus?" the other groom inquired in a tone tha marked the question as entirely rhetorical.

As it happened, Elaith had an answer. "The Mhao kiira Hadryad," he said bluntly. "A human adventure with Gundwynd's caravan has the dark kiira."

The elves stared at him with rounded eyes. "It ha been found? But how? It has been lost for—what? Thre centuries and more?"

Elaith folded his arms. "Would you like to discuss th

missteps of elven history, or would you prefer that I fetch this stone back before it creates any more trouble?"

The grooms gave him no further argument. One of them packed travel supplies, the other put harness and saddle on the protesting steed and led it out into the courtyard.

Mounting the beast took more time than Elaith liked, for the pegasus reared and snorted and pitched each time he approached her.

"You have not trained with pegasi, have you?" asked one of the elves in an apologetic tone. "She senses that."

More likely, thought Elaith, the winged horse had senses even more finely attuned. He carried with him the scent of vengeance and death. Undoubtedly it was this that spooked the fey creature.

The grooms kept cajoling her. Finally the pegasus quieted long enough for Elaith to climb onto her back. Immediately the enormous white wings unfurled, and the pegasus leaped into the air.

The elf clung to his seat as the pegasus rose in dipping, swooping loops. She tested him, responding too sharply to the reins, careening from one side to another, but Elaith was nothing if not determined, and he clung to her like scales to a snake. Eventually the winged horse seemed to sense, and then to absorb, her rider's urgency. When Elaith gave the pegasus her head, she set a steady, determined course for Waterdeep.

Beneath them the miles fell away as swiftly as autumn leaves before a strong wind. The day grew old, and soon Elaith had to shield his eyes against the setting sun. Though the pegasus's white sides were lathered and heaving, Elaith urged her on, hoping to find before nightfall the clearing where the caravan had made camp on the first night of the trip to Silverymoon.

He saw the caravan before he saw the clearing. Silhouetted against the purple and gold of an autumn sunset, they were already in descent, whirling down toward the valley and the clear, cold water that spilled from the mountain into a deep pool.

Elaith's gaze swept the valley, setting up the battlefield in his mind's eye. That he would have to fight, he did not doubt. The caravan guards might not fight to protect Bronwyn's safety and virtue, but they would not allow her to be robbed by a rogue elf. Elaith could possibly expect assistance from the elves in the caravan, but that was a last resort. Already he regretted confiding in the Gundwynd grooms. The more elves who learned that the Mhaorkiira had been found, the lower his chance of keeping the gem until its task was done.

His eye caught a bit of color and movement near the waterfall, where there should be neither—several feet from the ground, in what appeared to be sheer rock. Elaith understood at once what that meant. The northland hills were riddled with caves and passages. The elf peered closer, squinting so that his vision would pick up not the fading daylight, but heat patterns.

In the forest, almost indiscernible even to such eyes as his, were several telling patterns. He made out a group of men crouched near the mouth of a small cave, looking like hunting cats awaiting a chance to spring. Others waited on ledges and behind trees, draped in capes dyed to match stone and stump.

The caravan—*his* quarry—was about to land in the midst of an ambush.

Eight

The mansion belonging to the Dezlentyr family was among the more modest structures of the North Ward. A pair of massive elms flanked the iron gate, and the house beyond was small and graceful, crafted from stone and oddly shaped timbers in such fashion that it appeared to have grown there. It was unique in this human city devoted to excess and splendor, and it reminded Arilyn of the homes common in faraway Evereska—a community of moon elves who hunted the forests and guarded the secrets of the Greycloak Hills.

For a moment homesickness assailed her, though it had been many years since she had left the Greycloak Hills as an orphaned girl. There was no place for her there now. Nor, she reminded herself firmly, was there much of a future for her in Waterdeep, unless she could resolve the problem at hand.

The last three days had yielded nothing but frustration. Lord Eltorchul had sent a message asking her and Danilo to hold secret the news of Oth's death while the family came to a decision concerning possible resurrection. Honoring that request made it virtually impossible for Arilyn to ask the sort of questions that required answers. Isabeau Thione had run to ground. Bronwyn had yet to return from her trip to Silverymoon. Dan had gone to the libraries of Candlekeep and was deep in a study of the history of moonblades in hope of finding something that might explain the continuing capriciousness of her sword's magic.

Arilyn, who was running exceedingly low on patience, had decided to search for answers in the past.

She gave word of her errand to the Dezlentyr guard. In a few moments the gates opened, and a young servant came to meet her. He was roughly clad in tunic, breeches, and well-worn boots, but he was nonetheless a strikingly handsome male—tall, golden, and so fine of feature that he would be considered beautiful but for his sun-browned skin and a slightly raffish stubble of beard. He gave the impression of a prince playing at peasant. As he drew near, Arilyn noted that he was half-elven.

Not a servant, realized Arilyn, but Corinn, the Dezlentyr heir. Half-elves were not common in this city, and he and his twin sister were unique among their noble peers.

His eyes lit up as he regarded her, and he called her name and held out his hand for a comrade's salute. "We met some time ago, at one of Galinda Raventree's parties," he recalled, then flashed a brilliant smile. "Good to see you again, under better circumstances!"

Arilyn appreciated his point, and she clasped his wrist briefly. "I hope you'll still think so after you hear me out. I wish to talk to your father. Tell me if this tale will be too painful for him to hear."

The young noble's face turned grave as she related the story she'd prepared: a battle with a band of assassins and their elven victim, followed by repeated attempts on her own life.

Her implication was not lost on him. "You are often

seen in the company of Danilo Thann," he said thoughtfully. "He is a highly visible member of the peerage. If my father's fears are grounded, there might be those in this city who would take mortal offense at such a pairing. Yes, my father should hear of this."

He took her to a small side parlor and promised to return soon. Arilyn paced about, pausing before a portrait of a golden-haired elf woman.

Corinn's mother looked younger than her own twin children. Had she not fallen to an unknown assassin, she would undoubtedly look much the same now, some fifteen years later, like an undying flower watching the garden around her wither and dry.

Arilyn understood all too well how difficult that could be. Half-elves were eternally out of step with both their human and elven kin. Though she was nearly twenty years older than Danilo, she could expect to outlive him by nearly a century. She could expect to watch their children grow old and die. Not an enviable destiny, but she vastly preferred it to that suffered by Sibylanthra Dezlentyr. Arilyn had no intention of falling to assassins hired to safeguard the human bloodline of Waterdeep's nobility.

Arlos Dezlentyr came in with his son. He was a small, slight man who appeared to be nothing more than a shadow cast by his son's bright light, but the voice with which he greeted her was deep and resonant, and it possessed a beauty that might well have caught the fancy and then the heart of an elven woman. He possessed a graceful charm, as well. He bowed over Arilyn's hand with courtly grace that would have done honor to a queen.

"Corinn has told me your tale." He sighed and sank onto a chair. "If what you fear is true, my children could also be in danger."

"I will find the truth and bring you word," she promised. "I understand Corinn and Corinna are seldom in

Waterdeep. Until we have the answers we seek, perhaps it is well to keep them from the public eye."

"A good thought." Lord Arlos glanced up at the portrait. "My first wife was a mage, you know. I had hoped that Sibylanthra's children would take after their mother's art, but so far they both have too much taste for adventure. Now I see the blessing in it."

He turned to his son. "Corinn, you may follow that scheme of yours to sail around Chult and seek to establish harbors to the south. Corinna may take that commission she was offered. Better the uncertainties of Tethyr's seas than the proven dangers of this city. Make the arrangements at once."

The half-elf flashed another of his incandescent smiles. He bowed to his father, then lifted Arilyn's hand to his lips. "Thank you," he said softly and fervently. He was gone, like a golden bird in glad flight.

Arilyn spent an hour with the old man, exchanging reminiscences about Evereska, which had been his wife's childhood home. She learned only that Sibylanthra had been found in the garden, inexplicably dead. There were no wounds, no sign of illness or struggle, none of the usual marks of poison. Yet her husband had been convinced, and was still certain, that this was the work of an assassin. Lord Arlos would have talked until moonrise, but finally Arilyn rose to go. She asked him to show her the kitchen gardens before she left.

The nobleman was surprised but willing. They walked down rows of late cabbages and drying herbs. Arilyn headed for the potting and drying shed and there found what she sought. A large cistern opened into the tunnel below, allowing the kitchen staff to toss husks and parings into the sewers below.

"I'll leave by this way. An assassin would have," she explained.

He started, then shook his head in disbelief. "Why did no one think of this sooner?"

There was an answer, but it was not one Arilyn wished to speak aloud: to find an assassin, you had to think like one. She had spent too many years doing just that. She busied herself with the heavy lid, then raised a hand in farewell and dropped into the dark opening.

She found the small footholds carved into the stone and climbed down into the tunnel. As she expected, the openings continued along the wall, so that it was possible to skirt the tunnel floor. Such things were closely held secrets in the guilds that cleaned these tunnels, but Arilyn had long experience with the sort of folk who used these dark passages for other purposes.

It troubled her, how easily she fell back into the mind and the steps of an assassin. The role had always been an uneasy one, but it was doubly so now, after her years as an honored, acclaimed champion of the elves. Perhaps this was the only role destiny would permit her to play among the humans.

She thrust aside these thoughts and addressed herself to the task at hand. After a hundred paces or so, the tunnel floor rose at a steep angle. Arilyn leaped from her perch and began to climb.

The tunnel was clean and dry, and it appeared to be relatively new. This was interesting, given the reappearance of tren in the city. After the Guild Wars, some of the old tunnels had been sealed, barring dangerous underground races from the city. These tunnels had been magically warded, but it was possible that someone determined enough could have made new passages.

As Arilyn considered the matter, certain other pieces fell into place. Watch Alley in North Ward was exceptionally safe but for the fact that single, severed human feet were occasionally found discarded in its shadows. The first such occurrence had been about fifteen years ago—about the time of Lady Dezlentyr's death. Tavern talk claimed that severing feet was an old thieves' guild punishment and perhaps a signal of the guild's return to Waterdeep. Arilyn had heard the bad jests about " 'defeeting' one's enemy." In light of recent events, however, it seemed likely that tren, not human thieves, were behind these killings. The question was, who was paying their hire, and if this was a single source, what purpose prompted over fifteen years of costly, clandestine activity?

Arilyn examined the walls as she walked, searching for the telltale carvings that tren left as signals to each other. The tunnels turned out to be as convoluted as a cow path. The half-elf followed the faint markings for what seemed hours, finding them here and there but never quite able to distinguish a pattern. Finally it occurred to her to follow to its end the one passage that was *not* marked.

This proved to be worth doing. Arilyn found a hidden door in the wall of the unmarked tunnel. Beyond it a ladder rose into what appeared to be a large wooden shed. She climbed it and peered cautiously around.

The shed was permeated by a complex fragrance, a blessed respite from the dank tunnels. Bunches of drying herbs hung from the rafters. Piles of citrus peels and dried flowers stood on raised wooden platforms. Rows of shelves held bottles filled with colored liquid, into which flowers and herbs and vanilla beans and dozens of other fragrant substances yielded their essence.

Arilyn crept through the shed and eased out into the alley. She recognized the street ahead, and the shop that the small shed served: Diloontier Perfumery. Rumor had it that the proprietor also sold more lethal potions, but no one had ever caught him at it. Diloontier's prices kept out all but the most wealthy patrons—nobles who could afford to put down bags of gold for delicate scents. Who could afford to have new tunnels dug, and to hire reptilian assassins. It seemed to Arilyn that Diloontier's client list could be very informative.

To Arilyn's eye, this path was so clear that she thought it incredible that no one had thought to explore it. However, this was precisely the sort of thing to which this city turned a blind eye. All of Waterdeep loudly proclaimed that assassins held no guild, no power, no numbers, no threat.

Arilyn had reason to know the damage that could be dealt by a single, unseen blade. Perhaps it took someone like her to deal with such matters.

Old habits fell easily into place. Arilyn slipped away into the shadows, as silent as a hunting cat.

* * * * *

Elaith's dismay grew as he surveyed the certain ambush in the valley below. He cursed and drove his heels into the flanks of his winged mare. Leaning low over her neck, he urged her into a plunging dive.

Wind roared in his ears until he feared he might never again hear anything else. Even as the thought formed, an eagle's shriek rent the streaming air, tearing through the deafening noise. This was followed by an even more chilling sound—an undulating elven battle cry. The Eagle Riders had spotted the ambush.

From the four corners of the wind they came, moving in with a perfectly coordinated attack. Their eagle mounts dove in with the instincts of raptors, their golden eyes fierce and their talons outstretched to snatch up their prey. It was a glorious, terrifying sight: a classic elven attack.

It was also the worst possible strategy.

Elaith's cry of protest was swallowed by the wind. He could not hear his own voice. Nor did he hear the whir and thump of the catapults, but he knew in his blood and bones that such weapons lay in wait. After all, these bandits knew the caravan's route, they had found this remote site. They would know what forces they would face and how they might best be defeated.

Golden feathers flew back toward him like giant leaves torn away by a wintry blast. Among the feathers were deadlier missiles: bits of metal and stone hurled as grapeshot.

Elaith instinctively ducked as the spray rose toward them, pulling back hard on the pegasus' reins. The winged horse threw back her head. Elaith caught a glimpse of the steed's wild, white-rimmed eyes—and the ugy metal shape that protruded from her neck.

He leaned forward and eased it out. It was a caltrop, a ball covered with wicked, triangular spikes. Fortunately the thing had embedded itself more in the harness than the horse.

The giant eagles had not been so fortunate. They had caught the full force of the deadly volley. Two of the wondrous birds lay on the ground like discarded rags. A third spun down, one shattered wing hanging limp. Elaith heard Garelith Leafbower's furious battle cry as the last of the Eagle Riders dove in for the attack.

The first volley was quickly followed by a second, and a third. Elaith's pegasus strained upward, her wings curved almost to breaking to catch the rising winds. She leveled off and circled, whinnying with what sounded very much like concern. Elaith understood completely, though he did not know what kind of bonds pegasi shared. With senses heightened by battle, the elf felt the death of the young Eagle Riders as keenly as a wound to his own flesh. He urged the frantic beast to circle down so that he might assess the situation.

Utter chaos filled the valley and the sky above it. The tethered pegasus teams frantically fought to be free of their traces. Sky chariots spun out of control, spilling contents and riders to the valley floor. Griffons reared, pawing at the air with their leonine paws as they attempted to fight their way through the lethal spray. The bandits swarmed the valley, cutting down the wounded and gathering up the spilled booty. Few survivors were in any condition to give resistance. Seeing the loss of his treasure, Elaith once again urged his steed into a dive.

Stony, blood-soaked earth leaped up to meet them as the pegasus plunged. At the last moment she leveled out and swept into a wide circle, wings out wide. She hit the earth at a gallop. Elaith reined her to a halt and leaped to the ground. He drew his sword and headed toward the thickest part of battle.

"Stand and fight!" roared a too-familiar dwarven voice overhead. "Lost your stones in that slingshot, did you?"

Elaith ducked as Ebenezer's pegasus swept in low, her teeth bared in a fierce grimace. Her rider did not wait for the landing but launched himself into the air, his stubby arms outstretched. The dwarf flopped onto a trio of fleeing looters, bringing them down like stomped-on flowers.

A slender, autumn-colored figure staggered out from the midst of a melee. Using a broken piece of harness as a lash, she beat the bandits away from a wounded elven groom as she looked frantically about for a better weapon.

Elaith cut his way through to Bronwyn's side. Pressing a dagger into her hand, he fell into place at her back.

She lashed out at a short, black-eyed bandit. The thief ducked and darted out of reach, losing a hat in the process. The elf marked the sudden spill of long, black hair, the lavish curves revealed when the thief stooped to retrieve the fallen hat. A spray of blood dragged his attention fully back into battle. He pushed aside the man whose throat Bronwyn had just cut.

"Thanks," she panted out, lifting the bloodied weapon.

"Don't," the elf said coldly. "There is a price."

For several moments there was no time for speech.

Elaith stopped a high scimitar blow with his knife, then drove his sword up into the bandit's barrel chest. He kicked the man off his blade and lunged at the next attacker. With four quick, short strokes he left a bloody lightning bolt of a gash on the man's torso. The man fell to his hands and knees. Bronwyn took advantage of the moment to leap onto the man's back. Using the surprise—and the extra height—she easily cut down the bandit who came in on the heels of Elaith's victim.

They fought well together. Bronwyn did not exhibit Elaith's training or skill, but neither was she hampered by his rage. Whenever the elf began to be carried along on the icy tide of battle, she stepped in and finished the matter with grim practicality. Elaith soon found himself responding in kind, protecting her by fending off attacks that she alone could not have parried.

To his surprise, the heat of battle burned away his desire to take vengeance on this cunning wench. It was nearly impossible to desire the death of someone after working so long and so hard to keep her body and soul on speaking terms with each other. The Mhaorkiira he must have, but if he could find a way to let Bronwyn live, he would take it.

Finally Elaith and Bronwyn stood alone, in a silence broken only by a few scattered, tired clashes and by the groans of the wounded. She regarded him steadily with eyes that seemed to understand, and thus affirm, his change of plan. Before words could be spoken, Ebenezer sauntered up, one eye swollen shut and his tunic dark with blood.

Bronwyn regarded him with dismay. "Any of that yours?"

"Might be you could say that. I *earned* it, leastwise." The dwarf touched his puffy eye and grinned proudly.

This was neither the moment nor the company Elaith would have chosen for this discussion, but he could not afford to wait. "The ruby. I want it back."

A faintly smug expression touched the woman's chocolate-colored eyes. "I wasn't aware it was yours when I bought it. At any rate, I don't have it."

Seeing his doubt, she nodded toward a small leather bag, lying empty on the ground. The strings had been cut, and the bag lay flat and slack. She strode over and scooped it up. Her face suddenly went very still, and she jerked open the bag and thrust one hand in.

"Stones!" she spat out.

The dwarf pricked up his ears. "Troubles?"

Bronwyn drew out a small, round crystal and showed it to him.

"Trouble," the dwarf agreed.

"What is this?" Elaith demanded.

Bronwyn shook the offending sack. "This is a bag of sending. Everything I put in it should be in a safe place in Waterdeep. The magic isn't working!"

A possible explanation for this occurred to Elaith, one so fraught with dire possibilities that it blunted the loss of the kiira. He put out his hand. "That crystal."

Ever the merchant, she countered, "In exchange for a truce. We've both lost what we sought. Call it even."

Since this fit in with Elaith's inclinations, he responded with a curt nod. She dropped the globe into his hand. The small, iridescent crystal nestled into his palm like a living thing. His elven senses picked up the captured magic. He quickly dropped it into a bag, understanding at last the enormity of the risk—and the opportunity.

All magic came from somewhere. The dream spheres gave a dream and took one, but the magic power that fueled this exchange was drawn from nearby magic. Apparently the dream spheres stole magical power, drained it off and reformed it in much the same fashion as the legendary magic of spellfire.

Elaith's initial purpose for the Mhaorkiira remained, but here was a new and enormous potential. Not only could hidden knowledge be his, but also he could possess the potential to confuse defensive spells and confound mages. All that he lacked was the kiira gem.

He would have it and would not count any amount of blood too high a price.

* * * * *

In a cavern hidden behind the waterfall, deep within the mountains that surrounded the blood-soaked valley, the surviving bandits threw off their masks and hoods and began to paw through their loot.

Isabeau Thione strode through the crowd, looking like a pirate queen in her dark breeches and crimson shirt. She was in rare high spirits, joking with her hired band and dispensing portions of the loot with a lavish hand.

Appalled by it all, Lilly hugged the shadows on the far side of the cavern. Although she had not taken part in the battle, she had witnessed it all from the shadows of the trees. Never had she seen anything like it.

No, actually that was not entirely true. A former cook at The Pickled Fisherman once bought a small flock of chickens for stew. For sport, he penned them in the back alley and hacked them apart with a machete. The cook had long ago drifted off. Rumor reported that he'd ended up in Mystra's Arms, one of the houses that cared for Waterdeep's insane. Such places catered mostly to those driven mad by magic gone awry, but they also tended the occasional soul who found his way to lunacy by a more convoluted path. At the moment Lilly felt perilously close to madness herself.

She had not anticipated any of this. A letter, stolen from the large, bearded man she and Isabeau had robbed together the night they'd met, gave the route of this caravan. A simple theft, Isabeau had argued, only the pigeon was a caravan rather than a single nobleman. Lilly had fallen far short when she'd taken the woman's measure, and her lack made her as guilty of bloodshed as any of the hired killers.

She could not stay in partnership with Isabeau. The woman was as rapacious as a troll. Who knew what she might do next? No, Lilly could not stay—not with Isabeau, and perhaps not even in Waterdeep. She needed a place to hide, to start anew, a place to come to terms with what she had done, to find a way to make amends.

A bright, ringing clatter tore her from her guilty thoughts. Two mercenaries stood toe to toe, staring stupidly at the half sack each of them held. For a moment they watched the spilled coins roll away, then they began to pummel at each other. Isabeau shouted for the others to break up the fight. Most merely joined in.

All was chaos. Lilly knew what to do in such moments—she had done some of her best pickings during tavern brawls.

She eased her way into the melee and faked a stumble. With a quick swipe she gathered up some coins and gems and dropped them into her pocket. When she stood up, a blow caught her in earnest.

Her jaw exploded with pain, her head snapped back, and the ground slammed up to meet her.

Lilly awoke to the sound of dripping water, which kept an eerie rhythm with the pounding in her temples. Cautiously she opened one eye. Isabeau was stretched out beside her, a smug little smile on her face and a pile of treasure beside her.

A heap of gleaming white globes dominated the hoard. Longing swept through Lilly like a healing tide. She sat up and reached for one, clenching her hand around the comforting magic.

"You know those?" asked Isabeau.

Lilly tried to move her aching jaw, and decided that a nod would do the job.

Isabeau smiled. "Perhaps you would like to take your share in these? Say, seven?"

It was a ridiculously low payment, even at the cost of dream spheres, but Lilly considered it a fair enough way out.

"That will do," she mumbled.

Her words seemed to ring in the empty cavern. The silence struck her, numbed her. Like a dreamwalker, she rose and stumbled in growing horror through the too-quiet cave.

Everywhere the mercenaries lay in twisted, tortured positions. Blackened tongues protruded through mouths stretched open with silent screams. Their pockets had been turned, their gear bags sliced open and looted.

Lilly's hand flew to her mouth. She whirled back toward Isabeau, hardly believing what her eyes told her.

"You're wondering how we will move the cargo," the woman said, misreading her partner's dismay. "The porters I've arranged know the tunnels well. They can have the goods moved to Waterdeep's undercity faster than an overland caravan could cover the same ground."

One of the shadows moved and broke away into the torchlight. Lilly backed away, shaking her head in terrified disbelief at the monstrous sight.

Isabeau did not seem concerned by the sudden appearance of an enormous, bipedal lizard. She strode forward and handed the creature a fine short sword that held the sheen of a newly made weapon.

"An Amcathra blade," she said. "There will be four more when you get to Skullport."

Enormous claws closed around the hilt, and the creature grunted in apparent satisfaction. Isabeau looked to Lilly and seemed amused by the woman's reaction.

"Meet the tren," she said casually. "You might as well get used to them. We will be doing a considerable amount of business with them from this point forth."

She cocked her head and regarded her horrorstruck partner. Her eyes narrowed in speculation, and she turned back to the monster. "Lilly does not appear to approve. Show her what happens to those who speak of matters best left in shadows."

The curved, fang-lined jaws parted in a reptilian smile. With a grunt, the creature hunkered down beside one of the dead mercenaries. The enormous, clawed hand closed around the man's protruding black tongue. One yank, and the tongue came free with a wet, tearing sound. The tren grinned again, then tossed the tidbit into its fanged mouth.

Through the whirling haze that gripped her, Lilly heard the grunting echoing throughout the cavern. More tren emerged from the shadows, and they crouched down to feed.

Lilly began to scream. Dimly she was aware of Isabeau scolding her, slapping her, but she could not stop. She sank to the stone floor, hands fisted against her ears to block the sound of the horrid feast, and she screamed and screamed until the merciful blackness closed in again.

Nine

The scent of autumn was strong in the wind that whipped along the city streets, whirling the bright fallen leaves in small eddies and tugging at the skirts of passing women.

Danilo clapped one hand to his head to keep his hat at the angle dictated by current fashion. "You picked an unfortunate time to develop a love of the shops," he told his companion.

Arilyn impatiently brushed a dark curl off her face. "What if street rumor is right? What if the perfume merchant sells more than scents and ointments?"

"It is hard to credit. Diloontier has a fine reputation. Many of the merchant families do business with him. His scents hold true, and the few potions he sells are harmless and reliable. Believe me, the wizards' guild keeps a wary eye on his affairs, as they do anyone who traffics in minor magic."

"What of the tunnels?" Arilyn persisted.

"My dear, this city is built over a veritable anthill. Creatures of all sorts have been digging tunnels under

Waterdeep Mountain since dragons ruled the land. It does not signify."

Arilyn shrugged and pushed open the door to the shop. She stopped so abruptly that Danilo bumped solidly into her.

Cassandra Thann regarded both of them over the exquisite bottle in her hands. After a moment's hesitation, she handed it back to Diloontier.

"The blend is not quite right. Too much spice. I have no wish to go about smelling like a winterfest pudding."

"I will see to it at once," the merchant said. He made a quick bow to her, then turned aside and snapped his fingers at one of his apprentices. "You, Harmon. See to this gentleman while I repair this perfume."

He bustled off, leaving the two women eyeing each other like swordsmen in need of their weapons.

"I'm fond of winterfest puddings," Arilyn commented. "Since that perfume didn't suit you, perhaps I should buy it."

Cassandra looked nonplussed for a moment. She quickly covered her reaction with a cool smile. "My dear, that scent is far too . . . formal for you. Surely there is something in this shop that would suit you better."

The subtle insult held an opportunity. The noblewoman was aware of Arilyn's dark reputation. The half-elf decided to play upon that knowledge. She folded her arms and let her gaze go flat, cold, and deadly—the stare of a hunting hawk or a hired killer.

"So I hear. I have no immediate use for such things, but I would be very interested to know who might."

They regarded each other for a long, measuring moment. Cassandra glanced back at her son. She took a small vial from the shelf and handed it to him. "Take this as a gift for your . . . lady, and go. You would do well to heed my advice."

Cassandra pulled on her gloves and sailed out to her waiting carriage.

Danilo waved away the perfumer's assistant. He led the way out into the street, then turned an apologetic gaze upon his friend. "I suppose you realize she was not referring to perfume," he murmured.

"The thought occurred to me," Arilyn said with a touch of sarcasm. "Does Cassandra have a general aversion to half-elven assassins, or did she have some other, more specific advice in mind?"

"I'm not entirely certain," he admitted. "She was most insistent that I not involve myself with Oth's death, but I put that down to her abhorrence for scandal. She is concerned about my choice of companion, probably for much the same reason. As you have observed, some of the nobility look askance at alliances between their peers and other races."

This was the first time Danilo had openly admitted that a problem might exist. Arilyn decided it was time to put her cards on the table. "I spoke with Arlos Dezlentyr yesterday."

Danilo looked at her sharply. "He told you about his first wife?"

"So you have heard that story," Arilyn said. "I'd wondered. Yes, her death made quite a stir among the elves. Many were indignant when no real attempt was made to find her killer."

"If, indeed, she was murdered."

"Sibylanthra was a young elf in apparent good health and happy with her work, her husband, and her young children. What else could it be?"

When Danilo offered no argument, she continued. "You admit that your peers are unhappy to see you with a half-elf. Someone was unhappy that Arlos Dezlentyr married an elf woman. Tren tunnels link the Dezlentyr estate with Diloontier's shop. Shall we find out why, or would you rather spend the rest of your life checking shadows for a tren ambush?"

"There is something in what you say," he said slowly.

"Do we have any reason to believe that the tren attacks were directed at anyone other than Oth Eltorchul and those who happened to have recent dealings with the man? Once the truth of his death is known, there will be no further need for concern."

Arilyn sniffed.

"Truly," Dan continued earnestly, "no one among the nobility wishes you ill. Some might be displeased by my choice of companion, but they could hardly see our future children as a threat to the peerage. After all, the line for the Thann family title is as long as a dwarven ballad."

They walked in silence for several moments before he spoke again. "Your mention of Lady Dezlentyr took me aback. Lady Cassandra reminded me of that story a few nights past," he said slowly. "At the time it was apparent she meant it as a cautionary tale. Although it pains me to say this, I am not certain whether it was intended as warning or as threat."

Arilyn did not respond at once, giving him time to absorb the impact of his own words before she added another painful layer. "That perfume your mother recommended. Would you recognize the bottle if you saw it on the shelf among others?"

"I suppose so. Why?"

"Lady Cassandra was quick to give it up when she saw us. If we wish to prove that Diloontier sells things other than simple perfumes, this might be a place to start. You heard what I said to her in the shop."

"Heard, yes. I'm not sure I understood what went unsaid between you."

"I implied that her potions or others in the shop might be poison. I told her I had no use for them *at the moment* but was looking for those who might. An assassin hunting down assassins. She heard and warned us."

"I know people who can test it for me, see what it is and how it works. It will take a few days for me to get back the answer, but it would be information worth having."

Danilo digested this in silence. "Do not misunderstand me when I say that testing the perfume would be effort wasted."

"But—"

He cut her off with an upraised hand. "Diloontier took the bottle into the back room, promising to 'repair the scent.' By now the contents have been altered. We must look elsewhere."

Arilyn could not refute his logic. She gritted her teeth and acknowledged it with a curt nod. There was no more speech between them, though she could not help but wonder if Danilo was relieved at finding a wall at the end of this particular alley.

She had her moonblade and her duty to the elven people. Danilo had title and privilege and a nobleman's loyalty to family and peers. Of one thing she was grimly certain: Before this matter was settled, either she or Danilo would be called upon to sacrifice something of deep value. She only hoped it would not be each other.

In all truth, though, she did not see how it could be otherwise.

* * * * *

Lilly walked quickly down the streets of the Castle Ward. She seldom had reason to come to this posh district of Waterdeep, but her determination sustained her, just as it had through the horrid trip back to the city.

This ward was almost as foreign to her as the tunnels and caves had been. There was little work to be had in the Castle Ward, since the taverns hired serving girls with more polished speech and manners. Nor did she dare ply her trade as thief so close to the castle and the horde of guards and watchmen who patroled the area.

She nervously smoothed her hands over the skirt of her best dress and hoped that she did not look too conspicuous. More than one masculine glance lingered upon her and followed her as she turned onto the Street of the Sword. Usually Lilly would look upon such things as nature's course, a compliment paid without words. Today she feared the stares meant she was out of place.

Worse yet, under scrutiny.

The thought sent her blood skittering through her and set up a humming in her ears like that of a dozen whining mosquitoes. "I'm in a dither, that's all. No call for it," she assured herself in the most stouthearted tone she could muster.

Tossing back her head, she walked the rest of the way with feigned confidence and entered Balthorr's Rare and Wonderful Treasures as if she did so twice every tenday.

The proprietor glanced up. Lilly rocked back on her heels, unprepared for the man's scarred visage. She'd heard that Balthorr had lost an eye in a battle with a chimera, but she didn't expect that he would flaunt his loss as proudly as a family crest. He wore a glass eye, striking in that it was nothing but a white sphere. To Lilly, it was eerily reminiscent of the dream spheres.

"I have come to sell," she said, more abruptly than she had planned.

Balthorr studied her with his one good eye. He rose and jerked his head toward a curtained room.

Lilly followed him, then quickly spilled her coins onto the table. "These are platinum. Not many will accept them from the likes of me without asking questions. Can you exchange them for lesser coin?"

The man studied one of the large, shining disks. "Two hundred silver," he offered.

She worked out the exchange in her head and decided the deal was fair enough. "This, too," she added, placing the ruby on the table.

Balthorr picked up the gem and studied it. "Very pretty. Too big to be real, though."

For a moment Lilly's heart sank, but she quickly gathered herself, bolstered by her conviction that this stone was something very special, almost a living thing. It was not so very big—not much bigger than the nail on her smallest finger. "It is a precious stone," she said severely. "I heard tell you knew about such things."

The man spread his hands and shrugged, as if to say that she could not blame him for trying to make the best bargain. "Two hundred gold, paid out in trade-weight bars. Not a copper more."

Lilly's head swam with the enormity of it. Never in her life had she imagined owning such a sum! Why, with that money she could go as far west as Cormyr, with enough left to take lessons in speech and deportment and buy some respectable clothes. She could find work in a fine shop and make her own way without recourse to thievery.

"I'll take it," she said, knowing she should barter but not willing to risk that life-saving sum. She watched intently as the man counted out a hundred gold coins onto a scale, then balanced them with several small shining bars to show her the trade bars measured up in weight to the actual coin. These he placed into a small sack.

When he was finished, she fairly snatched up the sack, startled by how heavy that much gold could be.

Lilly was too eager to be off to be overly concerned with proprieties. She hiked up her skirts and attached the bag to the belt that cinched her chemise. The shopkeeper glanced in her direction, but he seemed far more interested in the ruby and platinum coins that he had just acquired.

With a fistful of silver coins at the ready, Lilly fled from the shop and searched about for a carriage. It was an extravagance, but one she could ill afford to pass up.

Under the watchful eye of Hamish Half-ogre, her tavern room was the safest place she knew. Better to waste a few coins to ride back to this haven than to risk losing all among her fellow thieves.

Three guild carriages passed by without responding to her hail. Finally one drew up, and a pair of halfling grooms hopped down to help her up. The carriage was not empty, but Lilly did not expect to have it to herself. A man and woman sat nestled cozily together on one seat. She settled down on the opposite seat, keeping her eyes politely averted to give her fellow travelers a bit of privacy.

"Doing a little shopping, are we?"

The voice was darkly accented, edged with ice, and chillingly familiar. Lilly started and turned a guilty gaze upon her partner.

"That I am," she babbled, trying without success to hold Isabeau Thione's hard, black-eyed gaze. "Sold one of the dream spheres, I did, just as we agreed. The coins bought me a lovely dinner, and this new hat—"

"Spare me. I've been following you, and you went nowhere near a tavern or a milliner. I'm guessing you sold all seven dream spheres. I'd like to see what they are worth."

Isabeau nodded to her companion, whom Lilly recognized as the captain of the bandit band—and the only thief who had survived the raid. "Hold her."

Lilly lunged for the door handle, intending to leap into the street. A large hand clamped on her wrist and flung it high and back. The thug seized her other hand and raised it over her head. With one hand he pinned her firmly against the carriage wall.

"I'll scream," Lilly threatened.

"You'll die," riposted Isabeau. For good measure, she tugged a large silken kerchief from her pocket and wadded it. She seized Lilly's jaw and pinched it hard, then forced the gag into her mouth.

Lilly sat in silent, frustrated outrage as the woman's deft hands explored her, finding the hidden bag in a few quick pats. Isabeau pulled a small, narrow knife from the coils of her hair and sliced open Lilly's dress. She took the bag and dumped the contents into her silken lap. Her black brows rose in a supercilious arch.

"Quite the merchant, aren't you? I never dreamed you could get so much for a few dream spheres—which we agreed you would keep for yourself."

Lilly watched helplessly as Isabeau slipped the bars into her pockets. "Normally, I would insist upon an equal split," the woman said with a sweet, false smile, "but since you saw fit to change our agreement, I think I should take the whole as penalty. That is fair, hmm?"

The false smile dropped from her face like a discarded cloak. "Your greed and carelessness could have brought this back to my door. Do not cross me again—ever. I hope you realize you can never speak of what we did without condemning yourself to hang from the city walls."

Lilly nodded her head emphatically, though this threat was far less potent than the grim demonstration the tren monsters had given.

"Good. We understand each other. I'll contact you when I need you again." She turned to her henchman. "You can let her out at the next alley."

The bandit reached for the door of the carriage. Without waiting for it to stop, he wrenched it open and hurled Lilly through the door.

She hit the cobblestones and rolled, coming to a painful stop against a pile of wooden crates. The carriage moved smoothly down the street, its passage covering the brutal exit.

Lilly's head throbbed from the impact with the stone, and the world spun madly as she rose to her feet. She collapsed with a cry of pain—her ankle had been wrenched in the fall. Even without this injury, she doubted she could have stood for long. Quickly she took inventory of the damage. A long, raw scrape marked her arm, and one cheek stung. Her ears rang, and sharp sparkles of color popped and exploded through her vision. Her dress was torn, in addition to the rips Isabeau's knife had made. She had no money to ride, and her first tentative step sent bright shards of pain exploding through her battered body.

She had no choice, though. She told herself that as she struggled to rise, trying to beat back the waves of darkness. But her body would not obey her. She was only dimly aware of the approach of heavy boots, the smell of leather armor as two men crouched over her.

"What have we here?" one of them said. He twined a lock of pale red-gold between his fingers. "A strawberry tart, you might say, but a bit far from the bakery."

The other man slapped his hand aside. "You stupid sod! Look at that face. This is one of the Thann brood, or I'm a three-legged ogre. If Lady Cassandra hears you offered insult to one of hers, she'll have our stones set in silver and wear them in a tiara."

His companion grunted. "Best get her home, then. You got the price of a carriage hire on you?"

"Not bloody likely! The Watch doesn't pay that well. Wait—I've got three silver. You?"

As the men pooled their coins, Lilly tried to protest. The best she could manage was a little mewling sound as one of the men hauled her into his arms, hailed a carriage, and set a brisk pace toward the North Ward and the Thann estate. The thing she had wished for all her life was before her. She was about to meet her father, and the prospect filled her with terror.

Her father.

She had never really thought to meet him, much less ever once considered going to him for help. She fully expected him to reject her—if indeed she managed to find her way into his presence. Lilly would far rather be lying in that alley than faced with the disdain she anticipated. That thought followed her into the darkness, and haunted her dreams.

*   *   *   *   *

Lord Rhammas Thann turned the wooden device over in his hands, running his fingers over the raised carving of a raven perched on a horse's head. It was well crafted, but not a precious piece. A man might throw such a thing aside on any number of whims. "This is indeed my family crest, and I seem to remember this pendant. How did you come by it?"

Lilly put a hand to her throbbing temples and took a deep, steadying breath. "My mother passed it on, sir, along with her story."

"Which, I can only assume, you intend to share with me. My time is limited, so please get on with it."

Lilly was hard pressed to understand the nature of these limitations. The room to which she had been brought was a gentleman's study of sorts, but she saw no evidence that it had witnessed any serious study. A few books lay on a shelf, but their leather bindings were not creased and seamed by reading. A dusty quill tilted out of a glass inkwell that contained nothing but a dry stain. The only object that showed evidence of use was the set of dog-eared cards scattered about the table.

The gentleman himself showed similar signs of ennui. Rhammas Thann must have been a handsome man once, and he still cut a rather dashing figure. His hair was thick and silver, and his eyes, though rather bleary—whether from an excess of morning ale or a lack of interest in the life he led, Lilly could not say—were a striking shade of silvery gray. She could understand why her mother had spoken so wistfully of this man.

"My mother gave this to me, along with my name. She said to seek you out and tell you both these things if ever I was in dire need. I am that, but you can believe me when I say I never intended to come."

"You said your name was Lilly," he remembered. "I am sorry, but I do not see the significance."

"Do you recall a place called the Dryad's Garden? It was a tavern in the Dock Ward, long since closed. All the girls were given names of flowers. Marigold, Pansy, Rose. My mother's name was Violet. Her hair was of like color to mine, if that helps."

Memory flickered in the man's eyes, and then wide-eyed chagrin. He looked at her closely for the first time. "Violet's child—and mine, I suppose. Yes, of course. The resemblance is there to see."

"So your steward said, as he rushed me out of sight," Lilly said in a wry tone. When she had been presented at the servants' entrance, the steward—an austere fellow who looked as if discretion was the sum and essence of his moral code—took one glance at her face and then hustled her into a private room. He'd tended her injuries, fed her a vile-tasting healing potion, and heard her tale. Next he'd hurried off to arrange the interview, not even asking to see the pendant she offered as proof.

"Good man," the lord murmured absently. He sighed and fixed a troubled gaze upon her. "Now that you are here, what is it that you want?"

A family. A home. *A name.*

Lilly spoke none of these things. "I'm in a bit of trouble, sir. I don't want to bother you, but it's needful that I leave town as soon as possible."

This idea clearly appealed to him. "Yes, that would be best. I'll have someone see to it. Stop by on your way out and speak to the steward—no. No, that won't do at all," he muttered. "Cassandra keeps the accounts and would mark any unusual sum and not rest until she knew the whole of it. No, that is impossible."

Lilly's heart sank. She rose and dipped into a small,

graceless curtsey. "Then I'll be on my way, sir, and it's sorry I am to be bothering you."

His eyes focused on her again, and this time there was a bit of emotion in the gray depths, and a hint of regret. "I won't turn away any child of mine, however begotten. I'll send someone to you who can take care of this."

She bobbed another curtsey and turned to leave.

"One more thing," the lord said. Lilly sent an inquisitive look back. "Your mother. She is well?"

"As well as any dead woman can be, sir. She is long gone, but I'm sure she would appreciate you asking about her."

The words came out as a reproach, though she had not intended to speak them. Rhammas merely nodded, as if he expected—deserved—this jab.

The bleak acceptance in the man's face disconcerted her more than would a cruel denunciation, or accusations of fraud. She had expected both. She had not expected to find this shell of a man, worn down to nothingness by relentless petty concerns and easy luxury.

This was not the father she had imagined or the life she had dreamed of living. Lilly turned and fled back toward the servants' quarters and the discreet rear exit the steward pointed out for her. For the first time since the theft, she did not regret the loss of her coin. If this was the price of wealth, it was too dearly bought.

* * * * *

Elaith strode into the enclosed garden late that afternoon, congratulating himself on his decision to use Greenglade Tower as a meeting place. A group of his mercenary captains awaited him. Some of them had been waiting for hours. It was never wise to have large groups gather all at once, for fear of drawing attention. One or two men at a time, their arrivals spaced over time, were less likely to raise attention.

The remnants of a feast lay scattered on the long table and littered the garden floor. Hounds gnawed at discarded bones, and serving girls cleared away the empty trenchers. A few women—and a couple of handsome youths—had been hired for other tasks. Some were draped across the mercenaries' laps, while others had quit the table entirely for the relative privacy of alcoves once tended by careful elven hands.

"Enough," snapped Elaith as he strode up to the table. The mercenaries stood like puppets pulled by a single string, some of them spilling their hired companions to the ground along with other discarded memories of their revelry.

This did not seem to bother the escorts. They gathered up their scattered belongings and the threadbare remnants of their dignity and slipped through the garden gate.

The largest of his captains—a woman of the Northlands with hair the color of flame and various passions of similar hue—cast a wistful look toward the departing youth. Elaith settled his ire upon her.

"You, Hildagriff. Your report."

The woman hauled in her attention. "This from Castle Ward: Balthorr acquired the big ruby. He wants six hundred gold."

This was the news Elaith had been waiting to hear. The dream spheres he had already located, and the kiira gem was the last, vital part of Oth Eltorchul's scheme. The elf gave no sign of the importance of this intelligence, but he rushed his other captains through their reports and sent them on their way.

As soon as he was alone, he set a swift course to the fence Hildagriff had named. This was a task too important to entrust to an underling. No one else could be trusted to handle the Mhaorkiira, the dark gem.

Later that day, Elaith was not certain that he himself could handle the elven gem. It was a beautiful thing—

far surpassing the images his mind had painted of it. Its color was clear and flawless, and it had been perfectly cut and faceted to catch light. The kiira was a marvel of elven gemcraft. And elven magic.

He was disturbed by the dark, compelling power in the stone. Not even the dire legends he had heard from his boyhood fully prepared him for the impact of the Mhaorkiira Hadryad. This stone had twisted and ultimately destroyed an ancient elven clan. Only the last-born, a mage of such utter evil that he might as well have been an orc or a drow or other such abomination, could bend it fully to his will. The gem had been found several times since then, but always slipped back into oblivion with the destruction of the elf who dared to take it up. This was an enormous gamble. Elaith knew he was quite literally putting his life on the line. Was it truly so important that he know his own deepest measure?

"You want it, or don't you?" Balthorr had asked, seeing his reluctance. "I could sell it easy if you don't. Two, three people looked at it this afternoon."

That had interested Elaith. "Any make an offer?"

"No," the fence had admitted, and Elaith had let the matter go.

The kiira was his. The gem settled into his hand with an inaudible sigh of contentment, as if it had found its proper owner at last. At that moment Elaith's hope died, his heart turned to stone. He had his answer. Nothing elven remained to him but the Mhaorkiira. That would have to be enough—that, and the power it would give him.

So be it. He left the gem in his most secure property, then hurried toward the Dock Ward to meet his waiting contacts. A second group would have gathered by now, brought in through the tunnel that ran between the tower and a nearby warehouse. The members of the two groups would not know each other if they passed on the street. Such precautions, he had learned many long years ago, were necessary to those who lived as he did.

He slipped into the warehouse and made his way through the labyrinth of aisles that wove among the high-stacked crates. Without warning, the pile ahead collapsed, crashing down to seal off the passage.

Elaith spun in a half turn, so that he could see both behind and ahead. A trio of hooded men leaped from the heights as another four closed in from behind. The elf scanned the stacked crates on either side. Several other men knelt in position, nocked crossbows aimed at his heart.

Chagrin poured through the elf as he acknowledged himself trapped. He lifted his hands to show that he held no weapons and turned to face the band behind him. He addressed his remarks to the largest form among the hooded men, knowing that brute physical size was deemed important in the sort of primitive hierarchies common among human thugs.

"If you had wished to kill me, you would have done so by now," he pointed out. "Now that you have my attention, speak your mind."

"We bring a message," intoned a gruff, familiar voice from beneath one of the hoods. "You have taken too much upon yourself. The elf lord, they call you."

"So I am, by right of birth and property," Elaith pointed out. "My concerns, both in this city and the one below, outstrip that of most of the merchant clans. Yours included," he added slyly.

The man's sudden jolt of surprise was gratifying— and enlightening. Elaith was not certain until this moment that Rhep, the Ilzimmers' mercenary captain, was beneath that hood. Well enough. At least he knew with whom he dealt.

"This is a city of laws and customs," the man continued, as if determined to put the discussion back on his terms.

"Really." Elaith smiled blandly. "I have not heard the law permitting armed trespass. This little visit must therefore fall under the banner of local custom."

"Mind your tongue, elf," snarled Rhep. "Your welcome in Waterdeep is wearing thin. Play tavern keeper if you will, but close up your Skullport trade. This will be your last warning."

"Good," returned the elf. "I find this particular custom rather tiresome. Please, bring my regards to your masters."

He reached into a pocket sewn into the shoulder seam of his jerkin and drew out a small, silver rod. This he pointed at one of the crates stacked high overhead, which had been marked with a curving rune that none of these louts could read.

A shower of sparks leaped from the tiny staff and coalesced into a single, arrowlike shaft. This sped toward the box and exploded into a second dazzling shower. This explosion was followed by a second, as the contents of the box—smokepowder, highly illegal and as unpredictable as a dryad's romantic fancy—caught flame.

Streams of burning light arced down, spitting and whistling in their descent. The archers dropped their bows and fell to their stomachs in an attempt to hold their perches on the swaying piles of crates.

Elaith drew his sword and ran at the trio guarding the blocked tunnel. He lunged and ran one man through the gut, then shifted his weight onto his back leg and lifted his bloodied sword to meet the second man's attack. A quick twist disengaged his weapon, another deft turn brought the blade slicing across the man's throat. On the backswing he caught the final man's blade. He pushed up, forcing the enjoined blades high, and leveled his silver wand at the man's chest.

Another tiny arrow of light sizzled forth, diving into the man's chest. Elaith dove aside as the magic weapon exploded from within, transforming the man into a crimson mist.

The elf ran up over the spilled crates and raced nimbly down the other side. Quickly he found the second hidden door, one known only to him, and slipped down into the tunnel that led to a tailor's shop two streets down.

As he emerged from the fitting room, Elaith heard the tolling bells that summoned the Watch to tend the fire. He was not particularly concerned: The warehouse was constructed of solid stone and would withstand the blaze. It held little of value, and he could well afford to lose a few empty crates.

Nor did he regret the survival of some of the "messengers." If a few escaped to bring word of his defiance to the merchant lords, so much the better. After all, he had the Mhaorkiira and the dream spheres. He now possessed the perfect weapon to strike back at those who had the best reason to send such a message.

That he intended to do. His vengeance would be lingering, highly amusing—and deadly.

The elf set a quick pace back toward his fortress home and the beckoning, compelling magic of the dark gem.

Ten

Arilyn led the way through the narrow streets of Skullport, with Danilo following close on her heels. Although the city lay directly beneath his native Waterdeep, and though both were port cities, she could not conceive of two places more different.

Here all was squalid, sordid, and ugly. Ramshackle buildings leaned and listed as precariously as scuttled ships. Creatures from at least two-score races, many of them outlawed in the city above, shoved past each other on the crowded streets. A one-legged beggar was toppled by the rude throng. He made no call for help, obviously realizing that none would be forthcoming, but struggled to right himself with the aid of a home-carved crutch. But like most of Skullport, the man's appearance was deceiving. Far from helpless, he nimbly sliced the ear off a sly-faced goblin who sought to pick his pockets. Like his intended victim, the goblin did not seek aid. He merely snatched up the bit of living leather, clapped it to his head, and reeled off in search of a healer—or possibly just a mirror and a needle.

Arilyn's companion took this in with growing dismay.

She'd had misgivings about bringing Danilo into this dank, dismal, lawless place. Though at her insistence he had donned rough clothes more suitable to a dockhand than a gentleman bard, he looked thoroughly, miserably out of place.

"I must say, this is no improvement on Oth's cistern," he commented. "At least *that* was dry."

Arilyn could see his point. In Skullport, water was everywhere. Although it was a port city, it was entirely underground, far below sea level. Water dripped from the cavern ceilings and puddled on the walkways. It gave sustenance to the strange creeping molds and glowing fungi that writhed on the walls of the ramshackle buildings or inched along the walkways. The scent of rot and mildew permeated everything, and foul mist clung to the lamplight. Even after a few minutes in the city, Arilyn's clothes clung damply to her, and her companion's mood was becoming nearly as oppressive as the thick air.

"You wanted to be part of my world," she said with only a moderate degree of exaggeration. "This is the sort of place I end up going."

Danilo glanced pointedly at her sword, which was dark and silent. "I would wager there are few forest elves in these parts. Shouldn't we go find some? Elsewhere?"

She pulled the neck of her clinging shirt away from her throat and dashed a damp lock off her forehead. "The sooner we're finished here, the sooner we leave." She nodded toward a row of dangerously tilting wooden buildings, lined up with all the precision of a patrol of drunken orcs, and started toward the narrow street that snaked between them.

Behind her Danilo cursed with impressive creativity. "For what, exactly, are we looking?"

"Perfume," Arilyn said dryly as she skirted a rather suspect pile. She recognized it as the spoor of a manticore and quickened her pace. It was relatively fresh, and she had no desire to confront a monster with the body of a lion and the face and cunning of a man.

"Perfume. Good thinking," he congratulated her. "Given our current surroundings, I suggest we purchase it by the vat."

She shot a glare over her shoulder. "Do you intend to whine the entire way there?"

"Back, too, I should think. No sense doing half a job."

A trio of kobolds scuttled toward them from behind a pile of crates. They were hideous creatures, goblinkin whose bald heads came not much higher than Arilyn's sword belt. Their bulging yellow eyes held a frantic look, but their ratlike tails wagged in an eerily precise imitation of hounds eager to please their master. Their arms were full of fabric, not weapons, but Arilyn did not slow her pace.

"You look, maybe buy," one of them pleaded as it jogged alongside the half-elf. "Got lotsa good cloaks. Not much worn. Only one gots blood and guts on it, and them's already dried."

"Now there's a vendor's cry that any of Waterdeep's roving merchants might envy," Danilo murmured. He slowed down to address the kobold. "Blood and guts, eh? Does one pay extra for that sort of ornamentation?"

"Sure, sure. You want it, we put."

"Ah. An admirable arrangement, provided one is not the source of that particular decoration."

This bit of locution clearly baffled the small merchant. He settled back on his heels, and his rat's tail lashed about in apparent consternation, but the moment passed quickly, and the kobolds pressed in.

Arilyn elbowed one out of the way. "Don't encourage them," she told Danilo in a low voice. "Do you plan to die down here?"

"Oh, surely not. Three kobolds are no threat."

"Neither is one mouse. Problem is, there's never only *one* mouse. More are always hidden nearby. How do you think 'three kobolds' got their merchandise in the first place?"

This excellent reasoning prompted Danilo to pick up his pace. He kept step with the half-elf as she wove her way through the squalid town, toward the small shop where assassins purchased death by the drop.

"Pantagora's Poisons," Danilo said, reading the sign aloud. "Right to the point. No pretense, no dissembling. I find that quite refreshing."

Arilyn sent him a warning look and pushed open the door. The scene beyond was like something from a Northman's battlefield or a butcher's nightmare.

The air was thick with a distinctively sweet, coppery scent. Flies buzzed over sodden shapes. Dark pools seeped into the old wood of the floor. Somehow, blood had been spattered as high as the rafters. Here and there it had dried even as it dripped down, making it appear that the sodden timbers had wept long, black tears over the poison merchants' fate.

Never had Arilyn seen anything quite like it. She kicked at an empty boot, wondering how it had happened to come loose of its wearer. On impulse, she made a quick mental tally of bodies and footwear. This boot was an extra. To all appearances, its former wearer had been dissolved as surely as if he'd been hit by a blast of dragonfire. From the inside.

She stooped beside one of the dead men. To someone who had seen death as often as she had, a corpse could talk without benefit of spell or prayer.

The signs were there, but they were conflicting and deeply disturbing. Thin, precise cuts marked the man's body. Arilyn rolled the dead man over and tugged up his shirt. There was little bruising on his back. Small wonder. By the time he died, there had been little blood left in his body to settle. The fine, thin sword that had killed this man had left layers of wounds, dealing death by the inch, by the trickle and drop. Someone had toyed with the man, taking time to kill him so he lingered far longer than she would have imagined possible.

Strange behavior for a thief. It was possible, of course, that the killer was an assassin by trade, perhaps a regular customer whose skills and habits made it easier to kill than to pay. It seemed to Arilyn, though, that any assassin prompted by survival would never risk such an expenditure of time and vitriol. This killing held all the hallmarks of vengeance—or rage, or insanity, or an evil so intense that it no longer considered proportion or consequence.

Stranger still was the nature of the weapon. No human-made blade was so thin or so keen. The man had been slaughtered with an elven weapon. Of that Arilyn was grimly certain. Her mother's people were fierce, often merciless fighters, but few were given to such depravity. She knew of only two or three elves who would do such a thing. Just recently, in fact, she had seen Elaith Craulnober toy with a tren assassin, in very similar fashion.

Her sharp ears caught the sound of furtive footsteps on the walkway outside the shop. She rocked back onto her heels and rose in a single, swift move. Gliding over to the door, she drew her sword and gestured for Danilo to move to the other side of the frame.

Slowly the door eased open, and a small, furtive faced peered around the corner. Arilyn stepped in and pressed the tip of her blade against Diloontier's throat.

The perfumer shrieked and squeezed his eyes shut, as if he could block out the double terror of the looming sword and the carnage beyond. His face paled to the color of old parchment, and the bones of his legs seemed to melt to the consistency of jellied eel.

Before Arilyn could speak, Danilo seized the swaying man by the front of his shirt and jerked him into the room. He shook the perfume merchant as a vermin hound might worry a rat. This served to bring some color back to the man's face. When he started to struggle with a resolve and vigor that suggested he could stand on his own, Danilo released him.

Diloontier cracked open one eye and shuddered. "Too late," he mourned. "Gone, all of it!"

"That raises some interesting questions. We'll get to them in time," Arilyn assured him. She lifted her sword to his throat again. "What do you know about the tren?"

The man's eyes slid furtively to one side. "Never heard of them."

She gave her sword an encouraging little twitch. "Odd, that tunnels riddled with tren markings should converge beneath your shop. Strange that a door from the sewers leads into your drying shed. You can talk to me about this, or you can sit before the Lord's Council."

"Talking!" he conceded in a high-pitched voice. "Yes, it is true that sometimes I act as a broker for wealthy men and women who desire the tren's services. I make arrangements, but only through a second or third or twenty-fourth party! Truly! That is the agreed-upon method. It ensures I cannot give you or anyone else the name of my clients."

Arilyn wondered how the man might respond if presented with a name. She sent Danilo a look that mingled inquiry and apology. His lips thinned, but he gave a slight nod of agreement. She turned back to Diloontier.

"All right, then. If you can't name your clients, I'll do it for you. Lady Cassandra Thann."

"I am a perfumer. Many of the noble folk patronize my shop," he began evasively. His explanation broke off in a surprised yelp of pain, and he looked down in horror at the stain on the half-elf's gleaming sword and the blood dripping onto his shirtfront.

"Not an important vein," Arilyn said evenly, "but I know where those are."

"I cannot tell you anything! My customers prize confidentiality!" he protested.

"More than you prize your neck?"

Diloontier didn't need long to balance that particular scale. "Potions of youthfulness," he said, speaking so quickly that the words almost tripped over each other in their eagerness to emerge. "The Lady Cassandra has been buying them for ages, with the coming of each new moon. Forgive me, but how else could she keep the passing years from wresting her beauty from her?"

"I take it that you are not well acquainted with the lady," Danilo said dryly. "If anyone could stare down Father Time and win, it is she."

Arilyn lowered her sword. "What did you come here to buy?"

"It hardly matters, does it? There is nothing more here of value. Clearly, I did not kill these men. For all I know, you did!"

The half-elf's eyes went hard, but she realized at once that this was no idle threat. She was not the only one who would recognize the marks of an elven sword, and once again, here she stood over the work of an assassin. Fortunately, Diloontier had his own reputation with which to contend. "Mention our presence here to anyone," she snapped, "and the Watch captain will be reading an anonymous letter about your visit to this little shop. Now go!"

Diloontier darted for the exit. His boots beat a frantic, stumbling rhythm upon the wooden walk. The half-elf sighed and sheathed her sword.

Danilo looked sharply at her. "You let him go. Do you believe him?"

"About Lady Cassandra? Not a word of it. What does she need with youth potions, if she has elven blood? Although I suspect she would support Diloontier's lie rather than lay claim to her heritage."

He did not refute her. "There is nothing more to be seen here."

Arilyn was silent for a long moment. Actually, she suspected there was much, much more to be gleaned in this city. The tren came from these tunnels. So did poisons, which had most likely been used to kill Lady Dezlentyr. Arilyn had gone to considerable trouble to find out Diloontier's supplier, visiting acquaintances she had not seen for years and creating markers that she dreaded paying.

However, at the moment there was little more that they could do. This place had yielded not answers, but new and disturbing questions. "Whatever Diloontier came to buy is long gone," she agreed. She nudged at one of the corpses with her boot. "Whoever killed these men has it."

"Killing to procure poison," Danilo mused. "Seems rather an indirect way to go about things, doesn't it? This is not my sphere of expertise, mind you, but it seems to me that the affair would run much smoother all around if the middle merchant were removed from the transaction."

That was precisely what Arilyn intended to do, but she was not yet ready to voice her intentions. In many ways, Danilo embraced elven ways more wholeheartedly than she herself did. He trusted Elaith Craulnober and the pledge of Elf-friend. She could not bring herself to destroy that until she knew for certain that her suspicions described truth rather than her own bias.

Nor was she quite ready to confront the old patterns and roles into which she was falling with such ease. Every time she turned she was slapped with reminders of her dark reputation. If truth be told, she felt more at home in Waterdeep's underbelly than she did at a nobleman's ball. Her human side was coming grimly to the fore, while the elven magic of her moonblade was oddly sporadic. At the rate she was going, Danilo might not have to worry about the inconvenience of life with an elven hero.

Arilyn glanced down at the moonblade, half hoping that it would summon her to duty with faint green light. Of course it did not.

She wondered if it would ever do so again.

* * * * *

When they returned to the city above, Danilo took at once to his bathhouse. After an hour in a hot tub, the memory of the underground city's fetid stench began to fade. Danilo was soaking still when his steward came tapping at the door.

"Your pardon, sir, but you have received a most urgent message from Lord Rhammas."

News of an invading flight of dragons would not have been more unexpected. Danilo all but leaped from the tub, sending bathwater and soap flying like a flock of small, startled birds. He seized a towel and strode from his dressing room. "Is someone hurt? Sick? Or is it Judith? Gods! Her babe is due at any time. Her first!"

The halfling wiped a blob of scented foam from his forehead. "Your sister is fine, sir. She has another moon and more to await the child's birth," he reminded Dan. "This message regards a personal matter of highly sensitive nature. Your father bids you to attend him at The Laughing Mermaid with all haste. I will have your horse brought to the front gate."

Somewhat reassured but still mightily puzzled, Danilo quickly dressed and then rode the few blocks to the posh tavern.

The Laughing Mermaid was one of the few drinking spots in the staid North Ward. It was equally famed for its sumptuous gaming tables and its small, private rooms. Danilo knew that Lord Rhammas prized the tavern as a place to gossip and gamble with his equally idle peers, but he had never thought of his father having cause to employ one of the meeting rooms. Certainly, Danilo had never expected a summons to such a meeting.

His curiosity was near fever pitch as he dismounted in front of the enormous, ugly marble statue of a centaur. He tossed his reins to the attentive groom and hurried up the stairs to the front hall.

One of the minotaur guards nodded, recognizing Danilo as a member. The creature beckoned for him to follow, then trotted off, its massive haunches bunching with each stride. Its long, curving horns swept through a low-hanging chandelier, coaxing a hushed tinkle from the crystals that brought to mind a bevy of schoolgirls whispering and giggling behind their small hands.

The minotaur stopped before a thick oaken door and snorted insistently, as if to indicate that its mission was complete—or would be, once Danilo entered the room. The sound was disconcertingly like a bull readying for the charge, and Danilo got the distinct impression that he could attend this meeting under his own power or be tossed through the door on the minotaur's horns. He gave the creature a coin, then slipped into the room.

Rhammas Thann rose to meet his son, reaching his hand out in the gesture of one comrade to another. Danilo took his father's hand as if this were the most normal situation in the world. They sat down across a small table and for a few minutes engaged in the sort of meaningless talk that oiled the wheels of every such meeting the room had ever hosted.

Finally Rhammas got to the point. "You enjoy considerable personal wealth. The fund your mother and I started for you at your birth has increased a thousand-fold and could keep you in style for the rest of your days. You have also your share of the wine business and the increase on your investment in the bard's college. I hear both are doing exceptionally well."

Danilo nodded cautiously. "That is the shape of things."

"I have cause to ask that you part with some small portion of your ready cash," Lord Rhammas said stiffly, and with obvious reluctance. The man paused, grimaced, and squared his shoulders to steel himself for words yet to come. "A matter of some delicacy has been brought to my attention. It is one I would just as soon keep from your mother's eyes."

"Ah." Danilo settled back in his chair and considered the summons in this clear light.

Of all his siblings, Danilo was the least involved in the Thann family affairs—and the son least likely to report back to Lady Cassandra. Judith, the sister nearest him in age and temperament, also tended to follow her own mind and inclinations, but Judith's husband, a merchant sea captain who cut a dashing figure and who claimed distant ties to Cormyr's royal family, owed his position and wealth to the Thann family shipping concerns. He was therefore as devoted to Lady Cassandra's whims and moods as any lapdog. Judith was as yet too besotted to realize what manner of toady shared her bed, and she held back nothing from her husband. Lord Rhammas would get little discretion from that quarter.

"A personal matter?" Danilo took care to keep his tone even, to ask a question without offering censure.

"That is so. Before I proceed, I must have your word that this will not be bandied about in one of your inane ballads."

"So pledged," Danilo said shortly. The comment stung more than it should. As well accustomed as he was to his family's indulgent disdain, it was becoming increasingly difficult to maintain the role he had chosen to play.

"Very well, then. A woman of my acquaintance finds herself in distress and wishes to leave this city quietly and soon. Discretion is imperative. Your mother tells me you have some connections among the Harpers. You have managed such things?"

"Many times," Danilo assured him. Of course, never once had he considered that such skills might enable him to attend his father's mistress—and by the sound of things, a woman inconveniently with child.

Danilo was not certain how he should feel about the matter. Bastards were nothing new among the nobility, or among the common folk either, for that matter. Many marriages were made for gain or convenience, and children conceived outside such unions were usually acknowledged and granted some measure of acceptance.

Even so, he could understand his father's desire to keep this matter entirely from Lady Cassandra's eyes. If his father wished to discharge his responsibilities with extreme discretion, Danilo was not about to gainsay him. He was not certain, however, whether this unexpected request should rightly be viewed as an insult or an expression of confidence.

One way or another, it mattered not. This was the first thing his father had ever asked of him. Whatever Rhammas thought of him, Danilo could hardly refuse.

"I will see the lady safely out of the city in a matter of days and see that she does not want for anything. Will that serve?"

"Admirably." Rhammas pushed a folded bit of parchment across the table. "You can find her there. She is expecting a visit from you this night. I hope that will be convenient."

It was far from convenient. Danilo considered the day he had spent and the plans he had for the night ahead. His servants were preparing a private feast for two, then anticipating a night's holiday while their master and his lady had the house to themselves—a stolen hour or two before they tended Danilo's latest social responsibility.

Frustration swept through him. One more duty, one

more delay—and this time, he could not place the blame on Arilyn's moonblade.

"Convenient is not the word I would have chosen," he commented. "Nonetheless, all will be done as you ask."

* * * * *

When Danilo sent word canceling their evening plans, Arilyn had returned with the messenger and insisted upon accompanying Danilo into the Dock Ward. He seemed oddly preoccupied and was reticent about details of the task ahead.

A simple matter, he told her. He would make the first contact, then two Harper agents would see the plan through. That much was true, of that Arilyn was certain, but she could not guess what truths remained unspoken.

Her questions settled into certainty the moment the young woman opened the door to her chamber. This woman was not Rhammas Thann's mistress, but his child.

Arilyn glanced from Danilo to the girl. The resemblance was remarkable. Though her hair was an unusual shade of pale red-gold, her face had the same well-shaped features and sharply defined bones. Also familiar was the slender, graceful form reminiscent of dancers or—and this insight startled Arilyn—gold elves. The girl could probably claim an elven ancestor no more than two or three generations back. Arilyn had never seen the evidence of Danilo's distant elven heritage, but it was there beyond doubt in the mirror that was his sister's face.

Nor did the similarity end there. Familiar mischief lurked behind the girl's uncertain smile and intelligence was evident in the quick, observant glance she cast over her visitors. Arilyn would wager that the girl didn't miss much.

The tavern maid seemed reassured by what she saw, at any rate. She stepped back and swept a hand toward the poor room—a gesture that was at once sincere welcome and self-parody. "You are kind to come, Lord Thann."

"Lilly," Danilo said, studying the girl with puzzlement. "I did not expect to see you."

"I'll warrant you did not," she agreed. She glanced over at the half-elf and gave her a small, knowing smile—one that confirmed what Arilyn saw and gave a wordless, wistful commentary on the blindness of men. "Thank you for coming, lass. I'm taking it as a kindness that you came along with Lord Thann, seeing as how rough this part of town can be."

"You'll be safe soon enough," Arilyn assured her. She looked to Danilo to explain the plan.

His attention had been captured by a small object on the bed. "Is that what I think it is?" he demanded.

Lilly winced. "Aye, I'm guessing it is. A weakness of mine, I'm afraid."

"A dangerous one," he said sternly, sounding more like Khelben Arunsun than Arilyn would have thought possible. She debated whether to remark on this and decided to keep this observation on hand for a later time. It was always wise to have a hidden weapon or two.

After a few words about the risks of taking magic lightly, Danilo quickly explained the arrangements. Two Harpers, Hector and Cynthia, would come to the tavern toward the end of the late shift. Hector would bring a small covered cart to the back alley, and Cynthia would slip up to Lilly's room. The two women were to change clothes, and Cynthia would stay in Lilly's place. Hector would take Lilly to the North Gate and place her in the charge of a discreet caravan master, who would give her passage to an orchard village outside the city. From there, it was westward to Suzail along with the new-pressed cider. At each step, Lilly would be supplied with coin and lodging. A substantial sum would await her in

Suzail, enough to get her started in a new life of her choosing.

Lilly's eyes swam as she listened to Danilo's words. "This is your doing, not your father's. I'd wager my life on that," she said softly. A long moment passed, and she added, "It's more than I'd dare hope for, but for all that, I'll be sad to go."

"It is hard to leave home and family," Danilo agreed.

A wave of sympathy swept through Arilyn as she realized the pain these unwitting words would bring.

The girl's tears spilled over. She quickly dashed them away with the back of one hand and gave a shaky smile. "Aye, that it is."

As they rose to leave, Lilly dipped a curtsey to Dan and then held both hands out to Arilyn. It was a common form of leave-taking among women of the working class, a simple statement that the recipient was valued enough to warrant putting aside work entirely, if but for the moment. Arilyn understood the gesture for what it was: the only claim to sisterhood that Lilly would make.

On rare impulse, the warrior went one better. She gently pushed aside Lilly's offered hands and took the younger woman in a sister's embrace.

"The strength of Corellon, the beauty of Hanneli, the joy of Aerali," she said softly, speaking the traditional elven blessing in the language of their foremothers.

Lilly pulled away and managed a smile. "Many's the year since I heard those words. The same to you, lass, though I've more respect for the music of the thing than to wrap my caterwauling tongue around it. Now, off with you both, before Hamish misunderstands the nature of this visit and tries to charge you rent by the hour." She made little shooing gestures with her hands, as if herding recalcitrant chickens.

They shooed, walking down the creaky back stairs and into the alley beyond, where Danilo attacked the problem at hand with unusual vigor. He wanted Arilyn's opinion on the best spot for the cart to wait, her assessment of possible ambush spots, and what they should do to ascertain whether or not additional Watch guards were needed. With an attention to detail that would not have been out of place in King Azoun's court, they went over the small escape.

When that was settled, Danilo's supply of words ran uncharacteristically dry. They walked together in silence, and the young bard's expression was unusually pensive. Arilyn began to doubt whether Danilo was as oblivious to Lilly's identity as he had seemed. After a time the half-elf's curiosity overflowed.

"Does Lady Cassandra know about Lilly?"

He looked startled. "I for one do not intend to apprise her! If Lord Rhammas wishes to confess his mistresses, he must tend to the matter himself."

"It's a bit late for that," Arilyn said dryly. When Danilo sent her a puzzled look, she shook her head in astonishment and dug in her bag for the tiny bronze mirror she carried. This she thrust before Danilo's face.

"Take a good look, and try to remember where you last saw those features. I'm thinking that you—and your sister—both managed to get a bit of elven blood from your various mothers, but you both got your father's eyes."

His puzzled expression froze, then he nodded slowly as he understood the truth of it. "Of course. I should have seen it. Perhaps I did—Lilly is a merry lass, and I liked her upon first meeting. She was serving at the Gemstone Ball," he explained. Sudden anger flashed into his eyes. "She was serving in her own father's house! How could Rhammas countenance such an insult to his child?"

"Perhaps he didn't know. You only learned of it just now."

"There is that," Danilo admitted. A faint smile crept onto his lips as he pondered this revelation. "A sister.

How marvelous. You would think I had enough siblings that the novelty would have worn off, wouldn't you?"

"She needs you. The others don't," Arilyn pointed out.

Danilo looked surprised, then pleased. "That is so." He considered the matter and then cast a sidelong glance at her. "What would you say about wintering in Suzail? It is close to Cormanthyr. If the sages are right about a harsh winter to come, there will be the usual attempts to reduce the borders of the elven forest to firewood. Chances are, you'll be heading that way, anyway."

"True enough."

"It's settled, then," he said happily, taking her comment as assent.

Arilyn listened as he chatted on, full of plans for their time together and the life they would help his new-found sister build. It sounded so easy and hopeful that she could almost believe it might come true.

She glanced at the moonblade, almost afraid that it would be aglow with warning light or humming with silent energy. However, the elven sword was silent, as if content at last to reflect Danilo's high spirits and bright hopes.

Eleven

Midnight had not yet come, and already Danilo had borne witness to the death of some twenty barrels of wine and the subsequent birth of two new betrothals, a dozen covert business deals, and three challenges to duels scheduled to be fought upon the morrow. By these measures, Galinda Raventree's annual costume ball was its usual success.

Of course, there was the buzz created by Haedrak's arrival. A city obsessed with nobility could not resist the lure of the young man's claim to royalty. For many years, it had been common belief the royal house of Tethyr had been obliterated in the terrible wars. A few minor relatives survived, and from time to time one made a dubious claim, but Haedrak arrived in Waterdeep with unassailable credentials, not the least of which was the support of Elminster the Sage and the bard Storm Silverhand. Haedrak had expressed a desire to unite with Zaranda, the mage turned mercenary who had recently been acclaimed queen of the city of Zazesspur, and to join with her in uniting all of Tethyr. He was in Waterdeep gathering support for the Tethyr Reclamation from the wealthy, the bored, and the adventurous.

Danilo supposed Haedrak would do well enough. A dark, thin man with a serious face and a small pointed black beard, he looked more like a scribe than a warrior, but Waterdeep, enamored as she was by royalty, would no doubt flock to his banner. It was almost amusing how the nobles tripped over each other in their eagerness to be seen in Haedrak's shadow.

The most entertaining spectacle, in Dan's opinion, was Arilyn's participation in this frivolous event. The shopkeeper who'd supplied them both with costumes had outfitted Arilyn as Titania, the legendary queen of the faerie realm.

This had proven nothing less than inspired, for it built upon the half-elf's fey heritage, transforming her from somber warrior to a creature of heart-stopping beauty. The costume was a marvel of translucent wings and floating, glimmering silvery skirts, but the shopkeeper had not stopped there. She had dressed Arilyn's black hair in clusters of ringlets dusted with silvery glitter. The half-elf's eyes were remarkable to begin with—a deep vivid blue flecked with gold—but cosmetics made them appear enormous, exotically tilted at the outer corners, and startlingly blue against her white skin. Her face had been buffed with some iridescent powder, and it glowed like moonstone in the soft candlelight. In all, Danilo congratulated himself on having had the good sense to lose his heart to this marvelous woman years ago before the general rush began.

That was the second source of his private entertainment. More than a few of Danilo's peers had started to pay court to the apparent faerie queen, only to reconsider the notion when the half-elf turned upon them a flat, level gaze more appropriate to a battlefield than a ballroom. Faced with a forbidding Arilyn, even the most intrepid or inebriated man suddenly remembered pressing business on the far side of the hall.

This amused Danilo to no end. He supposed that evinced some serious character deficit, but he saw no immediate cure for it. He had always enjoyed Arilyn from their unpromising beginning to the complicated present, and he could not get out of the habit. He gave a nod of mock sympathy to the latest of her spurned suitors, then flicked a nonexistent bit of lint from the ruffle at his cuff.

"You're looking smug," remarked Regnet Amcathra.

Danilo's pleasure in the evening deepened as he turned to face his longtime friend. "Why should I not? Winning that lady's regard was no small accomplishment. I like to think that sterling personal qualities, which admittedly are well hidden, enabled me to accomplish this feat."

The nobleman chuckled. His amusement stopped abruptly as two men disguised as a centaur thundered past in pursuit of a coyly fleeing nymph.

Danilo studied the strange tableau. The centaur's head was undoubtedly that of Simon Ilzimmer, a black-bearded, broad-chested mage who looked so positively saturnine that Danilo would not have wagered whether or not the hoofs he sported were genuine.

The back end of the centaur was not quite as motivated toward pursuit, but he stumbled gamely along. Not nimbly enough, however, and the costume's fabric tore as the "creature" broke in half. Simon, nothing daunted, pounded off in pursuit of the nymph. The centaur's anonymous rump, a role undoubtedly played by a servant or possibly a family member of lesser rank and lighter purse, took a few staggering steps in pursuit of unity. He quickly abandoned the quest and went off in search of a full mug, apparently not overly concerned by the statement his partial costume made.

Regnet shook his head in disgust. "After that spectacle, I am almost inclined to believe what they are saying about the Ilzimmer clan."

It was on the tip of Danilo's tongue to ask what that might be, but it occurred to him that if he did, Regnet would probably tell him. Dan and Arilyn had attended this evening's affair for the express purpose of gathering information, but he saw little profit in the sort of salacious talk that Simon Ilzimmer inspired.

"Shame on you for spreading such tales! You have been spending too much time with Myrna," Danilo pointed out.

His friend heaved a heartfelt sigh. "On that, we are in accord. Speaking of the lady, she appears to be searching the crowd for me. You will excuse me while I run shrieking into the streets."

"Certainly," Dan replied. "I would offer to detain her, but the bonds of friendship go only so far."

Regnet snorted with good-natured scorn. "Don't worry, I wouldn't do it for you, either. Farewell, coward."

Dan chuckled and turned back to survey the scene before him. He was truly of no mind for festivities, but this would be one of his last chances to study the peerage for signs of enmity deep enough to inspire Oth's assassination. All of Waterdeep society gathered for the costume ball, which was one of the last large parties before many of the merchant nobility left for their country estates or southern villas. It was one of the most lavish affairs of the season, and one of Danilo's favorites.

At least, it had been until this year. Usually he enjoyed the pageantry and silly excess, but this year there seemed to be a decidedly sylvan flavor to the costumes. In addition to the usual pirates, orcs, Moonshae druids, drow, and such like, there were an inordinate number of revelers dressed as forest elves.

Even Myrna Cassalanter picked up this theme—if only as an excuse to bare vast expanses of the creamy skin that was her best feature. Nearly every exposed inch of the woman was decorated with the swirling brown and green designs that represented some artist's conception of what wild elf tattoos must look like. Myrna had taken the notion of wild greenwood hunters a bit too far, perhaps. She had woven peacock feathers into her bright red hair and hung a necklace of porcelain beads shaped like dragons' teeth around her neck.

All these imitation forest elves served to tweak at Danilo's more painful ruminations. Arilyn's response had been utterly unexpected and no help at all. She had taken one glance at Myrna and excused herself from the room. Danilo had found her in the cloakroom, clutching her sides and rocking with silent laughter.

"Not authentic, I take it," Danilo had observed.

She'd wiped her streaming eyes and subsided to a chuckle. "Not even close." She frowned and plucked at the diaphanous layers of her skirts. "Who am I to talk? When was the last time you saw a six-foot faerie?"

The answer to that, in Dan's opinion, was "not often enough." He and Arilyn had decided to go separate ways for much of the evening, assuming that Danilo's peers might be more forthcoming with gossip if the half-elf were not too close at hand. Her hearing was keener than any human's, so she could gather information in a different fashion.

Apart from talk of Haedrak's claim, most of the gossip Danilo had heard focused upon the party's hostess. He watched Galinda Raventree as she glided about the dance floor, deftly steering compatible guests toward each other and just as skillfully heading off possible confrontations. The woman was a marvel—he had often remarked to his fellow Lords that she would be a redoubtable diplomat.

His *fellow Lords*, was it? Danilo grimaced as he realized that he had yet to return the Lord's Helm to Piergeiron. So many other matters demanded his attention. He would be glad to get the city and its demands behind him and begin shaping his life in a pattern more to his liking.

This returned his thoughts firmly to Lilly and to the confrontation he intended to have with Lord Rhammas concerning duty to family—*all* members of that family, regardless of which side of the blanket they happened to be born on.

He handed his empty goblet to a passing servant and took off in search of his father. Not a difficult task—he merely followed the tang of pipe smoke to the room where Lord Rhammas and a dozen or so of his peers waged war with weapons of thick, painted parchment.

Danilo had never been one for cards, but courtesy demanded he wait and watch until Rhammas tired of the game. Finally the older man threw down a losing hand and announced his desire for air.

He did not acknowledge his son's tacit request for conversation, but he fell into step and they walked out to the garden together. Neither man spoke until Danilo was reasonably certain they would not be overheard.

"All has been done as you requested, sir."

The older man nodded. "Good. That's settled, then."

"After a fashion, yes. But I am curious: why has Lilly never come to light before? Did you not know of her?"

Rhammas sent him a quelling glance. "The matter has been handled. There are other, more important concerns to attend."

More important than a newfound daughter? Danilo did not speak the words, but he saw from the flash of anger in his father's eyes that he had not managed to keep the challenge from his face. Well, now that his opinion was known, he might as well be shorn for a sheep as for a lamb. "I cannot conceive of anything more important," Dan said softly.

"Then apparently you haven't heard of the raid upon the consortium's air caravan."

This was the first time his father had ever mentioned the family business in Danilo's hearing. The shock of this was quickly overtaken by the implication of his father's words. A feel of cold, creeping dread threaded its way through Danilo's irritation.

"The caravan was a joint effort among several of the noble families," Rhammas explained, oblivious to his son's stunned reaction to this news. "Fine cargo—gems, swords, small statues, and the like—were flown to Silverymoon, with the intention of bringing back more of the same."

Danilo's mind raced with dire possibility. Foremost among them was Bronwyn's safety. She had sent him word that she planned to join an air caravan organized by the Ilzimmer and Gundwynd famiies, in which both Elaith Craulnober and Mizzen Doar, the crystal merchant, had purchased passage.

"Flown," he repeated.

Rhammas took this single world as a question. "Griffons, pegasi, large birds. Ingenious notion, but we all warned Lord Gundwynd that he stood to lose a fortune should things go awry. Those beasts were at least as valuable as the cargo they carried."

"Were?"

This time Danilo did intend the question. The attack must have been devastating, if some of these fierce beasts had been lost in the fighting!

His father either missed the question or chose not to dwell upon such unpleasantness. "I must say, this economy of response is not your usual custom. Well done. Quite refreshing."

Danilo shook off what might have been either compliment or insult. If Bronwyn had traveled in that caravan, and Elaith as well, either or both might be dead.

"Were there survivors?"

"Oh, Lord Gundwynd came through just fine. Tough old bird—couldn't kill that man with a meat axe. So did some of the mercenaries, and most of the merchants. The caravan lost a few guards and some hired hands. And the cargo, of course. Bad business all around."

It was an unusually long speech. Lord Rhammas lifted his pipe in a gesture of unmistakable finality. He took a draw, frowned, and then held it out for inspection. The wisp of smoke had vanished. He murmured something unintelligible, then wandered off in search of fire.

Danilo scanned the room for a likely source of further information. Nearby, Myrna Cassalanter was busily plying her family trade. The gossipmonger spoke in low, hurried tones to a pair of young women—an incongruous pair, since one was clad as shepherdess complete with beribboned crook, and the other was wearing a fur wrap and carrying a wolf mask on a stick. The protector and the ravager of sheep listened with identical expressions of shocked delight, and the glances they slid toward their hostess left little doubt as to the subject of Myrna's spiteful tale. Nonetheless, Danilo moved closer. Myrna might be annoying, but she served a purpose.

"Our Galinda has debts, you see," explained the gossipmonger, "but to maintain appearances, she has been replacing her gems with false stones."

"Her jewelry looks the same as ever," observed one of the women, eyeing the emerald pendant that nestled in the hollow of Galinda's throat.

"What would you expect? Even the faux pieces are fine work—if you consider counterfeiting an art." Myrna paused to give weight to her next words. "Apparently the Ilzimmer family does."

She glanced up at Dan's approach, and a shimmer of malicious delight crossed her face. "Lord *Thann*. You've heard about the air caravan, no doubt? But of course you have, since your family had an investment in its *success*."

The emphasis she gave to the final word held a nasty insinuation. Of what, Danilo was not certain. He pasted a bland smile on his face. "Actually, I have come to inquire on that very matter. What more do you know than is commonly spoken?"

The woman cocked her bright head and considered him as a horse trader might size up a plow nag for possible resale. "I hear that this year's spiced winterfest wine will be extraordinary. Ten bottles would be a reasonable exchange."

Myrna's companions frowned, clearly displeased by this blatant display of commerce at a social event. They withdrew with frosty little bows and flittered off to spread tales of their own.

"Strange that you should be seeking answers from me," Myrna purred, clearly enjoying herself. "There are others who could tell you for a smaller fee, or none at all. I do not complain, mind you."

Danilo was in no mood to spar. "For a simple answer, speedily delivered, you might expect an extra bottle."

The woman pouted. "Oh, very well. The favored rumors suggest that the theft was the work of insiders. The bandits were too well and cannily armed, and they lay hidden in wait in the very place the caravan used as a rest stop on the way north. Most are suspicious of Elaith Craulnober, of course. He traveled to Silverymoon with the caravan but not back. Yet many saw him take part in the battle. He disappeared soon after, riding a Gundwynd pegasus."

This news was disturbing but not entirely unexpected. Whether the elf had a part in the theft or not, he would be suspected. "And Bronwyn?"

"Who?"

"The young woman who keeps The Curious Past. You have been in her shop at least a dozen times. Small woman, long brown hair, big eyes."

"Oh, her." The noblewoman's tone was dismissive, almost disdainful.

"Do you know how she fared?" Dan persisted.

Myrna shrugged, looking none too pleased to be presented with questions for which she had no answers—even if the subject of inquiry was nothing but a common little shopkeeper. "Ask the elf. He was there."

She pointed to the far side of the room. Danilo's eyes widened as they settled on a tall, slender figure clad in deep purple and silver. Elaith had chosen an elaborate costume of an era long past, worn by elves and humans alike in the ancient courts of Tethyr. Either the elf was being unusually diplomatic or his costume was the equivalent of a green cloak in the forest—an attempt to blend in. Many wore the purple of Tethyr in Haedrak's honor.

Danilo made his way across to the elf as quickly as he could navigate the crowd. "You have had an eventful trip, I hear," he began.

The elf gave him a faint, mocking smile. "Let us dispense with the usual pleasantries and get to the meat of the matter. When I left Bronwyn, she was in good health, if poor company. She is a most resourceful young woman. Most resourceful," he added with rueful emphasis.

Danilo was beginning to see the shape of things. He also felt more than a little guilty about agreeing to have Elaith watched and followed. "I am always glad to hear word of Bronwyn," he said carefully. "She is an old friend."

"And a new Harper," the elf said. "Spare me the sophistry. I am watched by the Harpers and others. This is nothing new. Whether you had a hand in Bronwyn's task or not, I neither know nor care. Either way, I'm sure you are interested in the outcome."

"Well, now that you mention it."

"Both Bronwyn and I lost treasure in the raid—for which, I assure you, I was not responsible."

These statements set Danilo back on his heels. "Well, so much for the deft feint, the clever exchange of attack and parry. I am disarmed before I draw my sword."

The elf lifted one silver eyebrow. "Is that so? You accept my word on the matter so easily?"

"Why wouldn't I?"

"Many people would name your credulity unwise," Elaith pointed out. "Not without reason."

Danilo shrugged. That was true enough, but his instincts told him the elf had spoken truth. He was very interested to hear what Bronwyn would have to say about the encounter, but he'd had no reason to doubt Elaith's word since the day the elf had made the pledge of Elf-friend. Indeed, Elaith had been amazingly forthright—in some ways, more so than Dan himself had been. He had arranged to have Elaith followed and watched, and now he found himself on the verge of abandoning the responsibility such pledges entailed.

"There has been some little excitement here, as well," he began. In a few words he told the elf about his new-found sister. "Arilyn and I will travel east to meet her in Suzail."

Elaith studied him, his amber eyes unreadable. "Why do you tell me this?"

"Apart from making polite conversation?" he returned with a grin. His smile quickly faded. "I must confess some regret at the prospect of leaving the city. You were attacked by tren and may yet be in danger. The pledge of Elf-friend binds two ways. I am hesitant to leave while this matter is unresolved. Arilyn, even more so."

"Arilyn?" This intelligence seemed to surprise the elf. "Not on my behalf, surely?"

"Not precisely," Danilo said, though the expression on Elaith's face made him wish he could answer otherwise. "As you know, of late Arilyn's moonblade has taken to summoning her to duty. Since it has been silent for some time now, she is convinced that her duty to the People lies here in Waterdeep. Perhaps your recent misadventures have a part in that."

"That, I doubt," Elaith said lightly. "Do not consider the matter. By all means, accompany your newfound sister to Suzail. Winter in Waterdeep is often a dreary affair. You would do well to escape it."

Danilo did not miss the hint of irony in the elf's tone—and the warning. He responded to both. "Somehow, I rather doubt that this year's freeze will be without diversion."

Elaith's smile never touched his eyes, which were as golden and full of secrets as a cat's. "Yes, I daresay you could be quite right."

* * * * *

Arilyn's respect for Danilo grew as the night wore on. She doggedly worked her way through her dance card, moving from one dance partner to another and trying to learn something of value from each. She kept telling herself it was not so very different from her days as an apprentice swordmaster. The intricate dances were more easily mastered than the scores and scores of forms and routines she had practiced in her youth. Anticipating the movements of a dance partner or an entire circle was not entirely dissimilar to battle. The feint and parry of the nobles' flirtatious banter had a great deal in common with duel, and the backstabbing jabs of their subtly brutal gossip were as keen and deft as any assassin's blade. By midnight, however, Arilyn was exhausted. Her jaws ached from holding her tight, false smile—and from holding back tart comments.

That was especially difficult when it came to discussion of the Tethyr Reclamation. Arilyn was still smarting from her involvement in that country's woes. She had spent months posing as a member of the assassin's guild, learning about the country's powerful and would-be powerful by sifting through the detritus of their secret actions, their worse impulses. Her last mission for the Harpers had been the "rescue" of Isabeau Thione. The removal of a possible heir from Tethyr solidified Zaranda's claim, as well as the power of the Tethyrian nobles who supported the new queen. Arilyn had been willing to do nearly anything in support of the Harpers, but she knew far too much about the people whom the Harpers supported. Her protests had been dismissed with arguments of political expediency, safe trade routes, and important alliances. Nor did it seem to matter to anyone that Isabeau quickly proved to be just as reprehensible as the worst of Tethyrian nobility. She was feted in Waterdeep, supported in part by Harper funds. Arilyn had quit the Harpers in disgust and turned her full attention to her elven duty. Yet here she was, dancing with Tethyr's next king and exchanging light conversation with a roomful of nobles, knowing all the while that someone in the room might have ordered and paid for her death.

However, at Galinda Raventree's balls, such grim topics seemed utterly foreign. There was still no talk of Oth Eltorchul's death. The only explanation for this that Arilyn could fashion was that Errya Eltorchul had elected to keep this news quiet as long as possible, hoping to peddle spells and potions created by the family's students and pass them off as her brother's work. One thing seemed certain: the Eltorchul fortunes would plunge when the news became common knowledge. Arilyn had liked the Eltorchul patriarch, and she doubted that he would resort to subterfuge, but it was possible that he, in his grief, gave too free a hand to his venal daughter.

On the other hand, the story of the ambushed caravan was the second-most popular theme of the evening—outshining even the tawdry, overfed imitation elves that strutted about in much green and brown paint and little else.

Arilyn listened closely to what was told to her and what was spoken nearby. She constructed two main stories from the disparate and often conflicting parts. One school of thought held that the theft was orchestrated by the elf lord. The other rumor, spoken in softer tones but having the extra appeal of conspiracy and betrayal, suggested that the traitor was one of the families in the consortium that sponsored the caravan.

Lord Gundwynd was the lowest on the list of likely villains—at least, on such lists as the merchant nobility might fashion. He had supplied the flying mounts and the elven guards, and his losses were enormous. On the other hand, the elven minstrels noted with considerable bitterness that Gundwynd had used his elven hirelings in much the same fashion that orcs deployed goblin troops in battle: to draw enemy fire and reveal position, buying time for the "more valuable" fighters to assess the situation. The elves were not claiming that Gundwynd had orchestrated the ambush—not quite—but their opinion of the man and his methods was not far above that mark.

The Amcathra clan, dealers in fine weapons, lost some of the valuable swords and daggers fashioned by their craftsmen in Silverymoon, but the fine, upstanding reputation enjoyed by the Amcathra clan held too high a gloss to hold much tarnish.

Ilzimmer, on the other hand, suffered from a reputation that had been quilted together from scores of small scandals. Boraldan Ilzimmer, the clan's patriarch and not a well-liked man, had expected to receive a small fortune in crystal and gems on the westbound caravan. Of course, after Myrna's rumors made the rounds, no one was certain how much of his stated loss was truly gemstone and how much of it was worthless bits of colored rock.

And then there was the Thann family, who seemed to have a finger in nearly every pie in the city, at least as far as the shipping of goods was concerned. Their loss, by all reports, was not great and was limited to their investment in this new mode of travel. It was an investment, if indeed they had also informed and funded the bandits, that might have paid off quickly and handsomely.

These speculations troubled Arilyn deeply. If she remembered her history, war among the families of Waterdeep was nothing new, and she did not relish the possibility of seeing old times return.

Arilyn sought Lady Cassandra in the crowd. The noblewoman was dressed in a shimmering silver-blue gown that suggested, but did not precisely imitate, a mermaid's scales. She looked as serene and collected as ever, and her demeanor gave no sign that she had heard the rumors at all, much less that they gave her any cause for concern.

On the other hand, Arilyn noted that the noblewoman gave her respects to Galinda Raventree at an unusually early hour. Arilyn followed the older woman to her carriage and slipped inside before the startled groom could bar the door.

"It's all right, Nelson," Lady Cassandra said in a resigned voice. She moved over to make room, pointedly eyeing the wings on Arilyn's costume. "Tell the driver to circle the block."

She did not speak to Arilyn until the creak and rumble of the carriage gave cover to their words. She batted aside a lazily drifting feather. "There is trouble in the Land of Faerie? Molting is often a sign of distress."

"Oh. Sorry." Almost glad for the excuse, Arilyn tore the annoying wings from her shoulders and impatiently flung them out the window.

"I trust this is important?"

"You tell me." She quickly apprised the noblewoman of the situation. Not once did Cassandra's expression give a hint of worry or dismay.

"The rumors are not entirely off target," she said cautiously. "Thann losses were not very great, that much is true, but it is inconceivable that one of the consortium partners betrayed the others."

"Oh? Why is that?"

"The answer should be obvious," the noblewoman said. "Consider our past—the devastation of the Guild Wars when the families battled in the streets. There is no clan so foolish as to believe they could succeed in such an endeavor, and so none would engage in so blatant a challenge. Only outsiders, those who attempt to wedge their foot inside the door, would attempt such a ridiculous thing."

"Not so ridiculous," the half-elf pointed out. "By all reports, at least twoscore men and elves died in that ambush. The cargo is gone. Some might call that success."

The noblewoman gave Arilyn a supercilious smile. "Rumors are like drunken men," she observed. "Most of the time they babble nonsense, but sometimes a truth slips out that would otherwise be unspoken."

"Such as?"

"Let us consider Elaith Craulnober. Few have dared accuse the elf lord before, or if they did, they often dropped their accusation before the Lords Council met for judgment. Those few who persisted in their suit were never able to trail the elf's misdeeds to the source. This time, however, Craulnober has overstepped, and the truth about him is being spoken aloud."

"That, I doubt," Arilyn said without hesitation. "I have known Elaith for several years. I certainly won't argue that he is without stain, but never have I known him to act so openly or foolishly. There is a reason why his misdeeds are so hard to trace. He is clever."

"So was the theft of the air caravan."

"I've seen better," the half-elf said bluntly. "The ambush required information and planning, but little cunning. I do not see Elaith's hand in this."

Cassandra affixed her with a look of cold incredulity. "You defend him?"

"I'm just trying to see all the runes on the page. There is something more going on than a single bandit attack. Danilo said that he told you Oth Eltorchul was killed by tren assassins. Elaith was recently attacked by similar assassins—in your villa."

The noblewoman's steady gaze did not falter at any part of this litany. "You hold Thann responsible for this, I suppose."

"Not yet," Arilyn returned, "but it is possible that Elaith might."

"I see your point," the woman allowed, "but that is all the more reason for him to take vengeance on one of our business interests."

The reasoning was logical enough, but Arilyn shook her head. "Do you know who died in that ambush? Elves, mostly. Among them were four young warriors not long from Evermeet. They were Eagle Riders and among the most respected elven warriors. Whatever else Elaith might do, whatever he might be, I cannot believe that he would condemn those lads to certain death."

"Why not? If there is any truth at all to the legends and tavern tales, Elaith Craulnober has slain hundreds in his misspent life and barely stopped to clean his blade."

"Never an elf," Arilyn persisted. "As far as I know, never that. I admit that might be scant virtue in this claim, but there *is* a pattern. Everything I know about Elaith Craulnober leads me to believe him guiltless in this matter."

Cassandra sat back and regarded the younger woman with an icy gaze. "You know what you are saying, of course. You are accusing at least one of the noble families of betrayal, theft, and murder. That is a very serious accusation."

The half-elf did not flinch. "Someone knew the caravan route well in advance, and laid ambush. Someone is responsible for the death of those elves. It is my business to see that they pay for it. If for some reason I do not, Elaith Craulnober most likely will. For once, you should pay heed to what rumors say. Do not take either of us lightly."

The woman's lips twitched. "I am put on notice," she said with an unexpected touch of dark humor. "I suppose I ought to thank you for the warning."

"Don't bother. Just don't pass the warning along."

"Bargain made," the noblewoman agreed. "In any event, I would hardly put about the fact that my son's companion—a suspected assassin, as you have taken great pains to remind me—is hounding among the peerage for a traitor. There is scandal enough without this returning to my door!" She gave Arilyn a wry, sidelong glance. "Is there any hope of turning you from this path?"

"None."

Cassandra nodded as if she had expected this. "In that case I, too, have a warning. Nothing good will come of this inquiry, either for you or for Danilo. If you must persist, keep your eyes open and your sword at hand, and see that you keep good watch over my son."

"As I have done for these past six years," Arilyn said stiffly.

"Really? That is a marvel, considering that you are so seldom in Danilo's company. Think nothing of that. Your dedication to the elven people is admirable, I'm sure. Ah, we are back at the gate. You will return to the party, of course."

It was an order, not a question. Since she could see little profit in prolonging the interview, Arilyn descended and watched the departing carriage.

Lady Cassandra's words troubled her deeply. Until now, she had shrugged aside Cassandra's small digs and genteel sarcasm as easily as she might wave away a persistent gnat. Arilyn was well accustomed to slights. When it came to subtle insults, not even the most supercilious noble could hold a candle to an elf, and half-elves were favorite targets for elven slings and arrows.

However, this time things were different, and the noblewoman was letting her know that beyond doubt. Like a master swordsman, Cassandra had slipped past Arilyn's guard and gone straight for her heart. She had used the sharpest sword that anyone could wield—the painful truth, plainly stated.

"Truth is the sharpest sword," Arilyn murmured. Those words steadied her resolve as she gathered up her shimmering skirts and headed for the Raventree mansion. She and Danilo would find the truth, and that weapon would serve to cut through the deceit and intrigue. That would put things to rights.

A small, fluttering movement drew her eye. The autumn wind was brisk, and one of her discarded wings had been blown against the stone wall surrounding Galinda's garden. It lay there like a dying bird, ghostly amid the darkness of the stone and the swirling dry leaves.

Arilyn was not superstitious, but it seemed to her that the false wings spoke augury. She had cast off illusion, and the result was death. Though she did not waver in her determination to find her way to the truth, she could not help but wonder who might yet fall to that sharp sword.

* * * * *

Lilly hurriedly packed her belongings in preparation for the trip from Waterdeep, and to freedom. It was not a large task—a few pieces of clothing, her precious dream spheres, an ivory comb missing only a few teeth, a dented pewter mug, and a small but well-kept assortment of knives and picks.

She hesitated a moment before placing her thieving tools in her sack, for they seemed ill suited to the bright future ahead. Upon consideration, she tucked them inside and folded the bundle securely shut. A girl never knew what might need doing.

The door flew open so hard that it slammed against the wall. Lilly jumped and reached for a weapon. Too late, she remembered they were packed away.

Isabeau blew in like a leaf on a gale, more disheveled and wild-eyed than she'd been in the heat of battle.

"You're looking as if you've seen a ghost," Lilly commented, "and not a particularly friendly one at that."

That brought a faint, sickly smile to the woman's pale lips. She collected herself somewhat, but she continued to prowl about the small room as if seeking something of vital importance. The burlap sack seemed to be of special interest to her. As she eyed it, she began to toy with the strings that held her own purse to her waist.

"You're leaving?"

Lilly thrust the burlap sack behind her. "Just taking some things to the laundress, is all."

The woman studied her for a moment, then smiled. "A man and woman were inquiring for you downstairs."

Lilly's heart sank. Isabeau knew of the planned escape!

"Of course," the woman continued, "when I learned what they intended, I pretended to be you. I have reason to leave the city for a few days. You won't mind if I take your place, will you?"

Before Lilly could move, the woman swung her purse and dealt Lilly a painful, ringing blow to one ear. The room spun, and she suddenly felt the hard floorboards beneath her knees.

Isabeau hiked up her skirts and delivered a kick that landed just below Lilly's ribs. Too winded to draw breath, the thief could not fight as Isabeau stuffed a scented handkerchief in her mouth.

The woman knelt beside her. She held her palm up to her lips and blew, as if she were blowing a kiss. Red powder puffed toward Lilly's face.

Lilly drew in a startled breath. Instantly she realized

her mistake. A languorous haze spread swiftly through her, obscuring the path between her will to act and her ability to move. It was like being in the throes of a dream sphere but without either the pleasure or the oblivion. Though Lilly could not command her body, she could definitely experience everything that happened to it. She registered the second stunning blow to the head, and she felt a cord tighten around her wrists. She smelled the dry scent of dust as the woman shoved her under the cot.

Through the immobilizing haze, Lilly heard the creak of the old wooden stairs announce the approach of her intended savior. She struggled without effect to find some way to make her presence known. Finally, she listened with growing despair as Isabeau fell into her role and took her place.

The Harper woman was as small and slight as Lilly, and although her red hair was not as thick and pale and lustrous, at least it was a reasonably good match. She donned the extra dress that Isabeau took from Lilly's bag and gave Isabeau the overtunic and trews she had worn to the tavern. Cynthia expressed puzzlement over Isabeau's dark hair, but she readily accepted Isabeau's story of a sudden impulse to disguise herself, abetted by a mage's apprentice and a five-copper spell. Lilly did not blame the Harper for her credulity. She knew, to her sorrow, how convincing the thief could be.

When the women had changed places, Isabeau slipped down the stairs to the alley, and the carriage waiting beyond.

The cot sank dangerously low as the young Harper sat on the edge. She hummed idly to herself to pass the time until the tavern closed and the streets grew dark enough for her to hold her guise as she slipped off.

Again the stairs creaked, this time with more protest. Cynthia rose and crept to the door. She stood with feet braced as the portal began to swing slowly open.

Lilly saw the creature first, and she knew it from the enormous clawed feet. She threw her will and strength into a futile effort at screaming a warning.

The silence was broken, not by her voice, but by the sudden scuttle of tren footsteps. The creature darted forward, pivoted, then grunted with the effort of a single, massive blow.

There was no time to scream, even if Lilly had been able to. The Harper hit the floor hard. Lilly's eyes widened in horror as Cynthia's lifeblood spilled out into a spreading pool. The red stain reached out toward her in wide rivulets. To the terrified girl, it looked like tattling fingers pointing the way to her hiding place.

Even so, she was startled when a large green hand thrust under the cot and seized a handful of her skirts. The creature dragged her out with a single tug, then jerked her onto her feet.

In some mist-veiled corner of her mind, Lilly realized that she could stand on her own. The poison Isabeau had administered was beginning to wear off. Her terrible fear, however, was nearly as immobilizing. She stood frozen like a mouse facing a raptor, staring with a wide, dry, unblinking gaze into the fanged smile of a tren.

"You have some very interesting dreams," observed the creature in a musical voice. "It is almost a shame to end them. However, it is necessary, you see. A step toward an end I highly desire. As is this."

The tren held up a bit of parchment. It was the note Isabeau had stolen from the bearded man. On it was written the details of the air caravan's route. A signature had been added to the page. The name was that of her secret love. "They will find you, and they will know what you did. Of course, they will blame your gallant lover. He will pay for every loss, every death. And your family, of course. Oh, yes, the Thann family will pay as well."

Lilly shook her head, a tiny movement of anguished denial. Her secret love had had nothing to do with this! She was the thief, not he! Never, never had she intended anyone to die!

Even as she tried to shape air into protest, the creature before her began to change. The thick body became longer and more slender, the features sharp.

Lilly remembered what she knew of Isabeau Thione, and she thought she understood what manner of foe the woman had fled. Isabeau had stolen her escape, though, and had left her to face this handsome monster.

The deadly visitor smiled, as if somehow pleased that she understood his true nature and his intention. Then his smile widened horribly and his face elongated into a reptilian snout. Scales erupted on his face, and an anticipatory string of drool dripped from the false tren's fangs. He lifted claws already stained with Cynthia's blood, and hooked them with slow, tantalizing deliberation. There was malicious pleasure in his eyes. He intended to feed on her terror as surely as a real tren would have fed upon her flesh.

Lilly would not close her eyes. A noble's life might have been denied her, but the manner of her death she could choose.

She fought the immobilizing poison with all the strength and heart and will she could muster. Her chin lifted with a mixture of pride and courage, and she regarded the creature with steady calm as the deadly claws slashed in.

Twelve

The next morning dawned fair and bright. To the west of Waterdeep, past the north gates, lay a fair expanse of gently rolling meadow and a pleasant wood beyond. It was a favorite playground of the city's privileged class, a fine place for riding and hunting. In the distance, the baying of hounds and the excited halloos of pursing riders spoke of a fox run to ground. The blue skies were dotted with the small, wheeling forms of hunting hawks. A dull, faint thumping spoke of beaters flailing the trees to startle game into the path of waiting hunters.

Despite the evidence of nearby sportsmen, no human parties marred the immediate landscape. There was a scent of autumn in the air: the tang of drying oak leaves, the elusive perfume of late-blooming flowers, the sweetness of apples and cider wafting from the carts that trundled toward the city markets on the hard-packed dirt road. Elaith Craulnober tried to concentrate on these pleasant things and forget his distaste for the woman who rode at his side.

This should have been an easy task on so fine a day. He had his best, silver horse beneath him and a peregrine falcon riding—unhooded and untethered—on a perch on his saddle's pommel.

The small "lady's hawk" that Myrna Cassalanter carried was confined according to human custom and rode on the leather bracer on her wrist. The elf refrained from comment. If he could endure this dreadful woman's company, if he could smile pleasantly as she gleefully slew the reputations of her peers, then surely he could overlook her treatment of her hunting birds. What was such a thing, anyway, to an elf whose inner darkness both surpassed and controlled that of the Mhaorkiira?

Finally the woman lifted the little hawk's hood and tossed the bird into the air. The tiny raptor winged off gratefully in search of game and an hour's freedom.

"You are wise to pursue this matter," Myrna said, turning back to the matter that had brought them to this discussion. "Rumors abound concerning the poor treatment suffered by the Gundwynd family's elven employees. It is whispered that Lord Gundwynd knew of the attack on the air caravan and used the elves as cannon fodder."

She smiled unpleasantly. "Surely you can make good use of this situation. There will be a number of elves leaving Gundwynd's service and seeking other employ. You should be able to engage their services for far less than the going rate."

Elaith did not comment on this advice. "Important information," he allowed. It was, too. He wouldn't have started the rumor, if it were not.

"The Ilzimmer clan is also under scrutiny," Myrna said with relish. "You might find a way to make use of that, as well. There is a particularly juicy tale making the rounds about Simon Ilzimmer, a minor mage who likes to visit courtesans in shapeshifted form. Only a handful of the city's hired escorts will have anything more to do with him."

"That is hardly the sort of thing likely to bring

profit," Elaith said dryly, "and spreading such stories could make you rather unpopular."

"To the contrary! The appetite for such tales is immense."

The elf had to admit, privately, that Myrna's assessment of human nature was distressingly on the mark. "Perhaps I can repay my day's debt with a similar story," Elaith offered. When Myrna nodded eagerly, he added, "Rumor has it that Lord Gundwynd is furious with his youngest daughter, Belinda, who has been dallying with one of the family's elven grooms."

The woman clapped her hands with delight. "Oh, that is priceless! Belinda Gundwynd, of all people! To look at the prissy little wench, you'd think that a necklace of ice wouldn't melt on her bosom. A stable hand is scandal enough, but an elf! You don't know how the peerage loathes that notion."

"Oh, I have some idea," he commented, thinking of five tren assassins and the noble family who had hired them to kill him. That debt would soon be paid, the attempt on his life avenged. His business in Skullport and in Waterdeep would continue unchallenged, for those who had reason to stop him would be extremely busy elsewhere. Once the dust of battle settled, it was likely that those people would be in no position to challenge him, at least, not for a very, very long time.

An extreme measure, perhaps, but in his mind it was payment long in coming.

* * * * *

The costume ball lasted until dawn. Galinda Raventree's guests toasted the new day, then wandered off intending to sleep it away. Danilo and Arilyn took their leave as well. After shedding their costumes for less fanciful garb, they went to The Curious Past to check on Bronwyn.

The young merchant was less than happy with the results of her trip. "I got one of the crystal spheres you were looking for," she said. "The others were gone before I reached Mizzen's shop. But I did find a most interesting gem."

She told them about the ruby—and her suspicion that it might hold some sort of magic.

Arilyn, who had been listening to the tale with scant attention, sat bolt upright. "This stone: Was it about the size of a dried bean, perfectly round, with small facets whirling up to a flat surface?"

Bronwyn nodded. "Yes. You know it?"

The half-elf rose and began to pace. "There is hardly an elf who does not! You have heard of kiira gems?"

"I believe they are some sort of memory stones," Bronwyn said slowly. "Artifacts from ancient times, they are family gems passed down through the generations. Legend claims they contain the combined wisdom of their forebears."

"Not legend," Arilyn said tersely. "Fact. Long ago, one of the kiira's owners turned to evil, and his family gem was somehow twisted to reflect its bearer. The ruby became a thief of memories—other people's memories. The Mhaorkiira, as it is commonly known, was lost centuries ago. More than one adventuring party has spent years searching for it. Trouble follows it. Most who hold it are twisted by its power."

"And this was taken by bandits," Danilo said, his voice rounded with outrage. "Most likely the bounders will sell it as a common gem, not understanding what they have!"

"That has already happened," Bronwyn told him. "I've traced the ruby to a fence here in Waterdeep. After a little persuasion, he described the woman who sold it to him."

Bronwyn gave a concise description: a young woman, pretty and curvaceous and strawberry blonde, neat but not well dressed. Well spoken, but bearing a strong accent of the docks. "Does that sound at all familiar?"

Arilyn and Dan exchanged a troubled glance. "It sounds disturbingly like a young woman of recent acquaintance," he admitted. "I will look into the matter at once. About the gem, though—I'm assuming that it was no longer in the fence's possession, else you would have procured it. What did the fence tell you of the buyer?"

"Nothing could induce him to part with that information, but I'm guessing Elaith Craulnober had a hand in the purchase. He mentioned the stone during the trip, and he does have a gift for intimidating people," Bronwyn concluded.

A long, troubled silence followed her words. After a few moments, she asked, "Is there anything more I can do?"

Arilyn shook her head and rose. "Stay clear of this. It's a marvel that Elaith let you live. Don't push him, especially not now."

She left the shop with a quick, purposeful stride, setting a course for Blackstaff Tower.

"Where are we going?" Danilo said in the wary tones of one who already knew the answer and was not at all pleased with it.

"You mentioned that Khelben has elven blood. He knows more of magical items than anyone else I know, so he should know a thing or two about the kiira stones. We're going to talk to him."

"On purpose?" muttered Dan.

However, he offered no further complaint and quickly cast the small spell that took them through the solid black stone of the curtain wall and another that led them into the tower of the archmage.

Khelben was at home, busy with a trio of apprentices. He left the students in Laerel's care and showed his visitors into his private study, where he listened to their story with grave attention.

"My concern is this," concluded Arilyn. "Is it possible

that the Mhaorkiira and the dream spheres might be linked?"

"Entirely possible," the archmage agreed. He was silent for a long moment. "For that reason, you must leave this business strictly alone."

"That is hard to do. If Elaith does have the kiira, he should be warned of the dangers involved," Danilo protested.

"He knows," Khelben said flatly. "The Mhaorkiira is legendary. Its involvement makes the cost of simply using a dream sphere incredibly high.

"There is more," the archmage added. "You must understand that this particular kiira has the power to twist the user to evil. I daresay your friend has already taken the first few turns along this path of his own accord."

"I agree," Arilyn said. "Mhaorkiira is incredibly dangerous in Elaith's hands. It could distort and destroy what little elven honor remains to him." She turned to Danilo, her face grave. "The pledge of Elf-friend is a pale thing compared to the power of this artifact. Whatever Elaith's game is, he would not thank you for meddling. I'll give you the same advice I gave Bronwyn: Stay clear of him. He must be dealt with, but not by those who are tempted to trust him."

Danilo hesitated, then yielded before the weight of evidence. "I will do as you say," he said with deep regret.

*　*　*　*　*

Danilo went from Blackstaff Tower to the small tavern where he often met with the Harpers once under his command. Hector was there at the appointed time, wearing a look of satisfaction on his narrow, much-freckled face.

"All went well, I take it," Danilo said as he slid into the wooden booth across from his comrade.

The small man nodded. "I've yet to see my sister, but that is of little concern. Cynthia said she'd wait out the night and the morning if needs be to convince any watching eyes that the woman was still in her room."

"Was our charge delivered safely to the orchard house?"

"Been and gone," Hector confirmed. "She didn't much take to the country, though. Set up a pretty steady flow of complaints, I hear. Our man set her up with horse and harness, and she rode off on her own." He shrugged. "They were glad to be rid of her, truth to tell. I saw no reason to argue with this arrangement. Figured she was safe enough, once she was well out of the city."

This did not sound at all like the warm and merry lass Danilo had met. A feeling of deep unease assailed him. "This woman. Describe her."

Hector let out a short, humorless laugh. "Promise first that you won't repeat the language I'm about to use to my wife, my mother, or my priest."

Danilo's concern deepened. "If her character is that distressing, focus on her person."

"An easy thing to do," the man allowed, "and the same rules of discretion apply. Gods help me, the shape of her! The only thing I ever saw that stood so high and proud with less to bolster it was that Moonbridge over in Silverymoon. She has a handsome face, though it takes a while for a man to drag his eyes up to that height. Eyes the color of winter stout in a clear mug. Hair like a dark cloud."

Danilo stood up so abruptly that the wooden bench toppled over. "Damn it, Hector, you took the wrong woman!"

A look of utter horror crossed the young Harper's face, a distress so profound that Danilo longed to explain the situation, to assure Hector this mistake was not his fault. That would have to wait.

He raced from the tavern and rode to the Dock Ward like one pursued by demons. He leaped from his horse and left the steed untethered in front of The Pickled Fisherman, then ran through the tavern and up the back stairs.

A half-ogre tavern guard shouted at him to stop and followed him up the stairs. The guard's progress was halted by the tip of Arilyn's sword. Holding the glowing weapon at arm's length, she stood at the head of the stairs and blocked the half-ogre's passage. Her face was set and grim, her lips in a pale, straight line.

"The moonblade drew me here," she said to Danilo, "but the warning came too late. Prepare yourself."

Her words were not entirely unexpected. What he had not expected was a sense of grief that was staggering, nearly overwhelming. Danilo left Arilyn to deal with the half-ogre guard and slipped into the silent room. He stood for a long moment regarding the scene before him.

Cynthia lay sprawled out on the floor, her thin form clad in a barmaid's worn and patched clothes. Her throat had been slashed to the bone. Blood pooled on the floor beneath and flowed to converge with another river, from another source.

Lilly lay on her side. Her eyes were open, calmly staring ahead into the future that was no longer hers to claim.

He dropped to one knee and gently closed the young woman's eyes. Regret tore through him as he considered the waste of this blithe spirit, the joy he could have added to her life, and she to his.

His eyes were bright and blurred as he took a gold ring from his small finger, upon which was engraved the horse and raven of the Thann crest. This he placed on Lilly's hand, and then he raised the small, cold fingers to his lips.

Thirteen

How long Danilo stayed by his sister's side, he could not say. Time slipped into a meaningless haze. He was vaguely aware of Arilyn's low, musical voice as she explained matters to the half-ogre, who apparently had appointed himself Lilly's personal protector.

"I knew it," the tavern guard said, his voice suspiciously gruff. "Fine girl—too good to have sprung from this swamp. Too bad you took your time coming for her."

Danilo rose and faced the half-ogre's accusing glare. "I will not gainsay you, sir. Permit me to do for her what little service remains. If you have servants to spare, can you put them at my disposal? I intend to take her home," he said firmly, "but not like this."

The half-ogre nodded and then hollered for someone named Peg. A thin, dark-eyed girl crept into the room and began to tend to Lilly with a sister's care. Other servants set off on errands, declining Danilo's offer of coin as they gathered their last gifts for their lost friend.

Arilyn took his arm and guided him down to the tavern. Danilo waved away the bottle that the half-ogre, who was apparently the owner of this establishment as well as the guard, sent to his table. It was effort enough to push away the dark haze of grief and regret when his wits were clear and whole.

Their host had no such reservations. The massive tavernkeeper slumped at a table littered with empty mugs, morosely staring into the dregs of his latest cup and looking like a man whose last light had gone dim.

Finally Peg came downstairs and bade them come. Lilly was lying at peace, clad in the simple white gown that one of the serving girls had given her.

"A scarf is needed," the girl said in a dull, dazed voice as she regarded the wounds on Lilly's throat, "or flowers, maybe." She nodded wordless thanks when Danilo placed several silver coins in her hand, and she walked on leaden feet from the room.

"Tren," Arilyn said softly, nodding toward the four slash marks. "The width and spacing of the claws tell that tale."

The unspoken question hung heavy in the air. Neither of them cared to give words to it or to contemplate what had kept the reptilian assassins from completing the task in their usual fashion.

"A nobly born mage, an elven rogue, a half-elven woman, and now Lilly," Danilo murmured. "Where is the pattern to it?"

Arilyn held up a small, glowing sphere. "I found this in Lilly's room. If it was Lilly who had the kiira, the money she got for it is long gone."

He quickly took the dream sphere from her and slipped it into his boot. "Better this not become common knowledge. I will find whoever did this, but the fox is more cautious when he knows the hound has found the trail. Was there anything else in the room that might help?"

The half-elf hesitated. "A bit of parchment. A note of some sort, I suppose, but it was too sodden to unfold, much less read. Lilly must have reached for it in her last moment and drowned it in her own blood."

"What secret did she protect?" Danilo murmured as he studied his sister's still face. "Who absorbed her last thoughts?"

The half-ogre came to the door. "All is ready," he said gruffly. He shook aside offers of help and carried Lilly himself to the waiting carriage.

The closed, flatbed carriage moved with somber pace to the Thann estate. Danilo and Arilyn saw that it was placed in the carriage house, then started for the villa. Word of this arrival had already reached the lord and lady. Cassandra met them at the door, her face white with fury.

"How dare you bring this tawdry matter to my door?" she demanded.

Danilo ignored her—probably the first time this slight had been offered the lady—and looked over her shoulder to address his father. "My lord, Lilly was in danger. You must have known that, yet you represented this to me as a minor nuisance. Now the girl is dead. Your daughter, my sister. I am sorry for any pain this may cost you, my lady," he said to Cassandra, "but this matter should have come to light long ago."

Before she could respond, the family steward blew into the room like a storm-tossed scarecrow. Arilyn had never seen the servant in such dishabille. His shirt was untucked, the sash and emblem that proclaimed his position was askew, and the strands of his sparse sandy hair stood up like bits of straw. A slight puffiness of his upper lip lent his mustache an asymmetry that, on any other man, might have been mistaken for a wry and roguish grin.

"Lord Gundwynd to see you, Sir, Madame," he announced with stiff dignity and slurred diction.

"Not now, Yartsworth," all those present said in rare and perfect unison.

"He is most insistent," the steward observed, gingerly touching his fingertip to his swollen lip.

Cassandra took note of this, and her indignation rose to another stage. "Show him in."

The small, gray man burst into the hall. Before he could sputter out a word, Lady Cassandra bore down on him like a prevailing wind.

"This is beyond the pale, Gundwynd! You might mistreat your own servants and suffer no ill for it, but do not presume to abuse any person in my employ."

Lord Gundwynd fell back a step, some of the wind knocked from his sails, but quickly recovered his pique. "Your choice of words is telling," he said coldly. "You have heard of my trouble, but then, who has not?"

"Thann had losses as well," she pointed out.

"If only the loss ended with the ambush!" he exploded. "All the elves in my employ have left. Do you know how difficult it is to find riders for aerial steeds? As if that weren't enough, there is the threat that all those of elven blood in the city—and beyond, for all I know—will refuse to use Gundwynd transport and will not buy or sell goods carried by my family. Elves are few enough, thank the gods, but this scandal could mean my ruin!"

"My sympathies," Danilo said in flat, ironic tones. Arilyn noted that he shifted a step closer to her, wordlessly—and perhaps without thought or design—declaring his allegiance.

The lord whirled on him. "You will be sorry soon enough! I would not be surprised to hear that this whole affair is somehow your doing, you and that elf you keep company with. This one too, for all I know," he added, looking wrathfully at Arilyn. "Well, the truth will come to light. I will bring suit against Thann and Ilzimmer and let the Lords sort the thing through!"

A long moment of silence followed this pronouncement. Lord Rhammas turned so pale that Danilo feared he might faint.

Cassandra took a step toward her husband, as if her near presence might serve to bolster him. "Idle threats,

Gundwynd. You have too much to lose to take such action."

"My family faces ruin, disgrace! If it comes to that, do you think I care who falls with me? I will know how this came about, mark me."

Danilo saw a pattern emerging. According to Bronwyn, the dream spheres had left Mizzen's shop the very day Gundwynd's caravan returned to Waterdeep. She had reported to him the malfunction of her bag of sending, and the small crystal orb that had remained in the magic bag. Lilly, who had sold a ruby stolen from the caravan, had had a dream sphere in her possession when she died. It seemed certain to him that the answer to his sister's death was entwined with this string of events. Without thinking of possible consequences, Danilo reached into the hiding place in his boot and took out the dream sphere Arilyn had found in Lilly's room.

"Were there any such items among the lost cargo?"

Lord Gundwynd's face turned a deep shade of puce, and his eyes slid guiltily toward the suddenly wary Cassandra. He puffed and hmmphed for a few moments, then admitted there had been.

"We had an agreement," the noblewoman said coldly. "None of us would support the sale of these toys!"

"Arrangements for this delivery were made well before that agreement," he argued. "This was between Mizzen Doar and Oth Eltorchul. Take it up with either of them." His eyes narrowed into slits as he regarded the ball in Danilo's hand. "Where did you get that?"

"In an alley behind the bazaar," Danilo lied smoothly. "The thieves must be an efficient lot—the goods have already reached the streets."

The merchant snorted in disbelief. "I knew it!" he exploded. "The Thann family are behind this—you lot, and the elf lord with you. So much for your *agreement*, my lady! I'll see you all ruined before this is through." He sliced the air with one hand in a gesture of finality—or possibly execution—spun on his heel, and stalked out.

Cassandra took a long, calming breath and turned to her son. "Danilo, I am going to ask the same question Lord Gundwynd posed. Where did you get that infernal thing?"

"It was in Lilly's possession," Danilo said bluntly. "In light of Oth's death, it is reasonable to assume that the dream spheres at least in part led to Lilly's fate."

The noblewoman turned white. "Have you any idea— any at all!—of what you have done?"

"I know that I had a sister, that she was in danger and in need of my aid. I know that I failed her. Now she is dead, and I intend to know why."

"Sentimental nonsense." Her angry blue eyes settled on the watchful half-elf. "Can you talk no sense into him?"

Arilyn merely shrugged.

Cassandra hissed a sigh. "Let me paint the picture. Many caravans are waylaid. Pirates, bandits—these are hazards of the trade. This theft was unusual, but we could have quietly worked the matter through to its conclusion. For whatever reason, rumors are turning it into a parlor guessing game, in which all those involved are suspect. By presenting that . . . *thing* . . . while Gundwynd was ranting about the ambush, you gave him fuel for his fire. What do you suppose he will conclude when he learns what you've brought to the family villa? Do you think the pieces will not be put together? By your actions, you made it appear that Rhammas's little bastard was involved in this theft!"

"That was hardly my intent," Danilo began.

"Intentions seldom matter. Impressions, on the other hand, matter a great deal. This may well put the Thann family in an untenable position. Once this new scandal comes to light—and it will, for you've made sure of it!—no one will believe that the girl acted without the complicity of the legitimate clan."

"How can any reasonable person draw that conclusion?" protested Lord Rhammas. "I did not even know the girl existed until after the attack! From our scant acquaintance, I would venture to say that she could not possibly have had a hand in that sordid affair."

"Oh, and I'm sure all Waterdeep will accept your word as if Ao Himself had finally spoken," the noblewoman retorted. Her angry gaze traveled from her husband to her son. "You are a pair of children, blinded to the larger issues by a worthless trollop!"

"That is remarkably callous, even for you," Danilo said with equal heat.

"Think what you like, but obey me in this. The matter dies with the girl. You and Arilyn have already stirred up more trouble than the pair of you can possibly charm, buy, fight, or spellcast your way free of."

Danilo studied his mother for a long moment. "Forgive me, my lady, but I must observe that your words could be construed as a threat."

"Could they now?" Her thin smile was as sharp as a dagger. "I am gratified to hear you say so. Evidence at last that you are not such a fool as today's events would suggest!"

"But—"

"Enough," she said in cold command. She suddenly changed tactics. "Would you be content if we acknowledged the girl as family and buried her in the Thann tomb?"

This concession startled Danilo, and his anger softened somewhat. "Thank you, but in all honesty, that will not end the matter."

"Possibly not," murmured Cassandra, "but we will do what we can."

* * * * *

Arilyn rode out directly from the Thann villa, leaving Danilo to battle Lady Cassandra over the details of

Lilly's final arrangements. She tracked Isabeau to the orchard farm and confirmed from the farmers the tale that Hector had passed to Danilo.

Isabeau had left soon after her rescuers deposited her in the safe house—but not before she had managed to insult the farmers who risked their home and their safety for the Harpers' charge. As Arilyn picked up the trail of Isabeau's horse, she wondered where the woman was bound and what sort of reception she expected to get.

It would seem that Lady Isabeau's ambitions were lifting faster than a courtesan's skirts. Just a few moons past, when they'd found her on the road north of Baldur's Gate, she was happy enough to have left the remote gnome settlement that had given her shelter all her life. Waterdeep delighted her, as did the modest wealth that had awaited her there—most of it the legacy of her mother, who had been forced to leave the city without gathering her possessions. Now it seemed Isabeau was no longer content with her transformation from serving wench to lady of station and substance. She had progressed from thief to murderer.

This Arilyn firmly believed, regardless of the facts of Oth's death. Whether or not Isabeau was responsible for the Eltorchul mage's fate, she had left Lilly to hers. To Arilyn's way of thinking, that made Isabeau as guilty as if she herself had cut the girl's throat.

Nor was the woman any more merciful to the animals under her control. Isabeau had pushed her borrowed horse at a high pace, with callous disregard for the creature's safety. The moon had been full the night before, and each of the seven gleaming shards that followed the silver orb through the sky had been as bright as will o'wisps, but no amount of light, not even the brightness of highsun, could justify running a horse full-out on such rough terrain.

As Arilyn followed the trail, the road widened, and the forest gave way to fields. She rode past a few tidy cottages, through an orchard dense with late fruit, to the gates of an imposing country estate.

Whose lands these were, Arilyn could not say. Many of the merchant lords of Waterdeep had farms or stables or country manors in the northlands. One thing was certain: The owner possessed a rather dark streak of whimsy.

The manor and the wall around it had been fashioned from gray stone, a ghostly color that seemed to merge with the mist of coming twilight. Gargoyles, most of them winged cats with vampiric sneers, stood guard on the ramparts and towers. Arilyn did not bother to stop by the gatehouse to seek admission, even though the guards seemed more interested in their dice game than in their post. When a group of peasants came to the gate pulling a cart laden with late-summer produce, Arilyn left her horse in the shadows of the orchards and took a long, thin rope from her saddle.

She slipped around to the rear wall and tossed her rope. The first try fell short. With the second she snared one of the gargoyles. She gave the rope a tug to ensure it would hold, then quickly climbed the wall. Using a spreading elm for cover, she draped the rope down the inside of the wall and slid to the ground.

While the estate's cooks were haggling with the peasants over the price of carrots and cabbage and the guards' attention was absorbed by the cooks, Arilyn crept into the building through the kitchen entrance to await the coming of night. It proved to be a good choice, for the heavy tapestries and drapes intended to keep out the chill also provided ample places to hide.

When all was dark and silent, Arilyn slipped into the halls. Her passage went unchallenged, for the servants demonstrated the lax concern for their responsibilities that often marked those who labored under an absent tyrant's rule. She checked each bedchamber for occupants. Most were empty—the noble family was not in residence.

Most of the chamber doors were open. At the end of a long hall, near a balcony overlooking the garden, one door was firmly shut. Arilyn tried the door and found it locked. She took a bit of thin paper from her pack and slid it under the door handle to catch the key, then inserted a pick into the lock. To her chagrin, the key had been removed from the lock. Picking it would take several minutes more. The task felt familiar to her fingers, and she overcame the lock in short order. Carefully she eased open the door.

Moonlight poured in through the round window placed high on one wall, lingering on the sleeping woman and the abundant dark locks strewn about the pillow. It was without doubt Isabeau Thione. Before confronting the woman, Arilyn took a few moments to take stock of her surroundings.

The chamber was luxurious, but macabre. The bed was enormous, and it was covered with a heavy coverlet of blood-red velvet. Drapes of similar fabric shrouded the tall bed frame and the windows. A statue of a man with the head of a cat stood vigil in the corner, and winged cat gargoyles leered down at her from their perches on pillars and shelves scattered about the room. Other than the sleeping Isabeau, the only sign of life in the room was the gray tabby curled up at the foot of the bed. The cat raised his head and regarded Arilyn with a somnolent stare, then yawned hugely and went back to sleep.

Arilyn quickly scanned the room for hidden doors and found none. She parted one of the velvet curtains and discovered another balcony beyond. She affixed a length of rope to the railing in case a quick exit was in order, then turned to her quarry.

The half-elf pounced onto the bed and seized Isabeau's wrists, pinning them up over her head. The tabby cat yowled and disappeared under the bed, and the woman came awake with a startled, inelegant snort.

"Call out, and I'll break your fingers," Arilyn said softly.

It was a potent threat, for hands were a thief's most valuable tools. A dancer would sooner lose the use of her legs or an artist his eyes.

Isabeau went very still. "What are you doing here?"

"I was about to ask you that." Arilyn cast a quick glance around the room. "What is this place? It's got more cats than Cormyr."

"This is the Eltorchul estate," the woman said haughtily. "I am here by invitation."

"Who did the inviting?"

"Lord Oth, of course. He and I are . . . dear friends."

Arilyn considered the possible layers of deception that formed this boast. Oth obviously had not invited her, but was this claim meant to cloak a darker deed? She decided to go on attack, for people often stumbled over themselves in an effort to explain and justify their claims. "You're a liar," she accused.

Isabeau didn't take the bait. "You will have to be more specific."

"All right, how's this: Lord Oth is dead," Arilyn said plainly.

Panic jolted into the woman's eyes. "Let me up, and I'll tell you what I know," she said in a subdued voice.

Arilyn eased away. She rose to her feet and stood by the bed, arms folded. The former barmaid sat, pushing aside the heavy mass of her hair from a face that had suddenly grown pale.

"You are certain he is dead? Who killed him?"

Interesting, Arilyn thought, that she would immediately come to this conclusion. "How do you know his death wasn't illness, or accident?"

The woman scoffed, dismissing that notion with a small, spitting sound. "From what I knew of him, I'd say it's a marvel he lived so long."

"Yet you seemed upset to learn of his death."

"Naturally! Lord Oth was a wealthy man, a powerful man. He could have been useful. See this?" Isabeau brandished one hand, her fingers spread to show the pink and gold ring on her middle finger. "He gave me this as a token and bade me present it when I wanted use of the estates."

"You picked an interesting time to use it," Arilyn said coldly. "The woman whose place you took is dead."

Isabeau didn't so much as blink her heavy lashes. "What of it? The Dock Ward is a dangerous place."

"Especially when there are tren lurking about."

"Tren?" The woman shifted one silk-clad shoulder. "That word means nothing to me."

The half-elf tamped down her temper. "All right then, what is your connection to Lilly?"

"Who?"

Her bored, derisive tone did not match the defiant challenge in her eyes. Arilyn saw that she had two choices: she could play this woman's game by rules Isabeau understood, or allow herself to be played like a cheap fiddle.

She backhanded the woman across her lovely, sneering face, then hauled her up by her hair. "Let's try that again," she suggested in a cold, dangerous voice.

A measure of respect crept into Isabeau's eyes, and she eased Arilyn's hands from her hair. "You are speaking of the red-haired serving wench. Yes, I took her place. I overheard a man and woman talking about seeing a young woman to safety out of the city. Why should that be her and not me? I seized the chance, as a drowning man might take hold of a rope. Would you begrudge that man his rescue, demanding that he die while he considers whether someone else might be more worthy of it?"

Arilyn folded her arms. "Drowning, were you? In what cesspool?"

She tossed her dark head. "I fled the elf. You know the one. He was pursuing me."

The half-elf carefully kept her face neutral as she considered this revelation. She had to admit that Isabeau's story was plausible. Elaith had promised Danilo months ago that he would let Isabeau live. Perhaps the elven rogue thought that he'd kept the promise long enough. If indeed he had followed Isabeau, he was most likely behind Lilly's death. With all the weapons at his command, it would not be difficult to imitate the cutting patterns of tren claws. Certainly Elaith had some knowledge of tren.

Another, darker thought occurred to her. Perhaps the tren assassins she had come across in the Thann villa were there not for an ambush but for an arranged meeting. Errya Eltorchul had said that her brother had done business with Oth. Perhaps their dealings had gone sour, and the elf had intended to arrange for Oth's death. Once Elaith was discovered with the tren, it was not inconceivable that he would kill a few of the creatures to maintain his cover.

Even as the thought formed, Arilyn acknowledged this was an extreme measure. For one thing, it courted tren vendetta. For another, Elaith and five tren could have easily overcome her, and there would have been no one left to tell the tale. However, as Arilyn had told Lady Cassandra, she had never heard that Elaith had slain another elf.

She turned her attention fully upon the watchful Isabeau. There was room for truth in the woman's words, yet Arilyn did not trust her and did not believe her claim that she "just happened" to wander into Lilly's tavern. Arilyn knew what would have led Elaith to Lilly's door, and she could easily imagine Isabeau having a part in its acquisition.

"As you say, the Dock Ward is a dangerous place," Arilyn said, as if she conceded the woman's argument. "Lilly recently sold a large ruby to a fence and probably had ready coin."

Isabeau's eyes went dark with rage, and she pounded on the bed with both fists. "The little cheat!"

Immediately she recognized the error of her words, realized that she had been tricked into admitting more than she had intended to. The vindictive, malevolent rage that twisted her face robbed her of beauty and stole Arilyn's breath.

Arilyn fought away the instinct to take a step back. The last time she had retreated from anything was a chance confrontation with a wounded panther, and that was a tactical move rather than one motivated by fear. Nonetheless, she recognized this was a truly dangerous woman.

Even as the thought formed, Isabeau sprang, cat-like, from the bed. She lunged not at Arilyn, but at the statue with the feline head. This she shoved with all her strength, sending it toppling toward the pursuing half-elf.

Instinctively Arilyn ducked, but the statue never quite fell. One stone hand flashed up to catch its balance against the wall. The painted eyes took on depth, then a luminous glow.

It was clear that Isabeau had not been expecting this. She scrambled back up onto the bed, her back against the headboard and her eyes enormous.

The cat man leaped at Arilyn, fangs the color of alabaster bared in a deadly smile. She dove straight toward it, rolling under the spring and rolling again to put distance between herself and the magical guard.

She rose to her feet and drew her sword, although she was not sure how much good it would do her. The cat, for all its light-footed speed, was fashioned of stone.

A paw lashed out. Arilyn parried, and sparks lit the room as steel struck stone. The cat's other hand closed around the steel blade, and it wrenched the sword from Arilyn's hand. It threw the sword across the room and batted at the half-elf with its other paw.

Arilyn could not dodge the blow in time, but she rolled with it to minimize its force. She came up aching and bruised, but not badly hurt. The stone cat had kept its claws velveted. The statue was playing with her. Once it unsheathed those alabaster claws, Arilyn was done.

On impulse, she dove at Isabeau and tore the signet ring off her hand. Brandishing it at the cat, she commanded the creature to stop.

A heart-stopping moment passed as the magical guard studied her with its inscrutable feline gaze. It was an enormous gamble, Arilyn acknowledged, and if it didn't work, she would be dead.

The cat turned and returned to its post. It assumed a regal pose, and the light faded from its eyes. Arilyn's shoulders sagged in relief.

"Don't think this is over," Isabeau said, her dark eyes gleaming with satisfaction.

The half-elf heard the voices and hurrying footsteps of servants in the hall. They began pounding on the door.

Apparently this was yet another trigger for attack. The winged gargoyles began to stir. Arilyn dove for her sword, and came up in a battle-ready crouch. Unlike her first adversary, true gargoyles only looked like stone. These were living creatures, and what lived could also die.

She spun away from a diving attack and delivered a backhanded slash. Her sword sliced through the batlike wing. The creature plummeted into the bed, sundering the ticking and sending feathers flying into the air.

Isabeau edged toward the window, obviously intending to take Arilyn's escape route. "Not this time," the half-elf muttered. She lunged at Isabeau and caught her by the nightdress. She sent her spinning back into the room and took a stand in front of the window to block the woman's escape.

By now the manor's servants were at full alert. They had improvised some sort of ram and were pounding at the door with it. The wooden planks bulged inward with each resounding thump.

Arilyn paused at the window and sent a warning look at Isabeau. "We're not through."

"Oh, but I think we are." The woman gestured toward the door. The bar was beginning to splinter.

The half-elf swung herself over the balcony rail and slid down the rope. Though it galled her to do so, she had little choice but to retreat. Isabeau was in no position to bring a formal accusation against Arilyn, but if the Eltorchul servants found her on the estate, Isabeau would not have to speak out. The penalties for unwanted intrusion in a lord's home could be stiff.

She ran through the garden and to the rope she had left hidden behind the elm. Quickly she climbed the wall, and then made her way back to the orchard. Her mare awaited her, and she cantered toward her mistress.

Arilyn caught the saddle's pommel and swung herself up. She leaned low over the horse's neck and urged her on to Waterdeep. Isabeau would have to be dealt with, but the half-elf herself was in no position to do so.

An old question, one that she had not asked herself in years, floated to the surface of her mind: Who would take the word of a known assassin?

*   *   *   *   *

The door splintered and flew inward, sending a half dozen servants stumbling into the room. Isabeau gathered up the neckline of her gown in one hand and drew back, as if this intrusion were not so much a rescue as an affront to her modesty.

One of the maids snatched up a coverlet and draped it around Isabeau's shoulders. "What happened, my lady? Are you hurt?"

Isabeau sent her audience a tremulous smile. "No, thanks to your quick response. A man came in through the balcony. I think he just meant to rob me, but the statues came awake, and they fought. It was terrible, terrible!"

The maid clicked her tongue soothingly. "Rest, lady. As you've seen, the master's magic will keep you safe."

"I cannot stay here after this!" Isabeau exclaimed in astonishment. "Saddle my horse at once."

"But dawn is hours away," one of the men protested. He wavered before Isabeau's steady gaze and conceded, "We could send a guard with you."

"I would be most grateful. Perhaps you could see to the arrangements, while I dress?" she hinted.

The servants retreated, leaving Isabeau alone and furious. She threw open the doors of the wardrobe and began to toss rich garments onto the bed as she considered what her next step should be. Without Oth as a protector, she was in a delicate position. That wretched half-elf had surprised a reaction from her that might tie her to the theft of the air caravan.

Much good had *that* done her! The treasure was lost. The goods had been moved to Skullport, but they had been stolen before Diloontier could claim them for her. Or so he said. Isabeau would not be at all surprised to learn that the perfume merchant had double-crossed her.

So now what? She had no treasure, very little money, and a pair of diligent hounds on her trail. Isabeau had witnessed how relentless Arilyn and her handsome companion could be in pursuit of one of their little crusades. She muttered curses as she dragged a small traveling chest out from under the bed and began to hurl her new, stolen wardrobe into it.

"You are quick to take what is not yours," observed a cold, male voice behind her.

Isabeau gasped and whirled, one hand at her throat. A tall, slender figure stood in the shadows, smiling with icy amusement.

Her heart leaped painfully, then picked up the rhythm at a shallow, frantic pace. A strange giddiness overtook her, and the floor tilted as if it were an enchanted carpet on the verge of taking flight. She seized the bed curtain for support.

"You!" she gasped on a short, sharp breath. "It *was* you who pursued me!"

"Clearly, this is more of a surprise to you that it should be," the intruder said.

"What are you going to do with me?" she said in a tremulous voice.

His laugh was equally resonant of music and scorn. "Please. The role of delicate maiden does not suit you. I am not going to kill you."

"Then what?"

"This is a warning, nothing more. Do not pursue the dream spheres. I will brook no more interference."

Isabeau seized what seemed a likely distraction. "You will suffer interference regardless of what I do. Two meddlers are already on the trail. You know them well. Arilyn the half-elf, and Lord Thann."

This news was received in silence. He lifted one hand, displaying a small glowing sphere. "If they cross me, they will die—but not before I learn what death they fear most."

She laughed scornfully, a bit of bravado that went a long way toward restoring her spirits. "So much for the vaunted concept of honor among peers."

With the speed of a striking snake, his open hand shot toward her. Isabeau turned with the blow so that it barely grazed her cheek. The intruder reined in his anger with visible effort.

"Do not press me," he said in a low voice quivering with rage. "Heed well my words. I do not wish to see you again, but I might yet have use for you. The tides in the southlands have turned, and you will be welcomed in your homeland. Find your way there as soon as possible."

There was a puff of acrid smoke, then a soft hissing sound as air rushed to fill the void left by the shadowy figure's disappearance. The sudden wind swirled Isabeau's hair and nightdress around her and then was gone.

Isabeau brushed aside one of her dark locks and realized that her knees were trembling like aspens. She sank down on the bed and considered this new development.

Tethyr, the land of her ancestors. The suggestion had merit, and it fit well with her new and loftier ambitions. However, it was one thing to decide upon a trip to the distant south; it was quite another to manage it. She had no patron, little money, and slim prospects of getting more before the winter snows set in. The only solution she could devise was to return to Waterdeep and recover the lost treasure. When she had accomplished that, she could return to her homeland in style.

Yes, that was what she would do. Isabeau rose, her mind made up, and continued stuffing the garments owned by some Eltorchul woman into the traveling chest. She would have the dream spheres, and she knew just how to get them.

Let the half-elf and her courtier chase down the magical toys. She would follow them, as the desert jackal slinks after a pride of hunting lions. Jackals ate well, as a rule.

It did not concern her that many had died because of these spheres—some of them at her hand. She would not meet that fate. Arilyn and Danilo were powerful buffers. When they fell, Isabeau would know to retreat.

She began to hum as she finished her packing. The servants who carried her things to the stables and handed her up onto her horse commented with admiration on her courage and resilience.

"I will be fine," she assured them. "I will do very well indeed."

* * * * *

Danilo knew he was dreaming, but he took little comfort from that knowledge. Images, disjointed and surreal, chased each other through his shallow, restless slumber.

A small white kitten playing in a courtyard. The sudden descent of night, and the approach of an owl. He tried to intervene but found he could neither speak nor move. A child chasing a ball into the street, unaware of the carriage bearing down upon her. Again and again—grim variations on the theme.

A cool hand smoothed over his forehead. Still caught up in the tumble of dream images, Danilo responded to this new threat. He seized the thin wrist and tugged. It was a great relief to be able to act at last. On instinct, he twisted and pinned the intruder beneath him.

A familiar voice said his name. He emerged fully from the nightmare and looked down into Arilyn's face. She regarded him calmly, which made him feel all the more nonplussed at being caught so much out of countenance.

"Are my wards and locks so poor that you could easily overcome them?" he asked.

"Probably," she said mildly, "but Monroe let me in."

"Ah." Dan moved aside and let her rise. "Well, that's reassuring. I suppose." He rose and placed his hands to the small of his back as he tried to ease out the stiffness of his restless sleep. "Where have you been?"

"I went after Isabeau."

He froze in mid stretch. "She's dead, I suppose."

"No."

"You're unusually tolerant. In this case, I'm not sure I approve."

"She will get her due," the half-elf said with certainty. "Soon, I'm guessing."

He eyed her sharply. "Meaning?"

"Isabeau claims she took Lilly's place to save her own life. She says she was pursued by Elaith Craulnober. Dan, before you deny the possibility, remember that Elaith probably has the Mhaorkiira. Remember that Lilly might have sold it."

Danilo turned to the window. Dawn was near, but dark clouds blinded the setting moon. "Elaith went after Isabeau once, and it is conceivable that he might do so again, but I do not want to believe that Elaith killed Lilly."

"It is a possibility."

"I know," Dan admitted with a sigh. He rubbed both hands briskly over his face, as if to clear his vision. "Damnation. I've grown rather fond of the rogue, and I truly believed he would honor his pledge. Of late, though, I have discovered reason to doubt my judgment of those around me. I do not know what to make of Lilly's death, but I feel as if I am standing on shifting sands with my family."

"And with me," Arilyn added softly.

"No. You only do what you must," he protested.

"The end is the same. Promises made and not kept. You need to know where things stand and whom you can trust." She fell silent. For a long time she looked troubled, as if she were fighting some invisible battle.

"You must speak with her," she said abruptly. "Lilly. Get a cleric, summon her spirit. Find out who killed her, and put your mind at ease. Whether it was Elaith or not, you will know, and you can move on."

He regarded her with astonishment. "Elves do not believe in this. You fought me over Oth's possible resurrection."

"I do not like it, but it's a matter of elven tradition, not principle. Right now, it's something you need."

He was deeply moved that she would set aside her elven scruples, putting his concerns paramount. Gently he touched her cheek. "Thank you."

She twisted away and stalked toward the door. "Let's get it over with."

Danilo swallowed a grin. "Let's. If we linger any longer, we are in danger of finding ourselves in a sentimental moment."

The half-elf sent him a suspicious look over her shoulder, as if she half expected him to be laughing at her. "Later," she said shortly, "and that's a promise I intend to keep."

"In that case," Danilo said, trying to wrest what lightness he could from the situation, "I think I can promise this will be a very short conversation."

They rode to the City of the Dead, the vast walled garden where slept many, many generations of Waterdeep's folk, from the poorest commoner to the most fabled heroes of distant times. High walls surrounded the City, and guards stood watch at the fanciful iron gates. This protection went two ways: it kept treasure hunters from despoiling the graves, and it kept the inhabitants contained. In Waterdeep, the dead did not always rest quietly.

For a moment Danilo regretted the course he was about to take. Peace and rest—surely Lilly deserved that much.

"She deserves justice," Arilyn said firmly.

He sent her a quizzical look. "Since when did you start reading my mind?"

"Just your face. Let's do what we've come for."

They rode in silence to the gate and tied their horses to the rail provided. The guards admitted them, and they walked through the park-like grounds, past enormous statues and small, serene marble buildings. Here and there stood a building that was little more than a shallow facade, for the door led not into an edifice but into a dimensional gate.

Danilo paused before a statue of a white horse with a raven poised for flight on its shoulder. Never had he found the Thann family symbol so appropriate. Both creatures were part of the journey—the horse as a traveling partner in life, and, if legend had any basis in truth, the raven to guide the spirit into the lands beyond.

"Lilly will be in here," Danilo said, nodding toward

the small, low building just beyond the family emblem.

Arilyn tried the door. "It's locked. Want me to pick it?"

"No need." Danilo placed his hand on the raven's marble head. Magic guarded the tomb, and none but family members could pass. The door rolled back silently, revealing an empty room.

He took a torch from the holder beside the door frame and lit it, then peered into the chamber. The doors that lined the room were marked with the names of those who slept beyond. No new engraving marked Lilly's rightful place among her kin.

"This is not what we agreed," he muttered. "She was to rest here in the main chamber until her permanent place was prepared. Perhaps the Lady Cassandra had Lilly moved to the commoner's grounds, or even an unmarked plot. If so, she will answer for it!"

They sought out the groundskeeper, a rather stringy-looking dwarf who was relaxing on the grass beside a site marked by an eternal flame. The small fire cast a pleasant warmth into the crisp air, and the dwarf was taking full advantage of it. He lay on his back, with his hands behind his head and his boots propped up on a headstone.

When Arilyn cleared her throat, the dwarf scrambled to his feet and dusted off one hand on the seat of his breeches. This he thrust toward Danilo.

"Sorry for yer loss."

Frequent repetition had drained the words of any empathy they might once have conveyed. Danilo grasped the offered hand briefly.

"*Loss* is the word, in more ways than one. I can't find my sister's body. It was supposed to be in the family tomb."

"Hmmph. What family might that be?"

Dan told him. The dwarf scratched at his beard and ruminated. "Seems to me yer too late, boy. That family's quick to get rid of servants and such like, ain't they?

The ceremony was finished yesterday."

Dan and Arilyn exchanged a puzzled look. "That was not to have occurred until tomorrow. Where was she interred?"

"Not buried. Burned." The dwarf spat into the eternal fire and admired the resultant sizzle as if it illustrated his remark.

"Who was responsible for this mistake?" Arilyn demanded, clearly outraged.

"No mistake. We had our orders."

"Really," Danilo said coldly. "Who has the authority in this place to issue such orders?"

"She ain't from this place, and I'll be lighting a candle to almighty Clangeddin over that!" the dwarf said fervently. He placed a stubby finger on his nose and lifted it to a haughty angle in imitation of his recent nemesis.

Danilo began to get an extremely bad feeling about this. "You're not speaking of the Lady Cassandra Thann, are you?"

"You know her, I take it."

Without intending to do so, he shook his head. "No," he said in a wondering tone, and realized that he spoke truth. "No, I don't think I know her at all."

Fourteen

Danilo found his mother in the garden, deep in the contemplation of the thick tome on her lap. He quickly cast the spell he had prepared on the way over to the family home, one born of his anger and fueled by his haunted dreams.

He intended to reshape the words on Lady Cassandra's page, transforming the scholarly text into an accusing restatement of the agreement they had made just the day before, but the moment he shaped the spell, he felt the magic twist away from him and spin beyond his will and control.

The ink of the open page melted, flowed together. The black stain turned into the color of blood, then leaped up into flame.

Lady Cassandra jolted to her feet with a strangled little cry. The precious book tumbled, unheeded, from her lap. Smoke rose from the smoldering tome, twisting and swirling in a futile attempt to shape the words that Dan and his mother had spoken and that he had placed into the spell. Now their agreement was broken, his trust shattered, and the spell could not recall it.

The noblewoman regarded her visitor for a long moment as she composed herself. "You have my attention," she said at last.

"And you have my promise," Danilo returned with quiet intensity. "I will find out what happened to Lilly, despite your efforts to ensure that this could not happen. Why, Mother? Given the events of this day—the events of the last tenday!—one might reasonably ask what you have to hide."

"Why indeed?" she retorted. "This whole situation is disgraceful. A barmaid's daughter in the family tomb? What were you thinking?"

"You agreed to the arrangements!"

"For your own good," she argued. "If I did not grant some apparent concession, you would not rest until you had your way in every particular."

"Nor will I." Danilo studied her, trying to fathom what went on behind that lovely, composed face. "Aren't you at all curious about Lilly? Her life, her fate?"

"No. Nor do I want to discuss this further. Not now or ever."

"Damn it, mother, you're as stubborn as a *full*-blooded elf!"

Finally, his words had effect. A look of consternation crossed her face, quickly controlled. "You should choose your words with more care. There are those in this city who might read too much into your comment."

A terrible, impossible suspicion snaked into his mind. Perhaps Lilly was murdered because she was a child of a noble house who clearly carried more than a little elven blood. Arilyn had been attacked. Elaith. Perhaps someone was determined to separate the Thann family from any contact with elves.

Perhaps Cassandra's desire to deny her heritage was so strong that she struck out against anything that reminded her of it.

Quickly he thrust this thought aside. He could not

believe that of his own mother—he could barely fathom how he himself could have imagined it.

"You may hear that Elaith Craulnober had a hand in Lilly's death," he said as soon as he could trust himself to speak. "I do not deny it is possible, but I will find the truth of the matter. Until then, do not support any efforts against him." He paused, then added with difficulty. "Or any others of elven blood."

His mother was dumbfounded, speechless for the first time in Danilo's recollection. "You presume to instruct me?" she said at last.

"In a manner of speaking. Our elven heritage might be a faint and distant thing, but I want you to understand that I am proud to own it."

She shook her head in disgust. "Khelben!" she muttered, turning the archmage's name into a curse. "You must have gotten this notion from him. I must say, he picked a fine time to stop being close-mouthed and enigmatic!"

"Then it's true. Why did you never say anything?"

"Why should I? It has been forgotten for generations! There is no need to open the closets and let the skeletons cavort about."

"The Thann family fortune was built on the slave trade," he reminded her. "Are you saying that it is acceptable to have slavers as ancestors, but not elves?"

"Watch your tone," she said in a voice that simmered with anger, "and watch your step! Elaith Craulnober has overstepped, and he will pay for his presumption. Take care that you do not go down with him."

She stalked out, leaving Danilo standing alone amid the ruins of his long-held illusions.

* * * * *

Arilyn waited at the agreed-upon tavern until the moon rose and the fire burned low. Danilo came in, looking as windblown as a sailor and more desolate than she had ever seen him. He threw himself onto the bench and dashed his damp hair off his face. "I'm sorry. I was walking the Sea Wall."

She knew the spot. It was a good place of solitude. A sharp wind, laden with salt and spray and secrets, blew in from the sea on the mildest of days. Nothing provided shelter from the buffeting wind or offered much of a barrier between the path and the long, sheer drop to the icy water below. It was not a stroll for the fainthearted or those too fond of comfort. A person could walk the length of the wall at nearly any hour and not meet another soul.

"Looks to me as if you came in too soon," she commented. She tossed some coins on the table and rose. "Let's go."

He did not argue. They headed north and climbed the stairs carved into the stone wall. For a long time, they walked along the rim. The setting moon glittered on the restless waves. The receding tide exposed the expanse of barnacles desperately clinging to the wall. There was no sound but the crash and murmur of the waves. It occurred to Arilyn that she had seldom seen a more lonely, desolate place.

"I come here from time to time," Dan said suddenly. "The sound of the sea often serves to wash clean my thoughts, allows me to start anew and think with greater clarity. Tonight, it does not avail."

He related his conversation with Lady Cassandra, his terrible suspicions. "I have always felt somewhat apart from my family, but I never realized how little I knew them. I never conceived of the possibility that they could turn on their own."

"It happens," she said shortly, for Danilo's tale was too like her own early life for comfort. After a moment's hesitation, it occurred to her that he might find, if not comfort, then at least community in her story.

"My mother died when I was barely fifteen," she said. "A half-elf of that age is little more than a child. Her moonblade came into my keeping. She had always intended that it pass to me, and she had begun training me with an eye toward its demands, but as you know her time was cut short before she could tell me all I needed to know. My mother's family came to Evereska for the funeral. They were robed and hooded in traditional elven mourning. I never saw their faces, but I heard them argue about the sword and its fate. None of them thought I should have it, but they left it in my keeping. Much later, I realized why. No one thought that a half-elf could claim a moonblade. They fully expected I would die in the attempt and that the family could then reclaim Amnestria's sword. But they gave me no word of warning or explanation."

Danilo's lips thinned in anger. "I never knew that."

"It's not something I like to talk about. It took me a long time to realize that my mother's family are not evil or even thoughtless. Far from it. I was simply not a part of their world. Half-elves are not people to them and so do not merit consideration. That sounds harsh, but they have reasons for their way of thinking."

"Even so, you were left alone, and at a very young age. I think I have some understanding of how difficult that must have been."

Arilyn halted him with a hand on his arm. They moved without speaking into an embrace, two figures silhouetted against the night sky.

"You are not alone," she said softly. "Never that."

As they stood together a small tendril slipped into her mind, a presence that she had always sensed, but never so vividly. She recognized Dan's merry, blithe spirit, but behind it was a darkness that she had never glimpsed. She accepted them both, understanding what this meant. They were connected by elven rapport, a deep psychic and spiritual bond. It was far from complete—the soul-deep union of the feyfolk was beyond either of them—but still infinitely more than a meeting of flesh or even of hearts.

"There is that, too," he said softly, answering her unspoken thoughts. By that, Arilyn knew the elven bond encompassed them both. The joining was made, the circle complete.

Suddenly, he swept her up into his arms, as if she were a silk-clad maiden rather than a warrior. To her surprise, she found she did not mind. Danilo had his own patterns, and at this moment the alien urgency of a human's desire seemed as natural to her as the coming of spring.

She circled her arms around his neck. Magic engulfed them, and the roar of the sea was lost in the sweeping tide of the travel spell.

They emerged from the white whirl of the magical transport into a world that, to Arilyn's heightened senses, seemed just as enchanted. Apple logs crackled on the hearth fire, and lamps fueled by scented oil burned low. Globes of blue glass filtered the lamplight and cast an azure glow over the room. Arilyn glanced down, half expecting to find herself clad in the deep blue silk and gems of Danilo's preference.

"Not tonight," he said aloud as he set her gently on the floor. "As you are."

She reached for the buckle of her swordbelt and cast the elven weapon aside. It was an instinctively protective gesture, for even a casual touch from the moonblade could burn the careless. She let it fall without care or concern. The sword was her elven destiny, but tonight, she had another pledge to fulfill, just as sacred.

Danilo put her hands aside and tended her himself. He gently smoothed away the indentations on her forearm where the bracer and knife sheath pressed against her. Her skin fascinated him, and he explored it with exquisite, torturous delicacy.

"Moonlight on pearl," he murmured in a reverent tone, easing her shirt away from her shoulders.

Arilyn began to experience a very human level of impatience. Had she possessed any magic, she would have dissolved all impediments. She began to tug at the laces that bound the side of her leathers.

He caught her mood, and moved to help her, but urgency made them both fumble-fingered. Finally she pushed him away and bent, pulling a knife from a sheath hidden in her boot.

This she handed to Danilo. He deftly cut the laces, and she kicked the ruined garment aside. She kicked her boots off so emphatically that one of them hit an oil lamp. The blue globe rocked wildly, and the flame guttered, then disappeared.

The darkness suited her. Moonlight was all that was needed. It filled her, in a very tangible sense. Its silvery light began to gather, burning ever brighter as it rose. Her mind washed clear. There was nothing but this, no time but now. Elven rapport melded with very human urgency, but there was no discordance, only completion, and a shared sense of homecoming so poignant and sweet that she knew the memory would stay with her long after her life essence melded with the moonblade.

Later, they curled together before the fire and watched the patterns in the flames. There was no need for words, for those served to bridge a gap, and the communion they had shared made this unnecessary. Whatever came, Arilyn felt that neither of them would ever truly be alone again.

* * * * *

The morning came in slowly, for the sun was curtained with clouds and a faint rain whispered over the roofs and rustled the falling leaves.

Danilo turned to the sleeping woman beside him and woke her with a kiss. "As much as I hate to say this, we should rise. We have business outside this room."

She stretched, looking as smug and languorous as a cat. "Had I known what was awaiting me, I would not have waited so long."

He caught up her hand and kissed it. "My fault entirely," he said ruefully. Four years ago, when they had declared their love, he had been determined that all would be done as tradition demanded. Their union would be blessed by clerics of Hannali Celanil, the elven goddess of love. There would be a splendid ceremony, a lavish celebration. Theirs was no trivial fancy to enter into lightly.

"You just wanted to do things right," she consoled him.

"I picked a damnably foolish time to start," he said with a wry grin. After the depth and shattering communion of their joining, ceremony and tradition seemed paltry things. They were bound for life and had been for a very long time.

Nevertheless there was still a part of him that yearned for the ceremony, the symbol. He reached for the bedside table and took from the drawer a small box. Four years ago he had purchased a hoop of sapphires and moonstones, which he had planned to give her at the Gemstone Ball.

"You don't wear rings," he observed. "Perhaps I could persuade you to make an exception."

She held out her hand. "At the moment, I find myself more open to persuasion than is my usual custom."

He slid the ring onto her finger. "It's almost a shame that I can't take advantage of that! But I can think of nothing in this world that I wish to ask for, that we do not already have. With the possible exemption of a new pair of leather breeches," he amended, nodding toward the ruined garment.

Arilyn frowned as she tried to follow his reasoning. Then she remembered, with a smug little grin that delighted him. He chuckled and reached for the bellpull. Monroe came promptly to the call. The steward opened the door a discreet crack, and asked how he might serve. Danilo sent him off in search of a gown that might fit Arilyn.

Monroe returned with admirable haste. He draped a linen shift and kirtle over the back of a chair. "Simple garments, but they should suffice for the present," he announced as he left the room.

Arilyn eyed the practical garments with approval. "Your steward has sense. I suppose I should feel odd, though, wearing clothes that belong to another woman."

Danilo regarded her with astonishment. "There *are* other women?"

She sent him a mock glare. "Keep thinking along those lines, and we shall get along fine."

The peace and unity of that morning lasted until they were on the streets. Arilyn's eyes turned hard and watchful. An aura of battle-ready anticipation rose from her like mist.

"You're as nervous as a squirrel," Dan observed. "What is wrong?"

"I'm not sure." The half-elf looked genuinely puzzled.

"What of the sword?"

He spoke easily, with none of the resentment that had shadowed him for so long.

"There is no warning, but I feel as if we're being followed. Why, I couldn't tell you. I don't hear anything. I just sense it."

They skirted an open gutter, mindful of the attack that had followed the last time Arilyn had a presentiment of danger, and hurried onto a more populated street.

So close to the market, street vendors did a brisk business. Small meat pasties scented the air, and fragrant steam rose from baskets piled with small loaves of fresh bread. People ate these as they walked and stopped to wash down their meal with a mug of ale poured from the keg or fresh milk dipped up from a pail.

A woman's scream froze them in midstep.

Before Danilo could turn toward the sound, Arilyn already had her sword out. No fey light limned its length, but Danilo's attention was captured by the runes carved along it—one for each elf who had wielded the sword and who had imbued it with a new level of power. One of these markings glowed with eerie white light.

Never had Danilo seen the moonblade respond in such fashion. This was nothing like the blue glow that warned of coming danger, or the soft green luster that led Arilyn to aid her fellow elves.

The woman gave another cry, this one closer to a strangled sob. Danilo tore his eyes from the moonblade. A dairymaid stood beside her upturned stool and pail, her hands at her mouth and her eyes enormous, oblivious to the spilled milk pooling at her feet. The girl seemed to be in no immediate danger, but Danilo tracked her gaze to the source of her distress.

Behind Arilyn, almost indistinguishable from the play of light and shadows cast by the milling crowd, was the ghostly image of an elven woman.

Though the form was faint and as translucent as a soap bubble, Danilo made out the ghostly elf's stern expression, the sapphire-colored hair braided tightly in a practical, battle-ready fashion.

"Thassitalia," Arilyn murmured.

Danilo had heard that name, and he knew at once what it meant. This was an elfshadow—a manifestation of the moonblade's magic and the symbol of the spirit-deep link between elf and sword. Thassitalia had been one of Arilyn's ancestors, one of the elves who had wielded the moonblade and whose spirit lent magic to the elven sword.

He had seen the elfshadow before, but it had appeared more solid and it had worn Arilyn's face. That had been a time of uncertainty and danger, for the moonblade's magic had been twisted and exploited by an elven mage. Arilyn had confided once that she often had nightmares about the possibility that this could happen again. It would seem that her fears had come to pass.

The ephemeral shadow studied them, her insubstantial face awash with puzzlement and consternation.

Arilyn was equally dumbfounded. "I did not summon you," she said to the ghostly elf in the Elvish language. "Return to the sword at once."

The essence of the warrior Thassitalia merely shook her head, not in refusal, but as if to indicate that she could not hear or understand.

Danilo caught Arilyn's arm. "Let's move on before we create a panic," he said in a low voice.

She nodded and fell into step as he ducked down a narrow opening between two buildings. They followed a Harper's road, an intricate, hidden path through the back ways of the city, over rooftops and through the hidden entrances of shops whose owners were sympathetic to the Harper folk.

Each step of the way, the ghostly elf followed them like a third shadow.

* * * * *

Elaith Craulnober padded lightly through a similarly convoluted path, as quiet and anonymous as the occasional cat that prowled the alley for vermin.

For all his wealth and power, the elf still moved about the city without attracting much notice. He preferred it that way. This was one reason why his recent inclusion onto Galinda Raventree's social registry had been so ill advised.

There were many people of wealth and influence in this city who knew his name, but not his face. Elaith could deal with them or gain information in casual conversation that they would never knowingly confide to a competitor. To oblige the man he had named Elf-friend, he had yielded this advantage. The peerage knew him now—or at least, they thought they did. If they had true knowledge, they would not move against him by sending masked men and second-rate soldiers such as Rhep.

It was almost a shame that they would never know the shape of his vengeance, but that was the way of things. Elaith would never have achieved his wealth or success if he had dealt in an open and forthright manner. Nor would he survive now if too much attention came to be focused on him and his activities. It was time for the eyes of the merchant nobility to turn elsewhere.

He found Rhep loitering behind an Ilzimmer-owned warehouse, shooting dice against the wall with a trio of Ilzimmer soldiers. Elaith lingered in the shadows long enough to take the measure of his foe. A woman clad in a tawdry scarlet gown leaned against a discarded barrel and watched the game, not apparently much concerned about the outcome of the men's wager. From the coarse comments the men made, Elaith discerned that she was to be the prize. The men had pooled their coin to pay her rent.

It would be convenient, Elaith mused, if Rhep won the wager. He could then follow the man to his afternoon's entertainment and deal with him in relative privacy.

Rhep's luck, however, was not good. A short, ginger-bearded man with a peg leg stumped off in triumph with the woman. His comrades threw a few more rounds for the sport of it, all the while discussing the likelihood of finding a tavern that would extend credit. The elf managed to catch Rhep's eye as they turned to leave.

The man stopped abruptly and made a show of patting himself down. "You lads go ahead. Seems like I lost my best dice," he improvised.

As soon as the men were out of earshot, Elaith stepped from the shadows. "Your nose is healing nicely," he commented. "It's a bit bigger and flatter than it used to be, but why quibble about a drop in a keg?"

Rhep scowled. "Hold your tongue, elf. I'd just as soon kill you quick, but keep it up and I'll be getting ugly."

"It's rather too late to be concerned about that, don't you think?"

The big man wrenched open the door to the warehouse and jerked his head toward the opening. "Inside. We settle this now."

Elaith bowed and extended one hand, indicating that the man should precede him. The soldier flushed a dull red at this reminder of his earlier treachery. He drew his sword and made a point of backing into the warehouse rather than turning his back to the elf.

Elaith silently applauded him. As insults went, it was a rather good one. Any claim that he was on the same level as this thug was base slander.

"Only one leaves this place," Rhep said.

"Agreed." The elf drew his sword and began to circle.

Rhep turned to keep the elf in front of him, but he waited for the first strike. Elaith obliged, delivering a high, lightning flash of an attack.

Before the mercenary could parry, Elaith spun, stepping past the man. As he did so the sword whistled just short of Rhep's ear. On the backstroke, he brought his sword low and slashed once across the seat of the man's leather breeches.

Rhep howled and whirled at the elf, lunging as he went, but Elaith was no longer there. The elf moved with his opponent, keeping just beyond the edge of his side vision. His next attack came in high, cutting a thin, shallow line across the man's cheek.

The elf danced back a step and gave Rhep a chance to face him down. The mercenary advanced with a furious onslaught of quick, hard blows. Elaith deftly parried each one with an economy of motion that was contemptuous in its ease. For a long time he was content to defend, one hand on his sword's hilt, the other resting lightly on his hip, his feet never moving. His faint, mocking smile never faltered. He intended to enjoy this.

At last Rhep backed away. They circled each other, swords held in low guard position, while the human caught his wind. With one hand he reached around behind his back to explore his first wound. His hand came back bloodied. He wiped the stain on his tunic and sent the elf a defiant sneer.

"Always heard elves favored attacking a man from behind, if you catch my drift."

Elaith let the crude comment pass. "Consider yourself lucky. I could have hamstrung you," he pointed out.

This notion stole the sneer from Rhep's face. His bravado vanished as he realized the truth of the elf's words and saw the battle could have been finished that quickly and that easily. His eyes were dark with the image of himself lying helpless, unable to rise, impotent to do anything but await the killing stroke.

"No games," Rhep said grimly. "Let's have done with this."

He came in with a rush, sword held high with both hands. He smashed down hard toward the elf, wagering everything on his superior size and strength.

Elaith whirled aside, not bothering to parry the mighty blow, but Rhep kept coming, battering away at the elf, pounding at him with all his force and fury.

It was actually a good strategy, Elaith acknowledged. It forced him into a two-handed grip and slowed him down. He was smaller and faster, and Rhep's attack forced the battle into a contest of strength. To compensate, the elf came in close, dangerously close, so that he had to catch the furious blows near the hilt of his weapon. He was close enough now to bring a second weapon to bear once the opportunity presented itself.

Rhep saw the strategy and began to retreat. The elf pressed him, following him, matching him step for step and meeting each blow. With growing desperation, the man struck out hard and then followed the sword attack with a bare-knuckled punch. The elf leaned to one side to dodge the blow, then sliced his sword downward, cutting into Rhep's arm before he could withdraw it. The blade caught the inside crook of the man's elbow and dug deep. The soldier immediately fisted his hand and brought it up tight against his shoulder, closing his arm over the wound to slow the flow of blood. Grimly he kept on, though with less force now that he could only fight with one hand.

Slowly, determinedly, the elf worked the clashing blades up high. Their swords crossed overhead. Rhep managed to hook the curved guard of his sword under Elaith's blade. With a triumphant leer, he hauled upward with all his strength, trusting in his greater height to drag the weapon from the elf's grasp.

Elaith simply let go.

The soldier staggered back, too late realizing his mistake. Elaith crossed his arms and pulled twin knives from the sheaths on his forearms. He advanced with the speed of a striking snake, and slashed both blades across the man's unprotected throat.

Rhep's sword clattered to the wooden floor. He sagged against the wall, his mouth working as he tried to form a final curse. Crimson bubbles formed at the corners of his lips. Will and spirit and life itself faded from his eyes, leaving nothing but hatred. The elf watched until even that dark light went out.

Elaith glanced at the fine daggers in his hand. They were Amcathra daggers, the best human-made weapons in the city. Without hesitation or regret, he hurled first one weapon and then the other into the former Ilzimmer soldier.

"Let them make of that what they will," the elf murmured. He turned and melted into the shadows, pondering with great satisfaction the course this action would spawn.

Fifteen

The unlikely trio—the human bard, the half-elven fighter, and the ghostly shadow—wandered through the city for the better part of the morning. Finally Danilo called a halt on a rooftop garden, a place far above watchful eyes and visible to none but the griffon riders who circled lazily against the clouds. He hoped the legendary vision of the eagle-headed beasts was not so keen that it could discern the shadowy elf woman who stood beside Arilyn, resting on an equally shadowy sword.

"I have to find whoever killed Lilly," Danilo blurted out.

Arilyn gave him a long measuring look. She turned away, propping her elbows against the garden wall. "Have I tried to dissuade you?"

"No. No, of course not, but you must let me continue alone."

The half-elf straightened up and affixed him with a challenging gaze. "Forget it."

He shook his head and took the small, glowing sphere from its hiding place in his boot. "Don't you see? Something is disrupting magic. It has to be these dream spheres."

His eyes shifted to the far edge of the roof. Thassitalia was all but gone now. Only a faint outline remained, invisible when he looked at it directly. "I've been carrying this sphere with me since the day Lilly died. As a result, the magic of your sword has been seriously disrupted."

"So are your spells. That's what happened the night of the Thann party. Oth brought some of his dream spheres to pitch them to a group of wizards and merchant lords."

"I took one from Isabeau," he added. "Yes, I understand that now."

She took a step closer. "I am more than my sword," she said firmly. "You are more than your magic."

He regarded her with a faint smile. "You've always said that there was too much magic in Waterdeep. It seems we may have the opportunity to do without it."

"Let's get to it. We'll assume that Lilly was mixed up with the bandits who ambushed the air caravan, and start there."

They worked their way across the city's rooftops toward the Gundwynd manor. As they approached, Danilo caught sight of several detachments of the Watch milling about, conspicuous in their green and black leather uniforms.

They climbed down to the street and walked up to the manor.

"No one in, no one out," announced the grim-faced woman who stood at the side gate.

"What happened here?"

The Watchwoman gave Danilo a quelling look. "Move along, sir. The Gundwynd family is not receiving visitors at present."

Danilo turned toward Arilyn, but she had disappeared. He nodded politely to the Watchwoman and went on his way, circling the walled villa as he observed the placement of trees on that street. He stopped two blocks down, then sat under a stately oak.

Several moments passed before he heard a faint rustling in the branches. He glanced up as Arilyn climbed to the lowest branch and dropped lightly to the ground beside him.

"Well?" he inquired.

"One of the servants found Belinda Gundwynd, the youngest daughter, dead in the stables. She was with an elven groom, the only person of elven blood who remained in the family's employ. Seems he had a personal reason for staying around. Rumors have been circulating about Belinda and her lover. The servants overheard the family fighting over it. They were forcing her to give him up. The family is claiming that her death was a lover's pact."

"You don't believe this."

She shot him an incredulous look. "The servants who found them said that the bodies were in the hay, not dangling from the rafters."

"Still, is that reason to conclude that the Gundwynd family is wrong?"

"It's reassuring to know that you haven't strangled anyone lately," Arilyn said dryly. "The task demands considerable strength and will. Hard to do, when you're being distracted, and I'd say that being strangled yourself is a bit of a distraction. They could hardly manage to kill each other and die at the same time."

"They would need a bard's timing," Danilo agreed. "So the Watch is not buying the Gundwynds' story, I take it."

"They are not hearing anything but the Gundwynds' story. The servants who told me the tale were encouraged not to talk. Let's move on—there's a Watchman over there who's starting to take note of us."

As they walked, Danilo struggled to sort through

this. Like Arilyn, he doubted that Belinda Gundwynd and her lover had contrived their own deaths.

Then who? The Gundwynd family, motivated by the nobility's bias against alliances with elves? If that were so, then Danilo had lived his entire life among creatures more vicious than tren.

"They eat their own," he murmured. "It's a matter of honor."

Arilyn sent him a sharp, concerned look. "Do you really think that's what happened?"

"The possibility is hard to ignore. If I can suspect my own family of attempting to rid itself of elven alliances, why not the Gundwynds?"

"That doesn't account for Oth," Arilyn pointed out.

"No. No, it doesn't, and this will only deepen the scandal regarding Gundwynd and the elven folk. This could mean the end of the Gundwynd fortunes." Danilo stopped short as his mind replayed the angry confrontation between Lord Gundwynd and Lady Cassandra.

"It could mean the end of the Gundwynd fortune," he repeated. "The death of Belinda and her elven love gives substance to every rumor spoken against the family. Who would have reason to do such a thing?"

"One name comes to mind," Arilyn said. "Someone who saw elves die in the ambush and who might want Gundwynd to suffer for it."

Danilo shook his head. "Not Elaith," he insisted. "It simply does not make sense."

"It might not need to," she pointed out. "Remember, he may have the Mhaorkiira. In the past, those who fell under the dark gem's power acted in twisted ways that made sense to no one but themselves."

"It's possible," he allowed. "Certainly some people will believe it to be true, but Lord Gundwynd will not. He will look elsewhere for blame."

"Oh?" she said cautiously.

"Thann, Ilzimmer, Gundwynd, Amcathra," Danilo

said, ticking off names on his fingers. "Four families sponsored the ill-fated caravan. All suspect each other of betrayal and ambush. Perhaps the tren are not the only creatures who take vendetta against attacks on their clan."

Arilyn nodded slowly, following his reasoning. "If so, none of these recent wounds are self-inflicted."

"If so," he added, "then the time of the Guild Wars could soon be upon us once again."

* * * * *

Arilyn considered Danilo's words for a long time as they left the Gundwynd villa behind. "If you are right, I suspect that this will be a very different type of war," she said at last. "No armies, no open bloodshed in the streets. As Cassandra pointed out, the noble families are very mindful of those times and are not eager to see them return. Any clan that came out in open aggression would be swiftly quelled."

Danilo considered this, then nodded his agreement. He had sat through enough meetings of Waterdeep's secret Lords to see the truth in it. The Lords had been chosen from every corner of the city, every strata of society. As a result, very little happened in the city that did not reach the ears of the hidden rulers. Their decisions were enforced by the Watch as well as a small standing army of guardsmen and some of the most powerful wizards in the Northlands. The days when wholesale war could rage within the city walls were over.

"So what, then?"

The half-elf sent him a measuring look. "You play chess, I suppose."

"When I cannot avoid doing so without bloodshed, yes," he said in a dry tone. "Is that what you think this is? A chess game?"

"It is possible. Waterdeep is a large city, with thousands of games played out on every street. Who notices the loss of a single pawn on a single board? Even Oth Eltorchul's death could be explained in that light. He had ties to the caravan. He arranged to have his dream spheres quietly shipped into the city."

"A plan that Gundwynd carried out, against Lady Cassandra's strong objections and despite an agreement the families had made," Danilo concluded. He sighed and cast a sidelong glance at Arilyn. "In that case, what was Belinda's death? A warning?"

"The Gundwynd clan will probably think so."

"I cannot accept your argument," he said quietly. "You imply that the merchant families maintain order with a brutal hand. Why would this be necessary? There are laws enough in Waterdeep, and many and powerful are those who ensure these laws are kept."

Arilyn was silent for several moments. "You've just answered your own question."

He lifted one brow in a supercilious arch. "I did? Perhaps I should start listening more closely to myself."

"Let me put it this way: You've heard the old saying about honor among thieves. I wouldn't go that far, but there is definitely a code. The same could be said of assassins. If someone starts getting too greedy or too careless, the others pull him back or do away with him. They can't afford to have too much attention focused on their activities, you see."

"I do indeed, but how does that signify? We are talking about some of the most respected noble houses in Waterdeep!"

"We are talking about merchants," she said bluntly. "None of them wanted to get behind Oth's dream spheres because they knew the sort of attention these would bring. The wizards would have opposed them even before they found out about the disruption of magic, and they would have ferreted out everything there was to know about the trade. Who knows what might have been uncovered in the process?"

Danilo did not answer at once. He sidestepped a pair of street urchins who thundered past in a race as old as Waterdeep itself. The boys rolled a pair of old barrel hoops down the street, sticks in their hands and grins on their dirty faces. Their carefree innocence drew Dan's eye, and for a moment he watched them and wistfully recalled the comfort of long-held illusions.

"Your words are hard to accept," he murmured.

"I could be wrong," Arilyn said. She hesitated, then added, "It would explain why your mother was so concerned when Lilly was linked back to the Thann family after her death."

It occurred to Danilo that perhaps Cassandra had fallen short of the full truth. "Lilly was linked to the Thann family *before* her death. That is why she died," he said with sudden bitter conviction. "It was a strike against the family. The killer was removing a pawn."

"Yes, but Lilly evidently saw the danger coming. Why else would she go to your father, when she had never made any claim on him before? Until that time, none of you knew her as family."

"Someone else did. Someone she knew well, confided in."

They considered this in silence. "I have been thinking about the manner of Lilly's death," Arilyn said after a while. "By all appearances, she was slain by a tren assassin, but the killer did not . . . follow the usual tren custom."

His lips thinned to a grim line at the inference. "Yes? So?"

"What if the killer wasn't a tren? What if he only appeared to be, and took this guise either to displace suspicion, or from twisted sport?"

Danilo looked sharply at her, understanding at once her reasoning. "Twisted sport," he repeated slowly. "By any chance, was Simon Ilzimmer at Oth's presentation the night of the Gemstone Ball?"

"Possibly. His cousin Boraldan was there. I heard several voices I couldn't name. One was very deep, with a bit of a rumble to it that almost hinted at dwarven speech."

"That does sound like Simon. Would you recognize that voice if you heard it again?"

"I think so," she said shortly.

Dan smiled faintly. "Judging from your expression, you would rather take another stroll through the city's sewers."

She did not deny his words. Actually, they expressed her feelings rather well. Among her contacts in the city were a number of women who worked in the taverns and bathhouses. After some of the stories she'd heard about the Ilzimmer lord, she could hardly imagine herself sipping wine and making polite conversation.

Danilo seemed less bothered by the prospect. They went directly to the small, brooding manor that was home to Simon Ilzimmer. The bells in the nearby Temple of Ilmater tolled solemnly as Danilo left his card with the servant. Arilyn idly counted the rolling peals, wondering as she did why anyone would devote his life to so dreary a creed as that of the God of Suffering. By the time the call to worship faded into silence, the servant returned with word that Lord Simon would receive them.

At first glance, Simon Ilzimmer did not fit his dark reputation. He was a tall, broad man who appeared to be no stranger to the disciplines of sword and horse. His manners were faultless, and he received his guests with every courtesy. He and Danilo sipped warmed zzar and chatted about mutual acquaintances and recent events with apparent candor and good humor.

Despite his genial manner, he was indeed one of the merchant nobility who had attended the meeting in the

Thann villa. Arilyn easily recognized the deep, resonant voice. Now that she faced Simon Ilzimmer, she found the man exceedingly difficult to read. Indeed, she doubted that he was entirely sane. There was an emptiness to his eyes, an utter lack of connection between his words and any discernible emotion. On the other hand, she sensed the seething energy of the man. His gaze seemed to skitter away without actually moving, and he had a sort of brooding intensity about him that reminded her of the portentous quiet before a sea squall. It was as if he were two men, one altogether too controlled, little more than a shell, the other a violent storm, likely to strike without warning.

His study supported this impression. Though the furniture was sparse and practical, the walls were lined with disturbing pictures—dark, twisted visions from a madman's mind. Danilo walked over to consider a rendering of two red dragons entangled in fierce mating amid the burning ruins of a village.

"Fascinating," he murmured. "Was this painted from life?"

Arilyn sent him a warning look. Chances were that the Ilzimmer noble was not overburdened with a sense of humor. "We are trying to retrace the goods stolen from the air caravan," she said frankly, for she was tired of the inconsequential talk and growing increasingly uncomfortable in Simon's presence. "Anything you could tell us might be helpful."

The storm behind the man's dark eyes kindled and flashed. "You accuse me in my own home?"

"No one is making accusations," Danilo said mildly. "We are merely trying to gather together the pieces of this puzzle. Since your family also suffered losses, is it not in our best interests to work together?"

Simon eyed him with deranged cunning. "Lady Cassandra is shrewd. Sending you here nosing about was a brilliant ploy. Everyone knows that you have little to do with the family's business, and all know you are her favorite son. A brilliant way for her to deny involvement."

"Why should she need to do such a thing? Thann had no part in the theft," Danilo said with as much conviction as he could muster. "For that matter, the Lady Cassandra does not know of my presence here."

The mage snorted. He was about to say more, but his eyes widened with mingled surprise and horror. He leaped to his feet, pointing with a shaking finger. "Threaten me, will you? Here in my own place, no less! I won't have it! All of you, leave at once! Get out, out!"

Simon's voice rose on the last words into near hysteria. "We should do as he says," Danilo said in a low voice. "He is a mage, and I'm in no position to challenge him."

Arilyn needed no urging. She turned to leave the chamber and immediately fell back onto her heels.

She stood nearly face to face with the ghostly image of an elven wizard. He was a tall elf whose silver hair had been woven into scores of tiny braids. He held a shadowy moonblade, point down, and he was leaning on the hilt as a wizard might rest upon his staff. His translucent blue eyes were watchful, and he was gazing at Simon with a quiet intensity that gave substance to the mage's fear.

They quickly left the estate, the shadowy mage walking soundlessly behind them. As soon as they were beyond the gate, Arilyn commanded the elfshadow manifestation to return to the sword. To their relief, the ghostly image dissolved into silvery motes. These swirled out into a neat line and disappeared into the moonblade one by one, like a row of ducklings slipping into a pond.

"This is getting out of hand," Arilyn muttered as they hurried back toward Danilo's home.

"At least the elfshadow is gone. You can still control

the sword," he said in the tone of one who was searching for good news in unlikely places.

"Not really," she said, then shot a quick glance over her shoulder. "I still feel as if we're being followed. The moonblade's magic is getting more and more unstable. How can I go about my business, knowing that one of my ancestors might come calling at any moment?"

"Look on the bright side," Danilo suggested.

"That is?"

"Well, at least we're not being followed by tren."

"Don't be so sure about that," she said grimly as she glanced at the cobblestones at her feet. "Remember, you're a sixth son. I'm your half-elven companion. Can you think of a more expendable target for reprisal?"

For a moment he looked as if he would protest, then his face turned thoughtful. "Belinda was the youngest Gundwynd child."

She turned to him, her face deadly serious. "That had occurred to me, too."

* * * * *

"The woman is a positive marvel," Elaith murmured as he read the note Myrna Cassalanter had sent by trusted messenger and fast horse.

Even the most unlikely of her rumors had borne fruit. Just that day, not more than a few hours before, Simon Ilzimmer had been arrested by the Watch for the murder of a courtesan—in one of Elaith's establishments, no less. Simon was noble, and the men and women who would give testimony against him were common servants, but the end result would be the same. A minor Ilzimmer lord would hang from the city walls.

It bothered Elaith not at all that Simon Ilzimmer was innocent of this particular crime. His death would be true justice, even if the facts did not tally in every particular. Best of all, no one would trace the man's death back to Elaith's door. His servants would give true and earnest testimony to what they had seen—or believed that they had seen. Magical examination would bear that out. Simon's reputation would supply the extra nudge needed to push him over the Hangman's Leap.

The pot was simmering nicely, Elaith concluded as he turned back to the note. Reprisals would be soon in coming, and the noblemen would be busily employed for some time to come.

His brow furrowed as he read on. With great relish, Myrna recounted the death of a tavern wench, a by-blow of Rhammas Thann. Rumor had it that the girl's body had been claimed by Danilo Thann, who insisted that she be laid to rest in the family tomb.

Elaith reached for the bellpull. His elven steward came promptly to the call. "Send a message to Lord Thann," the elf said. "Tell him I require an immediate audience at . . ." The elf thought quickly, then added. "The steps of the Pantheon Temple."

The servant bowed and disappeared. Elaith hurried to the temple complex, hoping that the unspoken message would not be misunderstood. Danilo had reason to distrust him, especially if he had pieced together the story of the Mhaorkiira. Bronwyn had no doubt reported back about the magic-rich ruby she had found in Silverymoon and about Elaith's interest in it. It was likely that Arilyn would recognize the kiira from its description and know those who held it could be twisted to evil. Reason indeed for concern—at least, to those whose knowledge of the kiira was limited to legend.

He found a quiet place in the courtyard just below the sweeping marble stair and fell into apparent contemplation of a statue of some goddess or other. This reflective pose did not at all mirror his state of mind, but it was common among the elves who came to the temple for a few moments' respite from the frenetic pace of the human city.

Even the dull sensitivities of the humanfolk perceived some of the tranquil calm of this elven haven. Those who strolled by softened their step and quieted their chatter. Elaith watched as Danilo reined in his horse at a respectful distance, then swung down and paced quietly over to the waiting elf.

"A matter of some urgency, your messenger said," Danilo prompted.

The human did not look well, Elaith noted. It was difficult to call him pale, in comparison to a moon elf's complexion, but the signs of several sleepless nights were etched on his face, and there was a deep sadness in his eyes. That, and nothing more. There was no warmth, no humor, none of the growing friendship that had come to mean more to the elf than he cared to admit.

Suddenly the task was harder than Elaith had anticipated. The elf turned aside and clasped his hands behind his back. "I heard of the loss to your family. I am sorry."

Danilo's eyes clouded with grief, as well as a flicker of anger. "No loss to my family," he said shortly, "but on Lilly's behalf and my own, I thank you for your sympathy."

"Sympathy is a cheap gift. In your position, I would prefer vengeance," the elf said. "You have the look of a hound that's picked up the fox's scent."

"A skunk, more like it. Yes, I will run this vermin to ground."

The elf expected this response, but he did not like the grim set of the man's face. He recognized that look of absolute, relentless stubbornness. Once, those traits had saved Elaith's life. He feared that now they could mean the end of Danilo's.

"Perhaps I can be of some assistance," he said, schooling himself to feel no remorse over the sudden leap of hope and gratitude in the man's eyes. Help he would give, but to the fox and not the hound. Better to send Danilo off following another scent than to allow him to come too close to the heart of the matter. If the hound lived to hunt another day, he reasoned, the Mhaorkiira's master would find a suitable use for him.

"You know that I do considerable business in the Dock Ward. I have some knowledge of the young woman," he said. "She had a sporting nature, and from time to time she found her way into my gambling dens. Since I make a point of knowing my customers, I learned her name, if not her heritage. But she has more in common with you than appearance might indicate."

"The point, please, and swiftly," Danilo implored.

"It will not be easy to hear," the elf cautioned. "More than once, I have seen her in the company of one of your peers. A friend of yours, I believe."

The flash of stunned recognition, the sudden bleak flood of loss and then the cleansing surge of anger, told Elaith that a name was not necessary. Nevertheless, he gave it. "Regnet Amcathra has been known to make an occasional visit to The Pickled Fisherman. He has been seen in Lilly's company, there and elsewhere."

Elaith let the man absorb this, then took a small package from the folds of his sleeve and unwrapped a blackened dagger. "One of my warehouses caught fire. The structure stood firm, but everything inside was burned, as was no doubt the intention. This was found between the charred ribs of a man in the employ of the Ilzimmer family. Do you recognize the workmanship?"

Danilo took the dagger and turned it over in his hands. He gave it back after a quick perusal. "My first sword was an Amcathra blade, as is nearly every weapon I own," he said evenly. "They are incomparable."

"Nearly as good as elven weapons," Elaith agreed. He saw the sudden leap of surprise and speculation in Danilo's eyes and wondered what it meant. The resolve returned, as suddenly as it had fled, now tempered by a new layer of sadness. "I am sorry to bear this news," the elf said. "What it means, I cannot say."

"Rest assured that I will find out."

The elf's resigned sigh and look of concern were not entirely feigned. "I thought as much. Have a care. The Amcathra clan is subtle and canny. Who would think them capable of such deeds?"

Those words were true enough to cloak the elf's deception—and hide another truth layered beneath it. Elaith knew full well that the Amcathra clan deserved its sterling reputation. There was no better quarry to set this particular hound upon, for Danilo would follow this path with dogged determination—and that would keep him and Arilyn out of Elaith's way. Of course, the cost to Danilo would be the loss of a lifelong friendship, but in Elaith's opinion Regnet Amcathra was a highly expendable pawn.

"Regnet Amcathra. Who would have thought?" Danilo echoed with a faint, pained smile. He extended his hand to the elf. "Hard words to speak, but I thank you for them."

Elaith took the offered handclasp and met the human's steady gaze. "What are friends for?" he said with apparent warmth and deliberate irony.

* * * * *

Regnet Amcathra lived in the Sea Ward, a sedate sector of the city that was nonetheless close to the roiling life of the docks. It seemed to Danilo that this contrast suited his old friend. The Amcathra family was obscenely wealthy, and Regnet, like Dan, was a younger son and not involved directly in family affairs. Although Regnet was as fond of luxury and as complacently serene in his position as any man of his class, he had a fondness for adventure. A few years back, he had founded the Deep Delvers, a group of bored young nobles who went into the tunnels beneath Waterdeep in search of adventure.

Dan had always admired this endeavor. At the moment, however, Regnet's deep-delving ways held too much coincidence for Danilo's peace of mind. Adventuring was often a convenient mask for roguery, and any connection with Undermountain in general and Skullport in particular was highly suspect. He sincerely hoped Regnet had not been involved with Lilly, that he'd had no part in the business that had led to her death.

He left his horse with the groom and walked through the iron gate, a daunting affair fashioned from three pairs of rearing pegasi. His friend's home was small, by the standards of the Sea Ward, and had once been a carriage house for a wealthy mage who owned a small fleet of pegasi. The mansion itself had burned down years ago—another casualty of magic created without thought of possible consequence—and it had never been rebuilt.

The door opened before Danilo could knock. He smiled down at the halfling steward—a hiring trend that had become all the rage since word of Monroe's efficiency had made the rounds of Danilo's social circle. This halfling wore a blue and red uniform that proclaimed his service to the Amcathra house, and his hair was as yellow as a dandelion. At the moment the comparison was particularly apt, for the steward's hair stood up as if he had raked his hands through it repeatedly and with great agitation.

Danilo regarded the little fellow. "Is something amiss, Munson?"

"You might say that, sir."

Before the halfling could elucidate, a jaunty step behind him spoke of his master's approach.

"Dan! Welcome. How long has it been since you've stopped by? Longer than a dwarf's beard, I'll warrant."

Though Regnet's words were a fair reflection of fact,

there was no reproach in the man's face or voice. Danilo took the offered handclasp and returned his friend's smile with genuine warmth—and deep sadness. Regnet was an affable soul, handsome in a roguish sort of way, with curly brown hair and laughing hazel eyes. He had his faults, including a hot and ready temper, but Danilo could not believe he could be part of something as vile and needless as Lilly's death.

His need to know deepened and settled his resolve. "Have you time at present for conversation?" Danilo asked.

"I am at leisure this whole day and yours to command. We must have a drink. Munson, is there any zzar in the house?"

"Of course, my lord, but—"

"Fine. Splendid. Bring some to the game room. Dan, you haven't yet seen my new trophy." Regnet clapped an arm around his visitor's shoulders and began to lead the way.

The halfling's eyes bulged, lending him a distinct likeness to a panic-stricken trout. "My lord, I must have a word with you."

"Later," Regnet said firmly.

Dan fell into step beside his friend, listening with only half an ear as Regnet chatted about his latest adventure—something about icy tunnels, and caverns so sparkling with crystal and ice that a single torch seemed to transform the place into a house of mirrors.

Danilo was more interested in whatever caused the halfling so much consternation. The steward followed them a few steps, his small round face a study in indecision. This Danilo could understand. Despite his good humor, Regnet had a demon of a temper—this Dan could attest to, as he had been on the receiving end of it twice or thrice. Like many men of his class, Regnet paid scant attention to his servants as long as they followed his orders without question or hesitation. It was a combination that might well give pause to the most stouthearted halfling. After a bit Munson gave up the effort, sighed, and veered off into a side passage, no doubt in search of the requested liqueur.

They reached a set of double doors. Regnet threw them open with a flourish. "What do you think?" he demanded proudly.

Danilo peered into the room. Fine, deep chairs were scattered about, and tables of polished wood held gaming boards and neat stacks of cards. Small bowls of semi-precious gems or brightly polished crystals stood nearby as an aid in placing wagers. The most notable feature of the room was the collection of trophies. A splendid stag gazed down from over the mantle, its enormous rack casting shadows against the flickering glow of firelight on the floor beneath. A wild boar grinned wickedly from its place over the dartboard. Dangerous tusks the size and sharpness of daggers lent the beast an air of dignity that was not in the least diminished by the pair of darts that bristled from its snout. A narwhal was mounted against an enormous wooden plaque. The great fish had long been Regnet's pride, for the narwhal's size and the wicked, serrated length of sword on its snout made it the most difficult and dangerous of game fish. The narwhal had been stuffed with its tail arched beneath it, the body curved and ready for a lunging attack. It looked like a master swordsman forever frozen in guard position.

The new addition to the game room was even more spectacular. A giant, bearlike creature loomed out of the shadows in the far corner of the room. The thing was taller than a man, with a strangely pointed head and fur the color of sooty snow. Its rubbery lips were pulled back in an eternal snarl, baring large yellow fangs. Clawed paws, long-fingered as a man's but padded on the palm like those of a cave bear, were raised in menace.

"A yeti," Regnet said proudly. "I took it in the ice caves this spring."

The taking of trophies was a common practice but not one that appealed to Dan. "An impressive collection," he said without much enthusiasm.

Regnet grinned and nudged his friend with an elbow. "Not as impressive as my *other* collection of trophies won, stuffed, and mounted, eh?"

Considering the nature of Dan's visit, the bawdy jest was as painful as a bare-fisted blow. It was also an unfortunately apt segue. "I regret to be the bearer of bad news," he began.

The nobleman's smile faltered. He sank down on a nearby chair and leaned forward, his elbows on his knees and his chin resting on his hands. Once Dan was similarly settled, Regnet nodded his encouragement.

"This regards a young woman known as Lilly. I know you have met her—she was at the Gemstone Ball, and you engaged her in conversation. Though you did not indicate to me at the time that you already knew the lady, it has been brought to my attention that you two were quite well acquainted."

Regnet's eyes widened in a moment of masculine panic. "Tymora take me! Not another bastard!"

This response was not what Danilo had anticipated. "You have others?"

The nobleman sniffed. "Surely you aren't claiming that you do not! Consider our misspent youth, and the long nights spent drinking and wenching. Only a special pet of Lady Luck, or a man as dry as a dwarf, could escape a mishap or two. But this is a most inopportune time. I had planned to announce my betrothal at winterfest."

Anger flared through Danilo, stealing his breath and almost blinding him with its intensity. From the corner of his eye he caught a glimpse of the stuffed yeti, which seemed to quiver in sympathetic indignation. He waited a moment until his vision cleared and he could trust himself to speak with control.

"Yet you toyed with this girl."

"As did others, no doubt," Regnet retorted. "For all we know, the brat could well be yours!"

Danilo surged to his feet and slapped both hands down on the table between them. He leaned in over the nobleman. "Lilly was not with child," he said in cold, measured tones, "and have a care how you speak of her. She was my sister."

Regnet jolted. "I did not know."

"Nor did I, until a few days ago. Nor will I know her." The reality of that brought an overwhelming tide of loss. He slumped back into his chair. "She's dead, Regnet."

"Gods above, Dan. I'm sorry."

The words were sincere enough, but they spoke of sympathy for a friend's loss. For himself, Regnet looked positively relieved.

Relieved. Not guilty. Danilo absorbed this, and decided that on the whole it was the best reaction he could have expected. Several moments of silence passed. For the sake of something to say, Danilo asked, "To what lady have you decided to pay court?"

"This may come as something of a surprise," Regnet cautioned, "but she is a fine woman, and she will see admirably to my business and social affairs."

Unlike a simple tavern wench, Danilo concluded grimly. He wondered if Lilly would have derived any sense of justice from the cool, practical description Regnet gave her rival.

"Business and social affairs, is it? Spoken like a true lover." Danilo's heart was not in the teasing, but at least he managed to keep the bitterness he felt on Lilly's behalf out of his tone.

Regnet grinned, not at all offended. "The lady has many charms, but those are the skills that come first to mind when her name is spoken. A redoubtable hostess."

"Is that so," Danilo said without much interest. "If Galinda Raventree were not so adamant in her refusal of suitors, I would think that you might be describing her."

"Indeed I am," Regnet said, not without pride.

At that moment, a feral shriek exploded from the far corner of the room. The yeti rocked back and forth, like a frozen creature trying to tear itself from a tomb of ice, and then it lunged forward.

Both men leaped to their feet. Danilo reached for his spell bag, and Regnet drew his dagger.

The yeti crashed to the floor, taking a table with it and sending ivory chess pieces flying like shards of ice. It rolled over onto one dead side and lay where it fell, leaving the real danger revealed behind it.

Myrna Cassalanter stood there, her hands fisted at her sides and her face as twisted and furious as a harpy's. She was dressed for seduction: Her henna-colored hair was arranged in an artful tangle to suggest—or invite—a lover's touch, and her gown was scarlet, clinging, and cut exceedingly low. Much of her snowy bosom was exposed and was, at the moment, quivering with indignation.

"You thrice-bedamned troll! Son of a poxed whore!" she shrieked. Her hands hooked into rending claws, and she came on like a rampant dragon.

Regnet tossed aside his dagger and leaped over the chair he had just quit, turning it so to put some barrier between himself and the flame-haired virago bearing down on him.

She leaped onto the chair in her frenzy to get at the man who had scorned her. Regnet dodged to one side, barely escaping her raking nails. The chair, no longer supported, crashed onto its back and sent Myrna tumbling over it and onto the floor.

She rolled toward the hearth but was on her feet with an agility that a traveling juggler might envy, brandishing an iron poker in a determined, two-handed grip.

Regnet backed away, tripping over the upended chair. "Munson!" he roared.

The halfling steward appeared in the doorway, wringing his hands. "I tried to warn you, sir," he began.

His next words were lost in Myrna's shriek as she took a mighty swing. Regnet leaned away from the blow, but the tip of the poker traced a sooty path across the front of his shirt. On the back swing, Myrna fetched him a glancing blow to the head. Encouraged by this success, she came on, shrieking like a banshee and flailing the poker with all the verve, if none of the skill, of an elven bladesinger.

Danilo settled back on his heels, folded his arms, and considered Regnet's dilemma. If Myrna had been a man—or for that matter, a woman trained in the fighting arts—Regnet could have settled the matter in a swift contest. Propriety forbade him to mishandle a gentlewoman. Even using force to subdue her was skirting the line. To all appearances, subduing Myrna would not be an easy matter. She bolstered this suspicion by smacking Regnet in the gut with enough force to double him over.

Danilo supposed he ought to come to his friend's aid. He firmly intended to do so. At the moment, however, he found the spectacle vastly entertaining. Moreover there was no denying that it held a certain justice. Danilo doubted that Tyr Himself could come up with a more fitting retribution for a casual and thoughtless lover than the wrath of one he had scorned. Who was he, the merest of mortals, to intervene in so apparently divine a pattern?

Just then Myrna landed another solid whack, this one a two-handed upswing that would do justice to a master polo player. It caught Regnet under the chin, and his head snapped painfully back. He dropped and rolled beyond reach just as another vicious, chopping blow clanged onto the floor.

The halfling steward rushed in and grabbed at Myrna's arm. She flung out an elbow and caught him in the face. He staggered back, clutching an eye already swollen and darkening.

"Do something," Regnet implored his friend.

Danilo relented and quickly formed the gestures for a cantrip—a small spell that would heat metal. The tip of Myrna's iron weapon began to glow with red heat, which slithered up the handle toward her white-knuckled fists. She took no notice, following Regnet's retreat as he rapidly crab-walked away from her, flailing away until the poker was entirely aglow. With a sudden yelp of pain, she released the weapon. It fell to the carpet, which began to smolder.

For several moments, chaos reigned. Munson rushed to douse the fire with the first available fluid—which, unfortunately, was the flagon of zzar he had fetched for his master. The potent liqueur set the carpet aflame. The halfling snatched a stuffed trout from its pedestal and beat out the flames.

Finally all was relatively calm—all but for Myrna, who looked ready for another round. "How could you have anything to do with that trollop!" she demanded of Regnet.

"Have a care how you speak," Danilo told her.

She sent him a withering look. "Not the barmaid. That does not signify. But Galinda Raventree! How *could* you offer me such insult?"

Myrna gathered up her skirts and stormed out. She whirled at the door to deliver a final shaft. "You will regret this. Both of you." Out she went, with the halfling sneaking behind her, suddenly less concerned about the visitor's spent wrath than that which was likely to ensue.

Regnet, though, was of no mind to scold his steward. He sighed in mingled relief and consternation as he rose to his feet. "I am sorry for that, Dan. What will come of this, I cannot say. Myrna can be vindictive."

That did not concern Danilo, and he said so. After all, what part could the gossipmonger have played in Lilly's death? She was a silly, shallow woman, venal in casual conversation but lacking the will and focus to do any real harm. He did not regret the conversation, for if it had shed no light on Lilly's fate, at least it had set his mind at ease concerning Regnet's involvement.

However, as Danilo left the gates, it occurred to him to wonder how Myrna knew Lilly was a barmaid. He had been careful not to refer to his sister in such terms. It seemed apparent that she had known about Regnet's involvement with Lilly—at least, she had not reacted to it with surprise and anger.

Danilo decided to cut though Regnet's property. It was a pleasant walk, shaded by large elms and lined with a hedge of lavender—leggy and outgrown this time of year, but still fragrant. It was a good place to think, and he had much to ponder.

Foremost in his mind was puzzlement over why Myrna did not show anger about her would-be lover's involvement with Lilly. Was it because a simple tavern wench just, as she'd put it, "did not signify"? Most of Waterdeep's nobles readily overlooked the small foibles and dalliances that were common among their class.

Or perhaps Myrna had responded with rage when the tale of Lilly and Regnet was newly told. If so, what form had her anger taken? In light of her display, Danilo had potent reason to believe that she was capable of ordering a rival's death—especially the removal of a person she considered to be without much consequence.

He was wondering still when the first blow came out of nowhere and sent him staggering into the fragrant hedge.

Sixteen

Danilo hauled himself to his feet. Through eyes swimming with stars, he made out three dark shapes dropping from the elm tree: three, in addition to the man who had already hit him.

He reached for his singing sword, for its magic served to galvanize the wielder and those who fought beside him, while disheartening those who fought against. Against four men, he would need that edge.

He pulled the blade free. At once it broke into melody, but not the ringing, comic ballads that Dan had magically "taught" it. The sword intoned a dismal little dirge in the nasal tones of the Turmish language.

The sword's magic had no power over the fighters. They fell into place around him. The man who faced him swept his sword in a taunting circle, then tossed it from left hand to right and back. It was a show meant to intimidate.

"And it succeeds," Danilo murmured under his breath.

He reached for his spell bag and called to hand the components for a slow-movement spell. To his dismay, the casting had no effect on the men circling him, but the falling leaves suddenly defied the brisk wind, dripping slowly through the sky like honey from a spoon.

The singing sword gave a ghastly croak and fell silent. Magic had, to all purposes, deserted him.

The man facing him sneered. "I *seen* rusty swords before. First time I ever *heard* one!" He lunged forward, his sword coming in high.

Danilo blocked. His sword groaned with the parry, a dismal sound that seemed to leech away his resolve. When the mercenary punched out, he could not move away in time. The heavy blow caught him below the ribs and knocked the wind from him, bending him nearly double.

From the corner of his eye, he saw another thug lunging in for his sword arm. He turned painfully, blocked, and riposted. All the while his sword whined, moaning and complaining.

A fiery streak flared across the surface of his mind like crimson lightning. His vision danced, and a heartbeat passed before he connected the flash of pain with the long rip in his left sleeve, the welling redness staining the emerald silk.

The man behind him kicked hard, catching him in the small of his back. He could not turn to defend himself. Nor would he, for another man was coming in, sword leveled for a lunging thrust.

Danilo blocked. He feinted low, then shifted his weight and lunged in high. His blade slid just wide of his opponent's parry, scoring a stinging cut on the man's cheek. Danilo felt a surge of satisfaction. The outcome of this seemed assured, but at least he would make some account of himself.

The next cut came from behind—a shallow, stinging jab to this shoulder. Dan whirled and thrust. His sword glanced off the man's belt buckle and sank in deep. He wrenched his blade free, shifted to his back foot, and parried an attack from another foe. At the same time, he kicked back and caught the third man on the side of the knee. The thug's leg buckled, and he stumbled, nearly falling.

The man caught himself and came in, his face a mask of fury. He leaped, his sword aimed for Danilo's heart. The first man, though, the one who had jeered at Danilo's sword, slashed out and knocked his comrade's blade aside.

"Not that," he snarled. He glanced at Dan and added, "Not yet."

Danilo suspected the last words were meant to cover a misstep. This attack was most likely not intended to be an execution but a warning. Still, he couldn't be sure.

He lifted his sword in guard position and faced down the three remaining men. The leader began to advance, and then froze in midstep. His eyes shifted down to his hand, and his puzzled gaze shifted from the sword that would no longer obey him to the broad, shining dagger tip that protruded from his beard.

Suddenly the dagger jerked to one side, and a crimson fountain exploded from the man's throat. He fell slowly, revealing the cold, amber gaze of the elf standing behind him. The man's comrades threw down their swords and ran.

Without pausing for thought, Danilo took off after them. Elaith swore and kicked into a run. "You are in no condition for this," he pointed out as he trotted along beside.

"Have to stop them," Dan gritted from between clenched teeth. "Have to know who ordered this."

The sound of fleeing hoofbeats resounded down the back streets, but Danilo did not slow. The elf hissed in exasperation. "You are depriving some village of an idiot, you know."

The rumble of a carriage caught the elf's attention. He glanced up as the conveyance ambled by and noted that it bore the guild sign and was driven by a halfling. Good. That made things easier.

Elaith leaped onto the running board. He reached up and pulled the driver from the box, sending him sprawling into the streets with a quick, careless toss. With the horses he showed a bit more care—he caught the nearest bridle and coaxed the team to a stop. He flung open the door and tumbled the shrieking passengers out, then shouldered Dan into the carriage. Slamming the door, he leaped onto the driver's box.

He shook the reins over the horses' backs. The frightened animals took off at a tearing run.

Danilo crawled through the window onto the box. "Don't think that I am devoid of appreciation," he began, "but—"

"Not another a word," the elf snarled as he guided the team around a sharp turn. "You wanted to catch those men. This is the only way you'll do so without bleeding yourself dry."

Danilo considered, then gave a curt nod. That was all he had time for, because another careening turn tipped the carriage onto two wheels. He seized the edge of the seat and braced his boots against the footrest to keep from sliding off onto the cobblestones.

"Hang on," Elaith said, belatedly.

They tore through the streets, tilting wildly first to one side then the other as they thundered along. The elf kept the hindmost rider in sight—no easy task, despite the fact that the man's precipitous flight emptied the streets.

Elaith followed him down a narrow alley, one that curved and twisted like a snake. The carriage tilted but did not fall. Sparks flew as the wheel rubbed against the narrow walls and showered down on them from where the upper edge grazed the opposite wall.

They burst out into the chaos of a crowded courtyard. A trio of barrels rolled toward them. One shattered beneath the horses' hooves. The scent of mead honeyed the air. Chickens fled, squawking in stupid indignation. A few merchants stood their ground, shouting imprecations and pelting the carriage with spilled and ruined produce.

Instinctively Elaith reached for a retaliatory knife. Danilo caught his arm as he was getting ready to throw.

"Listen," he said grimly.

The distinctive rise and fall of the Watch horn sounded over the noise of the street. Elaith swore and jerked the reins to the left, sending the horses careening down a side street. Four men in black and green scale armor formed ranks at the end of the street. "The Watch," Danilo said. "The penalty for attacking them is high!"

"Then let's hope they have the sense to get out of the way," the elf returned. He leaned forward, shaking the reins over the horses' backs to urge them on. Something of his grim determination transmitted itself to the team. The pampered carriage horses turned back their ears, lowered their heads, and charged.

At the last moment the Watchmen leaped aside. The carriage thundered through, veering off to the right with a screech of wheels and a wild chorus of snorts and whinnies—an equine cry that would not have disgraced a paladin's battlehorse.

"At least someone's enjoying this," Danilo commented. He sent a worried glance over his shoulder, then sighed with relief as all four men rose to their feet.

A shadow flashed over them, tracing a circle on the road below. "Griffon rider," Danilo supplied.

Elaith swore and pulled back on the reins, but the horses were too lost in their wild, newfound freedom to respond in time.

Wind buffeted them as enormous wings backbeat the air. A huge, leonine body pivoted in the air and dropped to the ground in a ready crouch. The creature's eaglelike beak snapped in percussive counterpoint to the menacing, feline growl that rumbled from its feathered throat.

The horses shied, rearing up to paw the air and whinnying in terror. The carriage tilted, spilling its occupants to the ground. Elaith was on his feet at once, alert for the attack, but he did not draw a weapon. From his position on the cobblestone, Danilo applauded the elf's good sense. At least twenty Watchmen and a dozen guards surrounded them with drawn swords.

Elaith cast a baleful look at Danilo. "Are you dead?" he demanded tartly.

Dan hauled himself painfully to his feet, giving the matter careful consideration. "Not quite."

"Good," the elf growled as the men closed in. "I should hate to miss the opportunity to kill you myself."

* * * * *

The door to the prison cell clanked shut. Elaith turned to glower at his companion. Danilo had been uncharacteristically silent all the way to the Castle. He slumped now onto the narrow cot. The elf noticed he cradled one elbow in his hand. "Your arm has come free of the shoulder?"

"I think so," Danilo admitted. "Hard to tell, though. Everything hurts, and it's difficult to sort one thing from another."

"There is one sure way of finding out." Elaith seized the man's wrist and gave it a sharp, vicious tug.

Danilo let out a startled oath, then rolled his shoulder experimentally. "That worked," he said, surprised. "There isn't a better way?"

"Of course there is, but I'm of no mind to use it," the elf returned. "That cut on your arm needs attention. I can stitch it if you wish."

"With what? A fishhook?" Dan retorted. "Thank you,

but I will await the healer." He paused. "You followed me. Why?"

Elaith considered what to say. The dream spheres were on the streets, sold to those who were likely to have knowledge that would aid the elf's chosen vendetta. He had picked up the dreams of one of these men, a hired sword who harbored a twisted desire to inflict pain on one of the city's privileged, wealthy men. Elaith had seen the man's mental image of his victim. Despite all that he had done, all that he was currently doing, Elaith could not allow a man he'd named Elf-friend to suffer this fate.

No, this was hardly the sort of explanation he could afford to give.

"Why were you following me?" persisted Danilo.

"Morbid curiosity?" the elf suggested.

"Very amusing," Danilo said dryly. "How did you know where to find me?"

"Not a difficult thing. I assumed you would go to confront Regnet Amcathra, considering that you two are longtime friends."

The man sighed and slumped lower onto the cot. "Of that, I am not so certain. The attack outside his house, so soon after I challenged him about his involvement in Lilly's death? I do not want to think ill of Regnet, but I no longer know whom to trust."

Elaith was silent for a long moment. "I saw Myrna Cassalanter leave. She looked angry. She is not without resources."

"She did threaten Regnet and me," Danilo admitted. "I suppose it is possible that she sent those thugs, although to date Myrna has limited herself to assassinating character."

"It is possible she took aim at your character, but missed so small a target," Elaith suggested pleasantly.

Danilo sent him a wry look. "Is that any way to address an Elf-friend?"

Elaith thought of the Mhaorkiira Hadryad. He could almost feel the heat of it, even though the stone was hidden. He could feel the compelling, twisting magic of the thing, and he answered from the heart. "I am doing the best I can."

* * * * *

In Arilyn's opinion, she had spent far more time in the company of Waterdeep's merchant nobility than any sane person should have to endure. Yet here she was, standing at the magic-blackened gate to the Eltorchul manor.

Isabeau was connected with the theft of the dream spheres. How, Arilyn was not certain. By her own admission, the woman had been involved with Oth. Errya Eltorchul had let slip that her brother had been doing business with Elaith Craulnober. Perhaps she would let slip something else that would enable Arilyn to start piecing together an answer.

However, Lady Errya was not receiving visitors. The servant made a point of sniffing at Arilyn's lack of a calling card, then slowly scanned the guest registry, glancing up from time to time as if to underscore the fact that the half-elf was not listed among those the family expected or wanted to receive.

After a few minutes of this, Arilyn lost patience. She shouldered past the servant and stalked through the halls in search of the noblewoman. The suddenly frantic servant followed close on her heels, imploring her to see reason.

"That will do, Orwell," said a cold, female voice. "I will handle this."

The servant bowed deeply and hurried off, clearly glad to have shed himself of this responsibility.

For a long moment the two women faced each other in silence. "What do you want?" Errya Eltorchul demanded.

"Information," the half-elf replied.

The noblewoman gave a scornful little sniff. "Have you no sense of propriety at all, to come storming in, making demands of a family in grief?"

"That leads nicely to my first question," Arilyn said. "Why does no one know of Oth's death?"

"That is no business of yours," the woman retorted.

"The creatures that killed Oth have followed and attacked me. That makes this very much my business." She remembered Errya's words about the death of the first Lady Dezlentyr, and added, "Nor am I the only person of elven blood who has been attacked."

A sly, cold smile edged on the woman's beautiful face. "I find it hard to weep over this."

"Why's that?"

"Nothing good comes of mixing with elves. You provide proof of that!"

Arilyn ignored the insult. "Yet your brother did business with Elaith Craulnober."

The woman's gaze shifted to one side. "Did he?" she said vaguely.

"That's what you said when we brought word of your brother's fate. I'd like to know more."

Errya tossed her head, sending her flame-colored ringlets dancing with indignation. "Go ask him yourself. The elf, not Oth," she added hurriedly.

This struck Arilyn as an odd statement. "Maybe I'll do that."

The woman's strange, sly smile returned. "If you hurry, you should be able to find him in the Castle. Danilo as well, for that matter."

"The Castle?" Arilyn repeated, not understanding where this was going. The Castle of Waterdeep was an enormous structure that housed the city guard, the headquarters and barracks of the Watch, the armory, offices for city administrators, and a host of other practical functions, including . . .

"The prisons," she concluded aloud, understanding the malicious delight dancing in Errya's green eyes. Anger and frustration washed through her at the realization that Danilo had ignored the warnings to stay away from the treacherous elf. "Both Elaith and Danilo? Since you seem to know so much, why don't you tell me what happened?"

"Didn't I make myself clear?" the woman said with false sweetness. "That's what comes of associating with the wrong people. Now if you'll excuse me, you've been here rather too long. I have no interest in courting Beshaba's fancy," she said, naming the goddess of bad luck.

Arilyn noted the woman's animosity, but her attention was more on the contents of her own purse. As she left the Eltorchul manor, she mentally counted her coin and tallied whether or not she had enough to pay damage fees for both of the offenders. If not, she was not entirely certain which of the pair she would leave to languish in his cell!

* * * * *

As it turned out, Arilyn was not forced to make that choice. Elaith had left the Castle within the hour, but despite Danilo's arguing and bargaining, he had refused to carry word of Danilo's predicament to his steward. "You are safer where you are," was all that the elf would say.

Judging from the grim set of Arilyn's face, Danilo was inclined to agree with Elaith. She strode along at a pace Danilo was hard pressed to match.

"Consider it a new experience," he suggested. "How many times have you had to sign pledge for a prisoner in the castle?"

"Too many," she muttered. "But you may get a chance to return the favor. Myrna Cassalanter doesn't inspire my better nature. I'm half hoping she'll come at me with a poker."

Danilo chuckled and slipped an arm around her waist, keeping it there until they reached Myrna's manor.

The maid ushered them into Myrna's presence and dropped her tray with a shriek. Her mistress was on her knees on the floor, both hands clutching at her throat. Her face was blue, and though her mouth worked frantically, no sound emerged.

Arilyn strode forward, reaching in her bag for the small vial she carried for just such occasions. She uncorked it with her teeth and spat out the cork, then seized the woman's chin and tilted her head back. She poured the liquid into the woman's mouth and held her head back until it ran down her throat.

Myrna slowly began to breathe normally. Her face turned a sickly green, and she rushed for the washstand.

She retched until she was as dry as the Anauroch, then wiped the tears from her streaming eyes. The look she cast upon her rescuers held more enmity than gratitude.

"Trying to clean up after your friend?" she croaked at Dan.

He and Arilyn exchanged a puzzled glance. "I don't understand," he said.

"Elaith poisoned me. I'm sure of it! I have had dealings with him of late," Myrna admitted, her voice growing stronger. "Some openly, some hidden. Payment for some of the information came in the form of elven coin," she said defensively.

"What reason would he have to do such a thing?" Danilo demanded.

The woman sniffed. "You are a fool," she said. "Do you know nothing of what goes on around you?"

Arilyn's face clouded and she seemed about to speak, but Danilo made a subtle gesture warning her to silence.

The gossipmonger's words were too close to his own thoughts for comfort. What she had to say, he needed to hear. He took a small purse of gold from his bag and set it on the table.

"Go on," he said evenly.

For once the sight of gain had no effect on Myrna. She caught up the bag and threw it back at him. "This I will do gladly," she said vindictively. "Lady Cassandra did well to keep you from the family business—you, who dance attendance to the archmage and play about with Harpers! What would you do, *Harper*, if you knew that the days of the Thann family's presence in illegal trade were far from over? Your duty?" she mocked him.

"Be careful what rumors you repeat," Arilyn said softly.

"Rumors?" The woman laughed scornfully. "Half the bards in Waterdeep speak of him as a Harper. As to his family, he believes me. I see it in his face!"

"Not just Thann," Dan said slowly. "There is much trade between Waterdeep and Skullport. It stands to reason that someone oversees that trade, someone who has the resources and the power to impose order on what would otherwise be lawless chaos."

"Huzzah!" Myrna applauded him mockingly. "He realized that his clan is not all powerful! Of course it's not just Thann. There are seven families, each with interests that are clearly defined and viciously protected. I will not name them, but surely you could come up with at least two of them."

"Eltorchul," Arilyn guessed, seeing Oth's death in this new light.

"Those potion-mixers and tinkers? Hardly!" Myrna cocked her bright head as she considered this. "Nonetheless, I would not rule out the possibility. The current struggle might make room for new faces—provided, of course, that those faces are not surmounted by pointed ears!" she added viciously.

Danilo began to follow her reasoning. "Elaith Craulnober has many concerns in this city, both above and below the streets."

"Huzzah again!" the woman said. "He is getting too ambitious, too powerful. The families have agreed to oust the elf lord."

"Yet you have had dealings with him," Arilyn pointed out.

Myrna smiled coyly. "Who is to say that I might not be behind some of these attempts?"

For a long moment no one answered. Arilyn stooped and picked up the empty vial. "To think I wasted a perfectly good antidote."

The noblewoman's face turned livid. "Mark me, you will not escape this. Do you think that the families are pleased with Dan's relationship with Khelben Arunsun? With the Harpers? With a half-elf?"

She stopped and made a visible effort to calm herself. "I have said too much, and I will no doubt pay for it. But every word of it is truth. If you ask my opinion—and many people in this city do—you're both in deep and wild water, and neither of you will swim to shore."

Seventeen

By unspoken agreement, Danilo and Arilyn sought out the beauty and solitude of his elven garden. They did not speak until they stood at the edge of the serene pool, and for a long time they stared into the water as if it were a scrying bowl that could show them their next course.

Danilo was of no mind for conversation. He still reeled from this revelation, which explained much, if not all, of the mystery surrounding recent events.

"Myrna Cassalanter is a spiteful woman," Arilyn said at last.

"I will not argue with that, but I daresay there is as much truth in her words as spite," he said. "Don't you agree?"

"Not completely. I doubt Elaith is responsible for poisoning Myrna."

Danilo looked at her in surprise. "Really."

"Elves seldom use poison. Elaith's methods, though twisted, are still elven."

"Twisted?" he prompted.

She told him her suspicions that Elaith killed the

broker down in Skullport in order to acquire the missing dream spheres. "The mark of an elven sword was unmistakable. One of the men had been dissolved into mist. Elaith is competent in magic, and he has a vast collection of magical weapons. It is the sort of thing he would do."

"But Myrna said she received payment in elven coin."

"What of it? That, more than anything, leads me to believe that Elaith is being set up. He isn't that stupid."

"No, he isn't," Danilo agreed, "but that makes him all the more dangerous. He will not take kindly to this treatment. It's possible that some of the recent events are his vengeance against the noble families."

They considered this in silence. A courtesan was dead, and Simon Ilzimmer had been blamed. The death count did not end there: Belinda Gundwynd and her elven love. Oth Eltorchul.

Lilly.

"And this is the elf I am pledged to defend," Danilo said softly. "Once, he asked me to prove his innocence. I have to find the truth of this, no matter where it leads. I owe him that much, for the honor he once did me."

Arilyn nodded and started for the gate. "We might as well get on with it.

* * * * *

Isabeau waited until Arilyn and Danilo were well out of sight, then sailed up to the door of Myrna Cassalanter's mansion as if she were a regular visitor.

She found Myrna pale, but unusually calm. The reason for this, the woman explained, was her new diversion. She showed Isabeau a wooden box filled with small crystal spheres.

Isabeau knew all about them—knew more than this silly woman could begin to suspect—but she listened with quiet contempt as Myrna spoke glowingly of using purchased magic to live a fantasy.

She, Isabeau, was determined to carve out her own.

The dream spheres were not the way. She saw that now. If they had already found their way into the homes of Waterdeep's wealthy and powerful, she had little hope of retrieving enough of them to turn a profit.

There was another way. Risky, certainly, but Isabeau saw in it her only chance.

She selected the largest, brightest globe from the box and took note of the greedy, territorial expression that leaped into Myrna's eye.

"I would like to try one of these wonders," Isabeau said. "Will you choose one for me?"

Myrna all but leaped for the powerful, expensive globe in her visitor's hands. "That one is for my own use. Any of these others you may have."

"We could perhaps share," Isabeau suggested. "You to your dream, and I mine? A pleasant respite to break up the day."

Her hostess nodded avidly. Once her guest was settled with a lesser magical dream, she took the powerful dream sphere for herself.

Isabeau waited until the woman was deep into the magical trance. She rose quietly to her feet and tipped the box of dream spheres into her pocket. Then she carefully unclasped the necklace from the entranced woman's neck and added it to her loot.

The larger and brighter the sphere, the longer and more powerful the dream. Isabeau had learned that much, but she took no chances. Moving as silently and swiftly as a dervish's ghost, she picked the chamber clean of any valuables and fled while the woman was still deep in her dream.

Isabeau had had no idea that gossipmongering paid so well—with the coins and jewels she had taken from this single theft, she could easily buy and bribe her way into distant Tethyr.

Elated at her success, she all but ran from the mansion and climbed into the waiting carriage. If the driver was surprised to hear that she wished to go directly to the South Gate, he did not state his opinion. An extra gold coin went a long way toward ensuring discretion. If she were careful, and lucky, she might yet make it safely to the southern lands.

Isabeau settled back against the seat and dared to begin dreaming a future far greater than any she might glimpse in one of Oth Eltorchul's magical toys.

* * * * *

Arilyn woke with a start, sitting upright beside her sleeping friend. After a moment her breathing returned to normal, but the dream that had awakened her did not fade.

She glanced at the moonblade, which lay sheathed beside the bed. It was dark and silent. In times past, she had awakened from such a dream to find the sword limned with green light, a sure confirmation that the dream was sent from forest elves in need of her help. This time, the dream was different. It was she who needed the help and her friends from distant Tethyr forest who came to her aid.

There was no trusting the dream, though. Evidence of that was plentiful. Five ghostly elves stood sentinel in the room, released from the sword by the relaxing of her will.

In fact, the moonblade's magic was growing ever more contradictory. Arilyn could almost count upon the elven sword to do the opposite of whatever function it had once performed. Warnings came not at all, or too late. Worse, its quick strike was growing unreliable—sometimes coming too fast, sometimes not at all. If this continued, she would not be able to use the sword in battle.

A discreet knock on the door roused the sleeping man

beside her. Danilo sat up and ran both hands through his hair. "What is it, Monroe?"

"A message for Lady Arilyn," the halfling said, his voice muffled by the heavy door.

"Well, bring it in."

The halfling entered and handed Arilyn a message marked with the seal of the Guard. She quickly broke the seal and read with growing wonder. "There is a group of forest elves inquiring for me at the South Gate," she said and explained in a few words her belief that the malfunctioning sword had reversed the direction of the dream summons. "They've come to help," she concluded.

"And?" Danilo prompted, seeing from her eyes that there was more.

Arilyn met his eyes with a steady gaze. "These are the elves from Tethyr's forest. You should know that Foxfire is among them."

Danilo absorbed this in silence. "You will want to meet with them at once," he said simply.

It was the answer Arilyn had hoped to hear—no questions, no reservations. This was part of her life, her duty, and he accepted it as such. He did not ask what path she would take when the task at hand was done. The time would come when Arilyn would have to answer that. She could not say how she would respond.

* * * * *

The night was nearly over, and Elaith had yet to decide whether his campaign to divert attention of the nobles from himself was success or failure. It was true that he had received important information through the combined magic of the Mhaorkiira and the dream spheres. However, word of the dream spheres was spreading fast—too fast. The powers of law and order were beginning to take notice.

Just that day, three of his dream sphere vendors had been arrested. The wizards of Waterdeep were furious at this profligate use of magic, and Elaith had received word that there were attempts to magically follow the spheres back to their source.

He wondered where those magical inquiries might lead. Given the distortion of magic that the dream spheres caused, it might be almost anywhere. He might not be the equal of Oth Eltorchul when it came to twisting magic, but he knew enough to ensure that no one could trace the sale of the spheres back to his door.

Certainly no one would come looking for him here. The Monster Pit was one of the best-kept secrets in the Dock Ward.

Through a two-way mirror, the elf looked out over his establishment with a mixture of distaste and satisfaction. Gladiatorial dens were illegal in Waterdeep, but this one was highly popular. It lay many, many feet under a smithy and a raucous tavern. By day, the clatter of hammers on metal, the hiss of the bellows and the gruff shouts and near-constant singing of the smiths served to drown out any hint of the noise of battle and the cheering of the spectators. By night, the tavern served the same purpose.

The Monster Pit was a large, round cavern that had been carved into the shale. The walls had been covered with wood to keep patrons from peeling layers off the rock and hurling them at the combatants.

As usual, it was an unruly crowd seasoned with strong spirits and a variety of entertainments not available in the market. Smoke from scores of pipes rose into a thick blue haze. Most of the patrons were shouting and shaking their fists at the fighters, but a few wandered off into back rooms for private wagers or games.

Tonight the betting was brisk, for few men knew how

to take the measure of the rare monsters that faced off. They were an unusual pair and had cost the elf considerable effort and expense to acquire.

The larger fighter was a fomorian, a member of a species of freaks in which no two were quite alike. This creature was male, a huge brute with four muscled arms and a vast torso that dwindled down to short, bandy legs. Despite his stunted legs, the fighter stood well over six feet tall. His face was malformed, dominated by an enormous eye that drooped low on one cheek. The fomorian's nose was a bearlike snout, and his other eye was small, red, and cunning.

His opponent was a yuan-ti, a snakelike creature with the head and arms of a man. At the moment, the snake man had the upper hand. His coils were wrapped around the fomorian. The brute's eyes bulged, but he continued to fight. With two of his hands, he squeezed the snake's neck, and with the other pair he desperately tried to peel off the crushing coils.

The monsters' faces were eerily similar, for both had mouths as wide as frogs. Their fanged teeth were bared in fierce grimaces, and their forked tongues flicked out in desperate, flickering gasps. It was all very distasteful, Elaith noted, but highly profitable.

The sound of a Watch horn tore through the din and shattered his comfortable musings. Three patrols—twelve men—pounded down the wooden stairs. To Elaith's consternation, they went straight for the mages who ringed the cavern and whose magic kept the monsters contained within the ring.

"Fools," Elaith muttered.

In the chaos that followed, the yuan-ti immediately loosed its hold and slithered off, disappearing into a small hole that led to its den. The fomorian roared and charged with the fury of a caged beast who sees a chance at freedom. Three of the Watch converged on the fighter. He resisted, easily lifting one in each hand and hurling them aside. The third was swept away as wild melee filled the room.

The creature's mismatched eyes swept the room, searching the crowd for Elaith, the elf who had captured and imprisoned him. He charged forward and smashed the mirror with three fists. His malformed eyes gleamed with wild delight as they settled upon Elaith. He backed off several steps, and kicked into a charge.

The monster's progress was halted by a shining elven sword. To Elaith's astonishment, Arilyn stepped into the fomorian's path.

"If you have a weapon, arm yourself," she said to the creature.

"You cannot be serious," Elaith began incredulously.

"I will not kill an unarmed being," she said sternly. "Give him your sword."

Still Elaith hesitated, but the fomorian settled the matter by ripping a weapon—and the arm that held it—from a passing gambler. Arilyn lifted her sword in challenge. The fomorian charged, seeing only the elf behind her and the prospect of cutting him down. Arilyn would not give way, though. For several moments the battle went on. Two of the Watch took notice and began to close in on the combatants. One of them came to an astonished halt.

"That's it. I didn't sign on for this." The man turned and headed for the stairs.

Elaith followed the man's line of vision, and gasped in astonishment. A tall, rangy elven woman stood at the edge of the ring, her translucent sword drawn and her ghostly face daring any to interfere with the challenge beyond. More of the patrons noticed the apparently vengeful spirit, and more took to the exits in frantic haste.

Elaith could not move so much as a step. He knew that elf. It was—or had been—Thassitalia, a warrior whom he had known on Evermeet. She had wielded the moonblade Arilyn carried and had bequeathed it to

Amnestria, the willful, wild-hearted princess he had loved. That was very long ago, though. Why was Thassitalia here? To help defend him, or to take vengeance upon him for his many misdeeds? Perhaps even to reclaim the Mhaorkiira and destroy the elf who dared to wield it!

Before an answer came, the ghostly elf faded away. Arilyn finished the battle and sprinted to Elaith's side.

"Any way out of here?"

The return to practicalities steadied him. Elaith used the points of his daggers to prod people out of the way. The two elves made their way to a back room. He threw aside a small carpet and opened the trap door hidden below.

They dropped into the opening and fled in silence through the tunnels. When finally they stopped for breath, Arilyn got right to the point.

"What do you have to do with these dream spheres?"

Perhaps it was the appearance of Thassitalia, perhaps the sight of a moonblade raised in his defense. "I have them," he said frankly, for he suspected that there was little she did not know. "When presented with the opportunity, I took it. In a way, this is self defense: I am using them to set my enemies against each other."

"Do you realize the implications of what you have done?"

"Things may have gotten out of hand." The elf felt more vulnerable and open than he had for many years, and he described some of the truly ugly dreams that had recently been coming through the magical spheres. "I can't begin to fathom where some of them are coming from."

Arilyn thought this over. A suspicion that she could not entirely grasp came to her. "Let me see the Mhaorkiira."

When the elf hesitated, she drew her sword and threw it aside, following it with the knife in her boot and the hunting knife in her belt. "I am unarmed," she said. "You can easily take it back."

"That was not my concern," Elaith said.

"I know what your concern is," she snapped. "A moment's contact won't corrupt me, even if I'm wrong."

The elf's face was deeply puzzled, but he produced the ruby from a pocket of his jacket and handed it to her.

Arilyn studied the stone, turning it over carefully and running her fingers over the glittering facets. It was a beautiful thing, deep red and perfectly cut. Magic vibrated through it—even she could sense that. All the same, she was certain that this was not the dark stone of legend.

"How much did you pay for this?" she asked.

Elaith looked startled. "Six hundred gold. Why?"

"That's a lot for a piece of crystal."

The elf looked as if he wasn't sure whether to be puzzled or outraged. "Explain," he requested coolly.

"You're still alive," the half-elf said with a faint, cold smile. "You know what I am—what I have been. There is enough anger in me to give the Mhaorkiira a foothold. I wouldn't need much of an excuse to kill you.

"More importantly, Dan is still alive. You even came to his aid. I doubt you would have done that if you were under the influence of the rogue stone."

His answering smile was bitter. "You do not know the entire legend, Princess. If there is a seed of evil, the rogue stone will make it grow, but creatures beyond redemption can handle it with impunity. I am still clear of mind and will, quite capable of making decisions that suit my whim. What does that say of me?"

Arilyn had never seen such emptiness in living eyes, or such despair. If anything, that only convinced her she was right.

"It is a counterfeit," she persisted. "Take me to the fence you bought it from and I'll prove it."

The elf conceded and led the way to a shop in Castle Ward. Arilyn stalked up to the one-eyed man and placed the stone on his table. "You sold this gem."

The man's gaze flicked from Elaith's face to Arilyn's as if seeking permission to speak. The elf nodded. "That is so," the fence said. "Why?"

"It's a fake. A crystal."

He drew himself up, outraged. "I know precious stones. That is a ruby. I stake my life on it."

"A bad choice of words, considering the company," Elaith said pleasantly. "Convince me."

The fence took up the stone and a glass. He began to study it. His confidence faded away by the moment, and he raised a horrified gaze to his visitors. "This is not the stone I sold you."

"I assure you that it is none other," Elaith said.

"Then it is not the one I bought."

Arilyn began to see through the problem. "Did anyone else look at the stone?"

"Two or three people. One I remember in particular. A young woman, very richly dressed and haughty. Her eyes were green, her hair a very bright red."

The half-elf snatched up the stone and seized Elaith's arm. Before the elf could protest, she hustled him out of the shop.

"That's Errya Eltorchul," she said tersely. "We need to speak with her."

Elaith nodded and began to climb the stairs carved into the thick stone wall of a cobbler's shop. The half-elf, understanding his intent, fell into step. They made their way onto the rooftops and set an unerring course for the Eltorchul manor, following a hidden path known only to those who made their way in the shadows.

Arilyn fell easily into the task and into the rhythms of the elf's quick pace. Without speech, they circled the rooftops around the Eltorchul estate until they caught sight of Errya.

The woman was in the garden. They dropped lightly from the wall, flanking her and closing in. Elaith pointed a wand at her. A shimmering ball darted toward her, enclosing her head and shoulders and cutting short her shrill scream. She turned to run, but the elf seized her and sat her none too gently back on the bench.

Arilyn's attention was elsewhere. A familiar-looking cat had vacated Errya's lap and was now sitting crouched a few feet away. The tabby's gray tail was lashing in agitation, but there was a decidedly unfeline expression of wrath in the creature's eyes.

It was the cat that Errya had held when they had come bringing word of Oth's death. It was also the tabby Arilyn had seen in Isabeau's chamber in the Eltorchuls' country estate.

It was, in short, one well-traveled cat—if indeed it was a cat at all.

Arilyn leaped, arms outstretched to seize the tabby. The creature vanished in a puff of acrid blue smoke.

"What the Nine bloody Hells was that?" demanded Elaith.

Arilyn looked down at the noblewoman and saw her suspicions confirmed in Errya's look of mingled panic and fury.

"That," she said emphatically, "was Oth Eltorchul."

Eighteen

"It all fits," Danilo said thoughtfully when they brought the matter before him. "That ring Isabeau had at the Eltorchul estate—was it like the one we found on the severed hand?"

"I had not considered that, but now that you mention it, the ring did look familiar," Arilyn admitted. "It was gold and had a pink stone."

"I'd wager that the ring we found was an illusion. The hand as well, no doubt." Danilo began to pace. "Remember the state of Oth's study? The tables were overturned, the floors littered with broken pottery and common spell components, but the shelves, with their valuable vials and scrolls and boxes, were untouched."

"No wonder the Eltorchul family kept Oth's death a secret," the half-elf said. "But why would he wish to appear dead?"

"I can answer that," Elaith said softly. "Much of it, you already know, thanks to Myrna Cassalanter's tattling tongue. The illegal trade in and out of this city is carefully, secretly controlled. For many years, I have been building an empire of my own." He smiled faintly.

"I suppose it is a tribute to my success that I have finally been perceived as a threat. The seven families have been sending me warnings for quite some time now. Some are subtle, some not quite so."

"Such as the tren attack at the Thann villa," Arilyn said.

"That lacked subtlety," the elf said dryly, "but set your mind at ease, Lord Thann. That was not your family's doing. Naturally, it was hoped that I would assume it was and would strike back. This would have given the Thann family reason to join the others in their attempts to have me ousted."

"So the Lady Cassandra has no part in this?"

"I did not say that," Elaith cautioned him. "She may have no choice but to take action."

"What form will that action take?" Arilyn asked.

The elf was silent for a long moment. "I thought that I held the Mhaorkiira. I had reason to think so. I arranged for certain people to use the dream spheres, and from them I gained information I used to take action against the two-city consortium."

"What kind of action?" Danilo said cautiously.

"I had nothing to do with your sister's death," the elf began.

"That was Oth," Arilyn said decisively. "If he can take the form of a cat, why not a tren? Of course Isabeau had reason to run from him—from what Elaith says, she stole from Oth not once but twice. She probably named Elaith from sheer spite. What of Belinda Gundwynd?"

"Ilzimmer, I suspect," the elf said wearily. "The path to that is rather convoluted. I had a fatal dispute with a mercenary captain, a retainer of the Ilzimmer clan. The killing blade was made by the Amcathra clan and was stolen during the ambush."

Danilo looked puzzled. "What has that to do with the Gundwynd clan?"

"It is common knowledge that the Amcathra family is

not among the two-city consortium. That is why I sent you to Regnet," the elf admitted. "It was a diversion, nothing more. The Ilzimmers assumed, as I intended for them to do, that the blade was a sign from Gundwynd. After all, it was lost from their caravan. Its use to attack an Ilzimmer soldier—especially considering that the man was the caravan master—could be seen as a direct accusation. The death of Belinda was intended to be a warning."

"So were the attacks on Danilo and me," Arilyn said. "What of Simon Ilzimmer?"

Elaith's smile took on a hard edge. "That was my doing," he said without the slightest hint of guilt. "The woman was in my employ and dying from a wasting disease of the lungs. A few illusions, a few well spent coins, and there are many who will swear that Simon Ilzimmer was seen coming from her room."

"I cannot shed too many tears over such a man, but I do not approve," Danilo said heatedly. "Let's set aside the consideration of whether Simon's 'innocence' is general or specific. What about those who give testimony? I assume that they were chosen to implicate some other family and to further fuel the flames?"

The elf admitted this with a nod. "I will undo what I can. You said that you had words with Simon Ilzimmer that same day—do you remember the hour?"

"The bells of Ilmater's temple were ringing," Arilyn recalled.

"That answers all," Elaith said with satisfaction. "The hour is close enough. You can speak for him. That will help build favor between the Ilzimmer family and the Thanns. It will be easy enough to blame this on Oth. We know he has done murder in other forms. Why not claim that he took on the physical shape of Simon Ilzimmer?"

Danilo started to protest, then gave up with a sigh. "We have to find Oth before we can accuse him of anything. The question is, how do we proceed?"

"I see several possible paths, none of them very attractive," the elf said. "We could turn this matter over to the Lords of Waterdeep, but these accusations would be hard to prove, and that might only deepen the animosity between the families. We could let the families settle this among themselves and hope that the bloodletting is minimal. This is the course I myself prefer, but for the fact that you and the princess are in line for reprisal."

Danilo grimaced. "Or?"

The elf's smile was cold and ruthless. "We could serve up Oth to the two-city families—but first, we will have to find and stop him."

"Not easy to find a dead man who can change his appearance at will," Arilyn pointed out.

"It will be easier than you think," Elaith said. He took the red crystal from his pocket and flipped it onto the table. "Oth has been sending information to me through this—things he wants me to know. He wants all three of us dead and he is trying to entrap us. Let's oblige him."

"I've heard better plans," Danilo said dryly, "but please, continue. This can only improve."

Elaith reached out and tapped the stone. "In two nights there will be a massive, coordinated tren attack against members of both the Thann and Ilzimmer clans."

"Why would Oth do that?"

"Several reasons. These families have longstanding rivalries. They will believe that the attacks come from their rivals and will continue to act upon them. They will fight until both are weakened. At some point, the other families will step in and settle the matter."

"Why would Oth want to create problems among these families?' Dan wondered.

"The Eltorchul fortunes are fading," the elf reminded him.

"No wonder," Arilyn put in. "New tunnels don't come cheap. Neither do the services of tren assassins."

"Or magical research," Danilo added. "The cost of developing the dream spheres must have been ruinous."

Elaith shook his head. "The cost would be a small thing compared to the profit Oth could make if he could worm his clan into the two-city trade. Using the dream spheres, Oth could learn enough bits and pieces of the illegal trade to make a convincing bid. Fortunately," the elf said grimly, "he failed in his most ambitious ploy. He drew me into the dream sphere trade, no doubt hoping that I would be tempted to use the devices myself and thus betray secrets that I entrust to no man. If he accomplished what the seven families could not do, and handed them both my ruin and my fortune, the other families would welcome him into their midst with open arms."

Danilo and Arilyn absorbed this. "There are still a number of loose threads," Arilyn said. "It is clear that the peerage does not embrace elves, but the Eltorchul family seems extreme in their dislike."

"Oth is an arrogant man," Danilo explained. "The thought that some magic might elude his grasp is deeply offensive to him. You should have seen his face at the Gemstone Ball, when he asked me to teach him spellsong magic."

"That is well said," the elf agreed. "A number of years ago, Oth tried to purchase elven spells from the priests at the Pantheon Temple. He was firmly rebuffed."

"Sibylanthra Dezlentyr was a mage," Arilyn pointed out. "Is it possible that she, too, rebuffed Oth? Perhaps he was working on the Mhaorkiira back then. If he thought that she understood too much of his intent, he might think it necessary to silence her."

Elaith looked startled, then grimly angry. "I would say it is very possible."

"That fits, as well," Arilyn mused. "She was most likely killed by poison. Diloontier deals both in poisons and the services of tren—clearly, Oth has some contact with the man. That could also explain the attack on Myrna Cassalanter."

"No, that was my doing," Elaith said candidly. He shrugged off their incredulous stares. "She had it coming. Who do you think ordered the attack outside of Regnet's house?"

Danilo massaged his temples. "Let us come back to that at a later time. I take it that you know where the attacks will be."

"I do." Elaith sighed in deep and profound frustration. "Unfortunately, I do not have enough men to counteract these attacks. Oh, there are many in my employ, but none whom I trust in this matter. The shipment of dream spheres I acquired in Skullport is no doubt a paltry thing compared to Oth's store of them. I would wager that dream spheres have made their way into the hands of every man, woman, and monster seen frequenting my establishments or taking payment from me."

The elf fell silent for a moment. "The only people I trust are in this room. I know of none others."

"I do," said Arilyn suddenly.

Danilo nodded slowly, understanding what she intended. "The elves from Tethyr came expecting to fight at your side if need be. There are other elves in the city. They might be recruited to this cause."

Elaith snorted. "Forgive me, but you do not understand the elven mind. Most of Waterdeep's elves are gold or moon folk like Arilyn and myself. Who would they follow? A band of forest elves, who to them are nothing but unknown savages? Or a half-elf? Or a rogue such as myself? The elves of this city know of my reputation," Elaith said, "and more than one of them has suffered vicariously because of my deeds. They will want no part of this. They have no reason to trust me, even less if they hear that the Mhaorkiira Hadryad is involved. No, I am sorry, but the People in this city have no reason to unite under any of those banners."

"Send out messengers," Arilyn said with grim certainty. "Gather all the elves you know. I'll do the rest."

* * * * *

Lady Cassandra regarded her youngest son with uncertainty. "No more flaming books?"

"Just a simple warning, Mother. I have come to the end of the path, and you should know what I have found."

She nodded as if she had been expecting this. Danilo told her what he had learned.

"I did not order the tren assassinations," she said in a tight, worried tone, "but if this comes to light no one will believe it and the Thann family will be anathema. How much more so, after the battle between the families is over!"

"It will not take place," he said adamantly, "at least, not in any way that touches Thann. For once, stay your hand and let someone else handle the problem. Take precautions to protect the family, but keep all your retainers out of this."

Cassandra did not agree, but neither did she disagree.

After a moment, Danilo spoke the one question to which he must have an answer. "Arilyn and I have shared the elven handfasting. We have bonded in rapport. She wears my ring, and we intend to marry. Know that she has my first and deepest allegiance. She is worthy of that and more."

"That I never doubted," the woman murmured.

"Then tell me why you have been so opposed to our union."

For a moment Cassandra looked weary, almost fragile. "You and Arilyn might have children. It is possible that one of them might be half-elven in appearance. That would raise questions."

Danilo nodded encouragement.

"When you spoke of your elven heritage, I thought you knew, but after the first moment of surprise passed, I realized that Khelben must have passed along some tale of distant ancestry. The son of Arun had a half-elven father. However, there is a closer tie."

She took a long breath. "I was born before my father came to Waterdeep. My mother died in childbirth, attended by none but my father. He remarried soon after. The Khelben whose name the archmage borrows was born of that union, and I always called his mother mine. Very few knew otherwise. None living know that she was half-elven."

"You were ashamed of this," Danilo said in wonder.

"Not so, but you have seen how the nobility regards those of mixed blood." She swept a hand toward the well-tended estate. "See what I have done. The family business was in utter disarray when I married your father. I have earned this place for myself. None of my family—not even those who have the magical gifts I so notably lack—have achieved nobility. It is what I have. It is what I am."

A faint tremor underlay the cool tones. Danilo considered it long and well before he spoke. "I have no desire to take this from you, lady."

She shook her head. "Without the two-city trade, all is lost. I am not speaking merely of fortune. Do you think the others would let Thanns survive, if we attempted to remove ourselves from this alliance?"

Danilo had already considered that. For good or ill, this was a secret he would never speak. "Thann will survive," he said.

Still Cassandra was not content. "What do you propose to do? And how will this not come back to our door, if it is known that you are involved?"

"Rest your mind on that," he said. "I have allies no one will connect with this noble house or any other."

She considered that, then let out a short, humorless laugh at the irony of the situation. "Do what you must, my son." She hesitated, then gave him a smile that was genuine—all the more so for its self-mocking edge. "Sweet water and light laughter until we meet again."

The traditional elven farewell surprised him, then left him feeling both confused and deeply touched. He did not understand this woman and would never find his way through the many layers and convoluted passages of her mind. This much he knew: she had given him her blessing, in words she knew would be meaningful to him. He took her hand and kissed her fingers, then turned and walked swiftly from the hall to prepare for the battle ahead.

Nineteen

The gathering at Greenglade Tower was far from cordial. Danilo soon realized that Elaith's assessment of Waterdeep's elves had been distressingly on the mark. Some of these elves had recently been evicted from the tower and were none too happy to learn that Elaith had given that order.

Nor were they willing to follow him. The mother of the elf who was slain at Belinda Gundwynd's side angrily demanded to know if Elaith had anything to do with her son's death. "Tell me, my lord," she said with bitter mockery, "was this part of your vendetta against the noble clans?"

Before he could speak, Arilyn stepped forward. She placed a hand on her moonblade. "All of you know what this is. You know it cannot shed innocent blood, and that it can never be used to harm the People. If the task Elaith Craulnober asks of us is a right and true path, if the elf himself is worthy of our loyalty, the sword will honor him. If he falls, you will follow me. Will you accept that?"

There were many doubtful faces, but a murmur ran

through the crowd as a tall male stepped forward from the small knot of forest elves. Danilo knew at once who the elf was. Arilyn had spoken of her friend Foxfire as a warleader. This elf moved with the fluid grace of a warrior. Dan had seen leaders before who possessed that quiet, indefinable strength that flowed like an aura, who inspired confidence in those around them. Never had he seen one who possessed this quality in such ample measure. If that were not proof enough, there was the elven naming custom in which given names were taken from an elf's skills or appearance. Foxfire was aptly named, for his long russet hair had the gloss and color of a red fox's pelt. Danilo noticed as objectively as possible that the elf was possibly the most strikingly handsome male of any race he had ever beheld.

Foxfire took a band from his arm and tossed it at the moon elf's feet. It was a ritual Dan had read of—no doubt the band carried the insignia of Foxfire's position as warleader.

"I will honor the moonblade's decision, and my people with me," he said in musical, deeply accented Elvish. The forest elves rose and came to stand behind him. Of course, they could not know that the moonblade's magic had been unreliable, even contradictory.

At that moment Danilo understood what Arilyn was doing. Fear rose in him like a tide. As if she sensed this, she turned and met his eyes. Gone was any hint of reserve. Her heart was in her eyes, and Danilo had no doubt that it was his. Nor did he doubt that this last, supremely honest gaze might well be her silent farewell.

Arilyn spun away and turned to Elaith. She drew her sword, raised it in challenge.

White-faced, the elf drew his weapon and mirrored her salute. There was no fear on his face, though he clearly expected to die. Danilo suspected that he wished for death. The answer Elaith sought from the Mhaorkiira had never come, but death by moonblade's decree would lay to rest the question that had haunted his soul. Danilo marveled at the unlike pair, the incredible courage of both elves.

Arilyn raised her sword for a powerful two-handed blow and brought it whistling down. She never got close.

A terrible flash lit the room. For a moment, Dan's horrified gaze perceived the outline of skull beneath Arilyn's face, the bones in her arms. Then the vision was gone, and the half-elf lay on the floor. Her hands were blackened. Her eyes were open and staring, but she was utterly still.

Before Danilo could move, Elaith threw aside his sword and dropped to his knees. He balled one fist and pounded on the half-elf's chest. He struck again, and then again. Instinctively Danilo moved to stop him, but Foxfire caught him and held him back.

"He does right," the warleader said softly.

Danilo realized the truth in it. He nodded to show that he understood, then put aside the elf's restraining hands and went to kneel beside his love and his elven friend. For several moments he could do nothing but watch as Elaith continued his brutal ministrations.

Arilyn suddenly drew breath in a sharp gasp. Her eyes shut as she struggled against the pain of her burns. When she had mastered herself, she opened her eyes and regarded the somber, watching elves.

"You have your sign," she said in a faint, ragged voice. "Do as the elf lord bids you."

A forest elf came forward, a small female, brown as a wren. "Go with the others," she told Danilo brusquely. "I am a shaman and will heal her." She looked to Foxfire to help her move the wounded half-elf. The warleader shook his head and nodded to Dan.

Danilo carefully eased Arilyn into his arms and followed the shaman out of the room. "You expected that to happen," he said softly.

She nodded once, with great effort, and turned to

Elaith. The moon elf followed at Dan's side, his eyes intent on Arilyn. His inscrutable calm was gone, shattered by the sacrifice his "princess" had made for the elven folk, the family of her human love, and for *him*.

"You did not get the Mhaorkiira, but you have your answer," she said. "Are you content?"

An expression of wonder suffused the elf's face. "All these years," he marveled. "The things that I have done. I am beyond regret—beyond redemption, or so I thought."

"Sometimes the difference between a rogue and a hero," she said carefully, "comes down to who is telling the tale. Ask these elves who I am. They will speak of the moonblade. Ask humans, they will say assassin. It could be the same for you."

"You're talking too much," scolded the shaman.

Arilyn's eyes drifted shut. "Needed to be said."

Danilo left her with the fierce little elf woman and returned to the main hall. Since Elaith did not seem to want to discuss what had just happened, he left that conversation for later and sought out Foxfire.

"That was a noble gesture," he said. "A rare kindness to offer a stranger."

The forest elf gave him an enigmatic smile. "I have seen you before, once, in a battlefield near my forest. Arilyn called all the elfshadows from her sword. Yours was among them."

"No longer. That bond is broken."

"Changed," Foxfire corrected. "Never broken. She has need of you."

This surprised Danilo. "How so?"

"Arilyn is courage. Never have I seen an elf who embodied courage so completely. However, she is half-elven, and so there are some qualities she lacks. Music and light laughter—these are as important to the elven soul as starlight. These she finds in you. See that you give them to her, and I will always name you a friend."

There was truth in these words, and also the answer

Danilo had long sought. He raised one hand in the elven pledge. Foxfire laughed and extended his hand for the salute that human comrades exchanged. They clasped wrists, then joined the others in preparation for the battle to come.

Twenty

Arilyn and the forest elves took to the rooftops. It felt odd, but amazingly right, to be back in the familiar company of her friends. The band took to the new challenge with ease, making their way across the uneven line of roofs as surefooted as squirrels.

They crept up to the Thann villa and circled the place where the tren attacks were to come: the garden shed with the false door that led into the tunnels. They got this in their sights and waited.

The night was dark, with a slim, fading moon and a thick mist. When the tren emerged from the shed, they blended into the shadows. Even to Arilyn's heat-sensitive eyes, they were little more than a cool blur.

"No one but elves would have seen them," the half-elf mused as she fitted her first arrow to her bow. "Oth wasn't expecting this."

At her side, Foxfire nodded and raised his bow. On his signal, all six elves fired.

The arrows dove in like silent, deadly falcons. A faint, rumbling cry drifted up to them, a sound that was abruptly and wetly silenced.

"We got at least one," Arilyn said.

"Two," the forest elf corrected. "There are three more. We should pursue?"

"No need. Listen." There was a faint hiss as the surviving tren dragged their slain kin beyond range. "They eat their own rather than leave evidence of their presence," she explained.

Foxfire shook his head in disgust. "All the same, some of us should stay here. You go along with the others."

She nodded and placed a hand on his shoulder in farewell, then was gone, running lightly over the rooftops toward the Ilzimmer estate. A large shape loomed up in front of her, springing up over the edge of the roof so suddenly that she nearly ran into it. It was the tren who called himself Knute, distinguished by the ridge of festering scar over one eye.

The tren touched the wound. "I think I die soon. Wounded clan chief doesn't live long—others will attack. But I will die wearing your blue hide."

Arilyn danced back and drew her sword. "Notions of fashion in this city," she said grimly as she circled in, "are getting entirely out of hand." She lunged at the creature, a quick attack that forced him back on his heels. Immediately she pivoted into a half turn and swept her sword in low.

Knute turned also, protecting his hamstrings and swatting away the blow with his thick, short tail. The blade sliced deep, but there was little blood. Almost casually, the tren kicked aside the severed appendage. He swiped at Arilyn, a knife in each clawed hand—two quick, slashing blows.

She parried them both, but the pain of the impact jolted through her hands. The prayers of the shaman had healed the blackened skin, but the blow from the moonblade's magic had dealt deep and possibly lasting damage. Arilyn fought aside a wave of weakness and fell back to prepare for the next attack.

To her surprise, it did not come. The tren looked confused, his tongue darting out and his huge head jerking back and forth as if he were trying to take stock of a host of new enemies. That, she realized, was precisely what he was trying to do. From the corner of her eye, Arilyn saw the ghostly image of a beautiful elf with enormous blue and gold eyes and hair the color of sapphires. The look that the elf gave her—at once bracingly stern and full of love—chased away any thought of weakness.

"Mother," Arilyn murmured, welcoming the apparition even though it was yet another sign that her sword's magic was breaking down.

She retreated another few steps and glanced around. All the elfshadows, all eight ancestors who had wielded her sword, prowled about the roof in battle-ready stance. The tren's gaze darted from one to another, his tongue flicking out to taste their scent. After a few moments of this, the creature began to advance. Unlike humans, he had no fear of spirits. If he could not smell them, they were not real enough to concern him.

Arilyn lifted her sword in guard position. The tren came in hard, slashing at her with both knives. She turned her sword this way and that to block the attacks. Each one throbbed through her battered hands, and the pain grew so intense that her vision began to blur into a red haze.

A musty, heavy weight sagged against her. For a moment Arilyn thought that she had taken too much punishment, that oblivion was claiming her. Suddenly the weight was gone, and the moonblade was torn from her slack hands.

For some reason, the sudden release steadied her. Her vision cleared, and settled upon Dan's stricken face. The tren lay dead at her feet, killed by three quick cuts of his sword.

She noticed her hands. Danilo held them both in his, gripping the translucent fingers hard enough to send renewed pain singing through her veins. Nonetheless, she did not let go, for she saw what he had seen when he looked at her. She could see *through* her own hands, almost as clearly as she could see the city below through the ghostly forms of her ancestors.

"Not now," Danilo said, his eyes defying the waiting shadows. "Not yet."

She felt him reaching through the link that bound them, and sensed new strength begin to edge into her battered form.

"I'm filling in," she said. It was an odd term, but it suited. Color and substance were returning to her hands. She pulled them free of Danilo's grasp and held them up for his inspection. Danilo caught one of her hands and gave the fingers a quick, grateful kiss. He then stooped and retrieved the blade. Dimly she realized that it dealt no harm to him, but that did not surprise her. The sword's magic was utterly distorted, so much so that it had turned upon her and was sapping her very lifeforce.

"The Mhaorkiira," she said, understanding what was likely at work. "It's close."

He stopped in midstride and threw the moonblade aside. "You cannot do anything to fight it. Stay here, or leave that sword."

Arilyn could do neither. She brushed past him and stood poised at the roof's edge. "Bring it with you," she said, and then leaped into the night.

Danilo's heart missed a beat, then he heard the light thud of her boots landing on the roof just a few feet below. He picked up the sword and followed her to Diloontier's Perfumes, and from there into the tunnels below.

It was there that the surviving tren were to meet. The elves had done their work well—there had been but few survivors. The bodies of tren and elves alike spoke of the final brutal battle that had taken place. All that remained of this band was the large tren facing off against Elaith.

"Easy victory," Arilyn said confidently.

Danilo was not so certain. Elaith's quick sword kept the tren's knife engaged, but the creature reached his free hand into a suspiciously familiar bag hanging from his belt—a fabric bag such as that worn by human mages, not the grim, fine leather fashioned from a tren victim.

"That is Oth, I'll wager my life on it," he said in a worried voice. The mage had the Mhaorkiira—the powerful dark stone that stole memory and magic.

Arilyn seized his arm. "I've got to get out of here," she said urgently. "Elaith is fighting for his life. I cannot help him, and I risk distracting him."

Danilo looked carefully at the nearest elfshadow, and understanding jolted through him. The face was Arilyn's, though if possible even more beautiful, and the ghostly image's hair was translucent blue.

"Princess Amnestria," he realized, seeing the wisdom in Arilyn's words. If anything could distract Elaith from battle, it would be the face of his lost love.

The warning came too late. Elaith's amber eyes settled on the beautiful elfshadow, and recognition tore a poignant, painful swath across his face. The elf seized control of himself at once, but the hesitation was all that the Eltorchul mage needed.

The "tren" flung aside his sword and made a short, sharp gesture with the thick fingers of both hands. A burst of crimson light exploded from his reptilian hands and caught Elaith full in the chest. The force lifted the elf off his feet and carried him back several feet. He crashed into the wall of the tunnel and slid to the ground.

Scales melted into flesh and fabric as the mage reclaimed his shape. The tall, aesthetic features of Oth Eltorchul came into focus, and in the mage's outstretched palm was a red stone glowing with malevolent light.

"You will die," the mage said almost casually, "but not before your memories are mine."

Danilo felt the sudden sharp tug—as if someone had reached into his chest and closed iron fingers around his heart. He felt the magic of the Weave shift as his place in it began to tear free, thread by thread.

A glance at Arilyn's white face told him that she was experiencing much the same thing. Her history, her magic was being stolen from her, but the manifestation was different: the elfshadows began to move toward the flame-haired mage, resisting each step, but struggling as if against a strong wind. Arilyn began to move, as well, fighting her way over to the place where her moon-blade lay in a desperate attempt to stop the twisted elven magic and the mage who wielded it.

Danilo gathered the remnants of his strength and will and formed it into the spell of accusation he had fashioned for the Lady Cassandra. As he anticipated, the spell went awry. Swirling lines and tendrils of flame danced into the air, swirling around the mage and then disappearing into the Mhaorkiira.

This distracted Oth, if but for a moment. The elf-shadows paused, uncertain. Danilo tried again, throwing at Oth the bubble spell that had contained the tren.

The mage again began to change form, this time to a giant hedgehog. The long, thick quills pierced the magical prison, sending shards flying like droplets of rain from a wind-shaken tree.

A howl of rage burst from the mage—a howl that lifted into a wolf's mournful cry and ended in the shriek of a hunting owl. The mage's body followed suit, shifting from one form to another in a spate of uncontrolled magic. Not all the transformations were uniform. The evershifting result was horrific, turning the wizard into a mirror reflecting the creatures that inhabited a thousand nightmares.

Arilyn finally made her way to the moonblade and stooped to pick it up. Her fingers closed around the hilt—and went through it. Her head fell forward in a gesture of resignation. The battle was over for her. There was nothing to do but wait and watch the spectacular spell battle rage between her love and the crazed wizard. It was the hardest moment of her life. Fitting, she thought fleetingly, that it should be her last.

She raised one ghostly hand to shield her still-sensitive eyes from the brilliant barrage of light. Danilo was throwing every fireball and lightning bolt spell in his memory at the mage.

No, not at the mage, she realized—at the Mhaorkiira.

Panic swept through her, and she tried to shout at him to stop, to flee. Such magic was dangerous at the best of times. In the presence of the dark gem, it could turn deadly.

The Mhaorkiira absorbed each of his magical attacks, growing brighter with each one. Suddenly it exploded, sending shards and sparkles of light into every corner of the cavern. There was no sound, there was no rumble or shudder or tremor. But the forces of the explosion tore through Arilyn's insubstantial form, sending her to her knees.

Never had she faced a foe to equal this one. A soundless, psychic maelstrom whirled through the cavern, made up of memories, magical spells, dreams, and nightmares. A lifetime of them—a hundred lifetimes! The force of it threatened to tear her away.

Amid the soundless howl, she heard a familiar voice and felt a familiar, golden presence. Danilo was equally adrift, equally buffeted. A moment's touch, and he, too, would be gone.

She felt the familiar clasp of his hand, as surely in her mind as she had ever felt it in life. With all her fading will she clung to that, lending to it her own stubborn courage. The storm raged about them, but together they found they could stand.

When at last the crimson storm faded, Arilyn slowly eased her grip on Danilo's hand. She rose to her feet and jolted with surprise when she noted that he was at least twenty paces away from her.

"Look," he said, nodding toward her elven sword.

The moonblade glowed with faint blue light. The elf-shadows were gone, but each of the eight runes glowed with serene power.

Danilo crossed over to Elaith and motioned Arilyn to his side. She heard the reassuring click of her boots on the stone, knew that her time as elfshadow was not yet come. A quick glance, however, told her that Elaith might not be so fortunate. His injuries were severe.

Oth Eltorchul was in considerably worse shape. The mage huddled at the base of the wall, his eyes as blank as a newborn babe's. At his feet lay the Mhaorkiira Hadryad. The light of life and memory was gone from it, leaving it a common gem. Arilyn picked it up and felt no trace of its malevolent magic. The kiira was as empty as the mage whose mind it had destroyed.

Epilogue

Two days passed before Danilo went to the Thann villa for what he suspected would be the last time.

There was much to do before he said his farewells to the life he had known. He had handed the Lord's Helm to Piergeiron and exacted from the First Lord a pledge to find a replacement who would champion the needs of Waterdeep's elven People. He had paid the keepers of Mystra's Arms for the care of Oth Eltorchul, whose mind seemed irrevocably destroyed with the Mhaorkiira. The dream spheres were also dead, their stored magic released by the final maelstrom of the spell battle. For years to come, small boys and girls would no doubt be shooting marbles with the crystal spheres, all the while dreaming the harmless, healthy dreams of childhood— dreams that would be earned not through magic, but through tears and time.

The tren's tunnels had been sealed, and Regnet and his Deep Delvers would be kept busy for some time to come hunting the last of the monsters down. Errya Eltorchul had disappeared. No dainty hand or foot had been found in the Eltorchul estate, but Danilo had his suspicions. Errya had all but admitted paying for the attack upon Elaith. Despite everything that had happened, it would be very like the elf to repay her in kind.

Best of all, Arilyn was at his side, as she would be from this point on. The spectre of renewed warfare threatened Tethyr, and they had both pledged themselves to Haedrak's cause—with one stipulation. They would fight with the forest elves and for them. Anyone in Tethyr who took arms against any of the People, even if that person were Haedrak himself, might face the small army of northern elves gathering under Elaith's command. Or—and Arilyn had been very clear on this—such a person might face one of the many assassins who still plagued the land and whose names were known to her. This "offer" had gained generous concessions from the would-be king. He had promised Elaith lands and title in the south, and Foxfire a place in the new order as advisor and ambassador.

"What of the forest elves?" Danilo asked.

"They're on their way back home. We have an invitation to stop at Tangletrees on our way north."

"North?" he inquired. "Last time I consulted a map, the forest of Tethyr was south of Waterdeep."

"True, but it's north of Zazesspur. From all I can gather, that's where Isabeau is headed."

"Ah." Danilo did not pursue this. The grim, determined set of Arilyn's face told all. She had fallen back into her assassin's role, this time of her own volition. Oth Eltorchul had been punished for his part in Lilly's death, but Arilyn still held Isabeau responsible for hers. She would pursue the woman into the glittering cities of Tethyr—or into the Abyss if need be. Danilo did not disapprove.

"Elaith is coming with us," she announced. "He asked to be released of his promise not to harm Isabeau. I told him yes—I hope you don't mind me speaking for both of us."

This time, Danilo was surprised. "I thought he would have his hands full with his new command."

"Will Elaith ever be too busy for vengeance?"

"Everyone needs a hobby," Dan agreed, "and as you pointed out, the difference between a rogue and a hero often comes down to who tells the tale. It seems to me that you have taken upon yourself the task of rewriting Elaith's path."

She shifted one shoulder in an impatient shrug. "He is what he always was. Nothing I did changed that."

"I disagree," Danilo said softly. "Do you know what he told me when he first regained consciousness? He asked about Amnestria. Apparently he found her in the storm and found strength in her as we did in each other. He did not understand what had happened and asked only if I thought he would see her again. I assured him that he would. I believe it," he said firmly. "An elf who is thinking about the afterlife to come is likely to treat this life with greater care. Indeed, any elf who would risk the Mhaorkiira's power to test his true mettle is worth as much in courage and heart as any three paladins you could name."

"He's out to kill Isabeau," Arilyn said, then shrugged again. "So am I. Who's to say that he is wrong and I'm right, just because I've got the moonblade to add its voice and judgment to my actions."

"Speaking of that," he said, "do you plan to tell Elaith that the moonblade's magic was running amok?"

She considered that, and shook her head. "No. I don't think so. I believe that Elaith is the same as he ever was, but what *he* believes is more important."

"Perhaps the moonblade spoke true. Perhaps he was not equipped to wield the Craulnober blade but is amply suited for another task that will serve the elven people as well."

Arilyn looked surprised, but she considered that. "Perhaps."

"The fact remains that Elaith is still a rogue," he pointed out, "a killer with great skill and little mercy."

"True enough," she agreed, "but let's see what else he can do."

Danilo found he was content to leave it so. They walked in silence to the Thann villa. He sought out the Lady Cassandra and faithfully recounted all, sparing her nothing of the battle and its outcome.

"You have bridges to mend, but I believe an all-out battle will be averted," he concluded. "Like all successes, though, this one comes with a price."

"I was expecting this," Cassandra said with resignation. Her ice-blue eyes flicked to the half-elf. "Very well. I will accept Arilyn into the family without reservation."

"You misunderstand," he corrected her. "Where Arilyn is concerned, there are no bargains. I have a debt to pay, and this time it comes out of family funds. The pledge of Elf-friend goes both ways. You will use your influence to see that the consortium makes no more attempts against Elaith or any other of Waterdeep's elves."

"That is too much!" she protested. "The family is already in a tenuous position without championing a rogue elf."

"I hold to my price." Danilo fell silent as he gathered the will to continue. It was not easy to know that his family controlled much of Waterdeep's illegal trade. It was harder still to contribute to it, but as Cassandra had pointed out, they were unlikely to survive any other way. This was one more reason why he had to leave the city—he could not betray them, nor could he be a part of their dealings. This once, and never again.

"I will give you this: There will be less risk than first reckoning indicates. Elaith will surrender some of his business interests to Thann control. He will remain the silent partner and collect a share of the gains."

Cassandra was silent for several moments. "Given

our recent losses, this might be a timely arrangement. I will have to work through the particulars, but I agree in principle."

It was an odd and ironic choice of words. Dan decided not to comment—at least, not directly.

"Then the matter is settled, but for this small remembrance."

He took his mother's hand, and slid onto her finger a wondrous ring set with a single perfect ruby.

"This is—or was—an elven kiira. I ask that you wear it always," he said softly, "as a reminder that not even the most formidable power can last forever."

Lost Empires

The series that uncovers the hidden secrets of the FORGOTTEN REALMS® world's most ancient, and most dangerous civilizations. Explore the ruins of Faerûn in:

The Lost Library of Cormanthyr
Mel Odom

To avenge the murder of his mentor, the ranger-archeologist Baylee must battle the Waterdeep Watch, a lich and his drow henchman, and the spirit of a centuries-dead elf, and find a storehouse of ancient knowledge lost for six hundred years.

Faces of Deception
Troy Denning

Atreus wants nothing more than to be beautiful again, and will travel to a hidden valley in the faraway Utter East for even the slimmest hope of success. Will the price of acceptance be too high?

Star of Cursrah
Clayton Emery

The sands of the Calim Desert hide many secrets, and powerful forces willing to do anything to keep it that way.

And coming in 2000 . . .

The Nether Scroll
Lynn Abbey

What lurks in the darkest corners of the haunted Weathercote Wood? A race for the possession of one of Faerûn's greatest artifacts is on, and the Beast Lord himself is in the running!

From under the waves of the FORGOTTEN REALMS® world's mightiest oceans comes a rising tide of war, hatred, and death—and the face of Faerûn will never be the same again.

"Odom does an admirable job of bringing the sea setting and its varied species to life. The novel's detailed fight sequences are tightly packed, making for a fast, exciting read . . ."
—*Publisher's Weekly*

The epic story of the Threat from the Sea continues in:

October, 1999

And coming in 2000: Featuring stories set against the backdrop of the sea invasion by R.A. Salvatore, Ed Greenwood, Elaine Cunningham, Troy Denning, Lynn Abbey, Mel Odom, and a host of your favorite FORGOTTEN REALMS authors!

The epic tale concludes in:

You'll never look at the blue spaces on your maps the same way again. . . .